Boss
meets Baby

CAROL
MARINELLI

NATALIE
RIVERS

MAGGIE
COX

⊙MILLS

Mills & Boon, an imprint of Harlequin (UK) Limited, Eton House, 18-24 Paradise Road, Richmond, Surrey TW9 1SR

BOSS MEETS BABY © Harlequin Enterprises II B.V./S.à.r.l 2013

Innocent Secretary…Accidentally Pregnant © Carol Marinelli 2010
The Salvatore Marriage Deal © Natalie Rivers 2008
The Millionaire Boss's Baby © Maggie Cox 2007

ISBN: 978 0 263 90673 8

011-0613

Harlequin (UK) policy is to use papers that are natural, renewable and recyclable products and made from wood grown in sustainable forests. The logging and manufacturing processes conform to the legal environmental regulations of the country of origin.

Printed and bound in Spain
by Blackprint CPI, Barcelona

INNOCENT SECRETARY...
ACCIDENTALLY
PREGNANT

CAROL
MARINELLI

THE BABY COLLECTION

May 2013

June 2013

July 2013

August 2013

Carol Marinelli recently filled in a form where she was asked for her job title and was thrilled, after all these years, to be able to put down her answer as 'writer'. Then it asked what Carol did for relaxation. After chewing her pen for a moment Carol put down the truth—'writing'. The third question asked—'What are your hobbies?'. Well, not wanting to look obsessed or, worse still, boring, she crossed the fingers on her free hand and answered 'swimming and tennis'. But, given that the chlorine in the pool does terrible things to her highlights, and the closest she's got to a tennis racket in the last couple of years is watching the Australian Open, I'm sure you can guess the real answer!

For Beryl with love from Carol
x x x

CHAPTER ONE

EMMA *had* been honest—had even admitted during her telephone interview that she was attending night school on a Wednesday night and studying art and that in a couple of years she was hoping to pursue it full-time.

Everything had gone really well, until the second Evelyn had walked out to greet Emma—and Emma truly didn't understand why.

She'd prepared so carefully for the interview. Reading everything she could get her hands on about D'Amato Financiers—about their spectacular rise, even in gloomy times. Luca D'Amato had a no-nonsense attitude—there was no secret formula to his success, she had read in a rare interview he had given—just sound decisions and fiscal transparency and the refusal to be swayed by hype. Yes, she'd read up on him and then gone through her favourite glossy magazines and followed every last piece of advice in preparation for this afternoon.

Emma had scoured the second-hand shops and found a stunning—if just a touch tight for her well-rounded figure—pale lilac linen designer suit, had had her thick brown ringlets blowdried straight and smoothed up into a smart French roll, and, horribly broke, she had, on the afternoon of her interview, as one magazine had cheekily advised, gone to the make-up counter at a department store and pretended that she was a bride-to-be and trying out looks for her wedding day.

Her brothers had always teased her about her obsession with magazines and her father had moaned about how many she had bought, but they had been her lifeline. Growing up without a mother, living in a rough-and-tumble house that the little girls she'd invited to come over and play had never returned to, Emma had lived her childhood and teenage years reading the glossies for advice, about friends and bullying and boys. It was the magazines that had taught her about deodorant and kisses and bras. The magazines she had turned to when at twelve she had been teased for having hairy legs. And though her devotion to them had waned somewhat, at the ripe age of twenty-four it had been the magazines she had immediately turned to for make-up and grooming tips to land her dream job.

She looked fantastic, *just* the image she had been hoping to achieve—smart, sassy, groomed—exactly the right look for a modern working girl in the city.

Evelyn clearly didn't agree.

Her interviewer was dressed in a stern grey suit, with black flat shoes. Her fine blonde hair was cut into a neat, practical bob and she wore just a reluctant sliver of coral lipstick. The antithesis, in fact, of the look Emma had been trying to achieve!

'And Mr D'Amato would also prefer someone who speaks Japanese...' Evelyn continued.

'It didn't say that in the advertisement,' Emma pointed

out. 'And you didn't mention it when we spoke on the telephone.'

'Luca—I mean Mr D'Amato—does not like to put too many specifications in the advertisements for one reason, and I rather agree…' she gave a small sniff '…that when the right person appears, we know.'

Well, there wasn't much Emma could say to that—clearly at first glance it had been decided that she wasn't the right person for the job.

Only…

Now, even though it had been an impossible dream, now that she *had* glimpsed it, Emma wanted it.

The salary was to die for—her family home, despite months on the market, hadn't sold and the nursing-home fees were piling up. Evelyn had explained during their initial telephone interview that Luca's staff burnt out quickly. He was a demanding boss, expecting complete devotion, and that this job and the travel would literally overtake her life, but that suited Emma just fine.

One year working hard and she could meet the nursing-home fees. Surely in that time the house would sell and pay off the backlog of debt? One year, burning herself out, and she would finally be free—free to pursue her dreams, free to live the life that had so far been denied her.

And now that glimmer of hope was rapidly being taken away. 'Now, if you'll excuse me…' Evelyn gave a thin attempt at a smile '…I have an important phone call to make.'

Well, at least Evelyn hadn't kept her guessing, at least she wouldn't be checking her phone every five minutes, or dashing to get the mail.

It couldn't have been made any clearer—she wasn't wanted.

'Well, thank you for seeing me...' She should just stand and go, shake Evelyn's hand and leave, except, inexplicably, she was dragging it out and for some stupid, stupid reason tears were threatening as yet another door closed on her push for a better future. 'Thank you for your time.'

It was her horoscope's fault, Emma told herself as Evelyn scribbled a note on her carefully prepared CV.

It had told her to *go for it*, reminded her that *you have to be in it to win it*. Told her that Jupiter and Mars had moved into her tenth house, which assured success in her career...

Stupid horoscopes, Emma thought as she went to retrieve her handbag. She didn't believe them anyway.

And then in he walked.

And the room went black.

Well, it didn't go black, but it might as well have, because *he* was all she could see.

Dressed in a tuxedo at four p.m., he strode over. Evelyn stood up, knotting his bow-tie as she gave him, in a couple of minutes, what seemed like a month's worth of messages, and all in a language that was foreign to Emma.

'Mr Hirosiko wants an "in person" next week.'

'No,' came his bored response.

'Kasumi was insistent.'

'He can have a face-to-face.

'And your sister rang, upset...she wants you there for the entire weekend.'

'Tell her that given that I'm paying for the entire weekend...' he had a thick, deep, Italian accent and

Emma felt her toes curl '...I can choose my schedule.' His eyes drifted around the room as Evelyn dealt with his cufflinks and then he gave Emma a bored glance that changed midway and utter disinterest shifted slightly.

He deigned to give her a second look, and it was one she recognised well. It was the same look her father and brothers had used on unsuspecting women—at the petrol station, the supermarket, school concerts, the pub, oh, anywhere...

It was a look that to Emma screamed danger.

Six feet two with eyes of navy blue, Luca D'Amato might just as well have had the word *danger* stamped on his smooth forehead. Jet-black hair was slicked back, but a thick, raven lock escaped as Evelyn declared him officially knotted, and with one manicured hand he raked it back through his hair and it fell into effortless shape. Oh, she'd seen photos of him, had known that he was good-looking, but a grainy newspaper photo didn't do him justice, could never capture the essence of him, just the shocking presence of him. A scar ran the length of his left cheekbone, but that one imperfection merely enhanced his general faultlessness.

'We haven't been introduced.' Full, sensual lips curved into a smile as he turned come-to-bed eyes on her, his deep, accented voice for her ears now. 'This is...?'

Emma was struggling to find her voice, but Evelyn did it for her. 'Emma Stephenson.' Evelyn looked as if she were sucking lemons, and it dawned on Emma then that the *real* reason she hadn't got the job was perhaps that Evelyn had been hoping for someone plainer, dowdier, older, bigger...in fact, someone who would withstand Luca's charm. Well, she needn't have worried. Emma could handle Luca's sort with her hands tied behind her back—she'd grown up surrounded by them! 'We were just concluding the interview.'

'For the assistant PA job?' Luca checked, holding his hand out, and, because it was the polite thing to do, Emma shook it, feeling his warm fingers close around hers. Then she looked up as he voiced what she was thinking. 'But I've got a cold heart!' He winked at her.

'I'm sure you do!' Emma retorted. He was shameless, utterly shameless, and Evelyn was welcome to him. 'Well, again,' Emma said, coolly walking to the door, absolutely refusing to be rattled, 'thank you for your time.'

She walked out into the foyer, took the lift and only as she went to sign out did she realise that she'd forgotten her bag. That, despite appearances, despite appearing utterly and completely unruffled by his stunning presence, one glimpse of Luca D'Amato and her stomach was in knots. He was devastatingly handsome, with eyes that stripped, undressed and bedded you in a matter of seconds, and she had deliberately not returned the favour.

Emma headed back up in the elevator, moving to step out, only he was stepping in...

'I wasn't expecting to see you again.' He didn't move to let her pass him, his broad frame barring the exit, just slightly, and there was this offer of conversation that Emma didn't want to take up. 'I hear the interview didn't go too well.'

'It didn't.'

'Shame.'

How loaded with meaning was that single word, and

Emma swallowed hard before speaking. 'I forgot my bag, I'm just going to get it,' she offered by way of explanation and as the lift door started to close she pressed the button to open it. There was this pang, this twinge, this snapping almost, this ending that she didn't want to happen, because he really was divine, and she wished for just a fleeting second that she had the looks, the confidence, the *experience* to allow him to pursue her.

But she didn't.

'Going down?' She pressed the 'hold' button for him, and he stood back as she stepped out and she caught the heavy scent of him, just the brush of his expensive suit as she passed by.

'No, up.' He grinned. 'To the roof.'

'Things that bad, then?' Emma called over her shoulder, safer now that the doors were closing, but he halted them with his hands.

'Do you want to join me?'

'I'm sure another job will come along,' she replied, watching a slow smile spread on his face as he got her dry humour. 'Things really are *never* that bad.'

'I'm actually going to Paris.'

'Lovely.'

'Helipad's on the roof.'

'They usually are.'

'Formal dinner, very boring, but maybe after… What are your plans?'

'TV dinner, a rerun of my favourite murder mystery.' Emma gave a sweet smile. 'So there's really no contest!'

He really was smiling now, thinking he'd got his easy way, holding the lift and waiting for her to step inside. So, *so* arrogant, so, *so* assuming, he really thought he could just snap his manicured fingers and summon her—he only seemed to get the message when she opened the doors to his office suite, his rich, assured voice just a touch perplexed.

'If you're worried that you've nothing to wear...'

'I'm not worried at all!' Emma laughed, and she could be as rude as she liked, could tell him exactly where to go with his smutty offer because, after all, he wasn't going to be her boss. 'As I said, there's really no contest!"

As the lift doors closed on him and she walked over to Evelyn's office, she was too irked to think before she knocked. Her hand rose, the door flung open and Emma stood there stunned as she took in the sight of Evelyn. The assured, pompous woman, who had dashed her hopes just a few moments before, was sobbing her heart out, first jumping up and shooing her out, appalled at being caught, then too upset to care.

'Negative!' she wept as Emma just stood there. 'I was so, so sure that I was.'

'I'm so sorry!' Well, what else could she say? 'I'm very sorry.'

And what could she do other than lead the sodden bundle to the nearest chair and peel off tissues as Evelyn gulped out her sorry tale?

Married five years.

Trying for a baby for four and a half of those.

IVF and injections and nasal sprays and tests and scans and egg retrieval.

And now she had to ring Paul and tell him, Evelyn had sobbed, had to ring her lovely, lovely husband, who wanted a baby as much as she did, and say that they'd failed to conceive through IVF for a second time.

Emma really didn't have to worry about saying the right thing, she couldn't get a word in. Instead, she just sat there and listened and poured water and offered tissues, and finally, when Evelyn had cried a river, she seemed to remember where she was and who she was talking to.

'You've been so nice—I mean, after I was so cool with you.'

'It's not a problem. If I'm not the right person…'

'No, you see…' Evelyn was wringing the tissue in her hands '…it has nothing to do with your experience or that you don't speak Japanese…'

'I know that now.'

'No, I mean—'

'I get it, okay? I admit, I assumed you must like him yourself, but…'

Emma giggled as Evelyn gave a watery smile and rolled her eyes. 'Not at all—I'm just sick of training new assistants, only to have them leave once he's bedded them. He's incorrigible, you know.'

'I know!' Emma groaned. 'He just asked me if I wanted to join him for dinner in Paris.' Emma smiled. 'Maybe you should look for a male PA.'

'They'd fall in love with him too,' Evelyn sighed, then she blinked. 'You said *no* to *Paris*?'

'Absolutely.'

'You don't find him attractive?' she gasped.

'He's divine,' Emma corrected her. 'He's side split-tingly beautiful and any woman who says otherwise is a liar.'

'So why did you say no?' Evelyn wanted to know.

'Because I know him,' Emma explained. 'Not Luca personally, but I grew up amongst his type—I've read their rule book from cover to cover. I grew up in an all-male household—an exceptionally good-looking all-male household at that. '

'What about your mother?'

'She died when I was four.' Emma said, and there was nothing in her voice that requested sympathy—she merely stated the facts. 'My brothers are all considerably older than me…' She gave a thin smile at the memory of her childhood. 'And my father, well, a good-looking widower attracts a lot of admirers—all wanting to change him, all assuming he's just waiting for the next Mrs. Stephenson to come along—and he played them all well.'

'Luca's a nice man,' Evelyn said, just a touch pink at her own indiscretion in discussing her boss so personally. 'Beneath it all, when he's not being horrible, he's a really nice man. Take this assistant PA role that's currently being advertised—that's so I can cut back on my travel and late work nights…he's great really.'

'So long as you don't love him,' Emma said. 'So long as you have absolutely no intention or hope that one day you might change him…'

'You really *do* get it.' Evelyn blinked in wonder.

'I really do.' Locating her bag, Emma plonked it on her shoulder. 'I'd best get going.'

'And I'd better ring Paul.'

And it *had* been no contest—not for a second had she considered accepting Luca's extravagant offer, but sitting in her pyjamas, eating her TV dinner and watching the credits on her favourite show roll, the house was too big and too lonely for one.

Lonely…

She had never admitted it, not even to herself.

Oh, she had friends and a job and was kept busy—but sometimes, sometimes she wished she wasn't so

wise, so cynical, so mistrusting where men were concerned.

She reached for a magazine, skipped straight to the
problem page and read about other people's lives, other
people's problems, and for the millionth time in her life
she missed her mum. Missed the chats that would
surely have happened about boys and men. Everyone
else seemed to find it so easy—her friends fell in and
out of love, skipped from relationship to relationship,
and some were even getting married, or moving in with
their boyfriends.

Yet Emma felt as if she'd been left at the starting post.

Too embarrassed by her brothers' teasing, too scared
of getting hurt, she'd hid her first innocent crushes, had
said no to dates in her teenage years, envying how others
found this dating game so easy and just dived in and said
yes.

Dear Barbara, she penned the letter in her head.

*I'm an attractive twenty-four-year-old, I have
friends, a job, a busy life and I'm still a virgin.*

*Oh, and I just said no to a night in Paris with the
sexiest man on earth.*

She'd make letter of the week!

And though it was great to have come home to no
messages from her father's nursing home or new bills
in the mail, all she felt was deflated. She flicked off the
TV, and for just a second she faltered.

A tiny, wobbly second, where she wished she *were*
stupid, wished for that impulse gene where men were
concerned that had been so sorely denied her.

Wished she'd just said yes to Luca's dazzling offer.

* * *

Luca flicked through the channels on the television.

Not that he was watching it. It was on all day for background noise for the dog, Pepper—not that the animal appreciated it.

The night stretched on endlessly and he stood there, rueing the fact that he had been yawning and bored at eleven p.m. in Paris, but thanks to the time difference was wide awake and thoroughly restless at five minutes to midnight in London.

He should be exhausted, he had been up since five—but his head was clicking like an abacus. Hemming's, a large shopping chain, had called him in way too late to stop them from going under.

Except he *could* see a way to save them.

He grabbed a beer from the fridge and tried not to think about it, tried to wind down—just fed up with all the travel, with the demands. Why did everyone want an in-person—why couldn't they just settle for a face-to-face on a screen in the meeting room?

Hell, an email would usually suffice.

Sex would be nice.

And there were plenty who would be willing.

But he couldn't be bothered to talk.

Couldn't be bothered tonight to even pretend to be interested.

His tie must have been soldered on, along with his cufflinks—because he had to put down his drink to deal with them.

And deal with Pepper.

He snarled at the ginger miniature poodle, who snarled back at him. He let him out on his vast balcony to do whatever dogs did.

His maid would see to it in the morning.

Martha, an ex-girlfriend, had, after a trip back to his home in Sicily, decided to move in uninvited, and had conveniently forgotten Pepper when Luca had asked her to move out—three years ago!

'You,' Luca said, wandering back to the fridge and selecting a few choice morsels, 'are the most pathetic excuse for a dog I have ever seen.'

He ripped a chicken leg off and gnawed it as he stretched out on his sofa, with Pepper quivering on the floor beside him.

'You're on a diet.' Luca reminded him. Half watching a detective show on the television, finally Luca relented and threw some titbits to the floor in reward for their new game—having recently found out that if he changed the word 'Paw' to 'High five' the outcome was the same, only much more satisfying.

It had been hellish breaking up with Martha—her tears and protests at the unexpected end had been unprecedented—as over and over she had asked how he could end something so good.

And she'd left Pepper—just hadn't taken him, sure that Luca would crack and ring, would make contact—but what she hadn't truly realised was that when Luca ended things, he ended them.

That Luca would rather deal with a senile, smelly old dog than face her again.

The detective show actually wasn't that boring…

Three minutes from the end of the final episode of the season, Luca decided it was something he might actually get into.

And then the credits rolled.

And he knew this was what Emma had been talking about.

Knew she was watching it too.

He just knew it. And he wished she'd said yes to Paris.

CHAPTER TWO

IT WAS a quarter to five on a Thursday afternoon and the entire staff of D'Amato Financiers, excluding Emma, seemed to be abuzz with excitement. As Emma walked back from a meeting with the manager of HR she could see make-up, slyly in some cases and blatantly in others, being applied at desks, and the general office area reeked of a clash of newly sprayed perfume. Even the guys were at it—appearing from the men's room with a generous dash of newly applied hair product and a glint in their eyes as the end of the workday approached.

Thursday night in London, and it seemed everyone had plans.

Everyone except Emma.

She remembered with a pang when Thursday nights had heralded the start of the weekend. When Friday morning had been spent huddled around the coffee machine, dissecting the previous night.

She'd be lucky if she was out of here by seven *and* she had to visit her father *and* she had to be back here by six the next morning, to meet with Luca and then fly up for an eight-thirty a.m. meeting in Scotland.

Evelyn had had second thoughts—offering Emma the position the following day—and she had been in her dream job for six weeks now. And though it was still just that, a dream job, it was also extremely hard work—as Assistant Personal Assistant to Luca D'Amato, it wasn't just her job title that took some explaining. Every minute of Luca's time was valuable, Evelyn had explained on her first day. Beyond valuable, actually—which was why he had his own travel team, two assistants and looking for a third, four full-time drivers, in fact a whole fleet of staff that took care of the details and allowed Luca to get on with doing what he did best—rescuing struggling companies, turning them around and making an obscene amount of money in the process.

Emma's job was varied, mostly exciting and yet also downright boring at times—dealing with his sister's wedding, his dog, his housekeeper's endless reams of days off. The list was endless.

Ducking into the ladies' room, Emma knew she ought to attempt a quick repair job on her hair and face before she headed back to her office and to whatever mood Luca was in, but it took for ever to elbow her way to the mirror and her curly dark hair had spent too long in an air-conditioned building because it was looking decidedly frizzy. She borrowed a squirt of serum from a snooty-looking redhead, re-tied her hair back in a low ponytail and then, sick of the coffee on the top floor, she grabbed a hot chocolate and a bag of crisps from the vending machine then headed back up in the lift, knowing that in all likelihood this would double up as dinner.

'Louse!'

As she walked out of the lift, Emma stepped back as

a stunning, raven-haired woman stormed out of Luca's office and into the lift, tears streaming down her face but watching his closed office door and just standing there, waiting for it to open, waiting for him to follow her out, to call her back, to no doubt tell her that it didn't have to end like this, that he'd had a change of heart.

Of course he didn't.

Of course he wouldn't—no one delivered an ultimatum to Luca and came out smiling, not even this rare beauty, who, with a sob of frustration, finally pushed the lift button, her desperate eyes peeking out of the closing gap, still hoping that Luca would change his mind.

'That,' he said, first peering around the door and making sure it was safe to come out, 'was not my fault.' He put up his hands in bemusement and said it again. 'Really, that time it wasn't my fault.' Still Emma said nothing, just watched with pursed lips as he helped himself to her hot chocolate, as he always did if she didn't pour it into her mug before he saw it. 'Honestly, it wasn't!'

'It never is.' Sarcasm dripped from Emma's lips, which might seem rude to some, and might be no way to talk to your boss—but it was because she did speak to him like that, because she did keep him at arm's length and because she was very good at her job, that, despite his stunning initial offer, in the six weeks she had worked there, Luca hadn't even attempted to flirt.

Well, the odd time perhaps!

But it was quickly, expertly, rebuffed.

'Did you get my messages?' Emma checked, because he never read them. 'A Dr Calista called—he wants you to ring him.'

'Fine.'

'And your sister too—she wants to know if you've looked at the ties.'

'Ties?'

'She sent you an email of some photos of ties—for the groomsmen to wear at the wedding—and she wants to know if you're staying. She's rung a few times today.'

'Remind her of my hourly rate,' Luca drawled, 'and if she keeps ringing, bill her.'

He didn't mean it, Emma knew that, but he could be so scathing at times.

'I *do* mean it,' Luca said as if in response to her private thoughts.

'You really want me to bill your sister for ringing you?' She *knew* he didn't mean it, knew he'd hit the roof if she actually did it, and just refused to play his games.

'I want you,' Luca said, very firmly, very clearly, 'to practise some of the assertion this job demands—I am not to be bothered with these details, is that clear?'

'Very.'

'Good.' Luca said. '*You* choose the ties, *you* sort things out and you have my full authority to tell her it was me.'

'Fine.'

He was turning now, heading back to his office, tossing the empty chocolate cup in the bin. Then he turned around.

'Are you doing anything tonight?'

'Actually, yes,' Emma said through gritted teeth, 'I've got plans.'

'Well, cancel them.' Luca shrugged. 'Ruby was supposed to be coming with me to some awful dinner dance at Hemming's. It's plus one, so I'm expected to bring someone.'

'I really *do* have plans!' Emma repeated, because she was beginning to get tired of this—she worked hard, more than hard, but this would be the fourth night in a row that she hadn't got to visit her father and it simply wasn't fair—surely she was allowed to have a semblance of a life? 'I need to visit my father,' she reluctantly explained, loath to let Luca in on her personal life. 'I told him I'd be over tonight.'

'So, tell him that you are working.'

'I've been putting him off all week.' She just couldn't do it to him *again*. 'I'd really like to finish on time tonight.' When Luca just frowned, she pushed a touch further. 'Look, I don't usually say no, but surely there's someone else you can ask?'

Which was a stupid thing to say. There were plenty of women Luca could ask, and there was one reason and one reason only that he was asking her! 'I was hoping for an early night,' Luca sighed. 'At least with you it would be just dinner!' Which was a rather strange compliment, but it bought a reluctant smile to her face. 'I'll ask Evelyn—where is she, by the way?'

'No, don't...' Emma flustered, for Evelyn had sneaked off to the doctor's to pick up her vials and needles for her final round of IVF, which she was starting in the morning. The last thing the poor woman needed was a night on the town with Luca. 'I'll just go. It's fine.'

'You're sure?' Luca frowned, just a touch guilty now that he had got his own way, as he knew full well where Evelyn was. 'Tell you what—we can visit your father on the way.'

'We can't,' Emma fretted. 'I'll be in evening dress!'

'So?' Luca grinned. 'Go on, get ready and we'll leave in an hour.'

It was testament to the nature of her job that she *could* get ready for a formal function within the hour. There was a bathroom on their floor and Emma stuffed her curls under a cap and quickly showered. She even had a wardrobe in her office—her day bag was already packed and ready for her jaunt to Scotland in the morning and Emma rummaged in it for her styling wand and spare make-up bag then set to work on her face, squirting drops in her eyes in the hope they'd sparkle and then working on her lips and cheeks.

With some difficulty she pulled stockings onto damp legs and then slipped on her fast-becoming-familiar little black dress and clipped on a string of black pearls, before coaxing tired feet into stilettos.

And then she tackled her hair. Spritzing her wayward, corkscrew curls around the wand and trying to coax them into shape.

It was a routine she was starting to perfect.

'You need some more evening wear,' was Luca's only comment when he saw that she was in her black dress again.

'Just as soon as I get a day off!' Emma retorted. 'Aren't you ready?'

He didn't answer but, then, Luca rarely answered pointless questions. Instead, he strode out to the lifts with Emma following behind, holding a small suitcase to take to her father and stuffing her evening bag with keys and lipstick and hair serum and sticking plasters as the lift plummeted down.

'I forgot to put on perfume.'

He sniffed the air. 'You smell fine.'

Men!

He glanced at the small case she was carrying, but didn't comment and neither did Emma, not bothering with small talk. She just sat in the back of the car with Luca as they moved at a snail's pace through the heavy peak-hour traffic, a knot of tension in her stomach, sure that at any moment he'd tell her it was too late to stop by her father's nursing home. Glancing at her watch, she realised they weren't going to be able to make it and it was actually a relief—she didn't want to explain her life to Luca.

'The old dog's home first!" Luca drawled, not knowing the nerve he was pricking as he let them into his apartment. The television was blaring as usual and Emma paced as Luca chopped up some chicken breast and added a spoonful of rice to Pepper's bowl.

'He's on a diet,' Luca explained.

She didn't quite get where Pepper fitted into the scheme of things. She'd been to Luca's apartment on several occasions and still couldn't work out what Luca was doing with a dog. Neither man nor beast seemed to particularly like each other and the last thing a person with Luca's schedule needed was a dog—and a lapdog at that.

But it wasn't her place to question. It was her job to just book the vet in for home visits, or make sure that the dog sitter knew when Luca was suddenly called away.

'Look in the bathroom,' Luca called from the bedroom. 'There is probably some perfume there that has been left behind—help yourself.'

It was like the beauty section in a chemist's shop—perfumes, lipsticks, body lotions, all left behind by their previous owners—but it wasn't them that caught her attention. In the mirror she could see Luca's reflection—dressed in black hipster underwear, he was selecting an evening shirt, and though she was getting used to Luca, she wasn't used to seeing quite so much of him.

He was stunning.

He was so pompous and arrogant that for the most part Emma was able to switch off from the fact he was, quite simply, the most beautiful man she had ever seen—only now she was *seeing* him.

He had long muscular legs that even managed to look sexy in socks. As he pulled on his shirt, she caught more than a glimpse of his chest, a smattering of black hair that made Emma's toes curl in her already too tight shoes. Dragging her eyes away, she selected some perfume and squirted it on, but her eyes wandered back to the stunning view of him, to those long lean legs as he sat on the bed and pulled on his trousers.

And then he caught her looking.

His eyes held hers in the mirror for an indecently long time, a ghost of a smile spreading on his lips, and then she snapped her eyes away.

'Ready?' So flustered was Emma that his voice in the doorway made her jump. 'If we want to stop at your father's, we'd better leave.'

He knew.

Cheeks burning, her back and thighs pressed into the leather seat of Luca's car, Emma knew that he knew.

That despite the banter, despite the rebuffs, despite her thoroughly cool demeanour around him—Luca D'Amato knew that he moved her.

And suddenly, for the first time in six weeks, Emma felt vulnerable.

CHAPTER THREE

'SO WHERE does he live?'

Emma gave the driver the address and sat back in her seat, her tension mounting as the car neared the leafy street, lined with huge impressive homes.

'It's nice here...' Luca glanced out of the window. 'So, is this where you grew up?'

He had no idea, must just assume that her father could afford a house in this area, but instead of answering she just shook her head, tempted to tell the driver to forget it and take them straight to the Hemmings' dinner dance, except her father would be devastated if she rang and cancelled again.

'After that red car on the left...' Emma instructed the driver. 'Just here will do.' Only he went past the red car and pulled up at the gates, pressing the button in the intercom. Emma could feel her cheeks burning as Luca took in the nursing home sign. 'Could you tell them Mr Stephenson's daughter is here for a visit?'

'I'll wait in the car.' She could feel Luca's eyes on her as he spoke, but couldn't look at him, just climbed out as the driver handed her the small suitcase.

'I shouldn't be long.'

* * *

'Hi, Dad!'

The way his face lit up when she walked into his room only made her feel worse. He looked forward so much to her visits, but lately they had been becoming fewer and further between.

'You look like your mum…' Frank beamed '…when we used to go out dancing.' And on and on he chatted as Emma put away his laundered pyjamas and replaced his deodorant and talc and filled up his little dish with money for a newspaper in the morning. And it seemed like a nice visit because her father was chatty and for once there wasn't a hint of malice about her mother, but it hurt more than she could explain.

His face had never used to light up when Emma had walked in the room—that had only started to happen in these past few months. Growing up, he'd practically ignored her, or when he did talk to her, it was to bad-mouth her mother, as if it had been her fault she'd died. So in all it had been a pretty wretched excuse of a child-hood and Emma knew she had every reason to walk away, to leave it to the system to look after him. Only now, since his stroke, it was as if her horrible childhood had somehow been erased. For the first time they had a father-daughter relationship, for the first time she was hearing little bits about her mother, about her history, and despite it all, he was her dad—and even if they'd left it rather late they did have a relationship and she could never, like her brothers had, bring herself to just walk away from him.

'I'm sorry I haven't been in more recently.' She broke his favourite chocolate she had brought him into pieces and put some on a plate in front of him. 'Work's so busy…but I'll be in properly at the weekend.'

'You have to go?' Frank's eyes filled with tears. 'You've only just got here.'

'Dad, I have to work.'

She felt awful leaving him so soon—except she had no choice. Until the house sold, it was her work that was paying for the home.

She knew what the nurses must think of her as she clipped past the desk in high heels, and she was so close to crying it hurt—she was tired, so tired of juggling things, of scrambling to get everything half done. At work she was calm and efficient, yet on the inside she was a festering mess.

'Miss Stephenson.' As the cool night air hit her she gulped it in, turning to see who was following her. Aware Luca must be watching, she died inside as the supervisor waved an all too familiar manila envelope. 'We've been trying to contact you about the account.'

'I spoke with Accounts yesterday...' Emma tried to keep her voice even, tried to lower her shoulders and pretend, for Luca if he was watching, that there was nothing wrong. 'I explained that I have a new job, that I'm catching up on the outstanding balance—they're putting a new payment plan in place.'

'I'm aware of that—it's here for you in writing.'

She took the envelope. 'Thank you.'

'Any default on this plan and I'm afraid...'

'There won't be.' Emma swallowed. 'You know Dad's house is on the market.'

'We have a long waiting list,' the supervisor answered. 'We're trying to help, Miss Stephenson, but we're not a charity.'

The car was full of music when she entered, and Luca was sending emails on his phone. She breathed out a sigh of relief that he surely hadn't noticed the uncomfortable exchange with the supervisor.

'How was he?' Luca checked.

'A bit teary,' Emma admitted. 'Still, I'll see him properly at the weekend.'

'Does he get other visitors…?' His voice trailed off. Evelyn had told him about her mother's death and, seeing Emma's tight lips, he changed tack. 'It looks like a nice place,' Luca commented, glancing up at the impressive building as the car crunched out of the driveway. 'Expensive?'

'A bit.' Emma shrugged. 'You do what you can.'

Unexpectedly, Emma found herself enjoying the Hemmings' dinner dance.

It wasn't an exceptionally lavish function they attended—that was the type of thing that had got the company into a mess in the first place—but it was a genuine, feel-good party and Luca was the man everyone wanted to greet. His prowess had salvaged a sinking ship and in the process had saved hundreds of jobs.

And Luca was a very nice date.

He turned off his phone the moment they arrived and he remembered to introduce her to enough people so that when he was circulating she didn't feel like a complete spare part. He even swapped his white chocolate and nougat mousse with her when she got landed with the almond torte, and when the dancing started he didn't ditch her just because she was a work date, even though on many occasions he could have. In fact, apart from one duty dance with the CEO's wife and a long conversation with some potential investors, Luca for once appeared off duty.

'Thank you...' He held her loosely in his arms as they danced. 'I know you had other things to do tonight.'

'It's actually been nice.'

'It has,' Luca agreed. 'I was worried, I admit.'

'I'm sure you'd have found someone else to join you.'

'I meant, I was worried whether I could salvage them from bankruptcy,' he explained, and he laughed at her blush. 'I do think about work sometimes.'

'Sometimes!' Emma laughed. 'I don't know how you fit it all in.'

'I just do.' He stared down at her. 'And so do you.' He looked down at her for a long moment. 'How long has he been there?' All evening he had made no comment about her father, yet the question had hung between them.

'Six months.'

'You are very young for him to be...'

'Dad was quite a bit older than Mum.'

'Oh.'

'He had a stroke at the beginning of the year...' Her voice trailed off, she didn't want to talk about it, she really, really didn't. Yes, tonight was work, but in his arms, swaying to the music, when Luca didn't push or press the point, really it was just a relief to be here, to be away from it all, even for just a little while.

'I am glad it is you tonight,' Luca said. And close to midnight, with champagne inside her, it would have been very easy to lean closer, very, worryingly easy to rest her head on that chest that was just inches from her, terribly, terribly easy to wonder at his words. So to stop herself, she reminded herself of the real reason that she was here, and couldn't help herself from asking.

'What happened with Ruby?' She spoke to his lips,

the same way that he was speaking to hers, and suddenly it wasn't working. Reminding herself of his appalling reputation wasn't keeping her safe—she was having to forcibly resist the urge to move closer to him.

'She said those four little words.'

'Three little words!' Emma corrected, because occasionally his excellent English slipped.

'No, four...' She could see the shadow of growth on his chin, his full mouth moving as he spoke, feel his breath and wished suddenly he'd just kiss her. 'Where is this leading?'

She could only smile at her own stupidity as realisation hit, and was so, so glad she hadn't quickly answered what she had briefly assumed was a question, because it took a second to work out he wasn't talking about them—he was answering her question about Ruby.

'So I told her—nowhere!

'Come on,' he said as the music ended and he broke away, 'let's go. I'm staying at the office. We have a helicopter to catch...' he squinted at his watch '...in five hours.' Which translated to about three hours' sleep if she went home. 'What about you?

That extra hour actually counted when you were operating on Luca time.

Ever the gentleman, he pulled out the sofa bed in her office then retired to his luxury suite. Emma lay staring at the ceiling, thinking about him. Not once had he pounced on her, had never made her feel uncomfortable, and apart from that blistering first invitation, there had been nothing else.

Except he'd caught her looking at him earlier.

Emma squirmed in embarrassment and then consoled herself that if she'd been standing in her bra and panties, he'd have had a quick peek too.

It offered no consolation.

'What's the point of it all, Em?'

His voice over the intercom penetrated the darkness and made her smile. He did this every now and then.

'So you can make pots of money,' she responded.

'I've made pots of money.'

'So you can have any woman you want.'

There was a pensive pause.

'I have any woman I want.'

'I don't know, then.'

'So why are you here?' Luca asked. 'Working yourself into the ground, that cruel boss never giving you a night off?'

'Because I love my work!' she duly answered.

'Rubbish!' came the voice over the intercom, and Emma smiled. 'Why *are* you here Em?'

She paused for the longest time—almost expecting the door to open and Luca to walk in. This conversation, despite taking place over an intercom, was surprisingly intimate. And lying in dark, she was almost tempted to tell him, about the bills and the house, about her dream of going to art school. About how this job was her lifeline, about how, one day, she hoped it might set her up to pursue her goals...

Which was hardly the conversation to have with your boss.

''Night, Luca!'

She could never have guessed but save for those two words her office door would have opened.

He liked her.

Luca stared up at the familiar ceiling, at the dimmed lights that never actually went off—and it was a measure of how much he liked her that he didn't go to her.

It had nothing to do with Evelyn's stern warnings—well, maybe a bit, as Evelyn was too good to lose, and her husband was getting less and less impressed with the hours his wife put in.

But it was more than that.

He didn't want to lose Emma.

He liked her.

Not just liked her, but actually *liked* her.

Liked having her in his day.

She was nothing like anyone he'd met before. She brightened up the office with her chatter and her fizz and she answered him back and made him smile.

And she liked him too. In *that* way.

He'd actually been beginning to wonder—he'd been a bit taken aback when she'd so coolly turned him down at their first meeting. Working with him, she was so on guard, so scathing of his ways, that he'd wondered if the reason he liked her was that she was the one woman who didn't fancy him.

Then tonight he'd seen her expression in the mirror, and in that second before she'd realised he'd caught her, he had seen the want in her eyes.

He lay racked with rare indecision.

His instinct was to let nature take its course.

With women, Luca always followed instinct—and instinct told him to go out there to where she lay, in those ugly pyjamas she wore. Luca became instantly hard at the thought of those curls on the pillow, and her soft skin.

So why the reticence?

Because it would last a couple of weeks, a couple of months perhaps—and then she'd want more from him, like they all did, like Martha had...

He closed his eyes on that sudden thought, but circles of light still danced before his eyes.

Martha had been the only one it had *really* hurt to let go.

It was a thought that till now had comforted him— that he had said goodbye to *the one*, that the hardest part of the deal he had made all those years ago was over.

So why, when he hadn't so much as kissed Emma, was he comparing her to Martha?

He hadn't seen anyone since Emma had joined the staff, had finally dumped Ruby, whom he'd kept dangling for weeks.

He thought about going out there to Emma—*how* he thought about going out there—but something stopped him: she really needed this job and for now, at least, he wanted her around.

He couldn't have both.

CHAPTER FOUR

'YOUR sister is insisting that she speak with you. She's tried your mobile, she's been calling all morning,' Emma said to the silence of the intercom. 'And now she is insisting.'

'I'm still in a meeting.'

Luca did everything the other way around from anyone else she had met: he didn't drop a thing for family! He had several mobile phone numbers—yet his family all went directly to message bank, no exception, no deviation. Emma knew he checked them—had seen him listen, scowl and hit 'delete', yet unless *he* was in the right frame of mind, Luca refused to pick up.

Which left Emma to deal with the fallout.

'I'm sorry, Daniela,' she said for the umpteenth time. 'He really can't be disturbed—is there anything that I can help you with?'

'You can ask why he no come, why all he can give me on my special day is two hours of his precious time, familia *is everything, my own brother...'* It really was rather draining to listen to, yet she was being paid fabulously to do so. And dealing with Daniela's histrionics was actually easier than dealing with Luca right now—

as the wedding approached his mood blackened. Oh, nothing had been said, he was still his fastidious, energetic self, barking orders, making her laugh every now and then, but there was this tension to him that was palpable—this grey, gathering cloud that seemed to be following him wherever he went.

'I'm going over to Hemming's.' Evelyn came to her desk. 'Luca needs some files and I have to speak with the accountant.'

'Sure.'

'Whatever you do, Emma—' Evelyn's voice was serious '—don't put Daniela through—with Luca in this mood, he'll surely say something he regrets and guess who will have to deal with it?'

'What is going on?' Emma asked for the fiftieth time. 'Why can't he just go for the weekend? He does it for his clients all the time.'

'I've no idea.' Suddenly Emma realised Evelyn wasn't putting her off with vague answers. 'I've worked for Luca for years now and have had little to do with his family, but since this wedding was announced, they're on the phone every five minutes, and it's doing nothing to improve his mood.'

'I had worked that one out.'

'Get me Dr Calista on the phone.' Luca's voice through the intercom was a brusque order and Evelyn rolled her eyes as Emma picked up the phone.

'Good luck.'

It was rather like knowing there was a wild bear in the building with the door unlocked.

Luca wandered out every now and then, snarling and sniping, giving his orders and then retreating. The phones were ringing red hot and with Evelyn out,

Emma rang the deli and had some sandwiches sent up for her own lunch. Luca had snapped, when she'd asked him, that he didn't want anything.

'What's in them?' He peered at her lunch and selected the smoked salmon and cream cheese without a word, but Emma was used to him now, and the second he slammed the door of his office she opened her drawer and pulled out her *own* smoked salmon and cream cheese sandwiches, smiling at her own foresight as she picked up the phone.

She wasn't smiling now—the sandwich like sawdust in her mouth as she faced a new challenge, wondering if she should ring Evelyn and check, completely unsure what to do.

'Luca…' she swallowed the mouthful of water she had quickly taken '…it's your mother on the phone.'

'I'll call her later,' came the curt reply.

Which she relayed, to no avail.

'Luca…' She felt as if she were pressing the demolition button as she pressed the intercom again.

'What?'

'She's crying. I don't know if something's happened…'

When he swore in Italian, Emma held her breath, hardly letting it out when she saw the red light on and realised he had taken the call, wondering if she had done the right thing. The thick door to his office meant she could hear nothing and Emma paced up and down, staring at the red light, knowing they were talking, wondering if she should go in and apologise afterwards, berating herself for not checking with Evelyn what she should do in these circumstances. And then, after an interminable time, the red light went off.

She waited a moment for his angry summons but, worse than that, there was only silence and a closed door.

She knocked—as he insisted she did.

And knocked again, ignoring that he didn't answer—deciding to 'practise some of the assertion this job demands'. Taking a deep breath, she walked in. Afterwards, she fervently wished she hadn't, but by then it was already too late.

He couldn't stand it—he just couldn't *stand* it!

For weeks Daniela had been ringing, every day, then every hour, and now and then his mother too.

And now had come the tears.

The pleading.

'Familia, Luca.'

He hated *familia*!

'Just this—all I ask of you, all I have done for you, all I have *suffered* for you!'

For him?

Always his mother twisted things—and she was twisting them now, telling him she had suffered for him, that she had taken the beatings, the hell, the agony—*for* him.

And now, supposedly, he had to repay the favour.

He *hated* this!

There was a rip of anger in him, this fury that sixteen years living away from home had only slightly dimmed, because it was always there, churning beneath the surface. His vast office was tiny, too small to contain his fury, his loathing, his hate.

Then he became distantly aware that his mobile was ringing.

Ma.

Ma.

Ma.

He picked the mobile up and threw it across the room—but still it rang.

He picked up his landline phone and tossed that too.

Ah, but soon would come the emails…

So with one swoop he cleared his entire desk of its contents, the computer, papers, his lamp, his coffee, everything, crashing in one swoop, a smash of glass and chaos, with no relief, no reprieve because Emma walked in.

'Out!'

He roared it at her, but she just stood there, frozen.

'Get out now!' Except she didn't, just stood there eyes wide in shock and then, worse, with tears in them…refusing to leave, refusing to go. So he stormed out of his office and on to the lift, pounded on the button and then gave in, resting his head on his forearm and dragging in air.

He would explain.

He must explain.

He hadn't wanted her to see him like that…

Luca turned and walked back, calmer now, together now, and then he saw her.

Kneeling on the floor, crying and scared and shaking, picking up the lamp, retrieving shards of glass—trying to clear up the chaos so that it might appear to have never happened.

It could have been his mother twenty years ago—only this time it was *he* who had caused the chaos, and *he* who had reduced Emma to frightened tears.

'I'm sorry!' Her voice was shaky as she took the

blame, and that was what almost killed Luca. 'I should never have put her through to you.'

It almost killed him, because Luca realised with a dread that had been building for years now—he *was* turning into his father.

CHAPTER FIVE

EMMA had grown up with men long enough to refuse to tiptoe around them—oh, she steered clear of Luca for a while and when Evelyn came back a new lamp was purchased, a few items replaced, and supposedly it had never happened.

Except it had.

Yet she refused to be silenced.

Refused to dance around him and refused not to question him when a ridiculous plan made itself known.

'Can you tell me why *I'm* booked to attend your sister's wedding?' Emma struggled to keep her voice even—after all, this was her boss and this *had* to be a mistake, but she wasn't going to take *this*!

It was six p.m. and Emma had spent the last two hours with Luca's travel team, working out the logistics of his impossible schedule for the upcoming fortnight, only to see her name appear on the flight list for Palermo and the transfer helicopter to his village. Worse than that, she'd had to suffer the thinly veiled smirk on the travel team manager's face when she'd asked why the hotel hadn't yet been booked.

There were no hotels in the village!

'Oh!' Luca had at least the grace to wince. 'I've been meaning to tell you...' Luca could read women as easily as a newspaper and as her eyes widened at his choice of words, he quickly corrected himself. 'I mean, *ask* you.'

'Ask me what?' she asked through gritted teeth.

'You know my sister is getting married soon.'

'Is she really?' Emma feigned surprise. After all, *she* was the one co-ordinating the lavish wedding gift—a pool, and not just any pool, an infinity pool cut into the edge of the volcanic rock no less. And *she* was the one who had been dealing with the Sicilian foreman and the architect and the insurance company, the tie selection people, the sister and the mother, not to mention Luca's appalling mood! Oh, yes, she knew his sister was getting married!

'Please,' Luca said. 'Sarcasm doesn't suit you.' He frowned for a moment, then added, 'Actually, it does—but not now. I need some help over the weekend. It's a bit hard to explain...'

She gave a tiny shake of her head. Luca *never* found things hard to explain—the Luca she knew always just came out and said what he meant.

'Well, I can't help. I actually have plans that weekend,' Emma said, her voice still even and calm. She didn't actually—even though it was her birthday, she'd made no plans other than visiting her father, but she certainly wasn't going to let Luca know that. 'And I know my job is varied, but playing the part of wedding planner is really out of my league.'

'The wedding is all taken care of.'

'So what do you need me for?'

'It would make things easier, to have someone there with me,' he admitted.

'You mean *with* you?' She was really shaking her head now. 'No, Luca, absolutely not. You could ask anyone…'

'But you're not going to go and get any stupid ideas,' Luca said. 'Emma, you understand me. The last woman I brought home…' He gave a small swallow before he named her. 'Martha. I explained to her not to get swept away, that my family would assume we were serious, that they would think that there was a wedding imminent. She assured me she understood, except when we got there…'

'Things changed?'

Luca nodded. 'I can't face going; I can't stand the thought of being in the same house for two, maybe three nights on my own.' He looked at her then, at her dark curls bobbing, at the mouth that could always somehow make him laugh, at the body he thought of at night now. *This* was the one way he could do it—with the one woman who could make hell bearable right now beside him.

Even if it meant he would soon have to say goodbye to her…

'I thought that with you there…'

'Did you really think I'd say yes?' Emma demanded. 'Well, obviously you did if the travel team already know about it.'

'I was going to speak to you later this afternoon. I didn't realise the meeting had been brought forward.'

'Well, the answer would have been the same—no!'

'You're making this a bigger deal than it is!' he protested.

'It's a very big deal to *me*! Anyway, there are any number of women who would be more than happy to accommodate you. Ask one of them.'

'My father's ill!' He played the sympathy card, but Emma just gave him a wide-eyed look.

'So is mine—but I'm not asking you to share a bed with me,' she retorted.

'He has just a couple of months to live,' Luca revealed.

'I'm sorry to hear that,' Emma responded, 'but I can't help. Look...' she was irritated now. More than irritated, she was angry at his assumption that he could just go ahead and organise something like this without even consulting her. 'I'm sorry he's ill, but—'

'I'm not sorry he's ill, Emma,' he interrupted her, his voice dark. 'I hate my father—really, the end cannot come soon enough. My mother has asked, pleaded that I come, that for one final time we put on the D'Amato show...'

'The D'Amato show?' Emma frowned, but Luca didn't elaborate.

'I cannot face it.' She'd never heard him anything other than assured and the plea for understanding in his voice momentarily swayed her. 'I'm asking you because I know you get it...'

'Get *what*?'

'Me!' For the first time he looked uncomfortable. 'I have no interest in marriage, no interest in settling down—not ever. You understand...' he gave an irritated shrug '...that this would be strictly business.'

'Sharing your bed isn't *my* idea of business!'

'You'd be well remunerated...' He took in her furious expression and hastily added, 'We could just say you're my girlfriend—I'm not asking for sex!'

'Just as well, because I absolutely do not fancy you!' Emma turned to go, her face burning. She'd heard enough, lied enough but she hadn't actually said enough. She turned back. 'You're right, Luca—I do *get* you. And, yes, I get your good looks and your sentiments where women are concerned. I get that you have no desire to settle down and that women want more— I get it all. Well, enough to know that you rarely sleep alone, and no matter how you introduce me to your family or what you think may or may not happen between us while we're away, but you and I, sharing a bed, well, it wouldn't work!'

'I think it would work rather well!' he retaliated.

And just then there was a tiny shift, a brief moment when they were both imagining it, both thinking about it, both visiting the same place for a very dangerous second. She suddenly felt hot and bothered—partly, to be honest, because he simply oozed sexuality—and yet it wasn't actually just about him and whether or not he deigned to lay a finger on her, whether or not he could keep to the spirit of any agreement they might come to.

It was also about the fact that she was twenty-four and had never had a relationship—sometimes she felt as if she was the last virgin around! Oh, she had made the excuse that she had been too busy looking after her father and in part that was true—but it was about more than that. She was far too guarded with her heart, far too mistrusting of men, and with Luca that was wise.

Except…

With Luca, at least she'd know where she stood from the very start.

He watched the small swallow in her throat, watched her cheeks dust pink.

And then she thought of his reaction when he found

out she was a virgin—which snapped her mind away from the very dangerous place it had been dwelling.

'The answer's still no.' Very firmly she said it.

'Can I ask you to at least think about it?' he pressed.

'I already have and I've given my answer. I like working for you, Luca.' She bared her teeth in a stand-offish smile. 'Let's just keep things professional, shall we? If you're able to!' And with that, she walked out.

Which told him.

For the first time Luca was the one blushing—not that anyone would notice, but he could feel his ears burn just a touch as she dismissed him, put him in his place. Just as she always did, Luca realised as he sat, smarting, at his desk. Unused to rejection, it didn't sit well with him at all.

He could have anyone he wanted! With that thought, he pulled out his phone and scrolled through the list of contacts, looking at the names of the many beauties around the globe he could summon right now, this very minute—only recently none had really appealed.

Emma did.

He sat there for ages, thinking, going over and over it in his mind, as the office darkened.

Emma could get him through these next few weeks—the wedding, the last stages of his father's illness. *How* much more bearable it would be with Emma around... And why did it only have to be for just a few weeks? He had no qualms that they would get on—despite her protests, he knew she was attracted to him.

So why would it have to end so soon? Maybe it could be a few months, or even as much as a year...

He went to turn on the desk lamp, but though Evelyn

had managed a close replica, the cord was on the other side, and in that second, as he reached for thin air, Luca was reminded why a relationship with Emma could never last even as long as that.

He pulled up a document on screen.

Position Vacant

Assistant PA

He read the guidelines and then added a few more words.

'Fluent Japanese essential.'

Save the changes?

Emma knocked and he called her in. 'I just need a file, if that's okay...'

'Sure.'

'I brought you coffee.' She didn't appear in the least uncomfortable when she came in and placed his strong brew on his desk. In her own way, Luca realised, she was setting the tone, heading over to the filing cabinet and carrying on efficiently, as if their previous conversation had never happened.

She was absolutely gorgeous, Luca mused. Her hair was working its way out of its low ponytail, dark curls dancing around her face, and he sat watching her thin jumper strain over her generous breasts as she pulled over the foot ladder and still had to stretch to reach the top file.

She had a fantastic bottom.

Round and curvy and soft.

What *was* this fascination with Emma?

She was nothing like the women he usually dated—he usually liked his women trim and groomed to within an inch of their lives and preferably without an opinion.

Emma had an opinion on everything.

'Go home,' he said, irritated with himself now. He just wanted the temptation of her out of there.

'Oh!' She glanced at her watch. 'Are you sure?'

'It's your art class tonight, isn't it?'

She'd missed the last two weeks, and Emma was touched that he'd noticed. 'Is there anything else you need before I go?'

He chose not to answer that one.

He'd get to that soon enough.

CHAPTER SIX

'EMMA!'

There were many ways Luca said her name, and with his rich Italian accent the first couple of thousand times he had made her rather plain name sound vaguely exotic.

Just not any more.

This was a short brusque *'Emma'* that came over her intercom and jolted her out of the notes she was compiling, a clipped order that he wanted her to come into his office now.

She had a nine a.m. meeting with HR that she *had* to be at in a five minutes—a meeting about which he would want a full written report on his desk by lunchtime, with question time after, no doubt. She was tempted to ignore his summons, let him think that she had already left.

'Emma!' The voice was just as curt, only this time it came not from the intercom but from the man himself—clearly she hadn't responded within the requisite two seconds.

'Didn't you hear me?'

'I was just coming,' Emma said calmly.

It had been a week since Luca had put forward his ridiculous proposition—and though he'd had the good sense not to broach it again, the mood between them wasn't great.

He wasn't sulking exactly but, as Emma had demanded, things were strictly businesslike and the chatter and banter had gone—and she missed it. Working such ridiculous hours, he consumed a large part of her day, and she missed that side of him, that was all.

'I need you to set up a meeting with Mr Hirosiko. I need all the latest figures...'

Luca had recently set his giddy sights on Japan—a difficult market to break into for an outsider, only Luca had seen it as a challenge, zipping through a refresher course of the language, instructing Emma and Evelyn to learn it too, and when Luca focused, he really focused. Not only did he brush up on etiquette skills but he was suddenly into *kaiseki ryori*, or Japanese haute cuisine, his restless mind constantly seeking challenges, new interests. He never tired; instead, he just absorbed the new energy and expanded, moving on to the next challenge while retaining the old.

'Set up the meeting room for a face-to-face.' He snapped his fingers as he tried to recall some small detail from his busy, brilliant mind. 'There is something I need to address with him first...'

'It was his mother's funeral last week,' Emma responded. She knew because she had arranged the flowers and condolences that had been sent on behalf of D'Amato Financiers.

'That's right.' He nodded brief thanks—he would start the difficult meeting with some friendly conversation, before heading for the jugular. It wasn't actually a tactic, Emma had realised after a few weeks of working for him. Luca could separate the business side of things from the social with alarming ease—his condolences would be genuine, his sympathy real, but when it came down to business there would be no concessions or momentary reprieves—which was why D'Amato Financiers were not just surviving but thriving. Luca dealt in money, serious money—his own and other people's—and, eternally vigilant, he preempted things with skill and ease.

And he was pre-empting now as she glanced at her watch.

'HR can wait,' Luca said. 'This is important.'

Kasumi, Mr Hirosiko's PA, was always sweet and unruffled whenever Emma had dealings with her, and this morning she was smiling into the screen when Emma finally found the right button to push. She chatted for a moment with the other woman, admiring her glossy blue-black hair in the video conferencing room as she arranged Luca's meeting desk and pulled up some figures he had asked for on his laptop.

'I will tell Mr Hirosiko that Mr D'Amato is ready for him,' Kasumi said when both women were sure everything was in order. And though she had done this many times now, there was still an awkwardness talking to the large screen, still a certain awkwardness in Emma's movements as she set up the room.

'*Konbanwa,*' Emma said, wishing Kasumi a good evening.

On Luca's instructions she had been learning Japanese in what could loosely be called her spare time. On the drive to work or to visit her father she practised the

difficult language with some CDs Luca had lent her—
but after six weeks she was still on level one!

'Have a pleasant day,' Kasumi returned the greeting,
but as Luca strode into the room, Emma realised that
the calm, unruffled Kasumi wasn't impervious to his
charms either. On the vast screen above the meeting
room Emma watched as the other woman's pale cheeks
turned pink—and who could blame her? Luca didn't
just stride into the meeting room and bid her a brief
good morning. No, he walked in and stood and gave her
his full attention, bade her good morning and chatted
in rather impressive Japanese, managing to keep full-
on eye contact that would make any woman squirm—
and then he treated Kasumi to one of his rare laughs.

'And that, I'm afraid, is as far as I can go!'

'You did very well.' Kasumi smiled. 'Your Japanese
is improving.'

'A bit,' Luca agreed. Walking to his desk and seeing
Emma's slightly rigid lips, he turned back to the screen,
catching Kasumi's waiting eyes again as thick heat
flared in Emma's throat. *'Saifu o otoshimashita,'* Luca
said, and Kasumi started to giggle. *'Isha o yonde
kudasai,'* he added, to Kasumi's obvious delight, and
Emma was appalled at the prickles that rose on the
back of her neck, at her indignation at their obvious
flirting while she was in the room. Well, she wouldn't
show it, of course; instead, she poured his water and
checked that the meeting was being recorded, as no
doubt Luca offered promises of dinner and breakfast in
bed on his next trip to Japan, or whatever it was that was
making Kasumi giggle so.

Still, the skittish giggles from the, oh, so professional Kasumi soon faded as her boss entered the room,

but it was Emma's cheeks that were still flaming even after she discreetly left the meeting room.

'Everything okay?' Evelyn checked as Emma collected some files for the rescheduled HR meeting.

'Everything's fine,' Emma said, forcing a smile, only everything wasn't fine. She was unsettled, restless—angry even—and she didn't want to acknowledge why. Taking her chair in the meeting, she eyed the pale pink blooms of an impressive display of orchids—Luca's choice of flowers for the week—her teeth grinding against each other as she choked on that alien emotion. It was jealousy that had flared when he had spoken with Kasumi, and it had no place in her life.

He was a rake, a born flirt, a serial heartbreaker and a self-confessed playboy. He'd crush her in the palm of his hand. Well, Kasumi was welcome to him—they all were. She'd been right to say no to his ridiculous offer. If she accepted it, well, her job would be as good as over. Whatever Luca had implied about nothing sexual happening between them while they were away, Emma didn't believe it for a second. And Luca didn't like looking at his mistakes afterwards. Evelyn had warned her of that from the beginning.

Yes, she'd been right, but then why at night did she lie there thinking, wishing it could be different, wishing she could pluck up the courage to say yes?

Her head buzzing from the HR meeting, she returned to find several personal calls that needed to be returned—and not one of them brought her joy.

The interested vendor that had been through her house at the weekend had put in a bid—on a different house.

And, though he insisted he wanted to help, her brother Rory had just found out that his child maintenance to his ex-wife had been increased, so, sorry, no, he couldn't.

'Rory!' Emma snapped. 'We agreed when we chose this home for Dad that we'd cover the fees between us until the house sold!'

'That was before we found out how much of a mortgage Dad had on the house. Look, Em, even if the house does sell, it's not going to keep him there for ever. He's only in his sixties. I've been talking with the boys and maybe we should look for somewhere cheaper...'

They'd do it, too.

As Emma hung up on her brother, she knew without a doubt that they'd do it—would move him from a home where he was, for the most part, happy, if it meant they could get their hands on some cash.

And then the nursing home rang to say that her father had been asking for her all morning.

'He's fine,' the nurse assured her. 'Just a touch anxious...'

'Look, I know I haven't been in as much recently.' Emma closed her eyes in exhaustion. 'It's not that I don't want to.'

'We're not trying to make you feel guilty,' the nurse said. 'You asked that we keep you up to date, and though he is confused, well...he does notice that you're not visiting as often as you were.'

'Tell him that I'll be in soon,' Emma said.

'Can I tell him when?'

They didn't mean to make her feel guilty—except guilty was exactly how she felt.

And at times it was completely overwhelming.

She pressed her fingers into her eyes in a bid to stem the tears, stem the urge to just throw in the towel, to let her brothers sort out the mess. To stop caring about a father who had treated her so poorly in the past.

When the house did sell, she'd be homeless. Oh, the profits from the sale would cover the overdue fees of the home, but it was the backlog of debt that was giving her nightmares.

'Problem?' Emma jumped, unsure how long Luca had been watching her.

'Not at all...' She forced a smile. 'The meeting went well; I'll write up a report and get the information to you.'

'I wasn't talking about the HR meeting.' Luca frowned. 'Is anything wrong?'

'Nothing,' Emma said, then realising what he'd seen she relented. 'I've got a bit of headache, that's all.'

'My housekeeper's not well.'

'Oh!' Emma blinked, reaching for the phone. 'Did you want me to ring the agency and arrange a replacement?'

'I'll survive for a day,' Luca said magnanimously, 'but I *am* going to be flying to Japan this afternoon. Evelyn's coming with me, she's gone home to get ready, so can you go over to my apartment and pack for me?'

It was a strange byproduct, Emma had realised, of being rich and in demand—there was very little personal in his personal life. There was a whole army of people ensuring that every minute of his valuable time was put to best use. Letting herself into his vast, luxurious apartment a little later, Emma bent down and went to stroke Pepper, who duly growled a warning, then waddled to the huge glass sliding door to be let out. Emma wandered out onto the balcony and stared at the spectacular view of the Thames, before setting to work. She headed into the bedroom, opening her organiser and locating the list that would tell her what was required for a two-night international business trip.

All the information was there in her folder.

His immaculate suits and shoes were packed, as was his equally immaculate casual wear, and then she opened his underwear drawer to see neat rows of folded hipsters and socks as if they were on display in an exclusive store. There was nothing personal about the choices she made—the list saw to that. These cufflinks were preferred with this tie and shirt, these shoes with that suit... It just felt personal, that was all.

'Hey!' Emma jumped as Luca walked into the bedroom unannounced, blushing as she held a handful of his hipsters. It just seemed wrong somehow to be going through his underwear drawer, even though it was her job to be in there.

He was completely at ease with it, of course.

Just kicked off his shoes and lay on the bed, chatting on his phone as Emma walked through to the sumptuous bathroom to pack his toiletries and to try and not listen as he made a couple of personal calls—cancelling his plans for the next couple of nights and, by the sound of it, breaking a couple of hearts in the process.

'Why?' Luca asked as she came back into the bedroom with his toiletry bag and was finishing off his packing, 'when I say I'm going to Japan, do they think it has something to do with them—why would they think that I'm lying?'

'Because you usually are,' Emma pointed out.

'Well, I'm not this time.' He ran lazy eyes over her, taking in the smudges under her eyes, the vague distraction that slightly displaced her more usual sunny nature. 'What's wrong, Em?'

'Ms Stephenson to you!' Emma instantly pulled him up, refusing, just refusing as she always did with him, to cross the line. 'But you can call me Emma.'

'What's wrong, Emma? And don't give me that rubbish about a headache.'

'Nothing's wrong,' Emma insisted.

He lay back on the bed, closed his eyes and gave a low laugh.

'Now that I've stopped, I realise I have a headache too!'

He did—right there at the front of his head. He could hear the sounds of her packing, and it would be so incredibly easy to just close his eyes and sleep. He didn't want to go to Tokyo. Incredibly, and not for the first time lately, he could hardly stomach the thought of the flight.

'We should *fare force*…' Luca smiled with his eyes still closed.

'Sorry?'

'You know…' he waved his hand, tried to come up with the English word for it, but it eluded him, and those gorgeous navy eyes finally opened to hers. 'Leave school…' He snapped his fingers, impatient with himself now. 'Not go back.'

'Play hooky!' Emma grinned.

'Play hooky!' Luca smiled at the term and closed his eyes. 'That would be good—we could get ice-packs from the fridge for our foreheads and lie in the dark and ignore the phone.'

'Sounds good.'

'And I wasn't being inappropriate.'

'I know.' Emma smiled, because she knew exactly what he meant, exactly how he felt, because she felt it too. 'But we can't.'

He looked as if he was dozing, except his mind was actually whirring.

He was sick of keeping things businesslike between them.

He was cross with himself too for his handling of things.

He wanted her.

And yet he didn't—because he actually liked working with her. Liked having her around, and once things moved, as they surely would, well...

There was no question of a future for them.

Not even a hint of one.

He deliberately didn't do long-term relationships—as soon as things got too comfortable, too nice, he cut all ties.

It was a promise he had made himself many years ago.

He lay there, head pounding, listened to her pad out to the kitchen, to the running of the tap, and for once he was torn with indecision.

He wanted her.

He didn't want to lose her.

Yet he couldn't have both.

'Here.' She was back, holding out a glass of water and punching out two tablets from a blister pack. 'Take these.'

'Only if you do.'

Emma punched out two for herself and they shared

the glass of water. Funny that he noticed a little thing like that—funny that to Luca it mattered that she didn't go and get another glass.

'We'll feel better in twenty minutes.' Emma smiled, glad that they seemed to be talking normally again after the strain of the past few weeks. 'It says so on the box.'

She zipped his suit holder and picked up the phone to summon his driver as Luca downed a quick shot of espresso from his coffee machine. He stuffed files and papers into his briefcase as he gave her a few last-minute instructions that would take about a couple of hours to execute.

'Any problems, ring Kasumi. It doesn't matter what time it is there—things have to be in place for tomorrow.'

'Sure!' He watched her bristle slightly at the mention of the other PA's name and inside Luca smiled.

'*Saifu o otoshimashita,*' Luca said, watching her cheeks go pink as he repeated the words he had said to Kasumi. '*Isha o yonde kudasai.*'

'You can tell her yourself when you see her,' Emma responded coolly.

'I've dropped my wallet!' Luca laughed. 'Can someone please call a doctor? I was practising new phrases!'

He made her laugh, but her little flare of jealousy was acknowledged and out there now—and she didn't know how to handle him, or this energy that swirled between them. His dangerous offer still dangled in the air and right there at that moment she wanted to reach out and grab it. Maybe she could fake it, Emma thought wildly, maybe she could pretend that she wasn't a virgin. Maybe her body would just *know* what to do. Evelyn buzzed and he picked up his briefcase. 'Don't bother going back to the office,' he said, nodding to a PC. 'Do it from here and then finish up for the day...' He frowned at her pale face. 'Actually, have tomorrow off.'

'I've got a full schedule tomorrow.'

'Cancel it—my orders.' Luca shrugged. 'Have a day off and sort out whatever "nothing" is, or, failing that, catch up on some sleep. I'll see you on Monday.'

And as always, he left home as easily as he left a hotel room—just turned and walked out of the door without a second thought.

As he handed his driver his bag, her voice reached him. 'Have a safe trip.'

He looked back over his shoulder, a throw-away comment, a rushed farewell on the tip of his tongue, and in that moment he glimpsed it.

Leaving.

How it *could* feel to leave home.

'See you Monday.' His voice was gruff and Emma stood there as he closed the door behind him.

Now that he was gone, she breathed.

She wanted to tell him.

For the first time ever, she actually wanted to confide in someone—to tell him what 'nothing' meant. To share, to reveal, not that he might fix it, because she knew no one could do that, not so he might wave a magic wand and make her father suddenly better, or the nursing-home fees smaller, or the anger at her father's past treatment of her disappear. It was none of that. No, standing in that bedroom, seeing him lying on the bed, those dark blue eyes concerned, all she had wanted was to do exactly what Luca had said.

Fare force.

To escape for a little while, to lie down beside him in a dark room and let the world carry right on without her for a little while.

As the door flung open again she stood to attention almost, snapped the smile back on her face as Luca hurried in and strode across the lounge towards her. He must have forgotten his passport or phone or…

And then it happened.

What she had been secretly thinking about from the very first time she had seen him.

What she had desperately been trying to avoid and ignore.

That bubbling, simmering tension between them finally acknowledged.

His arms pulling her in and his mouth pressing on hers.

Wrapping her in his embrace and crushing her with his mouth.

And it should have been unexpected, should have caused shock, anger, except it was just pure relief.

Sheer, sheer relief to be kissed and to kiss back.

His tongue was cool and he tasted of mint and man and coffee and escape—and Emma didn't at that point question it. All she did was feel it. The bliss of firm lips and the scent that had always made itself known captivated her as it intensified in their close proximity.

His body to touch was everything her eyes had promised—lean and powerful beneath her hands and against her own body.

His eyes were closed, she *had* to look, had to see

him, and it made her want this moment more because he was as lost in it as she. He moved from her mouth, his moist lips lingering on her cheeks, his hands on the small of her back pushing her hips into his, and then it was her ear he was kissing. Instead of moving her head away, with *his* kiss, she leaned towards him, curved into his touch, weaker in her body as Luca's mouth met her throat and thoroughly kissed it too—her neck was arching and his hands had moved, both now on the peach of her buttocks and pressing her heat into him. Then his mouth found hers again and she tasted his ragged breaths—and it was just like the first time she'd ever seen him, because the world was black again, everything diminished and nothing else mattered, just his kiss and his body. And who cared where it might lead or the damage it might do, because for the first time ever she wasn't thinking or fixing or solving or surviving—she was living, just alive and alert, but only for this, for him, for them.

And then the intercom buzzed—Evelyn warning him they would be late.

'That,' Emma said in a shaky voice as he pulled back from her, 'didn't just happen.' She put her fingers up to her lips, could feel them swollen and tasting of him, and what had been simple and natural a moment ago was suddenly very confusing.

And then he kissed her again.

'Or that,' Luca said, and he stared into her lovely clear eyes and saw the whir of confusion. She was wholly adorable and for a second he felt regret.

Real, wretched regret, because soon he'd have to get used to missing her.

But it was too late for regret, because he'd pulled

the pin now and the countdown to the inevitable end had started.

As Evelyn's voice on the intercom filled the room, warning she was on her way up, he gave Emma a quick frantic look that made her giggle. 'Don't tell her!'

'God, no…' Emma swallowed. 'Just go…' She was more than confused now, trying to assert herself, wishing she could turn back the clock, only Luca was upping the ante now.

'Think about Italy.' He was still holding her, his kiss this steam that wouldn't evaporate. She felt as if she'd been running, could feel her hammering heartbeat and the dampness between her legs. His knowing eyes were on hers, his hands on her hips, and he pulled her a little way in towards him once more, giving her just another small, decadent feel of what was there waiting there for her if only she could reach out and take it.

'What are you so scared of?' Luca asked, and after just a moment's thought she gave him a very honest answer.

'Losing.' She stared back at him, and it wasn't just the job, or the jet-set lifestyle, she was scared of losing, but him. 'Let's just forget that it happened.'

Futile words—and they both knew it.

CHAPTER SEVEN

'DAD, please don't cry.'

He always got upset when it was time for her to leave. She hadn't got to the nursing home till eight p.m., and so couldn't stay, but Luca left for Sicily tomorrow—he had finally agreed to stay with his family for a few nights so at least for a couple of days she'd be able to see more of her father.

It was worth it—even if her boss was barely talking to her! Luca was clearly smarting as, even after their kiss, she still had persisted in saying no to accompanying him to his sister's wedding.

'I just miss her…' Frank was staring at a photo of her mother and Emma just didn't get it—growing up, it had been practically forbidden to talk about her, and now it was practically all he talked about! Going over the past as if it had happened just yesterday, and it actually hurt to hear it. 'I just want my Gloria. Why did she have to leave us?'

'Dad, she didn't want to…'

'Off with that scum of a man…calling himself an artist! How could she walk out on her family?' Emma felt the blood in her veins turn to ice.

'She didn't walk out on us, Dad, she was killed in a car accident.'

'Out on the town with her fancy man, leaving her little girl crying at home,' Frank sobbed, and the night nurse came in then.

'We're going to give him his sleeping tablet now, Emma, and settle him down.'

'How could she walk out on four kids?'

How she wanted to press him for answers, to bombard him with questions, but the nurse was giving him his medicine, trying to settle him down, and he was just too frail and too confused to push it right then.

'Rory!' She didn't care if it was late, or that she was driving, she punched in his name and waited for him to pick up, not bothering to introduce herself, just blurting out her question. 'Did Mum walk out on us?'

'Emma?'

'Just tell me what happened.'

'You know what happened,' Rory sighed. 'There was a car accident.'

'Who was driving?'

Emma knew he was holding back, could tell by the uncomfortable pause before Rory next spoke.

'What's Dad saying now?'

'That she walked out on us.'

There was a very long silence and then came a truth she had never prepared for. 'Mum left us a month before she died.' As he heard her start to sob, Rory showed rare concern for his sister. 'Look, pull over, you shouldn't be driving…'

'She just *left* us!'

'She wanted to "find herself", do her damned art, see this new guy. Look, it was twenty years ago! I don't see what you're getting so worked up about,' Rory attempted. 'It doesn't change anything.'

Oh, but it did.

She clicked off the phone and threw it onto the passenger seat.

It changed *everything*.

She shouldn't be driving in this state...so she forced herself to concentrate, forced herself to be calm until she pulled up to her family home—the for-sale sign on the door, the home, the family her mother had walked out on—and only then did she see him. His car was there, waiting for her, and Luca climbed out of the back seat and walked towards her. His face was grey, and in the streetlight she could see the tiny lines around his eyes, the dark, weary shadows beneath them.

She could smell the whisky on his breath and hear the dread in his words, and it matched her soul.

'Come with me tomorrow.' He didn't touch her, he didn't make any demands, he didn't even ask, he just matched her need.

'Yes.'

He blinked just a touch at the ease of her answer, a smile spreading over his face, relief creeping in, because *now* he could stomach it, *now* he could face it.

'What took you so long?' Luca asked.

Her mother had left them...

This idol she had looked up to, the perfect woman, gone too soon, had feet of clay after all—and she was angry, but boy it felt good to contemplate living instead of mourning, to let go of the past and dive into the future.

And there it was—if only she had the nerve to reach out and take it.

'I've never slept with anyone before.' She watched his reaction, saw his eyes widen, and thought it was almost fear that darted across his features. 'Don't worry, Luca,' she said before he could respond, 'I haven't been waiting for Mr Right to come along and relieve me of my virginity.'

'Emma!' He hadn't bargained on this. Not once, not for a second had he considered this. He wanted relief, distraction, and instead this was responsibility, but Emma just laughed and kissed his cheek. She was in a strange, slightly manic mood he didn't understand, but it was actually a little bit catching. 'You know I'm not looking for serious…'

'I know the rules, Luca.' Emma's voice was steady. 'And I'm prepared to play by them. Now, if you'll excuse me, I have a weekend away to pack for.'

As his private jet lifted into the early morning sky, all Emma wanted to do was close her eyes and sleep.

The night had been spent packing and planning and then dreading, and finally weeping.

Weeping for a woman she didn't know at all, for a father she had always resented but was maybe, just maybe starting to understand.

She was resilient, though, she had always had to be, so she hid her swollen eyes behind huge sunglasses and pleaded another headache when Luca commented on them. She had, after a night of weeping, pushed away yesterday's news and was in a bizarre way actually glad to be getting away for a few days and leaving it all behind her.

They were served a sumptuous breakfast, pastries, waffles, meats and the thick treacly coffee Luca survived on, but Emma wasn't hungry and Luca watched her push her food around her plate and frowned over his newspaper.

There was something different about her. Oh, she was chatty and polite, only there was a vague distraction about her, a restlessness almost, something he couldn't quite pinpoint.

Her acceptance yesterday had floored him.

He had engineered this weekend—had been hoping the mutual attraction between them would be quickly sated, that she would be the solace that would get him through the difficult time ahead.

He had been dreading the wedding for months now—back to the family home, back to his father and uncles. Emma was to have been his relief.

But not now, and he had only himself to blame.

Breaking hearts he could deal with.

But breaking hers...he was having serious second thoughts about that.

He saw that she wasn't eating her food and, remembering her beverage of choice when she was flagging, ordered his crew to fetch it for her. Then he sat and watched closely as she took a grateful sip of thick hot chocolate.

'You have brothers, yes?' Luca checked, watching a small furrow emerge on her brow.

'Three,' she acknowledged briefly.

'And what happened with your mother?'

'I really don't want to talk about it...'

'But we have to,' he insisted. He finished with his breakfast and pushed his plate away. It was removed instantly, the conversation continuing when the steward had discreetly disappeared. 'You speak little of your personal life.'

'The hours I work hardly allow for much of a personal life!' she protested.

'Emma, for this weekend you are supposed to be my girlfriend—I am taking you to meet my parents. Surely you can see that I ought to know some of your background.'

He had a point. In the weeks she had known him, she had been privy to all sorts of information about him.

His diary had noted birthdays, anniversaries, his clothing preferences for the times when he needed an outfit at short notice, even the hairdresser he used for his regular trim. She knew, because it had been her job to hire a new housekeeper for him, how he liked things done, the sort of food he kept at home—had even downloaded some songs for him—so if she were put on the spot right now, she knew enough about Luca to bluff her way through, whereas apart from the fact her father was in a nursing home, Luca knew practically nothing about her.

That was the way she had wanted it.

But, as Luca pointed out, their stories needed to tally. She screwed up her courage, and then suddenly he came up with a compromise.

'Okay—I'll tell my mother you don't like talking about it.'

'About what?' she asked, bewildered.

'Anything I don't know the answer to,' he said, pleased that he'd managed to eke out a smile from her. 'We have been seeing each other for a couple of months,' Luca said, 'since you came and worked for me. We have both decided that working together is too much, so you will be finishing up soon.'

'To do what?'

Luca shrugged—trying to think what his girlfriends actually did all day.

'Modelling?'

'Please!' Emma snorted with laughter. 'If I'm to convincingly play the part of your devoted girlfriend, then at least there has to be a semblance of me in there. So...' She chewed on her lip and tried to imagine a world where this man loved her, tried for the first time to actually picture a world with herself and Luca as a couple, and glimpsed the impossible—being the sole recipient of his affection.

Yet even if it was impossible, it was still fun pretending.

'I'm applying to study art, you're organising a studio for me in your apartment, in that big room at the back that you don't use. It's supposed to be a surprise, but unbeknown to you I've guessed.'

'Are you good?' Luca asked. 'At art?'

'I've just started night school. My dad didn't like me pursuing...' Her voice faded for a moment, realising now why he might have hated that side of her so, but she refused to dwell on it, it was just too big to deal with right now. 'Oh, and by the way...' She gave him a wry smile. 'Just in case it comes up in the conversation, today's my birthday.'

'Really?' Luca frowned. 'You should have said.'

'I just did.'

'I am sorry to pull you away from your celebrations.'

'You didn't,' Emma answered tartly. 'It's really no big deal.'

'And how old is Emma today?'

'She's twenty-five!' It made her blush to say it, with

the information she'd so recently given him. She saw just the slight rise of one eyebrow, but thankfully he chose not to comment.

'So what about you?' she asked.

'You know about me.'

'I don't know much about your family.'

'My mother is Mia, my father is Rico. He was a policeman, and you know about Daniela...'

'And he's sick...' Emma probed. 'Your father?'

'Very.'

'And you don't get on?'

He gave a tight shrug and clearly it was Luca now who didn't want to talk about it!

'Anything else I should know?' she pressed.

'Nothing.' Luca shrugged. 'As I said, my father was the village policeman, I went to boarding school from ten...' He saw her frown at that. 'That is usual where I come from, as the school in the village only goes up that age. It was all pretty normal really.'

'Till their son became a billionaire.' Emma smiled, but then she was serious. 'Why, Luca? Why do you hate them so—?'

'Not Daniela,' he interrupted. 'And not my mother...' He shook his head. 'Let's just do what we have to, smile, enjoy, *familia*...' He sneered the word. 'Let's just get through it.'

There was a bedroom at the rear of the plane, but for the relatively short flight to Italy he just tipped back his seat and stretched out and Emma did the same. Hoping her swollen eyes had settled, she took off her glasses and lay back.

'I love these chairs,' Emma commented. 'I wish I had one at home.'

She squirmed in comfort as the attendant placed a soft warmed blanket over her.

'If I ever have to bribe you I'll remember that.' Then he added, 'Are you okay?' when it took her a second too long to smile.

'I'm fine.'

'Because if you're worried about what you told me yesterday—' he was direct as always '—well, you don't have to be—I'm not in anything for the long haul, and...' he gave a slightly wistful smile '...if you've waited this long for it to be right, I do understand.'

'I'm not upset about that,' Emma said, because right now she wasn't—Luca had wanted a fling and actually so now did she. She probably wasn't very good fling material, but she'd deal with it. It really was good to just get away.

'Then what *are* you so upset about?' They were lying flat, facing each other. 'You look as if you've been crying.'

'Not about you,' she retorted.

'Good,' Luca said, and he intended to keep it that way. 'Here.' He dug in his pocket and pulled out a black box and handed it to her as if it were a sweet. 'You'd better put these on—if we were going out, I would have bought you nice gifts.'

'Goodness!' Emma gasped and held up two earrings, the huge teardrop diamonds sparkling. 'They look so real.'

'They *are* real,' Luca said dryly.

'I'd better not lose them then.' She tried to sound as casual as him, but it felt strange to be holding his gift, strange to be lying beside him and very hard not to imagine that this was...

Real.

So she thought about other things instead. Silly things—like she used to when she was a child and couldn't sleep, not the grown-up things that she thought of now.

The steward clipped belts loosely around them and on leaving them dimmed the lights. Luca closed his eyes, but smiled when she carried on talking.

'It's like being in an ambulance.'

'Have you ever been in an ambulance?'

'No,' Emma admitted, but that didn't deter her. 'I'm in a coma, but I can hear, though no one knows it, and everyone I've ever fancied is going to dash to my bedside and beg me not to die, and say that they love me really.'

'What are you talking about?' He turned his head to face her again.

'Don't you do that?' Emma blinked. 'Make up stories before you go to sleep?'

'No.'

'What do you do?' she asked curiously.

'I close my eyes…' he shrugged '…and I go to sleep.'

'Just like that?'

'So long as there is no one talking.'

He'd wondered what to expect—if she'd be miserable, angry, but instead she was just being Emma.

He was glad that she was there.

He could feel the familiar knot of tension tighten in his stomach as the plane sliced through the sky—the same knot he felt every time he came home, the same sick dread he had felt coming home from boarding school on the holidays.

The same sick dread he had felt every night as he had lain in bed as a child.

Luca breathed out, suddenly needing to swallow, sweat beading on his forehead as he willed sleep to come.

His father was old and weak and dying, there was surely nothing to dread now.

And then he saw it.

Like a dog dashing into the street, his mind swerved to avoid it, but his father's fist was there, slamming into his mother's face, the image so violent, so real it was as if his father's fist had made contact with his own.

He jumped.

That horrible jump where you woke up with heart racing, only Luca knew that he hadn't been asleep.

'Luca?' Emma murmured. She was almost asleep, though, he could tell from her voice, and knew because in her right mind Emma would never reach out and hold his hand.

It felt like weakness to take it.

But it helped, it actually helped.

CHAPTER EIGHT

'WELCOME to our home.'

Landing at Palermo, Emma had enjoyed the helicopter ride that had taken them on the final leg of their journey to his small coastal village—and everywhere Emma looked the view was stunning. Houses perched on top of houses all staring out to the twinkling Mediterranean, and Luca's family home was the jewel in the crown—the basic home had been lavishly extended, and every room was angled to take in the spectacular sea view.

Luca's mother's welcome was warm and effusive, pulling Emma into an embrace and kissing her on both cheeks, then guiding her through to a large terrace that ran the length of the house while chatting non-stop in her rich accent, alternating between English and Italian.

'Luca!' The squeals of delight from Daniela had Emma smiling, and he was far more pleased to see his sister than Emma's own brothers ever were—hugging her warmly, teasing her about the face pack she was wearing and introducing her to Emma, who Daniela eyed with the same suspicious navy eyes as her brother, but she smiled and chatted in very good

English, before drifting back to her bedroom to get ready for her big day.

'*Dove Pa?*' Luca asked.

'*Dorme,*' Mia said, and then translated for Emma. 'He sleeps… Oh!' She gave a warm smile as her husband entered. Tall and thin, his once raven hair peppered with silver, he would have cut an imposing figure in his time.

'Luca!' He embraced his son, kissed him on the cheek as was the Italian way. Luca briefly hugged him back, but Emma could feel the sudden tension in the room. '*Comesta?*'

'This is Emma.' Luca's voice was just a touch short as he introduced her to his father. Despite Rico's fragility he took her firmly by the hands, kissing her on the cheeks and welcoming her to the family…making a kissing gesture with his fingers when he saw the impressive earrings, which made Mia laugh.

'Come, Rico…' She plumped the cushions on what must be his seat and fussed over him as he lowered his tall frame. Emma stood, suddenly awkward as Luca just watched, his face an impassive mask Emma couldn't interpret.

'Luca is upset.' As Emma did the right thing and helped his mother prepare coffee in the kitchen, finally there was an explanation for his strange lack of reaction. 'It is hard for him to see his father so ill. It is almost a year since Luca was here, it would be difficult for him to see the changes.'

'Of course.' Emma set up the tiny coffee cups on saucers and it should have appeased her, except it didn't. Luca had his own plane—his own travel team for heaven's sake, and even her selfish brothers managed a visit to their father once a month—there was surely a lot more behind this *familia* that kept Luca away so coolly.

It was a busy house. The drinks and pastries that had been set up were not just for Luca and Emma's benefit, but for an endless parade of guests, all wanting to meet Luca's girlfriend and to wish Daniela well for her big day. And Luca saw the strain showing in Emma's smiling face as the shadows lengthened, and he was proud of her, proud at how easy she had made it for him to be here, and he wanted to make it easier for her too.

'I thought I might take Emma out for dinner. I know you are busy…'

There were protests from Mia, of course, but not too many. Rico was tired and wanted to get back to his bed, and Daniela was calling for help from the bedroom. Just a typical family two days before a wedding, and, as pleasant as the afternoon had been, it was rather nice to get out.

They walked through his village, the scent of the sea filling the late summer sky, and he took her to a local restaurant. No matter how many Italian restaurants she had been to before, nothing could compare to the simple fare of fresh pasta swished in basil pesto and lavishly smothered in Parmesan. The wine was rich and deep and fruity, and they sat outside drinking it, bathed in citronella-fragranced candlelight. Though they had eaten out together on many occasions, both in London and abroad, this was nothing like a business dinner, because here no business was discussed.

Her eyes were huge in the candlelight, her laughter infectious, and for the first time at home Luca relaxed, till the conversation turned personal.

'So you brought Martha here...' She took a sip of her wine rather than look at him.

'It was a bad idea,' Luca finally admitted. 'Martha insisted it would change nothing.'

'But it did?'

'My family assumed we were serious—and then Martha started believing it too.'

'Is it so impossible?' Emma blinked. 'You talk as if you've no intention of *ever* settling down.'

'I don't,' Luca said. 'I would grow bored, restless...I would rather have my pick.' He gave her a smile. 'Italian men get *better* looking as they get older, so I don't think I'll be short of company.'

And it was honest, so why did it hurt her?

The thought of him in years to come, that jet hair dashed with silver, his distinguished features slightly more ravaged—this beautiful man walking the planet alone...yes, she couldn't deny that it hurt.

'I'm surprised you haven't built a hotel here, if you don't like staying with your family.' Emma refused to get morose.

'It is often suggested by developers, but it would ruin it. There are natural springs close by, so it would certainly be a tourist paradise, but...' Luca shook his head. 'No.' He had no desire to be here any more than he had to and no desire to discuss his family further, so he concentrated on their meal instead. 'There are two desserts,' Luca translated the menu for her. 'Tiramisu or tiramisu with cream...'

He liked it that she laughed, liked it that she didn't decline dessert and instead ordered it with cream, liked eating with a woman who actually enjoyed it!

'They make it once a week, and each night they soak

in a little more liquor, so by Friday it has reached perfection,' he told her.

'Then thank God it's Friday.' She smiled.

She had tasted many tiramisus—good and bad, tiramisu ice cream, tiramisu from the supermarket, even tiramisu from an expensive Italian restaurant Luca had taken her to with clients, but as the sweet moist dessert met her mouth Emma realised she had never *really* tasted tiramisu.

'It's gorgeous.' She closed her eyes and relished it for a moment.

And so are you, Luca thought, watching her.

She could feel his eyes on her, and dashed to the ladies to touch up her make-up, wrestled with underwear that was supposed to smooth out bumps and realised that maybe the tiramisu was more potent than it looked as she struggled to replace the top on her lip gloss.

Or she'd had too much wine with dinner, Emma thought, staring at her glittering eyes and rosy cheeks.

Or maybe it was just a reaction to the company!

Even if it wasn't real, it was so good to be away, to forget, to be twenty-five years old today and go out for dinner with the sexiest man in the world.

He signed for the bill and they wandered back, taking the sandy route. Emma slipped off her sandals, feeling a million miles from London, from everything, as her feet sank into the wet sand, and her ankles were bathed by the warm sea.

'How can you bear to stay away?' she murmured.

'You eventually get tired of the view,' Luca said, 'no matter how beautiful.'

'I meant from your family.'

'You've seen my schedule.' Luca shrugged, and then expanded a little. 'I ring, I send money, I try to get back when I can…' He knew it sounded lame, knew she thought him a selfish person, and that was completely fine with him.

They stopped walking, Luca picking up a handful of stones and skimming them out to sea, looking out at the rolling waves and the high crescent of a new moon. He relented a touch about his family—he told himself it was because he didn't want to kill the mood, but…she *was* nice to talk to. 'It's not just the view you get tired of—but the place, the people, the unspoken rules…'

'Rules?'

'*Familia.*' There was a scathing note to his voice. 'Everything is for appearances' sake—that is why I am here, remember! What *will* people think if the brother, the only son, just drops in for the wedding? That is the type of question you hear all the time as you grow up. They are so worried about how they appear, what people will think. There is shame that their only son has not settled down. Every time I come home, it's always the same questions…'

'And that's enough to keep you away?' She didn't buy it. 'A few questions?'

'You see a frail old man near death, Emma.' She felt the prickles on the back of her neck rise as he continued, 'And the village sees the patriarch of the D'Amato family, close to the end of a good and rich life…'

'What do *you* see, Luca?' she asked quietly.

'My mother's fear.' If it was only a hundredth of it, it was still more than he'd ever admitted to anyone, and there was this curl of trepidation in his stomach as for the first time he broke the D'Amato code of silence.

'How, even when he can hardly walk, she still jumps when he enters a room, still laughs too loudly at his jokes…'

'Was he violent towards her?' Emma asked.

'A bit.' His guard shot back up. 'Yet he is weak and pathetic now—there is nothing more to fear.'

'Is that why you stay away?'

Luca shrugged, a bit guilty now, embarrassed perhaps at admitting so much, and he tried to laugh it off. 'Apparently I should have married some sweet virgin, produced several children by now—no matter whether or not it makes me happy.'

'But you haven't,' Emma pointed out.

'Because there are no more virgins—no good-looking ones anyway.' His mouth curved into a smile at his own joke and then, appalled, he remembered. 'Emma, I'm sorry!' He had to run to catch up with her. 'I forgot, okay?'

'Just leave it.' She shrugged him off, angry, annoyed, embarrassed and very, very close to tears. She was sick of it, sick of it, sick of it!

'Hey.' He caught her hand and spun her around. 'I'm sorry if I offended you— I just never thought—'

'No, you didn't!' Emma flared.

'You're not ugly…you're gorgeous,' Luca attempted, 'and the guy who gets you will be a lucky man indeed.' Huge green eyes looked up at him. 'I'm just not sure that should be me…' He stared at the oh, so, familiar beach, dragged in the familiar smells, and though he so desperately wanted her, he didn't actually *have* to have her—there was sweet relief in just her company tonight and the knowing that she would be beside him tonight.

'Even if I *want* it to be you?'

'Emma...' He didn't finish so they walked on in silence, and it was Luca who finally broke it. 'Come on, let's get home. I'll text Ma and let her know.' Which to Emma seemed a strange thing for a thirty-four-year-old playboy to do, but she was too upset about how the night had turned out, and really never gave it another thought, especially when they stepped into a house that was in darkness.

'They must have gone to bed,' Luca said, and then the lights snapped on.

'Surprise!' She saw the usually deadpan Luca grinning at her stunned reaction, as shouts of 'Happy birthday' and *'Tanti auguiri'* rang out, and slowly the realisation set in that this was all for her.

Luca could never have known how much this might mean to her, how completely overwhelming this was, because there were gifts all prettily wrapped and a table set with glasses and liqueurs and, centre stage, a cake. A huge sponge filled with cream and iced on top and in shaky handwriting the words *Tanti Auguiri Emma*.

Her first birthday cake, her first birthday party—well, at least, the first she could remember.

'Sorry,' Mia said. 'Rico wanted to stay up but he was tired.' Emma could see the mood in the house was actually better without him, and then Mia apologised that the cake was home-made, which made Emma's eyes well up. 'Luca only told me yesterday, there was no time to order one—and—'

'Yesterday?' Her head whipped around to him—that he had known all along, before she'd even told him, and that he had thought to ring ahead and arrange all this for her...

'Did you really think I'd forget your birthday?'

She opened her gifts—first a stunning white lace nightdress from Mia. 'For your trousseau,' she hinted. There was some body lotion and perfume from Daniela, and from Luca a silver charm bracelet, with a diamond-studded 'E' and a pretty horoscope charm, The Virgo Lady, dangling on her bracelet, which he'd bought before he'd known she really was one!

Did everything lead there?

'Emma wanted to start a charm bracelet collection,' Luca said as he snapped it on her wrist and kissed her trembling mouth, and she wondered at what a convincing lover he made.

'Then we will know what to get you at Christmas.' Mia smiled and it was too much—the unexpected kindness, the care, the cake and the fact that there would be no family Christmas, that none of this was real...

Tiny thoughts, like flickering stars were there on the periphery of her mind, and she was almost scared to focus on them in case they flared.

Cakes and presents and the love that her mother had denied her. Yet a thousand miles from home and with people she didn't know, it wasn't the time to be exploring her feelings, so again she squashed them down, plastered a smile on her face and carried on with the celebration.

Except Luca noticed her anguish.

'Time for bed...' he announced, and there was an endless round of kissing and goodnights so that rather than being nervous of being led to his bedroom, by the time they got there she was actually relieved.

Relieved when he closed the door and it was just the two of them.

'What's going on, Emma?' He meant it this time, wasn't going to be fobbed off again, only she couldn't tell him, just couldn't go there with Luca—not with a man who didn't really want to get involved with her.

And then her phone rang

'Happy birthday, darling!'

'Dad?' She couldn't believe it—she had rung the home before dinner just to say goodnight and had been told that he was resting. Not for a minute had she expected him to remember it was her birthday. 'I couldn't sleep, Em. They let me come to the nurse's office and ring you...' Not once growing up had he made a fuss of her. Everything had been dismissed with words like, 'Oh, you're just like your mother,' and only now was she starting to get it, only now did she understand that maybe he had been terrified of losing her too.

'I love you, baby girl.' And those stars flickered brighter then as she recalled words used by him *before* her mother had gone, the love for her that had always been there in him but which had taken illness to help it re-emerge. 'Happy birthday.'

'That was Dad.' She tried to make light of it to Luca. 'Heaven knows what the nursing home will charge for a mobile call to Italy...'

He frowned at her pale face. 'Worth it, though?'

'Yes.' She sat on the edge of the bed for a moment, and then put her head in her hands.

'I found something out,' Emma finally admitted. 'About her.'

'Your mother?' And she couldn't speak. Tears that she had always, always pushed back were trickling down her cheeks. 'I always thought that she'd been living at home when she died, that she didn't want to leave us.'

He knew better than to ask a question now.

'Dad said something last night, and I asked my brother about it. It shouldn't really matter...' She attempted Rory's dismissive take, only it didn't work. 'She walked out on us—a month before the accident. She'd gone to *find herself*, apparently!' Her eyes turned to him for answers. 'I don't know how to feel any more—I don't know who she was. She walked *out* on us....'

'Emma, you can still mourn her, still love her. Who knows what would have happened had she lived? She could have come back, or come to get you...'

Oh, what was the point explaining it to him? Instead, she headed for the bathroom, brushed her teeth and slipped on her candy-striped pyjamas, and when she came out of the bedroom she looked so young, so vulnerable and just so lovely that for Luca there was no question.

Sex *was* off the agenda.

She was just too raw, too vulnerable right now. He did have some moral guidelines and to have her fall in love with him, only for him to then break it off, well, he didn't think he could do it to her.

He lay on his back, staring up at the ceiling, as she climbed into bed beside him.

Every laugh, every word, every chink of glass had him on edge—hell, he hated this house at night.

What did she have to be a virgin for?

He wanted to lose himself in sex, wanted to block everything out except the smell and feel and taste of her. He could hear her crying quietly beside him; he hated tears more than anything, resisted tenderness at all costs, and yet there was no avoiding her tears, nowhere to escape to tonight.

'Emma.' He spoke gently into the darkness. 'Do you want to talk?'

'No!' She was sick of talking, of thinking, and now she had started she couldn't stop crying.

God, he was used to women's tears, but usually when he was ending an affair. He chose women carefully. Yes, Emma had been a gamble, yes, he was attracted to her— to her fiery independence, to the humour, to the fire— and yet she lay beside him, suddenly fragile, and it unnerved him.

He put a hand on her shoulder—was that what he should do? He sort of patted it and she even managed a small smile at his strange attempt at comfort, realising he was exquisitely uncomfortable with her display of emotion.

So was she usually—yet tonight it came in waves, waves that had been building for nearly twenty years.

That first day of school when all the mums had stood at the gates and she had walked in with her brothers.

Her first period, when it had been the school nurse that had explained this terrible thing that had happened and had told her too late that it was all completely normal.

Her first bra, she'd shoplifted it. Long-buried memories were hurtling in, the one time in her life she'd stolen, but rather that than ask her father to buy one for her.

But always, in her heart, Emma had carried the memory of her mother, sure, quite, quite sure that her mother would have given anything to be there with her.

Only she hadn't, because she'd left her.

* * *

And now, lying in bed, she felt as if she was falling.

Anger for all the things she had missed out on was seething inside her.

And she lay in a strange country in a strange bed, with a playboy who didn't deal in emotions when hers were exquisitely raw.

She actually felt sorry for him.

His hand was still patting her in a sort of there, there motion, this slight note of horror in his voice as he felt her shiver at the prospect of the grief she must hold in for now. Yet it was leaking from her eyes, from her breath, this scream inside that was building, the tension in her muscles where she wanted to just run…to curl up, to howl and to weep.

He turned her over to face him.

'Emma, stop this!'

'I can't!' It was like a panic attack, as if she was choking, tears shuddering inside her.

She was this contrary bundle in his arms, tense then pliant, sobbing but distant. He felt her push him away and then he felt her head on his chest, felt the dampness of tears then her furious withdrawal as she wrestled away. And he let her go but she came back and so he comforted her in the only way he knew how—he kissed her.

It infuriated her that this was his answer, enraged her so she almost pushed him out of bed and then wriggled away, appalled. Except it had helped. His mouth, his tongue had flicked her thoughts from pain to pleasure and then he'd stopped.

'I'm sorry,' he whispered.

But Emma wasn't—the room was suddenly too small, the bed too small when her emotions were so big, and she couldn't think, she just couldn't stand to think, so she kissed him back hard. Pressed her red, angry face to his and kissed his mouth fiercely, forcing his lips apart with her tongue, because if he was so good, if this was where it was leading, then better it was now, better this playboy, right?

'Hey.' He pulled down her hands, that were clamped behind his head, and moved his head back.

'Worried you're being used?' Emma jeered.

'I'm not worried about me...' He held her hands and stared into her eyes, and at that second he recognised himself, those nights when he climbed into a woman rather than explore his thoughts—that need for escape, for release. He had just never expected to see it in her—but it was there, and you had to know it to recognise it. 'I'm worried you don't know what you're doing.'

'I want this, Luca.' Oh, yes, she did, she wanted comfort, she wanted *him*!

'I don't want you regretting it...'

'I won't.' She held his eyes and made her promise. 'I won't regret it, Luca. I want this.'

And she did.

She wanted comfort and hell, she was twenty-five! Some time in the future, some time never, when she'd got over him, she could step out into the world of men knowing what it was like to make love with someone.

She wanted to know that so much.

And she wanted him.

All of him.

There was a fuzzy logic in her mind—she was going to lose him anyway so she wanted all of him now. She just had to hold onto her heart, that was all.

'I want this,' she repeated. Of that she was certain.

'I know it's not going anywhere, I know that's not what you want from me...'

Luca stared down at her flushed face and glittering eyes and suddenly he wanted this too.

'One moment.' He stood to go to the bathroom, his condoms deliberately still unpacked in his toiletry bag, but she caught his arm.

'I'm on the Pill.'

He cursed in Italian. 'Emma...' Her naivety worried him. 'It's not just for pregnancy. You have to make sure he...' It made him wince to think that there would ever be someone else making love to Emma, that he was somehow breaking her in for others to enjoy.

'Do you?' Only she wasn't being naïve, she was bold. 'Always wear one?'

'Always.' Luca swallowed, understanding her meaning—he knew he was healthy and he knew she was too. She was offering him the golden key, yet he hesitated, this rare intimacy alien to him.

It was a tentative kiss, both holding onto their hearts, both refusing for a moment to melt into the sheer, utter bliss of each other.

'We can get rid of these.' Awkward for the first time in the bedroom, he unbuttoned her pyjama top and slid it over her shoulders, removing his own underwear and then sliding off her pyjama bottoms.

The sight of him naked did nothing to still her nerves. She had nothing with which to compare it, except the sealed section of a magazine, but she knew he was pretty spectacular.

'Should we put a towel down or something?' Emma

asked, and Luca felt as clinical as a surgeon setting up to operate.

'I'm scared,' Emma admitted. 'Nice scared, but...'

'Me too.' Luca grinned, staring down at his unusually less than responsive manhood, and then he laughed, because it was strange to be talking about *it*, sex, something that usually just, um, happened, and he realised that this had to be better than good—for her sake.

He turned to face her with a strange weight of responsibility on his shoulders, because he wanted this to be right for her. That last kiss had been awkward so he ran his finger along her cheek and then down her arm, and then he stared at the full breasts that had always entranced him, naked now for him to kiss. His hand cupped her lovely bottom and she could feel the wet warmth of his mouth, the tender suckling on her nipples, which made her stomach tighten, and it was a curious warm feeling as his mouth took her breast deeper. And she touched him, too—in awe of his unfurling length against her thigh. Nervous, curious, but brave, she reached down and touched him and Luca closed his eyes at her tender ministrations.

'Is this right?'

He couldn't speak so he nodded and he still couldn't speak so he kissed her instead, not awkwardly this time, and this not a kiss like any he had known—this a tender, slow kiss that led to much more. His hand slid around the front from her bottom, to her most intimate place, where she was moist and warm. He stroked her there until he could hear her slight involuntary whimpers, and then slipped his fingers inside, stretching her slowly, sliding in and out till she was moaning in his arms.

For Emma it was heaven, everything she'd hoped for

and nothing like she'd read about—no pain, just bliss, his hand working magic, his mouth back on her nipples now, and she could feel the scratch of hair on his thighs as he moved closer between her legs...

Suddenly there was a need for more contact and he read her thoughts because he pushed her with his body onto her back and he kissed her, not just with his mouth but with his skin, all of him pinning her to the bed, and for a while just the delicious, solid weight of him had her in ecstasy. Then he moved up on his elbows, her legs parting to accommodate him, and he was there at her entrance. She wasn't scared any more, just ready.

She had never been more ready for something in her life.

He was staring down at her with surprising tenderness in his eyes, a gentleness that she had never seen. And she felt as if they were starting something, as if they were going somewhere together. It wasn't just her body she had never trusted to another, but her mind too—and in that moment she let him in, she could feel the first slow, shallow thrusts, feel the stretch of her body as it tried to accommodate him, and the barrier of resistance, and she told herself over and over that she had to remember not to love him.

It hurt, this searing, this moment, and then it was gone—and whatever it was she had just lost, she had found so much more.

The feel of him inside her, the wonders of her own body, rising to greet him as he entered and then resisting each withdrawal—her hips moving to meet his. There was this pull in her stomach, little licks of heat in her thighs. She couldn't keep her eyes open, she was lost in the dark with him and she felt as if she'd been found.

He was moving harder now, and yet she could feel him hold back, only he didn't need to now. Her fingers ran down the length of his back, holding his buttocks and pressing him into her, and Luca had never been closer to anyone, had never been closer to himself, than he was at this moment. She was crying and he was kissing her, demanding, seeking and taking her all. He licked her tears and felt the coil of her legs tighten around him as she gave her urgent consent. He drove in, feeling her in a way he had never felt a woman, the delicious slippery grip of her, the first flickers of her orgasm beating like the first heavy raindrops of a gathering storm. He could feel her mouth on his chest, muffling the pleasure she felt, and he felt her moans vibrate through his heart. Suddenly she was climaxing and so now could he, spilling inside her as she swelled in rhythmic spasms tighter and tighter, dragging him deeper inside her.

He wanted them in this place for ever, could feel his body winding down from the giddy rush, hear his own ragged breathing that heralded the end. Then he did something else he never had before—sated, replete and utterly spent, he looked down at where she lay beneath him and he lowered his head and kissed her.

CHAPTER NINE

EMMA didn't know how she felt when she awoke alone in his bed early the next morning.

The house was already awake, she could hear several voices and the sound of activity as the day before the wedding dawned. In a little while she would join them, would shower and go down and play the part of Luca's girlfriend and help with the preparations in any way that she could, but not just yet.

Now she lay, naked under the sheet, her body tender from last night and her mind surprisingly calm—remembering from a calm distance almost, accepting now what she had always known.

That there could be no going back.

That having made love with Luca, the countdown to the end had started.

She had seen it so many times—with her father, with her brothers, and with Luca himself.

The thrill of the chase, the high on capture, the intense passion of a new relationship—and then, always then, the retreat.

She knew this, had accepted this, had factored it in coolly when she had delivered her demands, but there was one thing she hadn't counted on. As he walked into the bedroom, carrying a laden tray and smiling into her eyes, there was an emotion almost like fear in the eyes that smiled back at him, because she had never anticipated the full effect of him—the dazzling beam of Luca when the full power of his smile, his mind, his body was aimed in her direction.

He'd be hell to miss.

He was dressed in jeans and nothing else. Barefoot and bare chested, he walked across the bedroom towards her, and it was a Luca she had never seen.

Usually suited, clean shaven—even the times she had seen him dressed rather more casually, still there had been a formal air to him. But it was a different Luca in front of her now.

Unshaven, his hair damp from the shower, it flopped forward as he bent over her. Then he took the coffee pot from the tray and put it on the bedside table before placing a tray on her lap. He looked younger somehow, less austere perhaps, and for Emma terribly, dangerously, devastatingly beautiful.

'It is chaos out there.' His thumb gestured to the bedroom door. 'So we will hide in here for a couple of hours.'

'Shouldn't I be out there, helping?' Emma asked, reaching for the pot of coffee, but Luca got there first.

'I'll pour,' Luca said, then answered her question. 'No, as I just said to my mother, we would only get in the way.'

Only she wasn't really listening—instead, she stared at the cup he filled. It had been a seemingly innocuous gesture, yet for Emma it was huge.

He'd brought her breakfast in bed.

Oh, she'd had staff knock on the door of her hotel room at six a.m. when she was travelling with Luca and bring her in her order, but never, not once in her life, had someone who wasn't being paid prepared breakfast for her, brought it to her and expected her to just sit as they poured. Always she got up, always it was her...

And this morning it was *him*.

It was scary how nice it felt to be looked after, even in this small way.

'These are *pizelles*. Like waffles...' He smeared one with honey and handed it to her—and then lay on his side, propped up on one arm, his coffee in the other hand, watching her intently, scanning her features for remorse.

'How are you?' he finally asked outright.

'Good,' Emma said through a mouthful of *pizelle*.

'Any regrets?' he asked.

'None,' she shook her head. 'You?'

'None—so long as you're okay?' he pressed.

'The first time's supposed to be awful,' she murmured a little wickedly.

'Says who?' he asked, outraged.

'I read it in a magazine.'

Luca rolled his eyes.

'If that was awful...' Emma giggled '...I can't wait for bad!'

'Throw away the magazines, baby...' He took her coffee cup and her *pizelle* away and straddled her on the bed. 'I'll teach you everything I know.'

It was such a different Luca, as if she'd been looking at him through the wrong end of a telescope. His energy was lighter, funnier, sexier even, if that were possible.

They shared breakfast and then each other, and then they left the chaotic household and had a picnic on the beach.

This time she didn't slip away when it was time to ring her father, she just sat on the blanket and laughed and listened to him reminiscing, and it was so much easier with Luca lying there beside her.

'I'll sort out the back fees for the home,' Luca said as she clicked off the phone. She turned to him, appalled.

'How did you know?'

'I read the letter the nursing home gave you,' he admitted shamelessly.

'That's reprehensible!' She was furious, embarrassed... And then he kissed her.

'Sorted,' Luca said, and he caught her eyes, 'You've helped me—now I can help you. I absolutely insist on it.'

And it was probably no big deal to him, except for Emma it was.

She felt the lightness as six months of worry slipped away, felt the elation as they ran down to the beach and enjoyed the late afternoon, felt the joy of being a couple, having someone to lean on, helping each other out.

And then Emma did a stupid thing.

As he kissed her in the salty sea, as she felt the waves rush round them and the chase of his tongue in her mouth, she started to wonder.

Started to hope.

Their day at the beach had brought a glow to her skin and on the morning of the wedding Emma massaged in body oil, glad of the peace in their bedroom and the chance, for once, to take her time getting ready, without Luca snapping his fingers and telling her she looked fine as she was.

Most of the house had been commandeered by the bride and her entourage. The whir of the hairdryer had been continual from eight a.m. and there was a constant stream of flowers, including the traditional arrival of flowers for the bride from the groom, which Emma was summoned down in her dressing gown to witness. As Rico was conserving his depleted energy for the wedding, Luca had stepped into father-of-the-bride duty and Emma had a little giggle to herself to see the usually unruffled Luca, who could handle the most difficult client or tense boardroom meeting with ease, just a touch frazzled as he dealt not just with his sister's theatrics but vases and flowers and the hairdresser, who was trying to locate a free power point for heated rollers.

Yes, their bedroom was a nice place to be!

Because she could, Emma spent time on her hair, attempting what a hairdresser had once, when she'd been to her brother Rory's wedding—taking several curls at a time and wrapping them around her wand till it fell in one thick heavy ringlet. Over and over she did this and for once her hair behaved, for once Emma was pleased with the results.

The hot September weather meant foundation wouldn't see the service out, so she put just a slip of silver eye shadow on her lids, relying mainly on lashings of mascara, a quick sweep of pink on her cheeks and a shimmer of tinted lip gloss. In her dash to shop and get ready for the trip, Emma had relied heavily on the stylist's suggestion of a suitable dress, although Emma hadn't been at all sure that it was right for a wedding when she'd tried it on in the boutique.

The silver-grey dress had looked very plain, if a touch short, in the shop, but the assistant had assured her it would look marvellous with the right shoes and make-up.

It did.

It slipped over her head, the material shimmering more in the natural light and the superb cut of the delicate fabric turned her most loathed bits into voluptuous curves.

Staring at her reflection in the mirror, Emma was slightly taken aback by what she saw. It was as if she'd grown up in these few days—gone from young lady to woman, and Emma knew it had little to do with her birthday and a lot more to do with the man who was now walking into the bedroom.

'I must get changed...' His voice trailed off as she turned to face him—and he suddenly felt that walking into his room to find her there was like coming across a haven of tranquility in a madhouse.

He'd appreciated her all morning—so many of his girlfriends would have been demanding their hour with the hairdresser while simultaneously demanding yet more of his time, yet Emma had left him to deal with his family—no sulking, or pouting, just that lovely smile when she'd briefly come down, and now he'd walked into the bedroom to this. Oh, he'd seen her dressed formally on many occasions, only this was different—a wedding, a family affair, his Luca plus one.

His diamonds on her ears were as sparkling as her eyes and there was that glimpse again, that small glimpse of how life could be for him if he hadn't made the choices that he had.

Of a life he could have with her.

'We leave in ten minutes,' he said, his voice gruff with suppressed emotion. He'd already showered and shaved, so he quickly pulled off his casual shirt and trousers and dressed in the dark wedding suit and gun-metal grey tie that had been chosen for the men of the wedding party, or rather that Emma had chosen for them. He had refused, point blank, to consider the burgundy monstrosities his sister had insisted would match the bridesmaids, and Emma had found the perfect one.

Not *the one*, but the *perfect* one.

Making a rare effort, he combed some sculpting gel through his thick hair then splashed on cologne. He filled his pockets with various envelopes for the priest and the band and then, when his head was around it, when more rational thought had descended, he spoke.

'You look lovely.'

'Thank you.' She gave a brief smile at his clipped tone, insecure enough to worry that he privately thought she looked awful.

'I will be busy today, back and forth with relatives. With my father ill, that duty…'

'It's no problem.' Emma smiled, putting some tissues in her bag and then squirting her perfume—just as she always did last thing before they went out. It was *these* little things he was noticing, Luca realised, these small details that added up to Emma. Her perfume was reaching him and her entire being was too.

Today was a day he had been dreading for months, since the wedding date had been announced and the preparations had begun. It had hung over him like a black cloud—being with his family, *all* his family, smiling and joking and keeping up the pretence, the charade, that there was no rotten core to the D'Amatos—yet here in this room he could breathe.

He couldn't not kiss her.

He lowered his head and his lips gently found hers, just pressing a little into the luscious flesh of her mouth, and he felt a flutter of something sweet and good and right settle.

Only their lips met, gently touching, barely moving, just tiny pulse-like kisses as they breathed each other's air, and it was a kiss like no other, this rare, weary tenderness from Luca that made her feel beautiful and wanted and somehow sad too.

'This is so much better with you here.'

There was a sting at the back of her throat and she couldn't understand why something so nice should make her feel like crying.

'It could always be.' She'd crossed the line, she knew she had. She'd taken the present and hinted at a future—there was suddenly no breath on her cheek as Luca stilled, no acknowledgment as to what she had said, but it circled in the air between them.

'We must go.' He waited at the bedroom door as with shaking hands she reapplied her lip gloss, catching her eyes in the mirror and giving herself a stern reminder of the terms that she had agreed to.

It was the most gorgeous, moving wedding.

Even if she couldn't understand much of what was said, even if she was here under false pretences and was supposed to be playing a part, the tears that filled her

eyes weren't manufactured as the proud, frail father of
the bride walked his glowing daughter down the aisle.

There were only two dry eyes in the church and they
both belonged to Luca.

He stood, taller than the rest, his back ramrod
straight, and though he did all the right things, there was
a remoteness to him—an irritable edge that Emma
couldn't quite define, an impatience perhaps for the
service to be over. For the second it was, the first
moment that he could, she felt his hand tighten around
hers as he led her swiftly outside.

'These two will be next!' Mia teased, holding her
husband's hand, laughing and chatting with her relatives.

'When?' Rico's eyes met his son's.

'Leave it, Pa,' Luca said, but Rico could not.

'What about the D'Amato name?' he pressed.

'Soon, Rico!' Mia soothed. 'I'm sure it will happen
soon.'

There was an exquisitely uncomfortable moment,
because it was clear soon was far too long for Rico, but
his brother Rinaldo lightened things. 'They leave things
much longer now.' He squeezed his young wife's waist.
'Not like me…' He kissed her heavily made-up cheek
then murmured, 'I wasn't going to let you slip away.'

As Rico greeted other guests and Rinaldo and his
wife drifted off, Mia chided Luca for his stern expression,
talking in Italian then giving a brief translation for Emma.

'Luca was close to Zia Maria, Rinaldo's first wife,'
she explained to Emma, then looked over at Luca. 'You
cannot expect him to be on his own.'

'He didn't even wait a year,' Luca retorted, his voice
ice-cold on this warm day.

'Luca—not here,' Mia pleaded, then turned to Emma. 'Come, let me introduce you to my sister.'

Emma lost Luca along the way, chatting to aunts, congratulating Daniela—really, she was doing well. Through her work she knew enough about Luca to answer the most difficult questions, though it would have been far easier if he was by her side.

They were starting to call relatives for more photos now and she found him behind the church, walking between the tombstones, standing and pausing, his shoulders rigid, almost as if he were at a funeral rather than a wedding.

'You're wanted for the photos,' she said softly, her eyes following his gaze to the tombstone he was reading.

'My grandmother,' Luca explained.

'She was so young,' Emma said, reading the inscription. His grandmother had been little older than her mother when she'd died.

'I don't remember her really—a little perhaps.' He shrugged as if it didn't matter, but clearly from his grim expression it did. 'And this is Zia Maria. I *do* remember her...'

Emma licked dry lips as she saw the young age of his aunt too. 'Rinaldo's first wife...'

'She was a lovely woman.' His voice was tender in memory, and pensive too.

'I know what you meant about Rinaldo...' He closed his eyes on her as if she couldn't possibly know, but Emma did. 'About not even waiting a year to remarry. I hated how many girlfriends my dad had. I know now that Mum had left him and everything, but he started dating so soon after...'

Now that she knew, it was as if her brain was finally allowing her to remember—patchy, hazy memories that she couldn't really see but could *feel*—a woman who wasn't her mother kissing her father, women's *things* in the bathroom, the sound of female laughter drifting across the landing to her bedroom as she lay weeping into the pillow and wanting her mother.

'They make me sick!' He shook his head, then raked his hair back in a gesture of tense frustration. 'Just leave it.'

And she had no choice but to do that, because now really wasn't the time. 'We should get back anyway.' She turned to go, but he was still staring at his aunt's grave and Emma guessed he must be painfully aware that in a matter of days or weeks he would be back here in the graveyard to bury his father. Only she didn't understand what he was doing here today, when everyone was trying to be happy, reminding himself when he should be forgetting.

'Luca…'

'You go. I'll be there soon.'

'Luca, today is a wedding—your family are waiting for the photos. For now, surely you should try to forget?' she said hesitantly.

'I never forget.' It was a bald statement and his eyes met hers for the first time since she had joined him in the cemetery, but there was none of the warmth that had been there that morning. In fact, there was no warmth at all. 'Come—we have a job to do.'

And in that short sentence he both reminded and relegated her. This was just a weekend away to him, a deal that had been struck, a pact that had been reached—an act she had agreed to partake in. It was Emma who had forgotten that at times; Luca clearly always remembered it.

As they joined the rest of his family, as they stood side by side with her hand in his, never had it been harder for her to force a smile.

CHAPTER TEN

IT HAD been a long exhausting day and was a long exhausting evening—as weddings often are.

Rico made it through dinner and, as Mia watched on anxiously, he managed to dance with his daughter. After that, clearly unable to participate further, Rico took a back seat and it was for Luca to take up the baton.

There was nothing Emma could put her finger on as Luca took over the role of patriarch with ease. He chatted with everyone, sat with the men at a table for a while and she could see him laughing at jokes, raising his glass in a toast, joining in tapping spoons to demand that the newlyweds kiss—and when she came over, he was soundly slapped on the back for his choice in women.

'The D'Amato name goes on,' Uncle Rinaldo cheered, so clearly she would do! 'Salute!'

There was just something…

Something that filled the air between them as they waved off the bride and groom.

As they put his parents into a car and then stayed to say farewell to the last of the guests.

Something as he let them into the darkened house.

He climbed into the bed beside her and stared unseeingly into the darkness.

A shout from the house snapped Emma's eyes open, her body instinctively moving to investigate, but he caught her wrist.

'It is just Pa, calling for his pain medication.'

His fingers were loose, but there. That small contact became her sole focus, every nerve darting along its pathways to locate and gather where his fingers touched hers.

She listened to the sound of silence and thought how hard it must be, not just for Rico but for Mia with the exhausting, round-the-clock care she delivered. And Luca must be thinking it too, for she could feel him—the tense energy in the room, this state of hyper-vigilance this family must live with when dealing with someone so ill.

Had it been like this for him as a child too?

She had never known violence—oh, there had been arguments and, living with four men, yes, the occasional fight, but they had been storms that had blown over quickly. This was different. A thick tension had slowly built as they lay there together—yet he would have lain here alone as a child, and heard every creak, every bang, every word while wondering if...

'Luca?' She knew he was awake even if he was ignoring her. 'How bad was it?'

'Leave it, Emma.'

'You can tell me.'

'I don't want to.'

And it should have ended it. She expected him to turn away, except he didn't. Instead, he turned on his side, towards her. 'Emma, please...' He didn't finish what he was saying, or had he just said it? This begging for distraction.

He moved his body over hers, and then his lips were on hers, his kiss catching her by complete surprise. Luca's mouth was seeking an urgent distraction; it was a frenetic, heated kiss that urged her body into instant response. They had made love over and over, Luca initiating her into the wonders of her body, the marvel of his, only this was nothing like the tender, slow lovemaking of previous times—this an enthralling new facet. Urgency crashed in like a stormy ocean slamming onto the beach, and her body flared in instant response to his potent maleness. He was kissing her, hot, demanding kisses that she reciprocated, her fingers at the back of his head pressing his face closer to hers. His thighs came down hard on hers, his arms swept under her, circling her, craving more contact— as too did she.

She opened her centre to him, parting her legs, yearning for that first thrust of him with the hunger of an addict. Only it didn't bring relief, the feel of him driving inside her, his skin sliding over her, it just made her want more, energy building like a cyclone, swirling and obliterating and dragging her to its centre. He moved his arms from beneath her and there was the sensation of falling as her back hit the mattress and Luca leant in on his elbows. Over and over he kissed her, over and over he said her name into the air as he gulped it in, into her mouth as he licked her.

Her orgasms had, till now, been slowly coaxed from her, a learned thing, this gradual build-up as he taught her to let go, as he urged her on to lose her mind, herself, to new sensations. But this night in his bed she was swept into a maelstrom of sensation that was as desperate and urgent as Luca's fierce need.

The shudder of him inside her was met with sweet beats of her own—it wasn't sex, it was devotion, the intensity of her orgasm startling her. Her hips moved frantically upwards to escape from the relentless throb of her body, but Luca was in instant pursuit, his last throes tipping her to a place there could be no coming back from, to true abandon, to utter trust.

They slept together—the third night in his bed, and this time they truly slept together, coiled around each other in a fierce embrace that didn't abate with sleep.

Never did he just glance at his mother in the morning.

Never could he just accept that greeting and coffee without thought.

Always he checked.

And all these years later, still it happened—an instant check that, for Luca, was as natural as breathing.

A cardigan on a hot summer's morning.

Or the unusual sight of her in full make-up at seven a.m.

Or worse, an empty kitchen and the explanation of a migraine as to why she couldn't get up.

His dark eyes automatically scanned for clues or confirmation, yearning for that same rush of momentary relief he had sometimes felt as a child, that all was well—for today at least. That surely his father was too old, too sick, too frail to hurt her... Ah, but he had a savage tongue too—and words, if they were savage enough, could sometimes hurt as much as a blow.

'How was he last night?' Luca asked in his native language, watching his mother stiffen.

'It went wonderfully,' she replied evasively.

'I meant how were things when you got home? How was Pa?'

'Tired,' Mia said briefly. 'Where is Emma?'

'Still asleep.' Climbing out of that bed, feeling her stir, he had hushed her and kissed her back to sleep and then stood and watched her sleeping. Young, innocent, trusting—how could he do it to her? How could he take her by the hand and lead her to hell? He felt as if his home was built on a sewer—he could almost smell the filth beneath the very foundations as he sat at the table and his mother embroidered the lies.

'He did so well to dance with Daniela…Leo is coming this morning and his nurse Rosa. I am a bit worried, because he coughed all night—it was a very long day for him.'

'For you too,' Luca pointed out, and then added, 'I heard him shout in the night.'

'He just shouts, Luca, nothing else…' Mia closed her eyes. 'He is old and weak and tired…'

'Yet still he treats you poorly.'

'Words don't hurt me, Luca,' Mia said. 'Please just leave things alone—it is good that you came.'

The coffee tasted like acid in his mouth—her words rendering him hopeless.

Again.

For everything he had a solution, an answer. His logical, analytical brain could take the most complex problem and unravel it to the base solution. Yet nothing—not logic, not reason, not power, not brawn, not wealth—could solve this.

Nothing!

'Leave him.' He stood up, stared into her eyes and

even as he pleaded again, he knew it was futile, as futile now as it always had been.

'You know I cannot!'

'You can…' His usually strong voice cracked, and he saw his mother flinch—both of them realising that he was near to tears. It had been so long since he had even been close to crying that the sting in his eyes, the swell in his throat caught even Luca by surprise. The pain, the fear, the helplessness, the never-ending grief he had lived with as a child was still there—right there and ready to return at any given moment—the anguish waiting to floor him. 'Leave, Ma.'

'He is dying, Luca. How can I leave a dying man? What would people think?'

'What does it matter?' Luca burst out.

'It matters!' Mia sobbed. 'And he matters too. He is sick, he is scared…'

'He wasn't always sick! He can be moved to hospital.'

'Luca. Please. I beg you to stop this.'

She didn't want his help—she simply didn't want it, yet he could not accept that.

'He is a bastard, and he has always been a bastard,' Luca tried again. 'That he is dying does not change that fact.'

'He's my husband.'

Those three little words that had condemned her to a lifetime of pain and suffering.

The shame of leaving, the scandal attached to such an action had silenced her and in turn had silenced Luca too.

It hadn't always silenced him.

He had spat in his father's face many times as a child—and he still bore the scars to prove it.

He had tried to intervene when he was twelve years

old, and had been beaten to within an inch of his life for his trouble.

And always Mia had sobbed—always she had pleaded that he ignore what his father was doing, that he was making things worse.

So he had waited.

Waited for his moment, waited till he was taller, fitter, stronger—and then one night, when the inevitable had happened, an eighteen-year-old boy in the body of a man had intervened.

Eighteen years of tension and frustration, combined with a generous dash of testosterone, had exploded, and he had beaten and bullied his father that night as mercilessly as his father had beaten and bullied his mother over the years—sure this would end it, sure that finally it was over.

Yet the next morning, his knuckles bruised and bleeding, his top lip swollen, his left eye closed, his cheek a savage mess, something inside Luca had crumbled and died when his mother had walked into the kitchen—bruises that hadn't been there last night on her face, her arms a pitiful mass of red and blue. But worse than that had been the accusing look in her eyes as she'd faced her son, telling him that he had made things even worse, that his interference hadn't helped. And then she had said the words that would stay with Luca for ever.

'*Siete no migliore del vostro padre.*'

'You are no better than your father,' Mia had told him as Luca had sat appalled at what he had done and sick with what she said next. 'It is as I always feared—you are just like him.'

'Don't make things worse, Luca,' his mother said

now, and her words dragged him straight through the coals of hell from the past to the even more hellish, hopeless present. 'There is nothing you can do. Having Emma here has made things better.' Mia gave a tired smile. 'He is proud that perhaps his name will continue, and that has appeased him for a while.' Her eyes anxiously scanned Luca's face. 'She is a wonderful girl— I am pleased. It helps in other ways too...' Mia admitted. 'Seeing that you are finally happy. But please look after her, Luca, and don't let your past...' Her voice strangled off into silence, and Luca shut his eyes. 'Soon, one day, there are things I must tell you—about your past, your history...' she finally managed to add.

But he knew them all already, had worked it out long ago.

Vigilance and tombstones had taught him the unenviable truth.

And now, on this morning, discovering that his mother thought he might be capable of the violence of his father, that his mother, who loved him, worried for the woman who was starting to— That the most innocent of them all slept upstairs in his bed, was, for Luca, an added torment.

'There are things you need to know, things we have to face,' Mia said.

Not if Luca could avoid them.

Rinaldo's words rang in his ears. *'The D'Amato name goes on. Salute!'*

Not if Luca could help it.

The last D'Amato—he was it. He had sworn that on his Aunt Maria's grave, that night when he'd been eighteen. He had sworn that the D'Amato line ended with him.

If he could keep his heart closed, never fall in love, then he could never cause pain to anyone else.

It really was that simple.

CHAPTER ELEVEN

EMMA dressed in khaki shorts and a white halter-neck top and sandals and applied some light make-up, but gave up on her hair—if she brushed out the serum and lacquer, it would end up all fluffy, so instead she ran her fingers through it and tied it in a low ponytail, then tentatively made her way down to the kitchen.

'Good morning.' Luca stood and kissed her, but didn't meet her eyes. Instead, he introduced her to a rather formidable man who was sitting at the table. 'This is Leo, Dr Calista—he was called out yesterday to an emergency, so he could not make the wedding. And this is Rosa, the nurse.'

Rosa was at the kitchen bench, measuring out medication, and gave Emma a brief smile, then turned her attention back to her work. Dr Leo Calista was more formal than the people she had met so far. Instead of kissing her on the cheeks, as everyone else had, he stood as she entered and shook Emma's hand. He was also familiar to her and Emma frowned as she tried to place him.

'I was in the UK for a conference recently!' He smiled at her confusion. 'I dropped in to see Luca to update him on his father...'

'No, that's not how I know you.' Emma frowned, sure that she would remember.

'We have spoken on the phone.'

And that must be it. 'It's nice to meet you.'

'You too. And as a near local now! It is good to see Luca bring a friend here; you are welcome.'

'Thank you,' she replied, a little bewildered.

'*Gradite unirli per la prima colazione?*' Mia offered, inviting the doctor to join the family for breakfast, but Dr Calista declined, instead asking if he might see Rico.

'He seems nice,' Emma observed as the trio made their way out of the kitchen.

'He's a good doctor. He is from the village, he studied medicine in Roma, then returned, but always he keeps up to date. He has been good to my family,' Luca explained. 'His care has meant my father can be looked after at home.'

'That must mean a lot.'

'It does to my mother, but I think that my father should be in hospital—now that the wedding is over. I spoke with Leo before…'

'What did he say?' Emma asked.

'That it is not my choice. That my father wants to die at home and my mother wants to nurse him.'

'Then you have to respect their wishes…' Her voice trailed off as she saw his sharp expression, and there was a pause, a long tense pause as Luca made the decision, as he picked the fight…

And let her go.

'Don't tell me how to deal with my family, Emma— you can drop the concerned act when there is no one else present.'

'Act?' She had missed the change—was still working on yesterday's clock. Yesterday, when he had held her, kissed her, adored her, and it took a moment to flick to the new time zone Luca now demanded she adjust to.

'When we let people think we are together.'

'There was no one present in the bedroom last night,' Emma pointed out, 'but that didn't stop you making love to me.'

'Making love?' Wide eyes mocked her, a cruel smile on his face as he jeered, 'Why do women always call it that?'

God, but he could be sadistic. She could feel tears sting her eyes but she refused to let them fall. 'Because that's how it felt at the time, Luca.'

'It was just sex, that's what I'm paying you for, Emma, if you remember rightly. Remind me again, how much are the back fees for your father's home?' And then he was silenced, her hand slicing the air to meet his cheek, but his hand caught her wrist before it made contact.

'That would be extremely silly.'

'You're utterly despicable!' she gasped.

'Brilliant in bed, though. Tell me again, how much are the back fees for your father?' Luca drawled. 'Pillow talk is just that, Emma, you said yourself it is what men do.'

'This wasn't about *money*,' she denied, because his offer to help her had come after she'd slept with him. God, she hated him, hated what he was doing to her and that she didn't understand why he was doing it.

'I hate you!' she cried.

'Good,' Luca said calmly. 'Good—hate me, loathe

me. Better that than love me, because I will not love you back, Emma. I told you that from the start. I made it exceptionally clear. Don't go getting teary now and complaining, just because the sex is too good.'

There was nothing she could say to that, nothing because the door was opening and he dropped her wrist as Dr Calista walked in. Clearly sensing the thick atmosphere, he asked in English if there was a problem.

Emma didn't answer, appalled by Luca's words but more appalled by her action—if he hadn't halted her she would have hit him. She held her wrist where he had stopped her, his words still stinging as the doctor asked his question again.

'Is everything okay?'

'Yes.' Emma's voice gathered strength. 'Everything's fine.'

'Actually, it isn't,' Luca snapped. 'My mother is exhausted. How much longer must she nurse him at home before you admit him?'

'Luca, I am trying to respect your parents' wishes.'

'Which means you are only respecting my father's wishes.' Luca's lip curled as he added, 'That is all my mother does.' He turned to Emma. 'Can you excuse us, please?'

As she left the room they faced each other, two proud, impressive men.

'I am not leaving till my father is admitted to hospital,' Luca said.

'Then you may be here for a while, Luca.' Leo's words were born of exasperation. 'Luca, what is going on?'

'Nothing.' He was eighteen years old again, Leo slicing the needle through the raw flesh of his cheek and asking questions, Luca pretending that he had a hangover, that there had been a fight in the next village...

'I'm worried about you, Luca.'

'Worry about my mother.'

'That I do,' Leo said, 'and Emma too.'

'Emma?' Luca's voice was incredulous. 'You worry about *Emma*?'

'I heard you fighting, and I could see the bruises on her wrist. I know this is a tense time,' the doctor said, and Luca opened his mouth to make excuses, to lie, to cover up, to hide from it, except he didn't. It was like a fist in his stomach—he had done nothing wrong, logic told him that, he had been stopping Emma from hitting him, that was all—and yet he felt as if he were being handed the baton.

The D'Amato curse being passed onto him, when he had sworn the line would be finally broken.

Only, unlike his father, Luca faced it.

Stood there and faced the truth.

And knew he had to deal with it.

'I'm staying for a few days.' Luca walked into the bedroom where Emma lay on the bed, staring upwards. He could feel her pain, sense her confusion and he could see the purple marks his fingers had left on her tender skin. He flinched inside but let nothing of his horror show on his face or in his voice. 'You should pack.' Luca's head inclined to the wardrobe. 'I'll arrange the transport and ring Evelyn to cancel my diary for a week—I will stay on for a while. When you're back can you speak with Kasumi...' And he reeled off his orders, spoke of nothing but work and even managed to look her straight in the eyes as he did so.

'I take it that means business as usual?' Emma got his point—oh, she so got the point!

'That was what you wanted. I assured you that you wouldn't lose your job over this. Of course…' he gave a brief, mirthless smile '…if you choose to leave, I will provide an excellent reference. I have some contacts…'

He wanted her gone.

With no excuse or explanation, he just wanted her gone.

'What happened, Luca?' she wanted to know. She just didn't get it. 'Everything was wonderful…'

'For a little while, perhaps,' Luca said. 'But I'm bored with you now.'

'Should I send myself some flowers?' Emma sneered. 'That's what you usually make me do.'

'Buy yourself a leaving gift,' Luca suggested.

'Who said I'm leaving?' She damn well *wouldn't* give him the satisfaction. 'When did I say that I was looking for other work?' Deep beneath the pain of his dismissal, there amidst her loss, there was a small coup—a little surge of triumph as, though his expression appeared unmoved, she registered the slight bob of his Adam's apple and knew she had unnerved him. She felt a little flicker of satisfaction as she refused to dance to his beastly tune. 'I'm very happy where I am—unless you have any complaints about my work?'

She watched his lips tighten just a fraction before he answered.

'None.'

'Good, then I shall see you on your return.' She took off the earrings and attempting some dignity held them out to him, but Luca merely shrugged.

'Consider them a bonus.'

And just like that she was dismissed from his personal life, *they* were dismissed, everything they had shared these past days was cheapened and soiled.

'While we're still on personal time, before it's back to business...' There were no tears in her eyes, no waver in her voice, as she meant every word. 'I hate you.'

'You're repeating yourself now.'

'Just so you know,' Emma said, in a voice that was surprisingly clear. 'When I smile and bring you in your coffee, or laugh at one of your jokes, or join you at some function, or when you think that I've forgotten what you did...' Her eyes briefly met his. 'I haven't. Just so you remember... I hate you.'

CHAPTER TWELVE

SHE *was* preparing to leave.

Quietly, imperceptibly perhaps, but preparing all the same.

Like the lights being switched off in an office block, one by one, she closed the little doors to her heart—applying for other jobs, preparing her art portfolio, being more assertive with the real estate agent—all the while working alongside the man who had shattered her heart.

She had been back at her desk the next morning, ringing his clients, cancelling meetings, chatting with Evelyn, refusing to grant him his undoubted wish and immediately remove herself from his life so that he didn't have to look at his *mistake*.

She'd take small victories where she could find them, and absolutely refused to be rushed.

And when his father was finally admitted to hospital and he returned, it was *more* business than usual.

Efficient, competent, she got on with her work and, on his first day back, she brought him in coffee and offered a pleasant good morning—and very deliberately set the tone.

'Good morning, Luca.'

'Good morning, Emma.'

Had she not known better, Emma might have been fooled for a second into thinking this was hurting him as much as it was her.

He looked awful.

Oh, by any other standards he looked divine, but there was an ashy tinge to his complexion, a fleck of silver in his hair she was sure hadn't been there before, and the neck of his shirt was just a touch too loose, yet it looked as if it was choking him.

'Your client meeting isn't till nine. Evelyn has asked if I can go through your schedule for the next fortnight, if you've got time.'

She had been practising hard for this moment—Luca knew that. She didn't blush, or avoid his gaze, and there wasn't even a hint of aggression as she spoke. Never had he admired her more.

'Now's fine.' He nodded for her to sit and pulled up his schedule on his computer as Emma took notes.

'You've two international trips scheduled...'

'Three,' Luca said. 'We will need to stay overnight in Paris.'

'I thought...' Her pen was poised over the paper. As Evelyn had started another round of IVF, it meant Emma would be accompanying him on all trips—the prospect was almost more than she could bear. 'I mean with your father being unwell, Evelyn wasn't sure that you still wanted—'

'Paris is closer to Italy than London,' Luca interrupted. 'I won't be cancelling anything—in fact, after taking a week off, there is a lot to catch up on. I'll need one of you to stay back late tonight.'

'Of course,' Emma said evenly.

'Probably tomorrow too.'

Emma knew what he was doing—he was warning her just how difficult this would be if she chose to pursue it, because it was she who would be doing the bulk of the travelling—she was here to lighten Evelyn's load after all.

'Not a problem!' She gave him a smile. 'Was there anything else?'

Leave.

He didn't answer her, but it was the word that thrummed in his head during every meeting, every flight, every overseas trip.

Leave, his mind willed her—because it was killing him to be so close to her and not be able to have her.

He had thought it hard breaking things off with Martha—had thought for years that Martha had been 'the one', quietly safe in the knowledge that it would never be that hard again...

This was a thousand times worse.

Maybe she should just give him his wish, Emma thought over and over in the ensuing weeks as she worked alongside him, refusing to give in—it would certainly be easier to.

But she couldn't quite close that last little door, couldn't just sever all ties—and for one very good reason.

'What star sign would the tenth of June be?' Evelyn had given up trying not to hope—she had a blood test in a couple of days that would determine her fate, and was frantically working out dates.

'Gemini.' Emma smiled, then put her head down and got on with her work.

'What are Geminis like?' Evelyn pushed, and Emma hesitated. She'd seen Evelyn's devastation once and was dreading it happening again, yet was trying not to show it.

'Charming, happy, witty,' Emma said, wishing Evelyn wouldn't get her hopes up so, but, then, who could blame her? It was, of course, all Evelyn could think about, all that was on her mind, no matter how she tried to get on with her day.

Emma could empathise with that.

'I know I'm going over the top...' Evelyn stood up to join Luca for his two p.m. meeting and glancing over and seeing Emma's worried face, misconstrued it. 'I think sometimes you just know—I feel different this time, I just know that I'm pregnant.'

For Evelyn's sake, Emma prayed she was right.

For her own sake, she was frantically hoping that Evelyn was wrong because she was feeling different too. She pushed the thought firmly out of her mind and forced herself to concentrate on her busy afternoon.

Emma could hardly believe the variations in her work-load. One minute she was arranging seven-star hotels in Dubai, the next she was dealing with a hysterical house-keeper on the phone and a dog that was convulsing.

Just another day behind the scenes of Luca D'Amato's busy life.

Evelyn was with him in a meeting, so she texted her rather than rang.

There's a problem with Pepper.
Housekeeper has to leave soon.
Vet on way.

She hit 'send'—knew what the reply would be and

wearily picked up her bag and summoned a driver to take her straight to Luca's.

Somehow she hadn't been to his apartment since that day—since their first kiss.

Stepping inside, it was hard to recall her innocence, her naivety—that she had thought that she could handle things, could somehow deal with the force of his charm and his hot-and-cold affection and come out unscathed.

'The vet's coming!' Rita, his housekeeper, was in tears as she bent over the little dog. 'He's just a few minutes away. I have to get to school to pick up the children.'

Pepper was a sad sight, lying on the floor in obvious distress but snapping and snarling if anyone approached.

'You go,' Emma said. 'I'll wait for the vet.'

'Luca will be devastated,' Rita sobbed. 'He loves that little dog.'

'Really?' Emma couldn't keep the note of surprise from her voice. 'He's hardly ever here to see him.'

'But he liked to come home to him,' Rita said, emotion countering discretion. 'Oh, poor Pepper. I could never understand Martha just leaving him behind...'

Emma hated this.

Left alone with Pepper, she *hated* this.

These glimpses into Luca were killing her.

Working with him was bad enough, travelling with him too, but she could almost deal with business, only this job involved his personal life too...

Being in his home—amongst his things—sitting trying to comfort a little snapping, snarling, terrified dog that had belonged to a woman he had once loved, was more than she could take, more than she could bear...

'Where's the damn vet?'

She hadn't been counting on Luca arriving, she had never thought he would dash out of an important meeting for a little dog he didn't seem to particularly like.

'He's two minutes away—he just rang.'

He knelt down beside the little dog, his face grim and his voice not particularly tender.

'You're fine,' he said to Pepper in a gruff voice, and then glanced up at Emma. 'If I start being all nice he'll realise...' He put his hand out to the dog who bared his teeth and Luca ignored it, just stroked the little thing, and Emma watched as finally Pepper relaxed. 'You know you like it really, you know you won't bite me,' Luca said, and then, when the intercom buzzed, he addressed Emma.

'Can you let the vet in on your way out?'

'I don't mind staying.'

'There's no need.'

He was stroking the little dog with both hands now, soothing it and calming it and now saying nice things. She just didn't get him—never, ever would she get him!

'Should you ring Martha?' she asked and watched him freeze for a moment.

'She left him,' he snapped. 'It's not her dog any more.'

'Why did you two break up?' she asked curiously. Now maybe wasn't the right time for this discussion, but it was the only window she had, the only possible time to ask the question she had for so long wondered about.

'Things weren't going too well,' Luca said. 'Here's the vet now—let him in and then go.'

'Or they were going too well?' Emma stood up. 'What, you were too happy, Luca, so you had to break it off with her?'

'Just leave.'

But she couldn't, instead she said what was on her mind. 'Are you worried you might turn out like your dad?' His face was black with anger as he turned to her, except he didn't scare her. 'You're not your father, Luca.'

'Don't practise your high-school psychology on me,' Luca sneered. 'I don't love you, Emma—in fact, I don't actually like you.' His words were very deliberate and aimed straight for her heart. 'I slept with you because you wanted it, because you begged me for it. I warned you from the start an affair was all it could be. Now, when I tell you, as I did from the start, that it would not last, you have to find a *reason* why I ended it.'

'Okay, Luca,' she said, feeling sick, 'I get the message.'

'No, you ask, I answer—the reason I ended it is because, like the rest, you got too clingy, too needy…and frankly—' all his attention was on Pepper now '—you're not that interesting in bed.'

She closed her eyes and swayed on her feet.

'Out,' he said, without turning his head.

This time Emma went.

It was quick and it was painless and it absolutely had to be done.

Even with a dog-sitter and a housekeeper, there had always been a small dash of guilt at leaving him so much—but as the vet had often pointed out on increasingly regular visits, finding a home for a geriatric poodle with dementia would be a tough task.

It was his time.

'Do you want me to take him?' the vet asked.

'Please.'

'Do you want his collar?'

'No, thank you.'

He shook the vet's hand and thanked him, saw him out, and then spent ten minutes trying to find where Rita kept the bin liners. Walking around the apartment, he filled it with Pepper's things, kneeling and checking under the bed, in the laundry, under the sofa, making sure that every last thing of his was gone, then throwing the bag down the chute. Annoyed at the dog hair on his favourite suit, he stripped it off and changed, then threw his suit down the chute too.

Only when every last trace of Pepper was gone did Luca head back to the office.

CHAPTER THIRTEEN

'I'M SURE I'm pregnant,' Evelyn said firmly. If she said it assuredly enough then the universe wouldn't dare to argue.

'Let's just wait and see what the clinic says.' Emma attempted caution. 'You'll know tomorrow.'

'I've got all the symptoms,' Evelyn insisted. 'I mean, I feel sick all the time, my breasts are hurting…' It was like water torture—drip by drip, Evelyn listed her symptoms, each one causing a further stab of unease in Emma. 'I just want to know *now*.'

So too did Emma.

'Evelyn…' Emma picked up her bag. 'I'm going out for my lunch break, okay?'

'Out?' Evelyn frowned, as well she might. There was no such thing as a lunch break—it was either out with Luca and taking notes or a quick sandwich at the desk. The requisite lunch break in this place was non-existent. 'I've got some things I need to do…' Emma slung her bag over her shoulder '…and I doubt I'll be out of here by five.'

The public toilets in a department store wasn't the best place to find out the news, but somehow she needed to be away from Luca for this. Leaning against the wall, the short wait was interminable. Picking up the indicator, she stared at it, not trying to work out the hows or whys, as the internet had already told her that—new job, lots of travel, different time zones... She had been vigilant taking her Pill but sometimes, apparently, these things happened. Picking up the instruction leaflet, she didn't need to check it as the answer was perfectly clear—whether or not it was to her liking was another matter entirely.

She walked back to work, her heart in her mouth, not even attempting to fathom Luca's reaction to the news—she was having enough trouble fathoming her own!

'Where the hell have you been?'

Luca was not in the best of moods—in fact, he hadn't been in the best of moods for a long time. Since his return from Sicily the pretence of business as usual had soon worn thin, but since Pepper's death his mood had darkened further. Still, as she slipped off her jacket his harsh tone had no impact on Emma.

'I asked where you'd been,' Luca said. 'I've been ringing your mobile.'

'At lunch,' Emma said, 'and I forgot to charge my phone.'

'You went to lunch *two hours* ago.'

'And I stayed here till eleven p.m. last night,' Emma retorted, her head too full of the sudden news to feel threatened by Luca's tone.

Maybe she should just tell him now. *Oh, I just took a pregnancy test and was building up to giving you the happy news!*

God, men had it easy at times.

She looked up at him, at a face that had once appeared to adore her, at the stern lips that had kissed her, at the hands that had soothed her, and wondered how he could have changed so. How she could possibly ever work up the courage to tell him.

She couldn't.

So, instead of explaining herself, she peeled off her jacket and then made her way to the desk, not that her lack of response deterred him. Luca rattled off a list of orders that had even Evelyn frowning at the impossibility of it all.

But Emma just set to work, dealing with the most pressing emails and telephone calls, as Evelyn dealt with Luca.

His temper was palpable, she could hear it in the impatient buzz of her intercom, could feel it from behind the thick oak door, could see it when she knocked and entered and gave him the most recent list of figures he had demanded that she pull from thin air and that though deemed urgent were given nothing more than a cursory glance.

'And remember the midday meeting tonight,' he called to her departing back. 'Make sure I've got all the documentation I need.'

'Midday meeting tonight?'

'With the Los Angeles office.' He bared his teeth in a sarcastic smile. 'Evelyn has to leave at six tonight, so if you want your *break*, could you take it before then?'

'I've got plans tonight.' She did have plans, important plans—like seeing a doctor and trying to work out what the hell she was going to do. 'I really need to leave.'

'Would you excuse us a moment, please, Evelyn?'

His voice was dark and Emma was grateful for the sympathetic smile Evelyn gave her on the way out.

'When you were offered the position...' Each word came in clipped tones, his eyes never leaving her face as he spoke, but Emma wasn't going to take this.

'I know what you're doing!'

'When you were offered the position,' Luca said again, his voice icily calm, 'it was clearly stipulated there would be extensive travel and late nights.'

'You're trying to push me into resigning.' With every interruption, with every rise in her voice, Luca leant back further in his chair, a cruel glimmer of a smile on his lips as he calmly spoke over her.

'It was clearly outlined that the reason you were being hired,' Luca smoothly continued, 'was to lighten Evelyn's workload. I value Evelyn—'

'Unlike me,' Emma spat.

'I value *all* my staff,' Luca responded, 'but Evelyn is vital—that is why I have been so accommodating with her doctor's appointments and schedules. That is why you are here—to lighten her load so that she doesn't hand in her notice.'

'Which is what you want *me* to do?'

'Why would I want you to leave?' He was smiling now—utterly boxing her into a corner. 'If Evelyn gets good news tomorrow, we'll need you on board even more. It might even mean a promotion for you!'

He kept her at the office till ten p.m., and exhausted she fell into bed, but sleep evaded her. Her mind was a whir of scattered thoughts—that she was carrying his child was just too big and too scary to contemplate. Imagining telling him, dealing with him—telling the man who so clearly didn't want her in his life that she would be in it now for ever. Whether that meant monthly maintenance payments or access visits, there was a link now that couldn't be severed.

She lay there and wondered.

He had changed, yet so had she.

It had been like a beautiful seamless dance, and somehow she had tripped—had forgotten the rules, had tipped the scales from trusting to wary almost imperceptibly.

So she lay there, trying to pinpoint the moment it had ended, when, for Luca, the light had gone out on their relationship.

Trying not to ponder what she had done wrong.

Because she had done nothing *wrong*, Emma knew that.

It wasn't about wrong or right, or trying to please, or bending to fit—she had known from the start it would be short-lived, that Luca, by his own clear admission, would never loan his heart to anyone for long.

She had accepted the rules of the game, had gone into it utterly prepared—and had come out of it utterly broken.

Had been so sure that she could handle it.

Change him. Be the one.

Glimpse a future for them.

So, instead of sleeping, she lay there, rueing her own carelessness, because she had been taught, and she had learnt, and yet she had chosen to forget.

What a fool she'd been…

CHAPTER FOURTEEN

THE call when it came was unexpected. Luca had won, Emma finally decided. She had her notice typed up and printed off and it sat waiting in her bag for when the right moment presented itself. She simply couldn't do it any longer.

Evelyn had had her blood test that morning and the bad news that very afternoon. Luca had offered to let her go home, but Evelyn had declined. 'This will *not* be the last time,' he had said to her, as Emma had sat with her arm around Evelyn.

'Maybe it's time to see someone else. I have found out about a very good clinic. Their success rate with IVF is high.' He handed his PA a thick glossy brochure.

'We can't afford to go there,' Evelyn sobbed.

'I am to be sent the bills,' Luca said, 'and this time you will take the time off that you need and rest properly while you wait for the results.'

'Why would you do this for me?' Evelyn wailed as Emma wondered the same thing—he could be so nice, so charming, so very, very kind. Ah, but Evelyn was vital to Luca, she thought cynically, the last thing he must privately want was for his esteemed PA to be leaving—but his show of kindness *had* caught her off guard.

As he always did.

Her throat thickened with tears as he spoke to Evelyn, as she heard again the rare tenderness that *she* craved from him. 'Because you do so much for me, because always you have been loyal to me. Because I know that when your baby is here—and it *will* be here, Evelyn—that even if you come back to work for me part time, or even if you decide to never work again, I will be able to call on you, perhaps to train someone up, perhaps to help for a few days. And more than that, we are friends. I know I can count on you, and you can count on me too.'

When he was nice, there was no one nicer, Emma realised.

No one.

Evelyn was perhaps the one woman he could sustain a relationship with because there was no sex involved, no attraction, just mutual liking and respect.

Emma would kill to have the latter two from him.

Later, sitting at her desk, staring out at the grey autumnal sky that declared summer over, when Luca strode past her desk and to his office and slammed the door behind him, she felt like one of the trees waving in the streets below. Slight, every breeze exposing the bare truth beneath, and she couldn't do it to herself any longer.

Couldn't cling on when there was nothing left—couldn't stave off winter.

She didn't hate him after all, she only hated his behaviour.

Hated it that he didn't love her.

And she must remember this, Emma realised, when she told him about the baby.

If she told him.

She let out a slow breath at the *immoral* choice she was considering taking—denying him the knowledge of the child that she was carrying.

That she *would* carry until she gave birth to it.

Oh, she would love to be one of those stoic women, one who had never considered the alternatives to giving birth—except she had. Had scoured her magazines for information, had searched on the internet, had made a couple of phone calls—and yet it was Evelyn who had unwittingly halted that thought process. Evelyn's very real grief at what had just been lost that had reminded Emma of the miracle that had occurred.

That despite precautions, despite a man who wanted nothing more than a short-lived affair, despite a woman who'd had other plans, a life had been created. A life that she would cherish for ever.

It was taking some getting used to, that was all.

She had never felt closer to understanding her mother. She finally understood now how her mother could have felt trapped inside her role of wife and mother. Hopefully, for Emma, that feeling would one day soon be diminished by the overwhelming love she would feel for her child.

Would Luca feel the same?

Tears stung her eyes as she tried to predict his likely reaction—no doubt he would assume she was just after a monthly support cheque or, even worse, a wedding ring.

Well, a loveless marriage wasn't on her agenda—she was the product of one after all and would never expose her own child to it. So now she just had to tell him, only exactly which piece of information Emma didn't know yet—that she was leaving for good or that they had created a child together.

And so busy was Emma, wrestling with her decision, that when the call came, although it was not entirely unexpected, it *was* like a bolt from the blue.

CHAPTER FIFTEEN

'SIGNORA D'AMATO. COMESTA?' Emma responded to the familiar voice in very new Italian but the greeting faded as her mind registered Luca's mother's voice, and heard the effort and emotion behind the thickly accented English when she asked if Luca was in the office.

'I'll put you through.'

'No!' Mia's voice was urgent. 'Emma, please—the news is not good.' A strangled sob from Mia had Emma closing her eyes at the raw sound of pain. 'Rico has gone.' Emma held the phone and her eyes remained closed as Mia wept for a moment before speaking again. 'I do not know Luca's reaction, they were not close, but can you tell him...gently for me?' Emma could feel the beads of sweat on her forehead, as it wasn't her job to do something so personal. Except it wasn't about her job role—Mia thought they were in love.

But only one of them was.

'I will see you both soon for the funeral.' Mia's assumption had Emma's heart pounding, and more so when she continued talking, giving Emma details that only a fiancée should know. She concluded. 'Emma, this will be hard for Luca—I am so glad that he has you.'

The walk to his office was impossibly long, yet all too soon she was there. As were her instructions, she knocked and waited for his bored voice to summon her inside.

Had he looked up, maybe he would have seen her pale face and realised something was seriously wrong, but he was deep in the middle of a phone call, his long legs on the desk and crossed at the ankles, and he waved her to sit down, which Emma did, sitting quietly, going over and over in her head how she should break it to him.

'Yes?' As he replaced the receiver he also pulled his legs from the desk and adopted a more formal position, his curt word reminding her that Luca liked to be brought straight to the point—only she truly didn't know how to just come out and say it.

'I have something to tell you.'

'So tell me.'

'It's difficult.' Emma swallowed, then opened her mouth to speak, but Luca overrode her.

'Then let me make it easy for you—you've come to hand in your notice.' He opened a drawer and handed her a thick cream envelope, his relief evident. 'I have written a reference, as we agreed—'

'Luca—'

'There will be a bonus in your pay.' Again he spoke over her. In fact, for Luca the words were tumbling out. He had known this moment was coming, had engineered it, wanted it, needed it to happen, only when the moment had arrived, it was unusually hard, painful even, and he noticed just the smallest shake to his usually steady hand as he held out the envelope. 'It is for the best,' Luca said, more for his benefit than hers.

'Luca, will you please just *listen*?' she begged, wringing her hands in her lap. 'I just took a call from your mother.' And he could hear her voice, see her mouth move, only he couldn't quite process the words, his hand still holding out the envelope as somewhere he computed that his father was dead, that finally it was over... He had wished for this moment, Luca reminded himself as something catapulted him from his seat, had him striding to the window and turning his back to Emma. He had wanted this, wished for so long that it would be over, but he had never imagined mourning, grieving. He had never considered that it actually might hurt him.

He was dead, he was gone, it was over. Finally it was over, finally he should be able to breathe, only he couldn't. He actually couldn't drag in the air or push it out, even thought he might fold over in two, because it was all there in front of him—every memory, good and bad, playing out before his closed eyes, and futile questions playing over and over like a mantra in his pounding head.

Why?

Why had his father been like that?

Why couldn't he have just been happy?

Why?

He was almost doubled over with the agony of it all—shocked at the depth of his grief over a man who had caused nothing but pain.

'When?' he asked instead.

'Just now,' Emma said gently. 'Your mother has a

friend with her; she's staying in a hotel tonight and then coming home in the morning.'

He was obviously devastated, and she felt like an intruder almost, witnessing this most private moment, knowing Luca would never have chosen for her to see him like this. There were no tears, no outward, dramatic displays of emotion—they would have been easier to deal with somehow. No, it was his *pain*, this deep, wretched pain that sagged those strong shoulders as he had strode to the window then stumbled, bemused almost. She had sat there, torn—instinct wanting her to run to him, yet logic telling her to stay exactly where she was.

'And Pa?' She heard him attempt to inject strength to his voice. 'Did she say anything?'

'She asked if you could sort that out…arrange things.'

Only that wasn't what he'd meant. Everything was already sorted, things had been put in place weeks ago—all he had to do was pick up the phone, or ask Evelyn to. No, that hadn't been what he'd meant and he had never thought he would care enough to ask it.

'Did he suffer?'

'No.'

At one time he had wanted him to suffer—had wanted the agony he had inflicted to catch up with his father in death—but wishes were but flights of the imagination, Luca realised, reality entirely different.

'Your mother said it was very quick and peaceful at the end.'

That *did* give comfort, why he didn't know. And then he felt it, her hand on his shoulder, and he wanted to brush it off, ashamed at being seen like this, embarrassed that she should witness such private pain. Yet her touch helped, the bliss of human contact was like a rope to cling to in the dark, ferocious waters of grief. Luca turned and for the first time in his life and only for a moment so fleeting it was barely there he leant on another, felt her warmth, her kindness, felt *her* tears on *his* cheeks and accepted the bewildering fact that for a moment she shared his pain, divided it, lessened it even, just by being there.

And then he let her go.

Had to let her go.

'Organise the plane—I need to be there for my mother. When did you say she gets back?'

'Tomorrow, late morning.'

Which gave him space. He thought of the billion and one things he had to do—of the people relying on him, of things he *had* to do.

'Arrange that I leave at eight a.m. tomorrow. Now, if you will excuse me, I should ring my mother.'

'Of course, but—'

'Cancel my diary for the week—I have warned most people that this might happen soon.' He was back in business mode, standing tall and proud but unable to meet her eyes.

'Luca...'

He glanced at the envelope he was still holding. 'If you were thinking of leaving, I would appreciate it if you could stay on at least till I return.'

'Of course, but...' How to say it, how to just come out and say it? Finally, the words just flurried out. 'Your mother thinks that I will be coming with you—she is expecting me to be there for the funeral.'

'No.' His response was immediate. He could not do

this again, could not let her any closer, because it had already been hard enough losing her once—he couldn't do it again. 'I will explain you are needed here.'

'She thinks I am more needed there.' Emma was crying. It wasn't her place to cry, it was his father that was dead, but to see him so lost for that moment, to feel the weight of his pain momentarily rest in her arms, even if it would be agony, even if it was just another charade, she wanted to be there for him. She wanted this time with the man she loved, with the father of her child and maybe, just maybe, being with him, sharing in his grief, might bring them close enough for Emma to reveal her news. 'You don't have to do this alone.'

'No.' His response was final. He had done everything alone—always he had been alone. Oh, there had been women, so-called partners even, and they had shared in important milestones, family occasions even—yet in his mind he had always been alone. Now she offered a different path and Luca gazed into her eyes and down that unfamiliar route.

To have her with him, to get through this and have her beside him at night, to have that hand hold his as he tried to make it through…

Never had he been more sorely tempted.

'No.'

He dismissed her, picked up the phone and turned his back.

She quietly closed the door on her way out, and she held it together.

Evelyn was still in tears for her own reasons, so with just a little guidance from her senior, Emma put the plans for Rico D'Amato in place, and for Luca

D'Amato too. She struggled through the wretched day and then headed not to home but to visit her father.

'I loved her, Emma.' He was holding a photo of her mother and weeping when she arrived. 'I loved her.'

'I know, Dad.'

'I always knew she'd leave me. I knew that one day she'd go....'

Instead of taking the photo away, instead of filling up his little dish with chocolate, or replacing his laundry, Emma sat in the stiff leather chair by his bed— weary with new understanding.

Love hurt.

Love sucked.

Love made you do the unfathomable.

'I should have supported her with her art,' Frank wept, as Emma held his hand and closed her eyes. 'I should have been there for her. I should have been a better father for you...'

Round and round he went, trapped in a circle of dementia and bitter, bitter regret.

It was exhausting to listen to.

And exhausting to leave.

Bone weary, she stepped out of the nursing home and into the dark night, almost knowing Luca would be waiting for her, almost sensing what was to come.

'I went to your home.'

'I was visiting Dad.'

'We are finished, Emma.' He made himself say it, because she deserved better than lies, better than false promises.

Better than him.

'There can be no relationship.'

'I know that now.' And she did, finally she did, because he couldn't make it any clearer. His face was stripped of colour, just the blue of his eyes and the blackness of his words resonated in her heart. But love made you daft, love made you care, love made you weak at times, but true love, real love, actually made you incredibly strong.

'Your offer to come to the funeral, I would like to accept it now. It would mean a lot to my mother and also to me,' he admitted. One slight weakness and she blinked in confusion, because sometimes he sounded like a man who adored her.

'I said I'll come, but there can be no…' She couldn't finish but she knew he understood her. Unlike before, this time she meant it, because although she loved him, and wanted him, being intimate with a man who had confessed he didn't want her meant there was one rule that had to be voiced.

'I understand that,' Luca said, and he did. Always sex had been like balm, a release, a distraction, a pleasure— yet with Emma it had been something else, had taken him to places that had shown him all he was missing, all he must forever miss. Emma had been right too. His mother had naturally assumed Emma would join him, and at first he had reeled from even the thought. But to have her beside him… He knew he shouldn't but, selfishly, his need overrode logic.

'I am leaving in the afternoon now—Evelyn will come to your home in the morning to assist you.'

And in Luca's world no explanation was necessary—he could just give his orders and they would be followed. But as Evelyn arrived the next morning with an array of dour suits, as she helped her junior pack and pay last-minute bills and cancel plans and ring the nursing home, the mood was sombre. Black was Emma's safe staple—a suit, a jumper, a sexy little dress—but always it was lightened with colour. Pulling on black stockings, a thin black cashmere jumper and then the black suit, Emma felt sick. She had never been to a funeral before—well, just one, but she had been too young to remember her mother's.

They sat in silence in Emma's lounge, waiting for the toot of Luca's driver. Evelyn saw her junior's pinched face and restless foot that tapped a silent tune as she braced herself for whatever lay ahead.

'I know something happened in Italy,' the older woman said gently.

'How could it not have?' Emma gave a tight shrug.

'I warned you,' Evelyn said, but there was no accusatory note in her voice. She had seen it before and she would no doubt see it again—but it felt different with Emma. 'You don't have to go to this—'

'But I do,' Emma interjected.

'He'll hurt you,' Evelyn warned. 'Please don't get too involved... Luca's incapable of commitment.'

'I know that.'

'And he can't stand to look at his mistakes.' Evelyn spoke from years of experience. 'I've seen it happen so many times. Sooner or later, you'll end up leaving. Oh, you'll get a glowing reference, a fabulous payout...' Each word was like an arrow to Emma's heart, because it washed away the last dregs of the uniqueness that she'd been sure had been them. 'He'll hurt you,' Evelyn said again and then the car tooted its summons and they both stood, Emma tempted to follow Evelyn's advice—to just walk away now, before he hurt her even further.

'He already has,' Emma admitted finally.

'Then tell him you can't go with him, tell him that you've changed your mind.'

The doorbell rang and the two women stood in silence for a moment, but then Emma picked up her bag and opened the door. She stared into navy eyes that were glassy, and saw a taut, guarded face that, for a little while longer at least, needed her there.

Real love *did* make you strong, Emma realised.

It wasn't just for Luca she would go to the funeral.

It was for their baby. For the little bit of history that she would one day have to repeat to their child whose grandfather had just died.

CHAPTER SIXTEEN

EVERYTHING seemed different. As the helicopter swept them from the airport, Emma could see the bare vines and naked trees and as they made their way towards Luca's home, the Mediterranean pulsing swollen and grey as they came in closer to land.

They walked into the house. All the curtains were drawn and a wail went up, women dressed in black sobbing as Luca and Emma entered.

She had never seen such raw emotion and it made her flinch—this wall of pain that hit them with force. In the middle of them all was Mia, who sat dignified and silent. She stood as her son entered and accepted his embrace, and suddenly Emma experienced a stirring of memory within her. Tears and black and grief… She could remember holding her hands up to her father, who didn't notice, could feel again the bemusement she had felt as a child, seeing her brothers weep, her aunts, everyone… Emma had been holding Luca's hand for appearances' sake but suddenly he was holding hers.

Mia led them both past the kitchen where the men stood in strained, respectful silence and into Rico's study, where she spoke with her son about the arrangements. But despite what was expected of them, Luca put his foot down. For his mother he would do it, would stand in the kitchen with the men and drink whisky and play the dutiful son, would put himself through whatever was expected of him this one last time, but he would not do it to Emma.

'Luca!' She could hear his mother's annoyance, and had no idea what they were saying, but Luca seemed adamant, his voice, firm and non-negotiable, then he led her away, up to the bedroom, where she sat on the edge of the bed.

'What was all that about?' Emma asked. 'Surely now is not the time to argue with your mother?'

'You are expected to sit and weep with the women while I stand with the men.' He watched her eyes widen in horror. 'So, perhaps now *is* a good time to state my opinion, hmm?'

'Yes, thank you,' she conceded. 'What did you say?'

'That you are tired, upset…' He gave a thin smile. 'That you are English.'

Emma managed a watery smile back. 'We English have emotions too, you know.'

'Ah, but you hide them so well.' She was quite sure he was talking about them, about these past hellish weeks. 'When it hurts, when it really hurts…' His hand reached out, pushed a few stray curls back from her strained face and he just stood there, his hand resting on the side of her cheek as her skin warmed to his slight touch. 'You just keep it all in.'

'Crying and screaming doesn't change anything. I learnt that long ago.'

'You just get on with it?' he wanted to know.

'Yes.'

'Maybe living in England, some of your ways have rubbed off on me.'

She felt as if he was giving her a message, as if beneath his blandness, beneath the void of emotion there was a deeper meaning in his words—which was the edge of madness, Emma reasoned. There was no deeper meaning with Luca, he had told her that from the start, so she jerked her head, removed herself from his contact and wished him gone.

'I must go back down, I will bring you some supper.'

'I'm not hungry,' she told him.

He didn't listen, and returned a few minutes later with a plate of pastries and a large mug of hot chocolate and some liquor. 'My mother said to give you this—it's limoncello—made from the lemons from the family tree, it will help you rest.' He poured her a small glass and Emma took it, but placed it on the bedside table.

'I should join them,' he said.

'Go,' Emma replied.

'Thank you.' He stood at the door, then turned and added, 'For being here. It helps.'

'Does it?' Her eyes searched his. 'Luca, if me being here helps...' She watched his face immediately become shuttered, and knew now wasn't the time to demand answers—to ask why he shut her out over and over again, only to occasionally let her in, why he was so closed off to emotion.

'Rest,' Luca said instead, and once he had gone back to join his family, Emma undressed, feeling exhausted. Even if she weren't pregnant she wouldn't have drunk the limoncello, so she tipped the brew down the sink, hating his father's legacy. Then she undressed for bed, catching sight of herself in the mirror and noticing the slight changes in her body already. There was no bump, it was way too soon for that, but there was a softness to her belly and pressing her fingers to her pubic bone she could feel the firm wedge of muscle. Her breasts were rounder, the areolae darker—small, subtle changes that Luca would never notice. Not that he would see them because she pulled on her shapeless candy-striped flannelette pyjamas as if they were some sort of chastity belt—usually worn for a girls' movie night and certainly not seduction material.

She slipped between the crisp cotton sheets and willed sleep to come, wished it was morning and that this long night was over.

He came to bed before midnight, undressed and climbed in beside her. Silence would have been welcome, but wails of tears still filled the house at times.

'I hate this,' Luca admitted to the darkness, knowing she was awake beside him.

'I know.'

'This day has been coming for a long time.'

'You can never prepare for losing someone you love.'

'I don't love him.' She lay still beside him, her heart stopping for a moment as she heard his truth. 'I have *never* loved him.'

'Luca...' She shook her head on the pillow. 'You shouldn't speak like that on the eve—'

'So he is a saint now?' She heard the flash of anger in his voice. 'All those people out there think they are mourning a good man, a loving husband, a wonderful father, when the truth is...' He halted, but Emma wouldn't let him leave it.

'What *is* the truth, Luca? How bad was it?'

'He beat her.' Here in the dark, with her hand slipping into his, he said it. 'Over and over he beat her, yet she never cried, she just took it. Only even if she made no noise, you could still hear it...' The marrow chilled in her bones as he continued. 'Of course, we were not allowed to tell, of course Ma covered her bruises.'

'What was he like...' Emma swallowed '...to you and Daniela?'

'Daniela was his angel—people say children know, but I am not sure as Ma and I hid it well, even from her.'

'And you?'

He didn't answer, so she asked again, her hand reaching out to the scar on his cheek, and he held her hand against it for a moment.

'Did he do this?'

He didn't say anything more and it took a moment for Emma to realise that he was finally asleep—exhaustion catching up with him at last.

He reached for her in sleep, one strong arm dragging her that little bit closer, and she lay rigid in his arms, telling herself to pull away, except she had never felt closer to him, remembering his tension when they'd lain here all those weeks ago, when every noise, every creak of the house must for Luca have screamed danger.

Sleep didn't let him rest quietly, though.

With every noise she felt the slight jump of muscle still loaded with adrenaline, his arms pulling her further in until she could feel the press of his groin against hers.

She could feel the hardness of his erection, the tense heat of him, a need so demanding it must have woken him, because he turned away, moved onto his back, remembering their rules.

But distance didn't help it abate.

She knew that, could feel the thick energy in the room, could hear his tense breathing as he willed it to pass, for sleep to rescue him. For this hell to be over.

She turned on her side, and as her eyes adjusted to the darkness, she could see his were closed, could see the muscled outline of his stomach and the sheet that didn't disguise his need in the slightest.

Her hand reached out, resting on his stomach, and she heard his hiss of frustration as he thought inadvertent contact had been made, knew he assumed her asleep beside him—that, like himself, her body had forgotten the rules.

Well, it hadn't.

Slowly she traced the line of hair that snaked from his umbilicus, then nervous, tentative but bold she touched him, hearing his moan, running her finger along a thick vein, then tracing the path back, then doing it again.

'Emma…'

'Shh…' She didn't want questions and she didn't want answers. She was stroking him more firmly now, and then his hand was over hers.

'You don't have to…'

'I *want* to.'

'Why?'

Because she loved him, because she wanted him, because always, always she would—and despite her promises to herself, she could never lie in a bed beside him and not want him.

And because he needed this—in the thick of night, for Emma it really was that simple.

So she kissed him.

Kissed him in a place she'd never once have considered.

Licked his lovely length so slowly it took for ever to get to the top as he moaned again.

The dark made her brave, braver with each kiss, with each stroke of her tongue. She could feel his fingers in her hair now, guiding her, hear his breath quicken, her hair a thick curtain around his centre, shielding her from the world, to a place where she could just be, where it was just them and she could focus only on this. It was an act of pure giving and it came from the heart with no hope of return. She was crying when he climaxed, her salt mingling with his as he shuddered his release.

He pulled her up to his arms, and he held her, he spooned right into her and held her close and then he asked, 'Why would you do that for me?'

Only Emma didn't reply. She could feel him unwound and relaxed beside her now, felt his breath even out as he drifted into decent sleep. She knew her answer.

But it wasn't for Luca to hear.

She was embarrassed.

He was pretending to be asleep when she awoke, deliberately ignoring her—and Emma lay next to him for a moment, her body one burning blush as she remembered last night and the intimacy she had bestowed on a man who had so clearly told her this was for appearances' sake only.

Quietly she slipped from the bed and walked to the en suite, closing the door behind her, then sitting on the edge of the bath and resting her burning face in her hands.

She should never have agreed to this, should never have come back to Italy. Even if she had convinced herself that it was for all the right reasons—for Mia, to keep up appearances, for Luca even—in part, a very big part, it had been for her, for some time with him, for that chance to rekindle or reawaken in Luca some of the feelings that had once existed.

Instead, thanks to his silence this morning, she had found out what she had always known.

It was sex he wanted from her—and nothing more.

She showered, wishing the water could wash away her shame, her stupidity. She, Emma Stephenson, had been so sure she could handle it, so sure she would never succumb to his fatal charms. Eventually, like all the rest, she had. Bit by bit, each rule, each guideline had been chipped away—each time she had promised herself that this would be the last…

Till next time.

Turning off the shower, she shivered and reached for a towel that wasn't there. Walking across the bathroom, she stood naked as he walked in, her hands moving to cover herself as she leant against the sink.

'Don't you ever knock?' She attempted a smile to save face, and hoped the steam and the water from the shower would hide the evidence of her tears.

But he saw her.

Saw the body he had missed for weeks and saw the changes too.

Full, ripe breasts made his throat catch, and he noticed the dusting of weight on her hips, although there was something else too that he couldn't define, an added dimension to her femininity.

She was like a drug that kept beckoning. Never had

he cared for someone like this before—last night he had accepted the release she had offered, not for escape but to go back, to return, to savour the feelings they had once created in one another.

He had told her some of it, he had told her, and she hadn't blanched or turned away from his horrible past—and he was finally glimpsing a future, a future where bathroom doors were open, where you kissed and made up and you tried again.

Where you were there for each other.

'Why would I knock?' he teased gently.

'Because...' She was starting to cry and couldn't help it. 'Because...'

He pressed her against the sink with his kiss—naked, gorgeous, she made today possible. He had sworn to never again make love with her, he had sworn to just let her go, let her be, keep her safe, but he was finally seeing things differently.

She was safer by his side.

Safer with him than without him.

He kissed her as if it was the first time, relishing her all over again.

'You do make things better. With you things are better.' And that he remembered their words, that each conversation they'd ever had was in his head the same way it was in hers, brought assurance. 'You could *always* make things better...'

'This isn't just sex.' She wept out the words as he lifted her to the edge of the sink. His mouth lowered and suckled her swollen breast as her fingers knotted in his hair.

'No,' he murmured, because it wasn't. This was it, this was him and this was her and this was the place he always wanted to be. He lifted his head and kissed away her tears, kissed her mouth as his hands followed the curve of her thickening waist.

'Don't hurt me again, Luca...' she begged brokenly.

His eyes jerked up to hers, his mouth pulling away simultaneously with her words. Was that what he had done? Yes, he acknowledged. In protecting her, he had hurt her badly.

He could never hurt her again, never would hurt her again. Of that, at this very moment, he was absolutely certain.

'Never.' He growled out his truth.

'And tell me this isn't just sex,' she pleaded as his hips parted her thighs, because it wasn't just sex for her, because she could never be so real, so open, so exposed with anyone other than Luca. His fingers spread her pretty butterfly lips and he saw changes there too, and he was awash with this fierce surge of protection, assured in his answer.

'No.' His mouth was in her neck, he was as close to weeping as he had ever been. Her curls, wet from the shower, draped his face and as he slid inside her, he was certain of the moment. He was smelling her again, tasting her again, inside her again, and he was truly home, deep, deep inside her. His arms circled her, his mind wrapped around hers, and this was nothing like anything he had ever envisaged. Then she was arching towards him and he didn't have to hold back, he didn't have to do anything except love her, and that was so scarily easy.

The passion that blazed in his eyes should have assured her, but then he lowered his head. Nuzzling her shoulders, her neck, he drove deeper into her, only she couldn't give in, couldn't let herself be swept away by the building current, because she couldn't risk going under again.

Her body was twitching, her legs wet and wrapped around him, and it was Emma who sought release now. She could see his jet curls, see him slide in and out of her, and knew he was ready, knew he awaited her—but she was too scared to trust, too scared to hand over that last little bit of her heart to him.

She wanted his love, wanted a father for her baby, wanted him no matter how her head denied it.

She knew he was close and, locked into a rhythm, his body begged her to join him. He was saying her name over and over, his lips kissing the back of her neck, his hands cupping her damp bottom, and she could feel his abandon.

'*I love you.*' He groaned out the words as if it hurt to say them. She'd never thought she'd ever hear him say them, but he was saying them again and again, saying them over and over as he spilled inside her, rapid, urgent thrusts that took her to this heady place where she gave in to him, gave in to her body, and she was saying it too.

He was kissing her passionately, his tongue circling hers, as finally she joined him, and he dragged from her that last restraint. His mouth stifled her sobs as she gave that piece to him and then his tongue soothed her as he slowly kissed her back to the world.

'You,' Luca said slowly, wrapping a towel around her, holding her shivering body, comforting her on a day when it should be her comforting him, 'make this day bearable.'

CHAPTER SEVENTEEN

SHE was pregnant.

Of that he was sure.

That the baby was his there was no doubt.

He stood in the church, supporting his mother, his weeping sister, and stared beyond the priest to the baptismal font. He tried to comprehend the fact of the D'Amato name carrying on after all—his baby, the future, the family name continuing.

Tried to imagine himself as a father.

Could he do it—could he break every promise he had made to himself?

Today he did his duty, threw a handful of dirt on the coffin and then stepped back.

It should be over—and yet the cycle might now continue.

His mind was a blizzard of conflicting emotions, every tombstone reminding him of his history, of his legacy, of the true meaning of his family name. He wanted to go back to this morning, to the certainty he had felt then, the assuredness that no harm would ever come to someone he loved.

The priest was talking about faith and hope and love.

His faith had long since gone.

He desperately wanted to hope.

And he was terrified to love.

But he was dangerously close to accepting a different future.

He needed to think.

'Come...' Mia was calmer. Her tears had filled the church but now she seemed resigned. 'The cars are waiting.'

'I will make my own way back.' Luca looked over at Emma. 'You go to the house.'

'You need to greet the guests,' she pointed out.

'I want to walk.'

'You must come back to the house,' Mia said in exasperation. 'As his only son, it is tradition...'

'I will be back.' Luca refused to be swayed. 'But right now I need to be alone.'

He did, he needed so badly to be alone, because this was too big to leap into without serious thought.

Soon Emma would tell him, soon he would formally know that he was to become a father, and his response had to be right.

He walked around the graveyard then stood for a pensive moment.

He could hear his mother's bitter words from the past as clearly as though she'd just said them to him. *You are no better than him—you are the same. You are a D'Amato through and through.*

'Luca!' Leo stood beside him as he stared at his father's new grave. 'Can I give you a lift back to the house?'

'I am not going back yet—I want to walk.'

'Do you mind if I join you?' He was about to decline

the offer of company, only Leo was wise. Surely, at some point over the years, he must have treated his mother's wounds or at least seen what was going on—maybe the older man could give him answers.

They walked in silence—through the winding roads and to the next village, where finally they sat. Luca ordered coffee and whisky and wondered how to ask without telling.

'Emma seems a lovely woman.' Leo broke the silence.

'She is,' Luca agreed.

'It is good to see you two supporting each other, Luca. To know even in sad times you can find peace.'

'Can I speak with you as a doctor?' Luca asked bluntly.

'Of course.'

'I think she may be pregnant,' he revealed. The doctor didn't offer congratulations; instead he waited to hear what else Luca had to say. 'I have questions, Leo. Things I need to know about my past, about me…'

'Then ask,' Leo offered, 'and I will try to give honest answers.'

'Always I feel different from my father—my mother says I am the same, that I am like him…' He watched as Leo's drink paused near his lips. 'Do you understand what I'm saying?'

'I think so.'

'Is it true?'

'Is what true, Luca?' Leo asked.

That I will beat my wife, that the cruel streak of the D'Amato men is my inevitable fate—or Emma's? This was what he wanted to say, but instead he downed his drink.

'I should never have started this.' Luca stood up. 'I should get back to the house.'

'Sit, Luca.' Leo gestured to the waiter to fill his glass, but Luca remained standing. 'There are things we need to discuss, and it will be better for you, for Emma too perhaps, to know the truth.'

'I don't want to discuss it any more,' Luca said, because even if he had started it, he didn't want to go there, didn't want to face the inevitable, but it was coming at him now.

'There is a good counsellor in Palermo, one I highly recommend to deal with these things.'

'No!' He shouted it.

'Luca, you cannot escape your genes.' It was like hearing the guillotine fall, the truth was so appalling, and the horrible inevitability had Luca wanting to vomit. But instead he drowned the acrid taste in his mouth with whisky and willed the fear to abate as the doctor delivered his diagnosis that no matter the strength of Luca's feelings, his unenviable gene pool would claim, not just him but Emma and the baby he was sure she carried.

'No!' It was Emma's sobs that filled the house—and Luca had to restrain her flailing arms from making contact with his chest as he broke her heart again. 'You said you *loved* me.'

'Emma.' His voice was detached, matter-of-fact even, as she raged at what he was doing, at what he was saying. 'I was upset this morning, emotional...'

'You!' Emma sobbed. '*Emotional?* You're a cold-hearted bastard. You looked me in the eyes and said you loved me, and you *did* love me, I could see it.' She wanted to lash out again if he would just let go of her arms.

'People say that…' Luca's was the voice of cool reason. 'Men say that, you know that. Men say these things to—'

'Get what they want?' Emma finished for him. 'You already *had* what you wanted, Luca. You were already screwing me when you said it!'

'Don't talk like a tart.'

'Well, that's what *you* made me, that's what *you* did to me!' And then, because he was holding her arms, because she couldn't hit him again, she swore at him instead.

And then she swore again, using the most vile epithets she could think of.

He didn't even flinch.

She didn't tell him about the baby, didn't play her last card.

And for that Luca had grudging admiration.

She didn't cash in the cheque he sent her, which made Luca worry.

In the weeks and months that followed, every day he waited, for her letter, or her lawyer's letter, or a phone call—admiring her that it never came, eroding him that it didn't.

Back in his village for another tour of duty, for the three-month mass to mark his father's passing, it killed him to be back in the same room, only this time without her.

He lay in bed that morning, not wanting to get up, not wanting to shower, to walk into the bathroom, where he had told her his ultimate truth.

He *had* hurt her.

Not in the way that he had feared, but he *had* hurt her all the same.

He had never—except in this—doubted himself.

And he was angry now.

Angry for doubting himself, because after weeks of soul searching he knew—Luca knew—he would never hurt her. His grief on the night of his father's funeral and in the days that had followed had been real—except it had all been because of losing Emma.

Since she'd left, in the depths of his grief, this proud man *had* visited a counsellor—although not the Italian one Leo had suggested. Instead, he had sat in a bland beige office in the middle of London and had opened his closed heart to a stranger, explored his closed mind in a way he had never dared to do before, and he knew now.

Knew, despite his heritage, despite what Leo had said, despite the facts and figures, despite the anger of his youth and the unenviable history of the D'Amato men, he knew that his anger *would* never, *could* never be aimed at her.

For the very first time he trusted himself, except now it was maybe too late.

'Luca?' His mother knocked and then came into the bedroom, placed coffee on the bedside table and handed him the tray then headed to the window, opening the shutters and letting the sun stream in.

'You did not have to do that!' Luca protested. 'I should be looking after you.'

'You should be looking after Emma,' his mother pointed out.

She was dressed in black. This was a dark day, but

there was a lightness to her—the absence of fear, Luca realised. Oh, she would respectfully mourn her husband, but her duty was done now, there would be no feigned tears—life could be peaceful now.

For her.

'I thought I *was* looking after her,' Luca said, 'by keeping her away. I thought I was doing the right thing by her.'

'How?' Mia begged. 'I thought you were happy with Martha, but with Emma I just knew… How could you think you were helping her by ending it? Emma loves you.'

'I did not want to be like *him*.'

'I know I said hurtful things to you, out of fear, out of pain, out of guilt, and for that I am truly sorry. But you are *nothing* like him,' his mother said fiercely.

'I know that *now*,' Luca said. 'But I still wasn't sure back then.'

'Leo said you spoke with him.' Mia sat on the edge of the bed, her eyes sparkling with tears. 'I don't understand, Luca. He said you understood your past, and wanted to ask him about it. I know it must have been a shock, that it must have caused you pain to hear the truth, but to end it with Emma! Why, Luca?'

'Because Leo said it was in my blood, that I could not escape my genes. That the violent traits in my grandfather, my uncle, my father could not be denied. I said I felt nothing like them and he said he knew it was hard to accept, to face…'

A moan of horror escaped his mother's lips…a sound of such pain that Luca started with concern. She had always been silent, even when being beaten, but she was moaning in pain now, a pain he didn't understand, her eyes frantic and urgent and loaded with tears when they met her son's. 'To accept and face the truth that *Leo* is your real father...'

It was as if the sun had gone out. Everything suddenly went dark, as if the bed had been pulled from under him, as if the floor had just given way. Every rock, every foundation collapsed beneath him, yet he never moved, never moved a muscle, his mother's voice seeming distorted from a distance as his mind frantically tried to process the words.

'I thought you knew,' Mia pleaded. 'Leo thought that you knew, that you had finally guessed...'

As he looked back on their conversation with the knowledge the other man held, Luca closed his eyes. And as he did so, he felt the guilt, the shame, the *fear* truly unravel at last, and when he opened his eyes it was to a world that was brighter, safer. His only regret was that it was a world without Emma.

'*Devo sapere,*' Luca said. 'Tell me.' There was a flash of anger then. 'Did he know, did Leo know how he was treating you?'

'Never!' Mia sobbed. 'Only you, my son, only you know my pain. I was always promised for your father—our two families were friends. I knew I would marry him, but I did not like to think about it—sixteen seemed a long way off. Always I liked Leo—he was so clever, we all knew he was destined for better and sometimes, when he came home in the holidays, I felt his eyes on me. One time we kissed...' She sighed and then visibly shook herself and continued her story.

'I worked in the baker's, my marriage was two weeks away. The village was celebrating because Leo had passed his exams and was going to study medicine in Roma; he would return a doctor. I was sad. My wedding was soon and your father had slapped me, he had pushed me, he had made me do things that shamed me…'

'He is not *my* father,' Luca corrected her, and how good those words felt!

'*Rico* had hurt me.' Mia nodded in acknowledgment. 'We closed early one day and I was walking home and I met Leo. He was leaving the next day and he said he was sorry he would not be at my wedding…then he admitted he was not sorry. That it would hurt to see me marry another. We went to the river and I nearly told him…'

'Why didn't you?' Luca asked.

'How?' Mia asked. 'Leo was a good man, even as a teenager he was a good man, a man who cared for me. He would not have gone away to get his medical degree.'

'He could have taken you with him.'

'His family would have been shamed and would not have paid for his education. After all, I was another man's bride-to-be, and this town would have never forgiven that. How, in one conversation, could I change his life when neither really knew how the other was feeling?

'We kissed, and you were made that day, Luca. It was the best day of my life, and every night I fall asleep with that memory… Yes, in hindsight I should have told him, but we were young, and I loved him and wanted him to do well, to be happy. I would have brought him so much pain…'

'Did my fa—?' Luca stopped himself. 'Did Rico know I was not his son?'

'He never said, and sometimes I wondered if he had guessed, if that was why he was so angry with you, with me, but really he was angry with me and treated me badly before I was ever unfaithful to him.'

'And Leo?' Luca swallowed. 'When did you tell him?'

'I didn't for a long time. He was a man when he returned, and I was married with two children. He was married later too. I was friends with his wife.' The pain of her secret silenced her for a moment. 'He ended up being friends with Rico as well. No one knew the man Rico was in private. It was one time, Luca, and a long time ago, not much to ruin so many lives. When Carmella, his wife, died, Leo came over one night. He was chatting to your father and going through albums, talking of his wife, and there was a photo of you there when you got your degree. I remember him looking up at me, his eyes asking me, and I looked away, red and blushing—and from that moment he knew. He must have seen something of himself as a young man in that photo of you.'

'Have you talked to him about it?' Luca asked.

'I spoke with him a few months ago, yet we could not properly talk. He was treating Rico, his friend, but we knew we would talk one day soon.'

'And have you?'

'Soon,' Mia said. 'Still I have to break his heart by telling him all I have suffered, how you, his son, have suffered over the years.'

'How do you know it will break his heart?' he wanted to know.

'Love does not just go away, Luca.'

'I know.' He stared out the window at the Mediterranean.

'You can push it away, you can deny it, you can make excuses, give reasons, but once love has been born, once it has existed, it cannot simply cease to be.'

There were so many questions, so much more he wanted to know from his mother and from his real father, but he didn't need those answers right now.

It was Emma he needed to see and regardless of whether or not it was too late he had to tell her, which meant there was someone he had to speak with first.

'You cannot leave now,' Mia pointed out as he packed his case. 'There is mass tonight, one more duty, Luca—for *familia*…'

'No, Ma.' He kissed his mother's cheek to show he was not angry. 'My duty is to Emma—*she* is *familia* now.'

CHAPTER EIGHTEEN

'CAN I pay Dad's account?'

'Of course.' The supervisor was unusually friendly as Emma came into the office, just a little bit flushed in the cheeks and, well, just a little nicer. 'You've sold another painting.'

It was actually the supervisor who handed her an envelope with a cheque in it and there was a flurry in her stomach as Emma took it. That feel of her baby moving still caught her by surprise, and she smiled, not just at the kicks from her baby but that she had almost paid her debts—and all by her own hand.

All was well.

She chanted those words over and over to herself and out loud to her baby too at times.

All was well.

Her father's house had finally sold and she'd found a little flat nearby. Thanks to an excellent reference from Luca, she'd landed a wonderful job for three days a week and once the baby arrived they were happy for her to work a couple of days a week from home, which gave her time to concentrate on her art.

She was getting there.

Not quite thriving, but not just surviving either.

She missed Luca—missed him in her days, in her nights, in her life, and she missed him for their baby too.

But there was nothing she could do about that, so she poured her grief into her artwork and scared herself sometimes with her own mind—painting dark, swirling stories of loss and grief and hope and life.

And she'd sold not one but three paintings!

She'd put one up in her father's room at the nursing home, which a relative of another resident had liked, and things had taken off from there.

Oh, they hadn't sold for vast sums, but they'd keep the baby in nappies and bottles, and Emma knew that they'd be okay.

All was well, she told her kicking stomach.

They really didn't need Luca.

Want, however, was an entirely different matter.

She walked down the long corridor towards her father and wasn't really looking forward to it. He'd noticed her swelling stomach these past couple of weeks and unfortunately a stroke and a touch of senility weren't stopping him from asking awkward questions.

Emma pulled her coat around her and held a massive photo album over her stomach, hoping a few pictures from the past would be enough to distract him.

And then she saw him.

Saw six feet two with eyes of blue, sitting chatting on the bed and laughing with her dad, and she absolutely, completely didn't know what to do.

'Here's my baby girl!' Frank beamed as she made her way over.

She kissed her dad on the cheek and ignored Luca.

He watched as she put her father's pyjamas away and

sorted out his chocolate and put some money in a little dish for his newspaper—and he saw the swell of her stomach and the strain on her features, and finally, finally she faced him.

'Could we have a word?' Emma said. 'Outside.'

They walked out to the nursing-home gardens, along the winding paths, and finally she spoke.

'Don't...' Her voice was shaky. 'Don't you *dare* drag him into this! He's old and he's confused.'

'He's our child's grandfather,' Luca pointed out. 'I'd say he's already in this...and he knows, by the way.'

'Knows what?'

'That you're pregnant,' Luca said, and watched her cheeks burn. 'Were you ever going to tell me?'

'I don't know,' she said honestly.

'You don't *know*?' he repeated incredulously.

So she turned to him and just said it, too tired, too confused and too angry for his mind games this time.

'You knew anyway,' Emma accused. 'You *knew* that morning you said you loved me, and you knew it when you chose to let me go.' And it was agony when he nodded. 'So don't play the wounded party now—you chose not to be around, Luca. I *bore* you, remember?'

'Never,' Luca said, his face pale.

'And I'm *not very interesting* in bed.'

'That's not true either,' he said. How he hated hearing it, how he hated what he had done to her—and yet now he had to face it. 'All I think about is you. All I want is you—if you will give me this chance,' he vowed.

'Why would I?' She had loved him so much and he hadn't wanted that love. She could almost forgive him for herself, but she wouldn't be careless with her baby's heart. 'Why would I risk it again? We'll do fine without you.'

And she would, he knew that she would, but how he wanted her to do better than fine—with him by her side.

'I was scared I was like my father,' he admitted.

'Not good enough, Luca.' She turned her face away. 'I'm scared I'm like my mother—but deep down I know I'll never walk away. You did.'

'He beat her.' Luca closed his eyes. 'Badly, over and over.'

'I know that,' Emma pointed out. 'And I know you never would do that to me or our baby, so why couldn't you trust that?'

'My grandfather, my uncle, they were the same too. Emma, I didn't want to hurt you.'

'But you *did*!' She was trying not to cry, trying not to get upset, trying to stay calm for the baby, but it was hard. 'Over and over you did. It doesn't have to be a fist to hurt, Luca.'

Her words sliced his heart—bitter, bitter was his regret.

'My grandmother slipped and fell.' Luca's voice was a hoarse whisper, voicing dark thoughts that had never been said. 'That is what I was told, that was what I believed—I heard my mother sob one night that Rico was just like *his* father. "And look where my mother ended up" was Rico's response.'

It wasn't just his father, Emma started to see that now, and it wasn't just the beating...

'He killed her.'

'Oh, Luca,' Emma whispered.

'And Rico's brother, Rinaldo.' His voice was hoarse,

the filth of the past all spewing out now. 'He beat Zia Maria too. Daniela remembers her as glamorous, always wearing make-up—only, of course, it was to cover the bruises.'

Emma closed her eyes, recalling the well made-up face of Rinaldo's second bride.

'Maria came to our door one night, scared and crying, yet my mother sent her away—and she was dead the next morning. Kicked by a horse, my father, the policeman, announced after he'd *investigated*.

'I grew up with this secret—a secret so well hidden that not even the family doctor could see. My father was the trusted village policeman and yet in his home he did terrible things—his brothers and father too. And when I was younger, I promised I would never get so involved with a woman that I would marry her, give her children...' It was so hard to explain and yet he persevered. 'I thought there was this...inevitability, that the violence was in my blood, in my genes. That I had been passed not just the family name...' His eyes searched the gorgeous mound of her stomach. 'And I thought that I had passed it on too—and that the baby would have a better chance of a normal life with just you to look after it.'

'You should have told me all this,' Emma said.

'When?' Luca challenged. 'I don't come with a government warning. I made my choice to never get too involved with anyone, and then you came along and that simple resolution...' He swallowed as he recalled just how hard it had been to keep it in and how scared he had been to let it out. 'I was going to tell you. The day of the funeral, I knew somehow that I would do better, that I could not hurt you. For the first time I realised I had choices—and I also realised you had to make your choices too. It is not an easy family to marry into.'

'Marry?' Emma blinked. 'You were thinking of asking me to *marry* you that day?'

'And every day from the moment I met you—even if I didn't want to admit it,' Luca said truthfully.

'So why didn't you?' she wanted to know.

'I spoke with Leo.'

'The doctor?'

Luca nodded. 'I tried to tell him my concerns, I wanted him to reassure me, and instead he said that I could not hide from my genes. He offered me counselling. I thought he was talking about anger management…'

'How dare he?' It was Emma who needed anger management now. 'How bloody archaic, how dare he imply that you'd be like that too?'

'No.' He hushed her. 'Emma, I woke up this morning and I knew, no matter what he'd said, no matter what history dictates, that I would never, ever hurt you.'

'I knew that already,' she said, but she did understand because there was a part of her that had the same sort of fears—that she'd be a lousy mother, that she'd turn forty and some strange force would take over and she'd suddenly walk out on her family. Luca's words had rung that bell of fear that she'd heard many times before—that there was a certain inevitability to it all. 'I feel the same sometimes,' she admitted, 'that I won't be a good mum…'

'You'll be a *wonderful* mum,' he said with absolute conviction.

'You'll be a wonderful dad.'

'If you'll let me be,' he murmured.

'I could never stop that, and I know in the end I'd have told you,' she admitted.

He ran a hand over her swollen stomach, rued the moments he'd already missed and promised himself that he'd miss not a moment more.

'You're nothing like your dad,' Emma continued. 'You're like Pepper!' How she made him smile! 'Snapping and snarling, but you'd never bite. Luca...' She said it with absolute conviction. 'You're nothing like him.'

'Actually, I am *nothing* like him.'

'I just said that.'

'No...' He blew out a breath, because in all that had happened he hadn't even had time to really process the news, to even think about it, to explore it, so when he did that for the first time, he did it with her.

'I'm nothing like Rico because Leo is my real father.'

'Leo?' Emma gasped. 'The doctor, the one who said...?' She *had* thought him familiar when they'd met, and now she knew why! That assuredness, that arrogance that Luca possessed had to have come from somewhere—and now she knew where!

'That is what he was trying to say, about genes. He thought I had guessed, thought I was trying to tell him I knew. Guilt made my mother stay with Rico—and shame. Not just at what others might think but because of what she secretly knew—that she'd been unfaithful to my father even before she'd married him.'

Emma blinked in amazement, trying to take it all in.

'I love you.' And it was a different way he said it this time. Not something he dragged from himself, not something he didn't want to admit. Instead, he told her his truth. 'People make mistakes. I have just sat and listened to your father's regret about your mother and you—and I've heard my own mother's regret and guilt too. People bury their shame and fears in the past but they don't go away, they fester.' He smiled. 'Also, I have something else to tell you. Your father is not senile.' Luca gazed down at her. 'He told me that today. He knows you think he is, but his truth is that he remembers your mother now with love, and better still…' He looked at her kind, clear eyes that had never been loved and vowed to make up for all past hurts. 'Your father says he now has a second chance to love you.'

'He said that?' she choked.

'Yes.'

'He's not confused from the stroke?'

'No.' Luca grinned, the old Luca, the funny Luca, the Luca who had first won her heart. 'He's just a bit uninhibited,' Luca said, and then he was serious. 'And so now must I be.' He stared beyond her eyes and to her soul. 'I love you, Emma. I always have and I always will. I sat on the sofa that first night we met, after I came in from Paris, and there was a part of me imagining watching that detective show with you.'

He watched a pink flush warm her cheeks.

'When I left my flat for Tokyo that day, I imagined coming home to you.'

He watched as the colour spread to her little ears, saw the smile wobble on her lips, and so he told her some more.

'When you held my hand on the plane, I imagined lying next to you every night for the rest of my life.'

She could feel it, the warm glow of his love warming her icy veins, chasing away all the hurt, the fear, the loneliness—bathing her in this deep, rosy warmth and wrapping her in soft, infinite understanding.

'You can,' Emma said, her eyes open, staring into the eyes of a man who had made it so very difficult for her to love him. 'Every night for the rest of your life, you can lie beside me.'

'You too,' Luca said, because it was such a nice thing to know, such a nice thing to be told. 'Always, I am here for you.'

And he would be, Emma knew that. Luca was here, for her, for their baby—and finally, finally she had the family she had always longed for.

'Come on,' she whispered. 'Let's go and tell Dad.'

EPILOGUE

'ONE more push,' Luca implored—as if it were that easy, as if he knew how it should be done just because he'd read it in a magazine!

'I can't!'

It wasn't pushing that scared her, it was life, because in a moment the future would be here—and although she couldn't wait to meet it, she was scared she wasn't up to it.

That, by not having grown up with a mother, she might not be able to *be* a mother herself.

It wasn't one more push, it was four, and then this wait, this rush as a bundle of red was on her stomach and Luca was cutting the cord, was over. Ready or not, she was officially a mum, so she had no choice but to be able.

'A girl!' It was the doctor who spoke because Luca just stood, his face unreadable, watching his wife reach for their daughter, watching eyes peer at a very new, very big world.

He had hoped for a boy—not for the old reasons, not for a son or to continue the family name, which was a bit of a black joke between them. No, Luca had wanted a boy because Emma was so scared of having a girl.

And as he stared at this tiny little lady, so new and so raw and so fragile, he understood her fears—because he had them too. Their daughter was surely the most precious thing in the world and they had to do this right.

'A girl...' He picked up his daughter and cradled her close, hushed angry, startled cries and then, when he was sure Emma was ready, he handed her to her mother, and he watched nature unfold, and Emma feed her hungry baby.

Watched his wife become a mother to his daughter.

The midwife tidied up around them then opened the curtains on the beginning of a glorious new day, pinks and oranges and pretty lemons filling the window as if the sky had known it was giving her a girl.

'What a beautiful morning to become a mum!' the midwife said, and left the new family to it. Emma wanted to call her back, worried almost that she'd been left with her baby, that she should know what to do. What if she stopped feeding, or what if she suddenly cried?

But she was still feeding, making little snuffly noises as Emma stared down.

Girls were different.

Politically correct or not, scientifically based or whatever, in a hormonal haze Emma knew that they just were.

They needed cuddles and blankets and something else—something Emma had been denied and something she swore her daughter would never be without.

'If something were to happen to me...' Seeing her cradling their daughter, hearing the wobble in her voice, it would have been so easy to wave her fears away, but Luca wouldn't do that to her.

'There would be Daniela, my mother, Evelyn and her twin girls when they come... She'd be surrounded.' Luca stared at his daughter. 'But more than that, she would know about you and know how much I loved you and how much I love her.'

He left no room for doubt.

'What happened to my playboy?' she teased.

'He stopped playing.'

'What happens now?' Emma asked, because she had it all, here in this room. Here in her arms she had it all, and she didn't know quite what to do with it.

'We name her?' Luca smiled. 'Do you want to call her after your mother?'

She had thought about it long and hard and she thought about it again.

'No,' Emma admitted, because sometimes it still hurt. 'Do you want to name her after yours?'

'No,' Luca said. He had forgiven Mia, and he was happy to see her with Leo, but, well, it was all too new and too much just yet. He didn't even know what to do with his own surname, let alone pass on his mother's first name too!

'Aurora,' Emma said.

'Aurora?' Luca played with the word in his mind and liked it. 'It means dawn...'

'And new beginnings,' Emma said, gazing from her infant to her husband. They would follow their own course now. This precious clean slate they had been given deserved the very best they could give her, and that's what she would get.

A new beginning.

THE SALVATORE
MARRIAGE DEAL

NATALIE
RIVERS

Natalie Rivers grew up in the Sussex countryside. As a child, she always loved to lose herself in a good book, or in games that gave free rein to her imagination. She went to Sheffield University, where she met her husband in the first week of term. It was love at first sight and they have been together ever since, moving to London after graduating, getting married and having two wonderful children.

After university Natalie worked in a lab at a medical research charity and later retrained to be a primary school teacher. Now she is lucky enough to be able to combine her two favourite occupations—being a full-time mum and writing passionate romances.

For my editor, Sally Williamson

CHAPTER ONE

LILY shivered in the back of the water taxi as it travelled carefully along the foggy Venetian canal. The cold and damp sceped through her suede jacket, chilling her to the bone, but she was grateful for the fresh air. It was warmer inside the polished wooden cabin of the taxi, but it was stuffy, and the movement of the boat made her feel queasy. These days everything made her feel queasy, but at least now she knew why.

She was pregnant.

She closed her eyes and took a deep breath. Pregnant.

How was she going to tell Vito?

She'd been living with him for five months, and during that time he'd been the most amazing, attentive lover she could have imagined. But she'd always known that as far as he was concerned it was only a temporary arrangement.

From the start Vito had promised her complete exclusivity and, in return for his fidelity, he'd demanded the same from her. But he'd always made it plain that there was no future for the relationship. There would be no long-term commitment, and categorically *no* children.

But now she was eight weeks pregnant. The stomach bug that she'd thought was taking a long time to clear up was actually morning sickness. And presumably the same stomach bug was responsible for the failure of the Pill.

She shivered again and looked at her watch. Vito would be waiting at the *palazzo* for her, wanting to know what the doctor had said. She glanced up as the taxi passed under a familiar arched bridge. In only a few minutes she'd be home.

Suddenly, despite her apprehension about telling Vito her news, she couldn't wait to be with him. A baby might not have been his plan right now, but she hadn't got pregnant deliberately. Vito would understand. He was a rich and powerful man, used to things going exactly the way he wanted, but he wasn't unreasonable. He might be surprised, shocked even, but after he had time to absorb her news she was sure that everything would be all right.

She'd always wanted a family, and now that she thought about it she couldn't think of anyone she'd rather have as the father of her children. He was a successful and influential businessman, but she'd also seen the loving, tender side of him. He wouldn't reject his own baby just because it was unplanned.

It was eerily quiet as the taxi stopped at the watergate entrance of the *palazzo*. The fog muffled the sounds of the city, and all Lily could hear was the lap of the water against the marble steps. She paid the driver and gratefully accepted his hand as she climbed unsteadily out of the boat. Then she made her way upstairs, where Vito was coming out of his study to greet her.

Her breath caught in her throat, and she hesitated on the top stair, just staring at him—soaking up the absolute masculine perfection of Vito Salvatore, her lover.

Over six-feet tall and broad shouldered, he carried himself with the physical grace and power of an athlete.

His black hair was slightly wavy, and it was brushed back from his strong forehead to reveal his breathtakingly handsome face.

She'd often wondered if she'd ever get over how amazing he was. It didn't matter whether he'd been away on business for a few days or whether they'd just been in different rooms for a few minutes—whenever she laid eyes on him after they'd been apart, her heart fluttered and excitement coiled through her. After knowing him for ten months and living with him for the past five months, she was still overwhelmed by the pure thrill of being with him.

'You have returned at last.' Vito caught her with his blue eyes as he closed the distance between them and swept her into his embrace.

'Hmm.' Lily snuggled against his strong chest, pressing her face against his velvety-soft black cashmere sweater. She breathed deeply, drawing his scent into her lungs. Safe in his arms, she felt so much better. The nausea she'd suffered in the water taxi was already a distant memory.

'I tried to call you,' Vito said, lifting her face gently for a lingering kiss. 'But then I found your phone in the bedroom.'

'Sorry.' Lily looked up into his gorgeous face. As always his kiss had the power to make all thoughts fly out of her mind. 'I forgot to charge it.'

'Are you all right?' Vito asked, catching her hands in his. 'You're so pale and cold. Come and sit down. Would you like a warm drink?'

'I'm fine,' Lily replied, letting Vito lead her into his study. 'A glass of cold water would be lovely.' She smoothed her fingers over her hair, suddenly apprehensive again. Now she knew why she'd gone off tea and coffee—and in a minute she'd have to tell Vito.

'I thought Carlo was taking you to your appointment,' Vito said, looking over his shoulder at her as he dropped ice cubes into a glass and poured mineral water from a frosted bottle. 'I don't like you taking public taxis, especially when you aren't feeling well.'

'I was all right,' Lily reassured him. 'I thought I might want to walk a while—the fresh air makes me feel better.'

'Still, if I'd known you were going to dismiss Carlo I would have accompanied you myself,' Vito said, slipping his arm around her waist and guiding her over to a sofa by the window. 'I don't know how you persuaded me not to cancel my meeting.'

Lily ran her hand over her long blonde hair again as she sat down. The humidity of the fog had made it frizz. It was absurd to worry about what she looked like at a time like this, but somehow the enormity of the situation suddenly made it easier to focus on smaller things.

'What did the doctor say?' Vito asked, looking at Lily with concern. Her heart-shaped face really was incredibly pale, and there were dark smudges of fatigue under her expressive hazel eyes. 'Do you need antibiotics?'

'No,' Lily said.

She was smoothing her hands over her hair. Vito recognised the nervous gesture. Since they'd been together he'd grown used to her body language, but he couldn't imagine why she was anxious now.

'Then what is it?'

Fear that there might be something seriously wrong suddenly sliced through him like the blade of a knife. He dropped to his knee beside her, and took her chilly hands in his. The thought of Lily ill was unbearable. 'What did the doctor say?' he pressed. 'Do you have to go back for tests?'

'No.' Lily hesitated, looking at his expression. His

black brows were drawn down with concern, creating two vertical creases between his eyes. She was close enough to wonder at their amazing colour—the incredible vibrancy of sky-blue that made her feel like summer had come, rather than the cold and damp of early spring that still felt like winter.

But she'd worried him—something she'd never meant to do. She should tell him the truth at once.

'I'm pregnant.'

Lily could not have prepared for what happened next. She'd anticipated surprise, maybe even displeasure. But she'd *never* expected the sudden dramatic change in his expression—as if cold steel-shutters had dropped down over his features. Nor the brutal finality of his words.

'Pack your things.' He jerked abruptly to his feet, letting her hand fall from his fingers as if he could no longer bear to touch her. 'And get out of my house.'

CHAPTER TWO

LILY opened her eyes and looked groggily at the clock. Damn! She was late.

'Aren't you up yet?' Anna said, already smartly dressed for work, walking across the open-plan lounge to the kitchen area of her flat. 'I thought you had that presentation this morning. You know—the big make-or-break one.'

'Yes, it's at nine o'clock.' Lily pushed herself up into a sitting position on the sofa. She was so grateful to her friend for letting her stay since Vito had thrown her out, but this sofa wasn't exactly the most comfortable place she'd ever slept.

'Oh dear, you look awful,' Anna said. 'I thought morning sickness was only supposed to last the first few months.'

'So did I.' Lily moved and breathed slowly in an attempt to keep her stomach calm.

'Here,' Anna said, placing a glass of milk on the coffee table. 'Good luck this morning,' she added, already halfway to the front door.

Lily picked up the milk and took a careful sip. It was cool and comforting, and within a couple of minutes she felt her stomach start to settle enough for her to manage a quick shower and get ready for work. Thank goodness for Anna, who'd remembered one of her colleagues talking about how milk had worked wonders for the nausea she'd suffered from during pregnancy.

Forty-five minutes later Lily climbed out of a black cab she could ill afford, and hesitated on the wide London pavement, staring up at the imposing steel-and-glass building that was the home of L&G Enterprises. It was a subsidiary of the Salvatore empire, and a menacing shiver ran down her spine at the thought that Vito might be inside. But if she'd really thought, even for a moment, that there was any chance of him being anywhere near, she would *never* have agreed to make the presentation today.

She took a deep breath, gripped her heavy briefcase tightly, and walked into the building. A long blonde coil of her curly hair was bouncing in front of her eyes, so she tucked it back forcefully behind her ear. She'd been so late that there hadn't been time to straighten and style her hair properly. She'd settled for pulling it back tightly into a twist at the nape of her neck, but it was already showing signs of breaking free.

It was important she did well this morning. So far she hadn't managed to find the permanent job she desperately needed. But, if luck was on her side today, this could be the break she needed. She'd approached her old boss at the computer-software company she'd been working for when she'd met Vito, and as a personal favour he'd been prepared to offer her a chance. If she could sell his company's web-conferencing system to L&G Enterprises, he'd give her a commission and find her a permanent job.

'But didn't Suzy Smith set up the pitch?' Lily had asked, thinking of the flamboyant brunette who'd willingly stepped into her shoes when she'd handed in her notice so that she could move to Venice to be with Vito.

'She did,' Mike, her old boss, had conceded. 'But honestly, Lily, she won't be able to cut it. L&G are a notoriously hard sell. Trust me, Suzy will be glad to hand this one over to you—she even tried to persuade me to take it on.'

'Why don't you?' Lily had smiled wryly, realising she was halfway to talking herself out of this job opportunity.

'Because you're better,' Mike had said truthfully. He might be a computer genius, and was making a success of his small business, but sales spiel was not his greatest strength. 'You know your stuff,' he'd continued, pulling out all the necessary files and information for the presentation. 'And you won't let those stuck-up executives throw you off your stride.'

And now here she was, walking into a company owned by Vito Salvatore—the man who had thrown her out onto the streets of Venice like a piece of trash because she'd made the mistake of accidentally getting pregnant.

Six long weeks had passed since that awful day in March, but Lily was still in shock over the way he had treated her. Although at the time she'd hardly dared to believe her luck at being with such a wonderful man, she really had thought everything was going well with him. Until she'd discovered in the most appalling way that he *wasn't* really so wonderful—otherwise how could he have tossed her aside right when she'd needed his support?

With a determined effort she pushed memories of Vito and the way he had treated her to the back of her mind. Focussing her thoughts on the task in hand, she walked briskly up to Reception, and gave her name and the name of the company she represented. That was the only way she'd got through the last six weeks—by refusing to think about the brutal way Vito had betrayed her and their unborn child

She had no choice. She had to keep it together because she needed to find a job. Then she could make a home for herself and the baby.

'We've been expecting you.' The receptionist spoke without smiling, and handed Lily a visitor's badge. 'Samuel will escort you up to the meeting room.'

'Thank you.' Lily smiled brightly and pinned the badge onto the jacket of her ivory linen-suit. Then she glanced round to see a sullen-faced young man she presumed was Samuel walking across the lobby towards her.

He gave no sign of wanting to engage in small talk, so she followed him silently to the elevator and up to the executive floor, where he showed her to the room that had been booked for her presentation.

Vito had described L&G Enterprises to her as one of his smaller business interests, but there was nothing small about the glass-walled executive meeting-room that she found herself in. This certainly wasn't going to be a cosy pitch, she thought, looking at a vast smoked-glass table surrounded by black-leather chairs.

She had just finished setting up when she heard a voice behind her.

'Ms Smith, I assume?'

Lily plastered a bright smile on her face and spun round to see a short, balding man dressed in a dark suit. She recognised him from his photograph on the company website—he was the head of Corporate Communications.

'It's Lily Chase, actually,' she said, holding out her hand to him. 'I'm very pleased to meet you, Mr D'Ambrosio.'

'Decided to send in the big guns, did they?' D'Ambrosio asked. He let his beady eyes slide over her in assessment, and held onto her hand for far too long.

'You could say that.' Lily smiled. One of the most important rules in sales was always to appear bursting with confidence, even if it sometimes went against the grain. She retrieved her hand and resisted the urge to rub it vigorously on her straight skirt. 'L&G Enterprises is potentially a very important customer, and it was felt that I have the necessary experience to explain our product fully.'

'Hmm.' D'Ambrosio looked unimpressed. 'Let's get started,' he said, sitting down at the immense glass table as another group of suited people came in. One of them, a woman wearing scarily high heels, was talking on her mobile phone in a loud, insistent voice. Another, a young man in his twenties, sat down, opened his laptop and started scrolling through his emails.

Lily looked at the assembled executives, wondering if she should let the woman finish her phone call before she started. They were an arrogant bunch, and she'd long since learned not to expect much common courtesy from this type of person—if she didn't catch their attention quickly, it wouldn't be long before they were all talking on their mobile phones or looking at their laptops.

'What are you waiting for?' D'Ambrosio barked. 'We haven't got all day.'

Lily straightened her shoulders, smiled brightly, and started her pitch.

Vito Salvatore strode through the building in a thunderous mood. He couldn't get his recent visit to his grandfather out of his mind.

Giovanni Salvatore had always been such a force in

his life—a formidable head of the family, an important role model and, most importantly, a dependable father figure when Vito's parents had died in an accident.

But now he was a sick old man, clinging tenaciously to the last months of his life.

'Make me happy before I die, Vito,' Giovanni had said.

'*Nonno*, you know I would do anything for you.' Vito had sat beside him and had taken his grandfather's frail hand in his own. It shocked him to feel the weakness of his grip, feel the constant tremor in his fingers.

'Let me know my name will continue.'

Vito had squeezed his grandfather's hand in reassurance, but he hadn't been able to speak. He'd known what was being asked of him—but how could he promise something that was never going to happen?

'You're thirty-two years old. It's time to settle down,' Giovanni had urged, fixing him with a surprisingly sharp stare. 'You run through women like there's no tomorrow, but you need to stop and think about the future. My days are numbered. Before I die I want to know my great-grandchild is on the way.'

Vito had stood up and turned to look down out of the high-arched window at the many boats on the Grand Canal below. His grandfather was a stubborn old dog. Even as his health declined he'd refused to leave the baroque *palazzo* in one of the busiest parts of Venice.

It had been his home for more than seventy-five years, and he'd declared the constant noise of tourist and business traffic beneath his windows didn't bother him—what would finish him off would be putting him out to pasture in one of the family's rural estates on the Veneto plain. And in truth Vito liked having him in the city where he could oversee the care he was receiving.

He only hoped that he would be able to live out his

days at home. Certainly his fortune would cover the necessary costs of medical professionals to attend him.

'Everything will be all right, *Nonno*,' he'd said, turning to place an affectionate kiss on the old man's cheek. How could Vito break his heart by telling him that the Salvatore line would stop with him?

He pushed the memory aside and continued to stride along the carpeted corridors of the executive floor, unaware of how his expression was scattering employees in front of him. He wasn't in the mood to deal with the directors of L&G Enterprises, but nevertheless he would attend the board meeting.

Suddenly he stopped in his tracks and stared through the glass wall of the meeting room. He could not believe his eyes.

Lily Chase.

Seeing her standing there felt like a sledgehammer blow to the guts. Her betrayal was still a fresh wound and, as he looked at her, he could almost feel her twisting the knife. His heart started to thud furiously beneath his ribs, and he clenched his fists at his sides.

No one betrayed Vito Salvatore and got away with it—but that was exactly what Lily Chase had managed to do. The night he'd discovered what she had done, he'd been so shocked that he had simply thrown her out. It was *so* much less than she'd deserved.

And now, as if to rub further salt into his wounds, it was obvious that she'd fallen on her feet. Because here she was, bold as brass, coolly making a presentation to his communications team—as if she didn't have a care in the world. And as if she had nothing to fear from him.

He looked her up and down, automatically checking for signs of pregnancy, but there was no evidence of her condition yet. If anything she'd lost weight, making her look incredibly thin. The linen suit she was wearing was unflatteringly loose and baggy, and her hair was tied back in an uncompromisingly severe style.

But, even though she wasn't looking her best, he simply couldn't take his eyes off her. With her light-blonde hair and her pale clothing she stood out like a beacon against the dark-suited executives in their dark and gloomy conference room.

Why had she done it?

The question thrust itself forcefully into his mind.

He gritted his teeth, trying not to let his thoughts continue down that path. *He* was always in control. *He* was the one who called the shots, in his private life as well as in business.

All the women in his life understood how it was. Nothing permanent. No strings attached. But always absolute fidelity on both sides while it lasted. Up until the blow Lily had dealt him, that had never been an issue. He was man enough for any woman. Or so he'd thought.

He stared at her through dangerously narrowed eyes, watching her behind the glass. It only took a moment to figure out she'd gone back to her old job, selling web-conferencing software.

Although she looked pale and tired, she appeared calm and in control of the meeting, but he knew she was punching above her weight with this lot. He didn't like the head of Corporate Communications at L&G, and he knew he'd never invest in a new system, even though it was exactly what was needed to bring the company into the twenty-first century.

Why had Lily been unfaithful to him?

The question hammered persistently in his head.

Things had been good between them, both in and out of the bedroom. The time they'd spent together had been a wonderful counterpoint to the cut and thrust of his business life. And the sex... The sex had been nothing short of incredible.

She'd given him her virginity—something he'd considered a truly special gift. But that just made it all the more shocking that she'd fallen into another man's bed so quickly.

The thought of Lily with another man was unbearable. A vein throbbed in his temple and he surged forward, opening the door into the meeting room with a crash.

Lily looked up in shock.

Suddenly she couldn't breathe.

Her worst nightmare had come true—Vito was here.

'What...?' D'Ambrosio started to bluster at the interruption, but the second he realised it was his Venetian boss he fell silent.

Lily dragged a shallow breath into her lungs and felt her heart jolt back into life after the shock of seeing Vito. It began to beat painfully hard as she stared at him.

She'd missed him so much—but he'd hurt her so badly. Looking at him produced a physical ache in her chest. She longed to dash across the room and lose herself in the warm strength of his embrace—but she knew there was no warmth there any more. He'd made that clear when he'd thrown her away.

Despite the pain of seeing him, her eyes roamed urgently over his body as he stood in the doorway. He looked absolutely magnificent. His hand-tailored suit fit him to perfection, but did nothing to conceal his raw, masculine power. She recalled the athletic strength of his lean body only too well. Remembered exactly how it felt to be held close to his hard-muscled form.

But now she shuddered as she saw how intense his

expression was. His bronzed skin was pulled taut across his high, slashing cheekbones, and a muscle was pulsing on his strong angular jawline.

And his blue eyes were fixed on her, in a way that made her blood run cold. She looked straight back, matching his gaze with her own. An icy shiver skittered down her spine as she recognised the steely anger in his eyes. Apart from her final day in Venice, he had never looked at her like that. It was a nasty reminder of how brutally he had ended things between them.

'Tell me why L&G Enterprises should invest in your product.' Vito spoke suddenly.

Lily gripped her shaking hands together tightly and stared at Vito in surprise. She hadn't expected that. She'd thought he would throw her out, or perhaps call Security to do his dirty work for him. She didn't know what game he was playing, but she had no choice but to play along. She certainly wasn't going to turn tail and run from him.

Suddenly a strong smell of coffee assailed her nostrils and a wave of nausea washed over her. She looked down to see a steaming lake of black coffee spreading across the smoked-glass table from D'Ambrosio towards her laptop computer. Vito's dramatic arrival had obviously startled him into spilling his drink, but he was making no move to clean it up.

He looked at her, and with a shock Lily realised he was expecting her to do it. God, he was arrogant! But now, with Vito standing there staring at her, she had more to worry about than D'Ambrosio's spilt coffee.

She took a deep breath, inadvertently pulling the sickening smell of coffee deep into her lungs, and moved her laptop to one side. Then, looking straight at Vito, she began to speak.

Her voice rang out amazingly clear and steady in the ominous silence of the meeting room as she concentrated on delivering the presentation she had previously prepared.

'...and so this new system will give you the very best in web conferencing, saving your business both time and money, not to mention freeing you from the annoyance of using an outdated system that frequently fails to perform according to basic requirements.'

Lily finished her spiel and continued to match Vito's gaze. She knew it was pointless. Mike had been right—L&G was a hard sell. But now Vito had arrived it was more than hard—it was impossible.

The room was deathly silent as everyone waited for Vito to speak and, out of nowhere, her thoughts suddenly turned to her unborn baby. Vito's child. It still hardly seemed real. Some of the time she almost forgot she was pregnant for a few minutes. But then, even if the nagging nausea wasn't enough to remind her, the constant worry over getting a job so that she could provide for her baby slammed the reality home.

She remembered all the warnings her mother had given her about men, and now she was in exactly the same situation as her mother had once been—ruthlessly cast aside because she'd made the mistake of getting pregnant.

Lily's father had refused to acknowledge her, and had even threatened her mother if she ever revealed their relationship. He had his own 'real' family to protect—a wife and two daughters living in a lovely suburban home.

Lily and her mother hadn't been good enough. They'd been a potential embarrassment, always to remain hidden far away in the countryside where they couldn't do any damage to his impeccable reputation.

Lily knew her father was a first-class hypocrite and, as she'd grown older, she'd told herself she'd been better off without him. But it had been tough growing up without a father. Her mother had found it hard to cope, and that had made life difficult and unsettled for Lily.

'We will take your web-conferencing system on three-months-trial basis.' Vito broke the silence abruptly. 'D'Ambrosio, clean up here. Then take Ms Chase's equipment up to my office.'

'But…' For a second D'Ambrosio looked annoyed by his boss's snap decision, but then he recovered himself and jumped to his feet. 'Of course, it would be a pleasure to do business with you,' he said, holding out his hand to Lily almost desperately. 'Your company's system really does sound very impressive. We'll get it all arranged—my people will meet your people, and…'

In other circumstances, witnessing D'Ambrosio's turnaround from obnoxious to obsequious might have been amusing, but at that moment Vito turned his eyes onto Lily with a penetrating look that made the breath catch in her throat.

'Ms Chase, you will accompany me to my suite.' His voice rolled down her spine like thunder, setting her insides quaking. He'd never spoken to her like that before.

'I…I should make arrangements with Mr D'Ambrosio,' Lily prevaricated. Part of her longed to go with Vito, but the sensible part of her mind told her to keep well away from him.

He was not the man she'd thought she knew—the tender lover who'd taken care of her and made her feel safe. This was a very different man—a heartless beast who'd thrown her out of his house one horrible cold night in March.

That night had turned into an escalating nightmare. The airport had closed early because of the fog, leaving her no escape and nowhere to go.

'Come with me.' His words were nothing short of a command, and Lily found herself moving forward even before Vito's hand closed around her arm.

She gasped as he made contact, and her step faltered. It felt like an electric shock had jolted through her. She turned shakily to look up into his face.

Any hope that still flickered in her heart was extinguished as his hostile gaze knifed through her. The anger that glinted in his blue eyes was so cold and relentless that it felt like shards of ice were piercing her soul.

She wanted to get away, but there was no way out. She wanted to bolt for the door—willingly sacrifice the sale and her potential job—but Vito had her arm.

The glacial touch of his gaze ravaged her like a blizzard, but heat from his hand was steadily burning through the sleeve of her linen jacket, spreading insistently through her chilled veins, making her acutely aware of every single inch of her body.

It only took seconds to reach his private elevator and, before she knew it, he'd pulled her inside with him.

She exhaled with an involuntary whoosh as the doors closed, cutting them off from the rest of the world, enclosing them in a space that suddenly seemed too small to contain Vito. The sheer power of his presence was pressing out in all directions, bouncing off the mirrored walls of the elevator, becoming increasingly magnified with every moment that passed.

It felt like she was trapped inside a capsule with him, in a place that was completely saturated by his powerful presence. The air that flowed around his body, slipping underneath his designer clothes and sliding across his firm bronze skin, was moving sensuously over her too.

Every breath she took was laced with his achingly

familiar scent, setting her nerves alight, making the tiny space they shared more real and vibrant than the world outside.

His fingers still pressed into her arm, but from the way her heart was racing and her skin tingling it was as if his touch extended way beyond that. It was more like he was running his hands all over her naked body. And in a distant part of her mind she was aware of the elevator travelling up, further away from the outside world. Further away from escape.

Then suddenly the mirrored doors slid open and he stepped forwards, taking her with him. She blinked in surprise as he let go of her arm, momentarily disorientated by her new surroundings, and stared around at the cavernous space she found herself in.

'What is this place?' she asked, saying the first words that came into her mind. The floor was covered in a luxurious light-grey carpet, but there was no furniture apart from one imposing desk which was set to the side near the floor-to-cciling platc-glass windows.

'The penthouse suite,' Vito responded shortly. 'I have no use for it—it's being converted.'

She glanced around again, slowly regaining a little equilibrium as she put some distance between herself and Vito. She couldn't believe how powerfully her body had responded merely from being confined in a small space with him.

As she looked about, she noticed the marks where furniture had once stood, and shadows on the wall where pictures had been removed. It was a soulless space, like a home that had been gutted.

It didn't seem right that she was in this bleak place with Vito. In her mind her time with him was associated with his *palazzo* in Venice, or even just going out and about with him. It wasn't the level of comfort and luxury that was missing—it was simply being together. Being with Vito had always felt like being home. Now she had no home.

'Where are you living?' Vito asked, snapping her out of her thoughts.

'London,' Lily replied briefly. After the way he'd treated her, she didn't see any reason to let him know how unsettled her situation was.

'Alone?' he probed.

'That's none of your business.' He was standing only a few feet away from her, and she met his hard blue gaze with her own. She didn't want him to think that he intimidated her, even though she was feeling very shaky and uncertain. And she was sure he'd seen how being close to him in the elevator had affected her.

'The baby's father.' He spoke through gritted teeth. 'Are you living with him?'

For the second time that morning, Lily's heart skipped a beat.

Vito's words didn't make sense. He couldn't really mean what she thought he did—could he?

'What are you talking about?' she gasped, laying her hand protectively against her still-flat stomach. 'I know it wasn't planned—but *of course* you are the father.'

He was staring at her from beneath black brows, but the morning light flooding in from the massive windows caught his eyes, making them look almost metallic. For a moment she hardly recognised him. This really couldn't be the man she'd lived with for five wonderful months of her life.

'Don't bother with your lies,' Vito said. 'Just tell me if you are in contact with the father. Does he know you are pregnant?'

'You've made a mistake,' Lily said, still struggling

to process the implications of what he was saying. 'You know I've only ever been with you.'

'I may have been your first lover,' Vito said. 'But I wasn't your only lover.'

'But why do you think that?' Lily gasped. 'I don't understand. Did somebody tell you something about me?'

'Just tell me if the father knows,' Vito grated.

'You *are* the father!' Lily cried. 'There's no one else and there never has been.'

His eyes pinned her for a moment longer, as if he was assessing a cold, emotionless business situation.

'From that, I take it that he doesn't know—or maybe he doesn't want to know,' Vito said. 'Whatever the case, from now on, as far as the world is concerned, the child you are carrying is mine.'

'It is yours.' Lily said hollowly. She felt like she was banging her head against a brick wall.

Still holding her with his cold blue stare, Vito nodded once. The decisive movement of his head was strangely unnerving.

'We will be married immediately,' he announced.

CHAPTER THREE

'MARRIED?' Lily echoed, staring at him in utter shock. She couldn't believe what she'd heard. 'If that's some kind of cruel joke, I'm not falling for it.'

'It's no joke.' Vito sounded completely serious, and was looking at her with the hard expression she was starting to get horribly used to. 'We will be married at once.'

'How can you even ask me that?' Lily gasped. Six weeks ago she would have accepted willingly. A proposal from Vito would have been like a dream come true—but not any more. Now it was more like a nightmare. 'After the way you've treated me, I'd be mad to marry you.'

'I'm not *asking*,' Vito said. 'I'm *telling* you that we will be married. And, as far as the world is concerned, the baby you are carrying is mine. He or she will be brought up as the Salvatore heir.'

Lily's head was spinning and her stomach churning. With every passing second, Vito seemed more and more like a stranger.

Her mother, Ellen, had warned her how men could easily change. She'd had personal experience of it. Lily's father had gone from adoring lover to threatening brute overnight, when Ellen had told him that she was pregnant. That was when Ellen had found out that Reggie had been married all along.

He'd already had a wife and two children, and was steadily working his way up the hierarchy of his father-in-law's accountancy firm. Despite the sweet words of his seduction, he'd never been interested in anything more than a fling with Ellen. Her pregnancy had come as a wake-up call to him. He'd had too much at stake.

If his wife, or her father, had discovered his infidelity Reggie could have lost everything—his family, his professional status and, most importantly to him, the prospect of taking over a successful business when his father-in-law retired.

To protect himself, Reggie had set Ellen up in a tiny country cottage. He'd paid her rent and had made measly maintenance payments for Lily, but it was based on the strict understanding that Ellen could never reveal herself or her illegitimate child to his family.

'Look, I don't know what game you're playing with me.' Lily put her hands on her hips and met Vito's gaze straight on. Her childhood had been blighted by her father's duplicity, and suddenly she felt she'd had enough of dishonesty and secrets to last a lifetime. 'But, whatever you're playing at, I don't have time for it. If you want to buy the web-conferencing system, that's good—I need the commission to get myself a flat. If you don't want it, that's fine too. Just let me leave so I can get on with my life. I have to go find a permanent job.'

She had to get a job so that she could provide for her baby. She couldn't let herself end up like her mother. Or in a situation that was even more financially precarious.

Ellen had been devastated when Reggie had showed his true nature. To find herself blackmailed into silence by the man she'd fallen in love with had been unbearable. But with no one to turn to for help, and a baby to consider, she had reluctantly accepted his financial support. Then, as the years had gone by, she had become increasingly dependent on it.

With her trust in people and her confidence in herself eroded, she'd found it impossible to find a job that fitted around caring for Lily. Eventually she'd found solace working as a volunteer at the local hospice. She'd poured all her energy and love into craft projects to bring enjoyment and satisfaction to the terminally ill patients.

Lily loved her mother dearly, even though her childhood had been extremely difficult. She knew it would break her heart if she found out that Lily was pregnant and alone. Whatever happened, she had to protect Ellen from the truth—at least until she was settled. And the first thing she needed to do was find work, so that her future seemed more secure—financially at least.

'You haven't listened to a word I've said.' Vito looked so cold and unmoving, standing there, that Lily felt a sense of foreboding creep over her. 'You don't need a job, or a flat.'

'I heard you talking, but you haven't said anything that made sense,' she retorted, struggling to shake off the uneasy feeling. She decided to tell him the truth about her current circumstances after all, to try and reason with him. 'I need a job and somewhere to live, because since you threw me out I've been sleeping on my friend's sofa.'

'You need a husband to provide for you and the baby,' Vito said. 'And I am offering far more than just that.'

'We're not living in the dark ages!' Lily gasped. His expression was forbidding, but she ploughed on regardless. 'What are you offering that's so great? Money? Of course it would be great to have a rich husband—but, if I can't have a husband who truly loves and wants his child and me, then I'd rather be on my own.'

'Is that really true?' Vito asked. 'Bringing up an illegitimate child on your own isn't easy.'

'I never said it was.' Lily knew only too well how tough her mother had found it. It had been very hard on her too, living with someone prone to depression and panic, someone who had been only truly happy when she'd lost herself in an art project.

'Think about your child,' Vito pressed. 'How can you consider denying him or her the possibility of growing up the Salvatore heir?'

'You're crazy.' Lily lifted her hand to touch her blonde hair in an exasperated gesture. 'First you accuse me of being unfaithful and deny that this is your baby—then you want to marry me and make the child your heir. What am I supposed to think? It just doesn't seem real.'

She looked up into his blue eyes, and suddenly the way he was looking at her sent a prickle of sensual awareness skittering across her skin. It was as if they were back in the elevator again, trapped in a tiny space that was buzzing with the supercharged electricity that was flowing between them.

'*This* is real.'

He stepped forward, covering the space that separated them in two strides. He still wasn't even touching her—but she knew exactly what he was talking about.

Sexual attraction. A wave of heat was swelling through her body, setting all her nerve endings on fire. Deep down she wanted him to touch her again, wanted to feel his hands moving all over her.

'Maybe it's real,' Lily said, horrified by how husky her voice suddenly sounded as his gaze swept suggestively over her body. 'But it's just hormones—it doesn't mean anything.'

'Your virginity meant something to me,' Vito grated. His eyes looked impossibly dark, and a muscle started pulsing on his jawline. 'Until I found out it was meaningless to you—how quick you were to give your body to someone else.'

Suddenly an expression that was almost savage ripped across his features and he seized her, bringing his mouth down forcefully on hers.

Lily's heart lurched and she reeled in shock as he kissed her, but he had her firmly in his powerful grip. He had never been rough with her before, but her body was responding immediately, hot desire for him building inside her.

Despite the feeble protests her mind was trying to exert, the tension in her muscles yielded until she was pliant in his arms. He pulled her tight against him, so that she could feel the wonderfully familiar heat of his body burning through her linen suit.

Her lips softened and opened beneath his, allowing his tongue to sweep inside.

Oh! How she had missed him—how she had longed to be close to him again. It wasn't just the physical intimacy that she craved, although she was kissing him back with a fervency that was making her head spin. She'd missed the amazing relationship that she'd thought they had together. She'd missed him so badly.

His hands were holding her head now, tilting it backwards as he plundered her mouth in a kiss that delved into the very depths of her spiralling desire for him. He had released his grip on her body, but she continued to press herself against him, revelling in the pure masculine power she could feel radiating from his hard form.

Her arms snaked around his back, slipping inside his jacket. Then, almost of their own volition, her hands started to tug at his shirt. She longed to feel his skin under her fingertips, feel his muscles flex and ripple under her palms.

Suddenly she realised what she was doing.

'Stop!' With a monumental effort of will, she broke away from his kiss and forced herself to take a step back from him. 'This isn't what I want,' she gasped, walking shakily across to the huge plate-glass window that overlooked the City of London.

'What do you want?' he asked abruptly.

'I want things back the way they were.' She was suddenly too emotional to guard what she was saying.

'Then you should have thought twice before cheating on me,' Vito grated.

'I never cheated on you!' Lily cried. 'But it doesn't make any difference now.'

'Of course it does—it changed everything!' Vito said.

'But our relationship… Nothing was how it seemed anyway.' She felt tears prick her eyes revealingly, and she looked down so that he wouldn't see. 'You weren't the man I thought you were, or you would never have believed lies about me. You would never have accused me so horribly of something I didn't do.'

She turned away and stared out of the window, but instead she saw her reflection staring back—wide eyed and lost, wearing a crumpled linen suit. Her hair was escaping in wild curls from the tightly pulled-back style she'd tried to impose on it that morning, when she hadn't had time to do it properly—but there was nothing she could do to fix that now. She smoothed her hands automatically over her creased jacket, then took a deep, steadying breath before turning back to face him.

'I'm leaving now.' She was proud at how level her voice sounded, despite the turmoil she was feeling inside.

'No. You're not leaving.' Vito's voice was cold as stone. 'You haven't thought this through yet.'

'There's nothing to think about,' Lily said. 'You've made it very clear what your opinion of me is. Why would I marry you?'

'For your child's sake,' he said. 'Do you want your child to grow up illegitimate? Without a father?' He walked forward and put his hands on her upper arms, holding her in place to emphasise the importance of his words. 'Do you want your baby to be somebody's *dirty little secret*?'

Lily stood stock-still and stared up at Vito. A horrible feeling of nausea was rising up through her, and his hands felt like cold inhuman restraints.

'Why would you say such a horrible thing?' Her voice trembled with emotion as she spoke. Vito's words were too close to the bone. Too close to her own insecurities about her childhood.

'Because *you* know what that would be like for your child,' he said. 'All your life, you've known what it's like to be Reggie Morton's dirty little secret.'

She stared at Vito in horror.

For a moment she forgot to breathe. Her heart forgot to beat.

Then all at once she had to escape—get out of there as fast as she could. She whirled away from Vito automatically, her hands flying up in alarm as she swayed against the window.

Her mind was spinning as her gaze plummeted dizzyingly down into the street far below. They were so high up that nothing looked real—tiny stick-figures, toy cars and model trees were hazy images that were almost out of sight. It was like she was in some kind of awful nightmare.

Then suddenly her vision blurred and she felt herself start to fall into blackness.

'Lily!'

Vito's voice cut through the haze, dragging her back to the harsh reality of her situation. Hands like steel gripped her arms to prevent her from falling, then virtually lifted her away to the huge leather chair by the desk.

'Lily.' Vito dropped down onto one knee in front of her. For a moment she almost made the mistake of thinking he was concerned about her—then as her eyes came into focus she saw that his expression was just as cold as before. He had simply adopted the best position to get a good look at her. And probably to make sure she was looking at him, paying proper attention to what he had to say.

'You're extremely pale,' he said. 'Have you eaten today?'

'Of course I'm pale.' Lily spoke through gritted teeth. Her stomach was churning horribly, and she really thought there was a danger that she might be sick. 'I've had a lot of nasty shocks this morning.'

'Have you eaten?' he insisted. 'What would make you feel better?'

'Getting away from you.' She stood up so quickly that Vito rocked back on his heels, but the rapid movement was a mistake. A wave of nausea rolled through her again, and she clung to the desk for support, feeling her head start to spin.

'Sit down,' Vito barked. 'I'm not letting you leave so that you can faint in the street—if you even get that far.'

One hand was on her shoulder, pressing her back into the chair, and the other snatched up the phone on his desk. Lily only half listened as he reeled off a list of instructions—but she understood that he was ordering food and drink.

She closed her eyes, breathing deeply. As much as she thought she hated Vito right then, she couldn't bear to disgrace herself by being sick in front of him. She already felt vulnerable enough, and that would just be the final humiliation on what was already turning out to be the worst day of her life so far.

Only a few minutes seemed to pass before she heard the elevator doors open, followed by Vito's quiet footfall on the thick grey carpet as he returned across the room. She opened her eyes to see him setting a tray down on the desk.

'Drink this,' he instructed, holding out a large glass of iced water.

She took the water silently, unable to speak for a moment, as the memory of him preparing iced water for her on her last day in Venice flashed through her mind. He might not be the tender, concerned lover she had believed him to be—but he still knew what she liked.

In fact, apparently he knew more about her than she had realised, as she thought about the heartless way he had thrown her troubled childhood in her face.

'You snooped into my background.' She looked at him accusingly, expecting to see at least a hint of embarrassment pass across his shuttered features. But there was nothing. He appeared as unmoved as ever.

'Of course I did. You were living with me—a thorough background-check was mandatory.' His voice was matter-of-fact. 'You had potential access to all kinds of sensitive material.'

Lily looked at him in disgust. It would never have occurred to her to pry into his life like that. She knew he'd been married before; that was common knowledge. But she'd never poked around, trying to discover why his marriage had ended.

'Perhaps I should have run a background-check on you.' Lily took a sip of icy-cold water. It was making her stomach feel a little better—but the rest of her was still a mess of unpleasant emotions. 'I might have found out in time what kind of man I was getting involved with.'

She pushed a coil of blonde hair out of her eyes and looked away from him distractedly. She couldn't believe how things were turning out, and her mind was a horrible whirl of conflicting thoughts.

She should never have come to L&G Enterprises that morning. She'd known Vito held controlling shares in the company. But he also had many other business interests in London. She'd thought, if he was even in the city, what were the chances that he'd be right there in the building? That he'd walk into her presentation?

Maybe a tiny part of her deep down inside had longed to see him again, despite the unforgivable way he had treated her, but she could never have guessed that things would end up like this. That Vito, the man she'd once foolishly believed she was falling in love with, would rub her nose in the humiliating misery of her childhood. And then propose to her.

'Being someone's dirty little secret is not a pleasant position to be in.' Vito's voice was cold and unfeeling as he broke the silence. 'Don't make your child suffer the same fate. You don't need to make the same choices as your mother.'

'You're the one making it dirty!' Lily responded hotly, her gaze flashing back to his impossibly inexpressive face. 'And leave my mother out of it—she's happy living in the countryside, working with the hospice patients.'

'But you're not happy,' Vito said blandly. 'And your childhood was far from happy.'

'You don't know anything about my childhood,' Lily threw back at him.

'I know that your father refused to acknowledge you,' he said. 'That he paid your mother off to keep her quiet. That you've never met him or your two half-sisters, and that it seems unlikely that you ever will. Unless you're prepared to let your mother lose her home and income, just to satisfy your curiosity about the man who didn't want you.'

'Why would I want to meet my father?' Lily responded automatically, despite the way she was reeling under the onslaught of Vito's words. 'He's nothing to me.'

'You mean *you're* nothing to *him*.'

Vito turned away to select a Danish pastry from the tray on his desk. Lily gripped her glass of iced water dangerously tightly and stared at him angrily.

'You are utterly vile,' she said, looking at the plate in his hand, because suddenly she couldn't bring herself to meet his gaze.

How could he eat at a time like this? Did dishing out heartless comments over something so important to her really mean so little to him that he thought he'd combine it with a light snack?

She'd spent a lifetime trying not to think about the way her father had discarded her. And she didn't want to think about it now. She could have searched for him, tried to make him acknowledge her. But she'd always known no good would have come of that. And, in any case, she would never, ever have done anything to cause her mother distress.

'Here, eat this.' Vito removed the glass of water from

her grip and handed her the pastry on a highly glazed black plate. So it hadn't been for him after all.

'I'm not hungry,' Lily said mutinously, trying to pass the plate back.

'Nevertheless, you must eat,' Vito said. 'You'll feel better if you boost your blood-sugar level. You really are exceptionally pale, even for you.'

'Even for me?' Lily snapped. 'Don't act like you know me. You may know my secret—a way you can coerce me into doing what you want. But that's not really knowing someone.'

'It's not coercion,' Vito said. 'I'm merely helping you to recognise the full implications of trying to go it alone with an illegitimate child. In fact, it's more of a reminder, really—after all, you know from first-hand experience what it can be like.'

'It wasn't as bad as you're making it sound,' Lily protested. But in her heart she knew it had been pretty tough—constantly dealing with her mother's depression and her own sense of abandonment and disappointment. She hated the thought of her baby growing up without a father, feeling unwanted and worthless.

'Don't you want to protect your child?' Vito asked. 'Marry me, and he or she will be free of the misery that blighted your childhood.'

'My childhood wasn't miserable,' Lily insisted. She could hear the doubt in her own voice, but suddenly it felt disloyal to her mum even to let herself think it.

'As my heir, your baby will have every opportunity,' Vito continued. 'And you won't experience the difficulties that your mother faced on her own.'

'I don't know,' Lily said. Vito's proposal was totally unexpected and overwhelming. She didn't know what to think any more. 'I don't know what to say.'

Two months ago she would have been unimaginably happy to have Vito propose to her. Now things were different. It was clear he didn't love her. He didn't even trust her. But he was offering her a chance for her child—and wasn't that the most important thing to consider now?

How could she deny her child the life Vito could give it?

'You do know what to say,' Vito said. 'You must agree to marry me. And, in the circumstances, we must arrange the wedding for as soon as possible. We'll fly back to Venice this afternoon.'

He looked at her, sitting so stiffly on the high-backed leather chair, and he thought that she had been right when she'd said he didn't know her. He didn't. The sweet, innocent girl he'd thought she was would never have taken a lover and then tried to pass off another man's child as his.

She didn't even look the same as the eager yet tentative lover he had shared his home with for nearly half a year. Her defensive body-language was completely new to him, and the amount of weight she'd lost made her appear all bony angles beneath her ill-fitting linen suit.

The dark smudges of exhaustion beneath her hazel eyes emphasised their size, making them look extremely large in her painfully thin face. And she was wearing her hair in a strange style that all through their five months together he had never before seen.

But, even though her appearance had changed, the powerful attraction he felt for her had not diminished one jot.

It was the same as the first time he'd laid eyes on her; she'd been standing up in front of another group of executives in another of his companies, pitching an earlier version of the computer software she'd been selling today. He'd walked into that meeting too—with no thought in his head other than the fact that he *must* find out who she was.

It had suddenly been imperative that he invited her to dinner, got to know her…took her to bed.

And the urgent desire that had stormed his body back then was still surging through his veins like molten lava.

He wanted to haul her to her feet and kiss her until the rigid tension in her body melted away. He knew it would—he'd felt the way she'd responded to him earlier. Despite her protests he knew she still wanted him as much as he wanted her.

He wanted to run his hands all over her body, until she was soft and pliant against him. He wanted to release the clip at the nape of her neck and let her hair fly out in crazy curls. It had been only at the end of their most passionate love-making sessions that he'd seen her hair in its natural, untamed state. She'd always spent ages straightening it and smoothing it down into sleek, sophisticated styles. He liked it when it was wild. It made him think of rampant sex.

'Even if I agree, I can't be ready to travel this after noon.' Lily's voice startled him out of his thoughts. 'There are things I must do, people I have to tell.'

'Of course you can be ready. Leave all the technical details to me. Once we arrive in Venice, you may call anyone you need, to inform them of your change of address.'

Vito suppressed a grim smile of satisfaction at her imminent agreement. He hadn't allowed himself to consider the possibility that she might refuse his offer of marriage.

The fact that she had been unfaithful to him, and

subsequently denied it, had proved him very wrong in his original assessment of her personality. However, he did know what her childhood had been like. And he was confident that his frank reminders of how their uncertain situation had impacted on Lily and her mother would be enough to bring her round to accepting his proposal.

He knew he'd hurt her feelings when he'd thrown her out, but he was sure her maternal instinct to protect her child's future would win out in the end.

'No, I need to—' Lily began.

'Presumably the equipment you brought with you for your presentation belongs to the company you were working for.' Vito picked up the phone to make a call. 'I'll have it returned by courier.'

He had her in his grasp. All that was left to do was to make the arrangements as quickly as possible. Then he would tell his grandfather the news the old man had been hoping to hear for years: the Salvatore family name was to continue.

His grandfather would end his days happy, believing there was a new Salvatore heir. Then afterwards, when Lily was no longer of any use to him, Vito would exact revenge on her by ridding himself of her. And the baby.

A swift divorce, and his life would soon be back to normal. Lily, and the proof of her infidelity, would no longer have any part of it.

'But I can't just disappear off to Italy,' Lily said. 'People will worry about me.'

'A short announcement that we are reunited and about to be married should deal with that,' Vito replied.

'They'll never believe it,' Lily said, wondering how her independent friend, Anna, would react to her decision to marry Vito purely to ensure security and stability for her child. How would she explain that she couldn't bear the thought of her baby enduring a childhood as tough as hers? 'Everyone knows how badly you treated me—they won't be fooled by any story I tell them.'

Or at least Anna wouldn't, she thought. Somehow she'd never really got round to telling her mother any details about how she came to be back in London.

'No.' The word cut through the air like steel. 'No one must ever know this is anything other than a normal marriage.'

'But…' Lily faltered as he took her hands and pulled her abruptly to her feet. She was standing directly in front of him, and she could feel the intensity radiating off him. Her heart jolted nervously in her chest. He was utterly serious.

'*No one* will ever know.' Vito's voice throbbed and his eyes blazed. 'You will make them all believe that it is a normal marriage, that the child you are carrying is mine. If you fail to do this, I will cast you and the baby out.'

Lily stared at him numbly.

She just couldn't let her baby go through what she had experienced growing up. Vito's words 'dirty little secret' rang in her mind. He had been agonisingly accurate in his assessment of what her childhood had been like.

Living with a mother who was depressed and frequently plagued by worries and self-doubts had been tough. Having very little money, no father figure at home, and, on top of everything else, dealing with spiteful taunts from other children had been a constant grind.

But realising that her own father didn't want to meet her—probably wished she'd never even been born—had quite simply been heartbreaking. She couldn't let her child grow up never knowing its father—and she knew for sure that this baby was Vito's.

She had to agree. For the sake of her unborn baby she had to agree to marry Vito.

CHAPTER FOUR

LILY placed the large vase of blue cornflowers on the table. She put her handwritten note to Anna beside them and stood back, biting her lip in consternation.

She didn't want to disappear out of her friend's life as abruptly as she'd arrived, but she had a plane to catch, and couldn't be there to explain in person. Besides, she had a terrible fear that if she talked to her friend face to face she would almost certainly break down and tell her everything. The future of her unborn baby depended on her playing out the charade that Vito was demanding. She couldn't allow herself to fall at the first hurdle.

The cornflowers were gorgeous, and she knew they were Anna's favourites. She'd spotted them outside a florist on the way back to the flat, and decided at once that she must buy a huge bunch for her friend.

Vito's driver had tried to pay for them, but Lily was having none of that. From her time in Venice she was used to his assistants popping up beside her, cash or credit card in hand. But these flowers were a gift for a dear friend, a friend who'd been there for her in a time of trouble. She wasn't going to let it be sullied by allowing Vito to pay for it. She might have agreed to marry him, but she wasn't letting him buy her off.

Lily looked round the flat that had been her home for six weeks. It wasn't really home, but she'd been so grateful for Anna's comforting presence. There would be no one to comfort her in Venice.

It hadn't taken her long to pack—she'd been travelling light since leaving Venice. She turned away and started carrying her bags down to the waiting limousine. The driver hurried to help her, and in hardly any time her belongings were stowed in the boot.

She stood on the pavement, staring at the keys in her hand, suddenly reluctant to go despite the fact that she must.

'Would you like me to take them?' the driver politely enquired. 'Is there a trusted neighbour I can leave them with? Or should I drop them through the letter box?'

Lily blinked and stared at him for a moment. All of Vito's staff were honest and ready to help with anything. But this was a task she had to do herself.

'No, thank you.' Lily smiled at him as warmly as she could, but she knew it couldn't look very convincing. She was utterly exhausted and felt sick to her stomach. 'I'll just be a moment.'

She made her way wearily back up the two flights of stairs and let herself into the flat one last time. She placed the keys on the table next to her note and the vase of cornflowers, then walked back out and pulled the door shut behind her. She pushed it automatically, just to check the lock had caught, and suddenly she felt locked out of her own life. As her fingers fell from the unyielding door, she knew she was saying goodbye to her freedom.

A few hours later she was sitting next to Vito as their plane circled the city of Venice, coming in to land across the water at the edge of the lagoon. It looked so different from the city she had flown away from six weeks ago, the day after she'd told Vito she was pregnant. By morning most of the fog had lifted, allowing the airport to reopen, but the city had still looked eerily colourless, and the wide expanse of water had been a pale, metallic grey.

Now the sun was shining brightly, low in the western sky, and the water of the lagoon was a luxuriant blue, tinged with the gold of the approaching sunset. The island of Venice itself looked amazing from the air—like a perfect miniature replica dropped into the open space of the lagoon. Famous landmarks stood out with incredible clarity, and for a moment Lily almost felt like she'd never left. Except now everything was different.

'Do you feel well enough to walk down to the water?' She heard Vito speak beside her, and she turned to look at him in surprise. It really wasn't very far down to the pier where his personal boat would be waiting for them. They'd always made their way on foot in the past.

'I'd like to walk,' she replied. 'Thank you for asking.' She was still wearing the high-heeled shoes she'd worn for her presentation, and her feet were starting to ache, but after the flight she could definitely do with some fresh air.

It wasn't long before they were zipping across the water towards the city. Lily loved being out on the lagoon, and she'd always been entranced by the idea that she was travelling across the water to arrive at the city in the same way people had for more than a thousand years. Then, all too soon, they were winding their way through the maze of Venetian canals, approaching the water gate of Vito's gothic *palazzo*.

She couldn't help remembering the last time she'd disembarked there. That afternoon the fog had chilled her to the bone, and she'd been worried how Vito would react to her pregnancy. But despite everything she had been optimistic. She could never have predicted the harsh and unfathomable way he would react, initially throwing her out, and then persuading her to return with him to become his wife for reasons she still didn't fully understand.

She climbed out onto the marble steps soberly. Leaving this *palazzo* and her life with Vito had been devastating—but returning under such circumstances was equally hard.

'No doubt you'll want to rest this evening.' Vito guided Lily towards the stairs as several members of staff appeared to carry her belongings.

'I think that would be best,' Lily responded, suddenly feeling tears prick behind her eyes. Coming back to the place where she'd been so happy was affecting her more than she had expected.

Vito took her up to the grand bedroom she had previously shared with him, then left without saying a word.

For a moment she stood rooted to the spot, looking round at the room that was so familiar, yet seemed so strange. Then, taking a deep breath, she walked purposefully across to her luggage to find her wash-kit and nightclothes.

She was tired and emotional, but she wouldn't give in to it. She wouldn't let herself think about what she had got herself into. Vito had made her play his game, but she was going to remain strong and positive. She would not let him see any vulnerability.

She reached up and released her hair from the clip at the back of her head. It had been uncomfortable on the plane, but she'd been reluctant to let her hair down in front of Vito. She walked through to the *en suite* to take a quick shower and get ready for bed.

Although it was dark outside now, it wasn't really

very late. But pregnancy and the stresses of the day had made Lily so tired that she longed for sleep. She had no doubt that Vito would join her later, but with any luck she'd be sound asleep before he made an appearance.

Lily was alone in the bed when she awoke the following morning. She gazed up at the beautiful painted ceiling and the antique Murano glass chandelier, realising that she'd actually slept very well. And, more importantly, she felt better than she had for days. Maybe her morning sickness was finally starting to ease.

She sat up cautiously, noticing a glass of iced water had been placed on her bedside table. Beaded with condensation, the water looked enticingly cool, and next to it someone had left a plate of her favourite sweet rolls from a local bakery.

She smiled grimly. Eating before she showered and dressed would help to keep her stomach settled, but it bugged her that for some reason Vito was still demonstrating how well he thought he knew her, and how he understood her condition. She picked up the glass and took a refreshing sip, rebelliously thinking that perhaps she should inform him that her new preference was cold milk.

She'd just finished one of the rolls when the door opened and Vito walked in.

As usual he looked absolutely amazing, and was immaculately groomed, right down to his freshly buffed handmade leather shoes. He was wearing smart trousers and a black cashmere sweater that fitted him perfectly. Somehow the luxuriously soft layer of wool encasing his hard, muscled form emphasised his raw masculine power in a way that made her heart skip a beat.

Lily remembered what it felt like to be enfolded in

his arms and held against that sweater. She pushed the thought aside and lifted her eyes to his handsome face.

'Good, you're awake.' He stood at the foot of the bed, letting his eyes run over her in assessment. 'You look much better than yesterday.'

'It's not surprising.' She returned his gaze steadily, resisting the urge to fidget under his hard stare. She was glad that she was wearing her old, cosy nightshirt with long sleeves and a high neckline. Vito had always hated it. He'd preferred her in the filmy, revealing garments he had seemed to enjoy buying for her. 'Yesterday was just about the worst day of my life.'

'There's someone you need to meet this morning,' he said, ignoring her jibe. 'My grandfather has been ill. A visit from us will cheer him up.'

Lily looked at him in startled silence. She'd lived with Vito for five months, but he had never once taken her to visit his grandfather. She'd known that he lived very nearby, and that Vito called in to see him regularly. But she'd understood that, as his lover, it was not part of her role to meet his family.

'You intend to tell him, don't you?' She found her voice at last, the realisation that everything was so different making her feel really unsettled.

'Of course, he's my grandfather. I didn't bring you here to marry you in secret,' Vito replied. 'I thought I made myself very plain on that point.'

'You did,' Lily said. 'It's just that it was rather a sudden decision. I thought you might take time to reflect on it before things get too complicated to change.' She folded her arms across her chest, thinking that, once other people knew about their marriage, there would definitely be no going back.

'The decision has been made,' Vito said. 'All that

remains is to tell those who are important to us, and to start the ball rolling with the preparations for our wedding. As I said yesterday, it will be at the earliest opportunity.'

Lily looked away from him, knocked for six by the thought of actually telling people that she was getting married. Her note to Anna certainly hadn't gone into details like that. She knew her friend would have found such a sudden announcement bewildering, especially after the way Vito had callously thrown her out.

She didn't want Anna to worry about her, so she'd kept the message simple and upbeat—just saying she'd run into Vito, they'd patched things up between them, and she was returning to Venice with him.

If she was getting married she ought to tell her mother, but she honestly couldn't bear the thought of sharing her news with her mother, or anyone else she was close to. Although she knew she had to go through with it because it was the best thing for her child, she still had misgivings about the way Vito had treated her. About the way he was continuing to treat her.

How would she manage to keep up the pretence that it was a perfectly normal, happy marriage in front of people who knew her well and cared about her? She simply couldn't afford to reveal the truth behind the marriage. Vito had made it plain that they must maintain a normal happily-married front. Her child's future depended on it.

'We'll leave as soon as you're ready,' Vito said, walking to the door. 'My grandfather is at his best in the morning. He tends to sleep in the afternoon.'

Lily pushed back the covers, got out of bed and headed for the *en suite*. Half an hour later, she was sitting at the dressing table, adding the finishing touches to her make-up while she waited for Vito to return.

She was apprehensive about meeting his grandfather, and had tried to ease her nerves by taking extra care with her appearance. Her hair was freshly washed and straightened, so that it hung down in a sleek blonde curtain well past her shoulder blades. Her make-up was light and natural looking, but the judicious use of blusher had given her a bit of colour in her cheeks.

She had chosen to wear her ivory linen-suit again. It was a bit creased from travelling, but everything else was still packed haphazardly in her bags and was not likely to look any better. She looked in the mirror and decided that, although she might not look very glamorous, she was perfectly presentable.

The door opened and Vito came into the room.

'I'm ready to go,' she said, standing up quickly and reaching for her handbag.

Vito looked at her, picking up small details that were different from the day before. She didn't look so washed-out and, with her hair brushed down in that shimmering veil halfway down her back, she was starting to look more like the beautiful young woman he'd shared his life with over the winter. But she was still wearing the ill-fitting suit from the day before.

'I know this outfit isn't perfect,' Lily said, as if she'd read his mind. Or maybe, he thought, she'd simply read his expression. Although her shocking act of betrayal had made her a stranger to him, he mustn't forget that they'd lived together for five months. Undoubtedly she'd got to know him quite well in that time. 'But I don't have anything else suitable,' she added.

'A dress would be better.' Vito turned to open the huge fitted-wardrobe on her side of the room. 'Preferably something with a bit of colour—to brighten my grandfather's morning.'

'But…' Lily stared into the wardrobe in obvious surprise. 'All my clothes.'

'You didn't take them with you.'

Vito selected a soft peach-coloured silk dress he had bought for her in Milan. Lily was always drawn towards natural, pale colours—her favourites were cream and ivory—and, despite the fact he knew they suited her, he'd always had the urge to liven up her choices. 'I had to assume none of the items I bought for you were to your taste after all,' he added.

'I didn't pay for any of them,' Lily said. 'They were all so expensive—I didn't think they were mine to take.'

'Of course they were.' Vito suddenly felt annoyed. He'd enjoyed buying things for her, and when he'd seen she'd left them behind it had been a brutal reminder of how she'd duped him—like a spiteful smack on the cheek, on top of her shameless infidelity. 'What did you think *I* was going to do with them?'

'I don't know,' Lily said, smoothing her hand over her hair in a gesture that revealed how unsettled she felt. 'Maybe sell them. Or give them away. I never expected to find them still in the wardrobe.'

Vito turned and looked at her, deliberately keeping his expression bland as he laid the peach dress out on the bed. He wouldn't let himself think too closely about why he'd never got rid of all the things she'd left in his room.

Over the years he had invited very few women to share his home. And, once he had decided it was over, it was over—completely. For the most part they had taken everything with them, especially anything of value, like designer clothes and jewellery. Then any remaining items had been disposed of quickly, eradicating any evidence that anyone had ever been in his home.

But when his housekeeper had enquired about Lily's

belongings, he had barked at her to leave them. After that the poor woman hadn't mentioned them again— and had left them well alone. Out of sight in wardrobes and cupboards. But not entirely out of mind.

'You left the clothes and the jewellery,' he said. 'But you were quick enough to take every last piece of the lingerie I bought for you.'

'The clothes, the jewellery—they cost so much,' Lily said. A pretty flush had risen to her heart-shaped face, making the blood flow faster around Vito's body.

'The lingerie was expensive too.' He took a step closer to her, getting a kick of satisfaction as she refused to back away, even though he had clearly invaded her personal space. 'You knew that.'

'What would you want with my lingerie?' A spark in her hazel eyes and a defiant lift to her chin challenged him. 'Even you wouldn't sell second-hand underclothes.'

'I didn't want to sell them,' Vito said, deliberately letting his voice drop to a seductive purr. 'I wanted them for myself. You were gone, the nights were long…'

Lily gasped, suddenly speechless as she stared at his handsome face. 'Don't be so…so…'

'Don't looked shocked. It's a natural desire. You know how good we were together…*physically*,' Vito said. 'There's nothing wrong with wanting something to remember you by.'

'Stop it,' Lily said, hearing an edge of panic in her tone. But Vito's voice was rumbling through her, making her remember what it had been like to make love with him.

'I wanted to hold the flimsy little things in my hand as I thought about the good times we'd spent together,' he drawled, with blatant come-to-bed eyes locked onto hers from under sultry, half-closed lids. 'I longed to smooth the silky fabric against my skin—thinking about the feel of your skin against mine.'

'Stop it.' Lily's cheeks were starting to burn. 'You could have gone out and bought some more lingerie if you were so desperate.'

'It wouldn't have been the same,' Vito replied, with a meaningful smile on his full, sensual lips. 'It was knowing that the silk had been next to your body, pressing close to your most intimate places…'

Lily bit her lip, trying to think of a suitably cutting remark to put a stop to this line of discussion. She wasn't used to Vito talking like this, but although it was unsettling there was also something strangely exciting about it.

A wave of warmth was washing through her body, putting her senses onto full alert in a way that hadn't happened since she'd left Venice, until yesterday in Vito's empty penthouse.

'Are you wearing something I bought you now?' Vito's eyes were running over her, as if with his X-ray vision he could see through her linen suit to discover what underwear she had chosen. 'Or have you discarded it all—along with the sanctity of our relationship?'

'It's none of your business what I'm wearing under my suit,' Lily said, appalled by how her breath was catching in her throat.

'It used to be my business.' Vito dropped to his knees beside her and placed his large, warm hands on her hips. He tugged her gently towards him so that his cheek was resting on her stomach. 'You used to like me to come home from work, take you in my arms and hold you close. You loved it when I ran my hands up your legs, slipped them under your skirt, and traced my fingers over the silk and lace that covered the most sensitive part of your body.'

'That's over now.' Lily struggled to keep her voice level as Vito's words set off an alarming chain-reaction of sensation through her. It was true that she had loved the touch of his hands on her body, had revelled in the way that he made her feel. 'That was before you treated me so horribly.'

'Yes,' Vito said, letting his hands start to slide slowly down over her hips and thighs. 'That time is over. But now we are starting a different stage in our relationship. We are soon to be man and wife.'

Lily stood absolutely still, acutely aware of the movement of his hands. The familiarity of his touch was triggering a mass of conflicting feelings in her. Her body knew him, knew what exquisite pleasure he could give her.

But her heart felt betrayed. How could she be responding to him after he had treated her so unforgivably?

'It won't be the same,' she said, thinking how special it had been to make love to him when she'd believed he cared about her. She'd always thought it was more than just sex.

'It will be better.' Suddenly his fingers were unzipping her skirt. 'It will be the cement that holds our marriage together. Neither of us wants this marriage to fail—there is too much at stake.'

Lily's heart skipped a beat as her skirt slipped to the floor. Part of her wanted to flee to the *en suite* and cover up with a warm, fluffy robe. But most of her was shamelessly enjoying the feel of Vito's eyes as he ran his gaze over the French lace-knickers she was wearing.

'Are you wearing the matching bra?' He stood up and started unbuttoning the front of her jacket.

It was almost impossible for Lily to stand still. Liquid desire was running through her veins, making her feel more alive than she could remember. It was as if she had merely been existing, waiting to be back in Vito's arms.

Since he had stormed back into her life, demanding that she marry him, she'd known that this moment was inevitable. He was a red-blooded male, with a powerful libido. Celibacy was not in his nature. If this marriage was to succeed, then sex would play an important part.

But his hands were moving so slowly. It was taking him too long to remove her clothes. She yearned to feel his hands on her body, to feel his naked skin next to hers. She ached for him to make love to her, because that was surely what was to follow. And then she could let herself pretend that things were back to normal—that he had never thrown her out, and the last six weeks had never happened.

At last her jacket fell away to reveal a plain stretch-lace camisole. He took hold of the hem and pulled it over her head. Then he stepped back and let his gaze slide all over her.

Lily stood in her lacy bra and French knickers, still wearing her hold-up stockings and high-heeled shoes. Hot anticipation pooled deep inside her. Her breasts felt heavy, and her nipples were diamond-hard points straining against the flimsy covering of lace.

He'd hardly touched her, yet a sensual tingle moved through her body, settling in her most intimate place, making her need for him almost unbearable. She could feel her exposed skin flushing, betraying her sexual readiness to him.

His blue eyes grew darker as he looked at her, and she knew exactly how the sight of her was affecting him. She could hear the change in his breathing, recognise the expression on his face that meant he wanted to make love to her. But he made no move towards her.

Suddenly a shuttered look descended over his features and he turned to pick up the peach dress from the bed.

'You've lost weight,' he said. 'But this style should be forgiving.'

'Forgiving?'

His choice of word was like a slap in the face.

At that exact moment she knew he would never forgive her for what he *thought* she'd done. It made no difference that he was mistaken, that there was no possible proof of her sin against him—her denial would continue to fall on deaf ears.

'You are the one that needs forgiveness, for the awful way you treated me. For the way you're still treating me!' She snatched her clothes up off the floor and held them protectively across her body.

He had never truly planned to make love to her. His intention that morning had only ever been to humiliate her.

But she'd spoken her mind before she thought about the consequences, and as Vito turned back towards her his fury was almost palpable.

'Don't pursue this.' His words were forced out through gritted teeth, and she could see the monumental effort he was exerting to control his rage. 'You won't win. You *can't* win. It would be better for everyone if you don't keep reminding me of your betrayal—of the fact that you are carrying another man's child inside you.'

'But—'

Vito didn't need to speak again to quell Lily's retort. As his gaze met hers, the tortured look in his eyes cut through her pain, and in a sudden instant of clarity she realised how he was being torn apart by his belief that she had cheated on him.

But it wasn't her fault that he thought she'd been unfaithful. Was it madness to stay with someone who thought her capable of such a thing? But she'd made her decision—she had to marry him to make a future for her unborn child.

Later, for her own sake, she was going to have to try to discover why he believed what he did. But for now she had to let it rest. From the anger and tension radiating from every ounce of his powerful body, she could tell that now was not the time to keep pushing him. There was no chance of having a reasoned conversation with him while he was so tightly wound and his anger so raw.

'Put this on,' Vito said, holding out the dress to her.

She slipped it over her head silently, gathered her long hair to one side, and turned to present him with the zip. She straightened her shoulders consciously, determined to show him that her will was as strong as his. She wouldn't fight with him now—but neither would she let herself be quashed by the brute strength of his personality.

He pulled the zip up slowly, not touching her at all. She exhaled quietly, careful not to let him know that she'd been holding her breath in case his fingers brushed against her sensitive spine. Then she turned to look at her reflection in the mirror.

She hardly recognised the girl who gazed back at her. The girl who'd worn that dress and lived in this bedroom—*that* girl—belonged to another time. A happier time.

If she was going to survive this marriage, she was going to have to assert herself. Show Vito that, despite his threats and undeniable position of strength, he couldn't walk all over her.

'That will do very well,' Vito said, his patronising tone setting Lily's nerves on edge. He passed her bag to her and headed towards the door. 'We must set off to my grandfather's.'

'Wait a minute.' Lily gripped her suede bag tightly and dug in her heels.

'What is it?' Vito turned back impatiently.

'That sweater,' she said, tossing her bag onto the bed and walking briskly towards him. 'It's not right. You can't wear a depressing black sweater if you're serious about cheering your grandfather up.'

'He won't be looking at *me*...' Vito's words petered out as she gripped the soft cashmere in her hands and started peeling it off his body.

'You must have something lighter and fresher. Maybe your pale-blue sweater?' It was an effort to keep her voice steady, but she was proud of how matter-of-fact she managed to sound. Especially when she discovered he wasn't wearing anything under the sweater, and an intoxicating waft of his pure, masculine aroma filled her senses, making her legs feel weak all over again.

She took a step back, and for a second let her eyes run over his magnificent form. A shiver of sensual appreciation ran through her, and she realised her ploy to regain some control was in serious danger of backfiring on her.

Vito turned and stepped towards his wardrobe. Try as she might, she simply couldn't tear her gaze away. She'd always loved to watch him without his shirt on— never failing to be fascinated, and frankly turned on, by the irresistible play of his well-defined muscles beneath his golden-brown skin.

'It's your choice.' He indicated the neatly folded piles of sweaters in his wardrobe—but for a moment Lily got the impression he wasn't simply talking about clothing. He'd seen the way she was looking at him. He knew how she was reacting.

Was he letting her know that, if she was prepared to

make the first move, he wanted to make love to her after all?

With an effort of will, she pushed the thought aside. He was probably playing with her again, and she certainly didn't intend to cause herself any more humiliation.

'This is a cheerful colour,' she said, tossing a blue sweater at him. 'That will brighten your grandfather's day.'

Vito pulled it on silently. Then, without even bothering to check his appearance in the mirror, took her hand and pulled her towards the door.

CHAPTER FIVE

CA' SALVATORE, the beautiful *palazzo* that had been the home of Giovanni Salvatore for more than seventy-five years, stood in the very heart of the city on a magnificent stretch of the Grand Canal.

It was possible to make the journey from Vito's home by water, using the impressive canal entrances of both *palazzi*, but Lily was pleased when he decided they should walk. She had missed strolling through the maze of narrow streets, along canals and over bridges. Although she had lived in Venice for quite a while, she'd discovered something new almost every outing, and had always taken pleasure from investigating unfamiliar areas.

Now she walked apprehensively beside Vito. He'd told her that his grandfather was old and frail, but she knew that for most of his life Giovanni had been a formidable Venetian businessman. Vito had often spoken of him with a great deal of respect, but also great love.

She knew that when Vito was a child he'd come to live with his grandfather at *Ca' Salvatore* after his parents had died in an accident. It was clear that Giovanni was still hugely important to him—as was this visit. For everyone's sake, she hoped things would go smoothly.

It didn't take long to reach the baroque *palazzo*, and for a moment Lily gazed in awe at the building's amazing façade, complete with marble pillars and statues.

'And this is just the back entrance.' Vito paused beside her to look up at the bold ornamentation. 'The side facing the canal is really something to behold.'

Lily smiled in surprise at his tone. He'd grown up in this grand historic palace, but he didn't take it for granted, and was obviously very proud of his family's heritage. She glanced sideways at him, and for a moment he looked like the Vito she used to know. He appeared relaxed and almost happy—as if coming to *Ca' Salvatore* was like coming home for him. Suddenly she had the feeling that he was genuinely looking forward to seeing his grandfather and telling him their news.

He took her hand in his. It was a gesture that could be taken equally as a sign of possession or affection, and once more she was reminded how important it was that she played her part well. He led her into the building and up to the second-floor room where the housekeeper had told them Giovanni was resting in bed.

The moment they entered the old man's bedchamber, Lily got a sense that something wasn't right. Vito stiffened beside her the instant he laid eyes on his grandfather, then he dropped her hand and crossed to the bed in two long strides.

'*Nonno?*' Vito bent down to speak close to his grandfather's ear. 'Are you feeling all right?'

Lily stood beside the door, not sure what to do. The housekeeper had said Giovanni was resting, but she hadn't implied that anything was wrong. And, from Lily's perspective, she couldn't identify what had made Vito react so strongly. Giovanni looked old and tired, but maybe Vito had spotted something more worrying in his appearance because he knew him so well.

'Vito?' The old man's voice was weak, but he was looking at his grandson's face with recognition. 'I'm tired, that's all.'

'I'm calling the doctor,' Vito said. 'I don't like the way you look.'

'Hmph!' Giovanni snorted. 'You don't have to like the way I look—I'm not one of your women.'

Lily smiled at the old man's quick humour. His comment on Vito's women was unsettling—but he clearly had his wits about him. And it was obvious that, even though he appeared to be bed-bound, he was still a man to be reckoned with.

Vito was leaning close, talking to his grandfather in a firm but kind voice. It was plain from his body language and tone of voice that the old man meant the world to him.

Suddenly Lily's throat felt tight, and a foolish tear sprang to her eye as she remembered Vito talking to her in a gentle and caring way. But he wasn't like that with her any more. She blinked and turned away, trying not to think about just how different things were between them now.

She looked around the chamber to distract herself, running her gaze over the impressively frescoed walls with admiration. The ornate decoration in the chamber was truly splendid—fitting for the main bedchamber of an important *palazzo* on the Grand Canal.

It was incredible to think that this was Giovanni's bedroom. The chamber wouldn't have looked out of place in one of the many magnificent Venetian palaces open to the public. And the fact that she could see no evidence of modern technological living made it even more like stepping back in time to a more elegant age.

A movement caught her eye, and she turned to see Vito striding towards her. Before she knew what he was doing, he took her arm and hustled her out into the hallway.

'Now is not a good time for you to meet my grand-father,' he said, guiding her towards the grand staircase.

'Is there anything I can do to help?' Lily said automatically, although she knew Vito well enough to know he'd already have everything covered.

'No,' he said shortly. 'Go home now. I'll see you later.'

With that he turned on his heel and went back into Giovanni's room, closing the door in her face.

Lily stared after him in consternation. She understood Vito was concerned about his grandfather, but she didn't like the feeling of being so peremptorily dismissed.

She walked slowly down the stairs, thinking again how much things had changed. The old Vito would never have sent her off to find her own way home without an escort. In fact, when she'd first lived with him, it had taken her a long time to persuade him that no harm would come to her if she strolled around the city on her own. No one else had ever showed so much concern for her welfare, and at the time she'd been deeply touched by it.

She headed back to Vito's *palazzo*, strangely surprised by how familiar everything still felt despite the time she'd spent in London. She was almost on auto-pilot, weaving her way through the maze of narrow lanes without even thinking about her route.

Suddenly she stopped in her tracks right outside a busy *gelateria*. There was no need to go straight back just because Vito had told her to. She should take some time just for herself and try to clear her head.

She joined the queue to buy an ice cream, and a few minutes later she was sitting beside a canal in the late morning sunshine, pleased that her appetite had returned so she could truly enjoy one of her favourite treats.

The steps leading down to the canal were a good place to sit, out of the main flow of pedestrians, and it was restful watching the water lapping against the buildings that edged the other side of the canal.

She ate her ice cream slowly, determined to relish every drop. Then, once she had finished, she let her thoughts return to the predicament she had got herself into with Vito.

Everything had happened so fast since he'd walked in on her presentation yesterday. His proposal had taken her completely by surprise, but in the end she had agreed to marry him for her baby's sake. She'd truly thought it would be best for her child to grow up part of a proper family, with two parents.

Also, deep down inside, she couldn't forget how wonderful things had been between them before he'd thrown her out. Maybe, once they were living together again, things would return to the way they had once been.

But there was a massive problem. For some reason Vito believed she had cheated on him, and that the child she was carrying was not his. That was why he was so angry with her and why he was treating her so harshly.

Lily had no idea what had made him believe this. No matter how hard she thought about it, she couldn't think of anything she had ever said or done that might have led him to that conclusion. There had been nights when they'd been apart, but that had always been because of his business travel. She had never spent a night away from the *palazzo* without Vito.

Suddenly she knew what to do. If she could prove to Vito that she'd never been unfaithful, maybe he would trust her again. Although he'd hurt her feelings with his lack of faith in her, presumably he did have a reason. It would have been better if he'd had the courtesy to tell her, but obviously he was upset by it.

She'd ask him for a paternity test. Then, once he was convinced of the truth, perhaps things could get back to normal between then. That would be best for everyone—for Lily and Vito. And, most importantly, for the baby.

Lily stood up with a burst of energy. She'd found the solution to the problem—soon everything would be all right.

Vito returned to the *palazzo* in the early afternoon. Lily was waiting for him in the bedroom, knowing the conversation she planned to have with him would be best in private. He'd been so concerned that no one should know there was anything untoward about their marriage plans that she thought he wouldn't appreciate her talking to him about paternity tests in a room where a member of staff might overhear.

'How is your grandfather?' she asked, standing up as he walked into the room.

'The doctor thinks he's fine. Well, as fine as he ever is.' From the look on his face it was clear that Vito did not agree. 'I'm not so sure. He doesn't seem right to me,' he said. 'Maybe he's coming down with something.'

'He's lucky to have you nearby,' Lily said. 'I know you'll make sure he receives the best possible care.'

Vito didn't respond. He appeared to be deep in thought as he opened his wardrobe and took out one of his many hand-tailored suits. He must be going straight to the office, Lily thought, realising she'd have to speak fast if she didn't want to lose her opportunity.

He looked so worried about his grandfather that she

longed to comfort him. But she knew she was the last person he would accept comfort from—not while he still believed the worst of her.

She hesitated, knowing it might seem insensitive to bring up paternity testing while Vito was preoccupied with his grandfather's health. But on the other hand, if she could make things right between them, she could be there to help him through his grandfather's illness.

'Vito.' Lily took a deep breath and steeled herself to start a conversation that she knew could be difficult. 'Have you got a few minutes to talk?'

Vito turned to look at her, holding a dark-grey suit on a hanger in his hand, and frowned. The last thing he wanted right then was to talk.

'Make it quick,' he said, laying his suit on the bed and going back to the wardrobe to select a shirt. 'I have a meeting in half an hour.'

'I will be quick,' she said. 'But you have to listen to me properly.'

Vito gritted his teeth and turned to face her. She'd been back in his life less than a day and already she was testing his patience.

'You are upset with me because you think I was unfaithful,' she said, shaking her sleek curtain of blonde hair back over her shoulders.

'Upset?' Vito repeated incredulously, watching her hair swing alluringly as it settled into place. Perhaps she was hoping to distract him with her feminine wiles. 'My God! You English really have mastered the art of understatement.'

'I'm not just going to let your accusation pass,' Lily said. Her voice was calm, but Vito could see her hands were shaking as she gripped them together in front of her.

'I was not unfaithful to you. And I don't know why you think that. I've never done anything to give you that idea.'

Vito stared at her, wondering how she was able to make herself sound so sincere when he knew she was guilty as sin.

'You are right,' he said. 'You covered your trail well. But that doesn't change the fact that I know you betrayed me.'

'I didn't,' Lily protested. 'And the fact that you could even think that about me is just as much of a betrayal. But I don't want to go on like this. I want a paternity test to prove you are my child's father.'

Vito stared at her, feeling tension knot painfully in his stomach. She wanted a paternity test—the one thing he dreaded.

But he'd known it would come to this sooner or later. Although Lily had obviously been sleeping with two men at once, as far as she was concerned it was possible Vito might be the father.

For Lily a paternity test was just a game of chance. There would be a delay until it could be carried out, and she was willing to gamble on the outcome being lucky for her. It was a risk worth taking, because from her point of view she had nothing to lose—he already believed she'd been unfaithful.

But Vito had everything to lose. For him, the test could not produce a good result. There was no way he could win.

He knew he wasn't the father—because he could not have children.

'There will be no paternity test.' Vito clenched his fists at his sides.

He would not allow himself to be subject to physical, public proof that he was not the father of Lily's child. If his grandfather ever found out that the baby was not a true Salvatore heir, it would destroy his happiness for ever.

That was the whole point of marrying Lily. And he had to live with it until the time came when he could discard her and the baby. Even though she continued to show no sign that she had done anything wrong, or take any responsibility for her actions, this was the perfect way for Vito to bring a baby into the family—to make his grandfather happy before he died.

And then there was the other reason he would not submit to a paternity test. The real, gut-wrenching reason that made his palms start to sweat and his blood run cold. He simply could not bear to think of it—he could not face having his inability to father a child thrust in his face again.

'Why not?' Lily demanded. 'Why not have a paternity test and put all this misery behind us?'

'*If* I turned out to be the father, that does not prove your fidelity,' Vito grated.

Only his ex-wife, Capricia, and her fertility expert, knew of his failure as a man. The memory of Capricia's scornful face as she'd waved the doctors report under his nose was almost as painful as his infertility itself.

He would *never* admit his failure to anyone else—especially not to Lily.

'But...' Lily hesitated, looking up at his troubled face. There was something different in his expression, something she hadn't seen before. But she couldn't ponder it for too long. It had been hard enough to make this conversation happen, and it wasn't over yet. She owed it to herself to keep trying to get through to Vito. And he owed it to her to give a proper explanation.

'Where does that leave us?' she continued. 'If we don't have trust—where can we go from here?'

'This isn't about *us*,' Vito said coldly. 'This is about saving your baby from a miserable life as an illegitimate child.'

'But you can't deny me a paternity test then not even tell me why you don't believe me,' Lily insisted. 'How can I defend myself if I don't know what proof you think you have against me?'

'What you've done is indefensible,' Vito said, picking up his suit and shirt and striding towards the door. 'I don't have to give you any more information to weave your web of lies around.'

In a moment he was gone, and Lily was left alone, staring miserably after him. The last two days had been an overwhelming series of shocks, and now she realised she was shaking with reaction to it all.

She sat down on the chair, feeling her hand settle on something soft and warm. Without thinking she picked it up. It was Vito's black cashmere sweater. She lifted it automatically to her face, pressing the luxurious woollen fabric to her skin, and breathed in deeply, inhaling Vito's aroma.

Tears suddenly sprung to her eyes as she remembered the last time she had been enfolded in his embrace while he'd been wearing that sweater. She'd come inside from the foggy city, holding a joyful secret inside her. She'd felt so safe and so secure in his arms—thinking that he cared about her and would protect her from anything.

But it had all been an empty illusion. Five minutes later he had turned on her. And from then on her life had been sucked into a whirlpool of misery, getting increasingly out of her control. And this last argument had been the worst, with Vito not even giving her the information she needed to defend herself.

But she'd had enough. She wouldn't put up with it

any more. She might not be able to fight Vito over his accusation of infidelity. But there was some control she could take. She wasn't going to keep looking back at the special relationship she'd mistakenly believed she'd had with Vito. From now on she was going to concentrate on her future and make the best out of her new life.

She looked down at the black sweater which she was still holding on her lap. It was a harsh reminder of how much her life with Vito had changed—a reminder she did not need.

She stood up decisively and carried the sweater across the room. She opened the window and tossed it out into the canal below.

CHAPTER SIX

'WE'LL eat out tonight,' Vito said. 'To mark your return to Venice.'

'That would be nice.' Lily spoke mildly, determined not to let Vito see she was still shaken from their earlier argument.

It would be good to get out of the *palazzo*. It was less than twenty-four hours since Vito had brought her back to his home, and so far she'd been a bundle of nerves.

It wasn't surprising that she felt on edge after what had happened, nevertheless she'd tried to take her own advice and stop dwelling on it. She'd spent the afternoon pointlessly trying to lose herself in a good book; but even a favourite pastime like reading hadn't distracted her from all the unsettling thoughts that were whirling round persistently inside her head.

'We'll go to Luigi's,' Vito said.

'Oh…I…' Lily drew an anxious breath and stared up at Vito, quickly trying to think of an excuse not to go to Luigi's. After what had happened on Lily's last night in Venice, bringing Vito and Luigi into contact could be risky.

The restaurant had always been one of their favourite places to eat. It was within easy walking distance of the *palazzo*, served some of the best dishes in Venice, and it had a wonderful ambiance. Luigi, the proprietor, was a true character with an expansive personality and a generous nature.

The night Vito had thrown Lily out, Luigi's kindness had been an absolute godsend for her. Trapped in a fogbound city, with every hotel she'd tried full and every mode of transport closed to her, Luigi had literally saved the day. He'd arranged for her to stay in his mother's guest room—no questions asked—and then he'd seen her safely to the airport himself the following morning.

'Not Luigi's?' Vito asked, a vertical crease forming between his brows as he studied her. 'Why not?'

'It's up to you, if you're set on going there.' Lily stumbled for words. She'd done nothing wrong, but Vito was a proud Venetian man, and she knew instinctively that he would not appreciate the fact that she'd accepted help from another man. 'But I'd really love to go out to that place on Burano. I've got a craving for fish.'

'Very well.' Turning to leave, Vito suddenly stopped and pinned her with his piercing blue gaze. 'This meal is a celebration,' he said. 'Wear something suitable for such an occasion.'

Lily stared at his retreating back in irritation, wondering if he'd deliberately meant to provoke her by being so autocratic. It was hard to get used to the way he was treating her now. He'd always been a dominant force, but he'd never blatantly ordered her about before.

She stood up and walked across the room to look out of the tall, arched window. Sleek black gondolas loaded with tourists glided past on the jade-green canal below. She watched the languid ripples glimmering on the surface of the water, thinking about how her life had changed.

She wasn't a tourist any more. She wasn't even a visitor. She was in Venice to stay.

She pulled her thoughts together and headed upstairs to dress for dinner. She'd show Vito that she understood the rules of the game. He wouldn't need to waste his time approving her choice of wardrobe—her instincts for self-preservation wouldn't allow her to put herself through that humiliation again.

She'd accepted that Vito was utterly serious in his intention to marry her, and although the circumstances were not what she would have chosen she was determined to make the best of the situation.

She owed it to herself not to let the virile, masculine power of his personality completely overshadow her. She must take on the responsibility of creating a life for herself in Venice, and to prepare a place in this family for her unborn child.

And she knew that the best route forward was to stop fighting against Vito, to find a way to work within his rules. The way to stand up for herself was to be proactive. It would be better to try to influence how things happened in the first place, rather than battle with Vito after the event.

A little while later they were zipping across the lagoon towards the island of Burano.

'I've missed being out on the water,' Lily said, glancing at Vito. The golden evening light gilded his jet-black hair and cast a warm glow over his face, but his features were set in a shuttered expression. There was no way of knowing what he was thinking. 'It was one of my favourite things about living here, even though it was winter.'

'You never did seem to feel the cold,' Vito said shortly. Then, despite the fact it should have been obvious she was trying to start a conversation, he fell silent again, his expression still closed to her.

With a small sigh, Lily turned to look at the view, determined to enjoy the rest of the boat trip. The low angle of the sun across the water was creating a beautiful effect—dark indigo waves rippled against golden-orange ribbons of reflected sunlight. It was true that she'd always loved being out on the lagoon, and she wasn't going to let Vito's brooding silence mar her pleasure in the amazing view.

Before long they were approaching the picturesque island. With its gaily painted houses and simple style, it seemed a million miles away from Venice. There were no hotels on the island, and as the evening drew in the tourists disappeared back to the city. The local artisans packed away their handmade lace and other crafts, and fishermen and their families came outside to enjoy an evening stroll.

The driver brought the boat to a standstill on one side of the harbour, then jumped out athletically to tie the craft up. Vito disembarked first, turning to offer Lily support as she climbed out of the swaying boat onto the quayside.

She reached for him automatically, but the instant their hands made contact a jolt of highly charged sensual energy ran through her. She snatched her hand away with a gasp, then stumbled awkwardly as the boat lurched with the movement of the water.

Vito's fingers closed around her forearm, his grip strong and steadying, but he didn't speak as she climbed out onto the quay.

'Thank you.' She tried to make her voice bright and breezy as they started walking towards the main street, but it sounded strained to her own ears. Why should simply taking his hand make her so sexually aware of him? Out of the blue her body was humming with desire for him—even though he hadn't done or said anything much since they'd left home. 'I should know better than to make sudden movements when I'm standing on the edge of a boat.'

She lifted her eyes to his face, and the way he was looking at her suddenly made her mouth run dry. She looked away skittishly, waiting a moment for him to speak, but it seemed he was continuing to maintain a charged silence.

'For goodness' sake!' Lily stopped in her tracks and turned to stare up at him. 'Stop giving me the silent treatment. You're the one who wants us to keep up appearances.'

'What do you want me to say?' Vito asked, with an infuriating lift to one black eyebrow before he turned and continued walking towards the restaurant. 'Should I reprimand you for acting foolishly at the water's edge? Or would you like to talk about how the simple touch of my hand on yours sent shock waves of sexual desire burning through you?'

'No it didn't,' Lily said indignantly, feeling hot colour flood to her cheeks as she hurried to keep pace beside him. The very mention of sexual desire was doing things to her that she'd rather deny, especially given Vito's current rather arrogant and hostile mood. She was glad now that they were walking along and he wasn't looking at her any more.

'Of course it did. And, if something as simple as touching hands turns you on, whatever will happen at the restaurant when I take you in my arms and make a show of how happy we are together?' His voice rumbled through her, setting her nerves alight.

His absolute confidence in his effect on her bothered her on more levels than she could say. Even thinking about the fact that he could turn her on was doing exactly that. She could feel her skin start to flush, and her heart rate had definitely speeded up.

'Why can't we have a proper conversation?' Lily protested, trying to ignore the way she was feeling.

'We could try,' Vito said, as he held the door for her to walk into the restaurant. 'But you might as well face up to it—not much else is going to hold your attention. We both know how this evening has to end.'

Mental pictures of Vito making love to her whirled through her mind, and she could feel her body buzzing with anticipation. Try as she might, it was impossible to ignore the images and the way they were making her feel.

Lily's cheeks were scarlet as the *maître d'* rushed over to them, fussing about how long it had been since their last visit, and showing them to the best table in the restaurant.

'Your usual glass of prosecco to begin?' he asked.

'That would be perfect.' Vito flashed Lily a lazy smile that sent a frisson skittering through her. 'After all, this is an evening of celebration.'

'I shouldn't drink more than a few sips,' she said. For some reason she shied away from mentioning her pregnancy.

'What is it you English say?' Vito asked, with a devilish glint in his eyes. '"A little of what you fancy does you good"?'

Lily's face was glowing and she could feel herself actually trembling. She told herself it was just nerves magnifying her reaction to his provocation, and buried her head in the menu to avoid his piercing gaze.

If she was going to get through the evening unscathed, she had to get herself in check. She forced herself to read the menu, concentrating very hard on all the options, to chase all other thoughts out of her mind.

She was feeling slightly more composed when the waiter came to tell them the special fish dishes available from the day's catch, and she was pleased at the extra distraction. By the time they had both made their selections, she had more or less clamped down on her wayward reaction to Vito, although she knew her control was pretty tenuous. She'd have to work very hard to keep the conversation neutral.

'We should discuss wedding arrangements.' Vito suddenly spoke, taking her by surprise with his change of tack.

'Of course,' Lily replied, overwhelmingly relieved that he had apparently given up his campaign to make her feel uncomfortable. She picked up her prosecco glass and took a sip of the sparkling white wine that the Veneto region was famous for. The delicate bubbles fizzed pleasantly in her mouth, and for a moment she felt the tension start to drain out of her body.

'It must be very soon,' Vito continued. 'And I think a relatively small family affair would be best. Is there anyone you wish to invite who would be able to come at short notice?'

'I don't know. I hadn't really thought.' Lily smoothed her hand over her long hair in sudden consternation. It was going to be strange enough going through with the wedding. And nothing had changed regarding her concerns about keeping up appearances with her mother or best friends being there. 'You know, I think it would be better to tell them afterwards. Maybe they can visit later.'

'Ashamed of your fiancé?' Vito asked. His tone was utterly neutral, and for a disconcerting moment Lily wondered if he was offended or being sardonic.

'No.' She looked him squarely in the eye. A couple of months ago she would have been so proud to call him that. 'I'm just not sure I'll be able to convince the people I love that this is real. I'm still getting used to it.'

'All right,' he said. 'If you think it would be best, we'll keep it very small. Just my grandfather—if he's well enough—and a couple of witnesses.'

He continued to hold her gaze for a long moment, his blue eyes looking smoky in the candlelight, and for a second Lily had a flash of how it used to be between them. She was glad he had accepted what she said without making more of it. She knew she had to make the marriage look normal—and she had very good reasons for going ahead with it. But it was still too soon to be confident that she'd manage in front of the people who loved and knew her best.

The rest of the meal passed smoothly. Vito kept the conversation light, for which she was very grateful, and by the time Lily had finished her ice cream she was surprised to realise that she had actually enjoyed a proper meal for the first time in weeks. Maybe her body was finally settling into the second trimester of her pregnancy and the misery of morning sickness was over.

'Let's go home,' Vito said, signalling for the bill.

Lily looked at him, suddenly remembering what he had said about them both knowing how the evening would end. A dark shiver of anticipation ran through her. She couldn't deny that she missed the nights of passion they had shared.

Her skin was flushing again, and she stared at the paintings covering the walls to take her mind off making love with Vito. On their earlier visits to the restaurant he had told her how previous owners had sometimes accepted paintings as payment for meals. As a result the walls were covered with an astonishingly eclectic array of artwork that she'd always enjoyed looking at—but right then it wasn't enough to distract her from the thought of lying in Vito's arms.

It was dark as they travelled back across the lagoon, and a beautiful crescent moon hung in the sky. Lily shivered, hugging her silk wrap tighter around her—not because she was cold, but because of the way Vito had started looking at her again.

It was too dark to see his features clearly, but she could sense his expression was the one she had seen so many times before when they'd been lovers. The expression that meant very soon they would be making love.

'You're cold,' Vito said, slipping his arm around her shoulder and pulling her closer to his side.

'Not really,' Lily responded, leaning against his hard muscled body with a ripple of pleasure. Half a glass of prosecco had gone to her head—or maybe she was simply intoxicated by her proximity to Vito. His spicy masculine aroma was filling her senses, making her body sing with remembered sensations.

'You're trembling,' Vito murmured, leaning close to her ear. She could feel his lips moving deliciously against her hair. Excitement knotted deep inside her, making her shiver in expectation of what was to happen later.

'I'm not really cold.' The words came out in a small, shaky voice, and she realised that although she yearned to lie in his arms again she was also extremely nervous. Would it be as good as she remembered? Would Vito be satisfied with her?

Their physical compatibility was the one thing that might create a genuine bond between them in their marriage of convenience. Or was she placing too much significance on it? Would it ever again be more than just sex to Vito?

'I've missed this, *bella mia*.' Vito's deep, sensual

voice rumbled right through her as he lifted his hands to turn her face towards him. His fingers slipped between the silky tresses of her hair, and he inclined her head slightly to one side, as if he was about to kiss her.

Lily gazed at him silently. Her heart was racing and she wanted to feel his lips against hers, experience the mastery of his kiss again. But for a long moment he didn't move.

'So have I,' she whispered, thinking about the time when it had been natural for her to pull him close for a kiss. Before she thought about what she was doing, she leant nearer and pressed a light kiss against his mouth.

For a heartbeat she held her breath. He hadn't kissed her back. Maybe this wasn't the way he wanted it to be now. But her lips tingled with the feel of his firm, sensual mouth and she was desperate for him to kiss her properly.

Suddenly Vito began to move and everything seemed to happen at once. His strong hands were under the hem of her full skirt, sliding rapidly up the outside of her legs, making the breath catch in her throat. Then, before she realised what he was doing, he took hold of her hips and lifted her so that she was sitting astride him.

She grabbed hold of his broad shoulders to steady herself as desire flooded through her, pooling at the very centre of her womanhood. Her most sensitive feminine place was now pressed intimately against him. She could feel his erection pushing powerfully against her through his trousers. They were in a perfect position for making love—and sensation stormed through her quivering body, as if that was really what they were doing.

The movement of the boat as it bounced lightly over the waves bumped their bodies together erotically, and Lily felt her breath coming in shorter and shorter gasps. In a distant, rational part of her mind, she couldn't believe how aroused she was. He'd barely touched her and he hadn't even kissed her. Yet her body was on fire.

His hands were still under her skirt, resting on her hips and pulling her into close contact with him. She longed to feel those hands glide across her, but for a moment they stayed perfectly still.

'I want to touch you all over,' he murmured as his hands started to move.

Her knees on the seat were supporting her, and there was room for him to slide his hands around the curve of her bottom. She bit the tip of her tongue lightly between her teeth. His fingers left a tingling trail in their wake—but she needed more.

'Kiss me.' His words were a command, but suddenly she wondered if he was playing a game with her. A moment ago he hadn't kissed her back. Would he respond this time? Or would he sit there as cold as stone—despite the fact he knew how turned on she was, and that she could feel how hard he was?

Her position astride him meant that her head was slightly higher than his. She leant forward and brushed her lips lightly over his. He was driving her wild with frustrated sexual need—she'd try to give him a taste of his own medicine.

But as soon as their lips made contact another rush of overwhelming desire stormed her body and, almost as if from a distance, she heard a low, sexy moan emerge from deep within her.

Suddenly Vito lifted his hand and cupped the nape of her neck. He pulled her mouth down roughly to his, and kissed her with a furious passion that matched the pent-up energy burning inside her. His tongue plunged in deeply and she took it willingly, inviting the rough, sensual invasion of her mouth. She wanted to taste him, feel him. She wanted to be as close to him as possible.

They'd never kissed like this before. All through the many wild or tender nights they'd shared, she had never experienced a kiss so intense. The blood was singing in her ears, blotting out everything but Vito and her over-powering need to be with him.

Then she felt his other hand push up between them, pulling at the buttons on the front of her dress. A moment later his hand was inside, slipping under the lace of her bra to cup her breast. A deep sigh of plea-sure escaped her, but he kept on kissing, delving deeper with his tongue as his fingers found her nipple and teased it.

Sensation spiralled out from her breast and she finally pulled back from his kiss, gasping for air.

'Oh, Vito.' She breathed deeply, feeling her body shuddering against him.

'You're ready for me.' One hand was still inside her bra, doing exquisite things to her breast, and he slipped the other under the curtain of hair that had fallen forward over them. He pushed it behind her shoulder, then pulled her silk wrap closely around her to cover the open front of her dress. 'And as soon as we are inside I'm going to make you mine, once and for all.'

His words of possession rolled through her body like an incredible promise. She wanted to be his. She'd always been his. From the moment that they'd met he had been the master of her body, able to lift her to heights she had never imagined possible. Able to make her world splinter into a million points of absolute bliss, where nothing mattered but being with Vito.

She made a murmur of protest as he slipped his hand gently from her dress, then she realised that the boat had already slowed down as it wound its way through the canals of the city. In a minute they would be at the *palazzo*.

The boat glided up to the gothic arch of the water gate, and Vito lifted her from his lap. Her legs were unsteady, and before she realised what he was doing he pulled her wrap tightly around her and swept her up into his arms. A lifetime of watercraft and canals had made him nimble on his feet, and within a moment he had whisked her off the boat and carried her straight up to their bedroom.

CHAPTER SEVEN

HE LAID her on the bed and stood over her, discarding his jacket and tie, before kneeling beside her and finishing off undoing the buttons on her dress.

She gazed up at him, smiling at the way his fringe had fallen forward over his face. She reached up to run her fingers through his luxuriant black hair, while he unbuttoned her dress.

Touching his hair suddenly seemed a curiously intimate thing to do. It was silly to think that, considering what had happened on the boat and what was about to happen. But for that moment she found herself thinking that everything would be all right. She could almost imagine the past six weeks had never happened.

'I've missed this,' Vito said, slipping her dress off her shoulders and pulling it all the way down under her hips.

He let his gaze wander over her as she lay on the bed dressed in nothing but a lacy bra, French knickers, hold-up stockings and high-heeled shoes.

She was gorgeous.

'You are beautiful,' he murmured, cupping one breast in each hand. They were deliciously warm beneath his fingers, and he felt her nipples harden instantly against his palms.

She was moving restlessly on the bed, and he knew it wouldn't take much to bring her back to a state of heightened arousal. She had been unbelievably responsive to him out on the lagoon, and knowing how he was affecting her had also been a powerful aphrodisiac for him. Not that she'd ever had to do much to turn him on—he'd been hot for her from the moment he'd first laid eyes on her. And tonight he planned to lay more on her than just his eyes. They were to be married, and he would make her his wife in every sense.

With skilful fingers he slipped his hands behind her back to unhook her bra, and as he tossed it to one side he saw her start to tremble again. Her pupils were dilated with her building need, and as she arched her back, thrusting her breasts up towards him, he knew exactly what she wanted.

'Oh!' Lily cried out as his mouth closed over her nipple. Glorious feelings rippled through her body, as his sinuous tongue worked magic on her tingling flesh. 'Oh, Vito!' She said his name again. She couldn't believe she was really here, that this was really happening. Vito was making love to her again, and everything would be as it had been.

His hands were moving over her body, burning a trail wherever they touched, removing her French knickers and stockings, urging her pulse rate up and up.

She lay naked on the bed, breathing raggedly as Vito finally lifted his head to look at her. A knot of sexual excitement twisted inside her as she gazed into his darkened eyes. She knew he wanted her as much as her body was aching for him.

But he was wearing too many clothes. She needed to feel his skin against hers, run her hands over his hard, muscled body. She reached up to undo his shirt.

'This is good.' Vito's voice was husky as he looked

down at her fingers struggling with his buttons. 'I should have remembered—eating out always made you amorous.'

'No, it didn't,' Lily protested, finally tossing his shirt away. Then she paused and stared at him, suddenly thinking back to when they'd lived together. Some of their most romantic evenings *had* involved an evening out.

'Ah—now you remember,' Vito drawled, lazily pulling his black leather belt through the loop on his trousers.

'It wasn't eating out,' Lily replied.

A strangely hollow feeling moved through her as she suddenly realised that it had been more about having his attention. When he'd spent an evening with her—rather than working—it had made her feel special. Wanted. Worthy of him.

When he'd slipped into bed beside her after a night spent in his office she'd always welcomed him into her arms. But it hadn't been the same. She'd taken pleasure from knowing that he sought comfort in her arms after a long day of work. But it was never the same as when he'd spent time with her.

'We'll test it again tomorrow,' Vito said, his voice tickling her stomach as he leant forward and scattered kisses over her sensitive skin. 'We'll go to Luigi's.'

Without meaning to, Lily felt herself tense.

Vito sat up and looked at her sharply.

'What is it?' he demanded, his voice cold and hard. 'When I mentioned Luigi earlier you acted strangely. Tell me what this is about.'

'Nothing,' Lily said, pushing herself up onto her elbows and suddenly feeling acutely conscious of the fact that she was naked.

'Tell me.' Vito swore and lurched angrily to his feet. 'Is *he* the one? Is he the one you betrayed me with?'

'No!' Lily gasped. She hugged her knees up to her chest and looked at him in alarm. A terrifying change had come over him, darkening his features and making the room crackle with angry energy.

'I'll ask him!' He snatched up his shirt and started to pull it on jerkily.

'No!' Lily cried in horror. She couldn't let Vito storm out to confront Luigi. He'd been her guardian angel that night—she couldn't bear him to suffer Vito's rage because of his kindness. 'Listen. It's not what you think—I'll tell you what happened.'

'Speak quickly,' Vito said, reaching for his jacket. 'Then, when I've heard your lies, I'll go and hear what Luigi has to say.'

'He'll tell you how he found me alone, with nowhere to go, on the night you threw me out!' She stared up at him, painful memories bombarding her.

'Continue,' Vito grated, his face dark with barely contained fury.

'The fog closed the airport.' She took a breath, but she knew her voice was still shaky. 'It was a few days before Easter—everywhere was fully booked. I couldn't find a hotel—'

'Are you trying to tell me every hotel room in Venice was full?' Vito demanded. 'Don't be absurd.'

'It was already late when I left here,' she said, remembering how sick and miserable she'd felt, dragging herself from hotel to hotel. 'I'd stopped for a moment, down the alley near Luigi's, trying to think what to do. He saw me standing there, alone with my luggage.'

'Go on.' Vito's frown was thunderous, creating a deep vertical crease between his brows and casting his eyes into dark shadow.

'He was very kind. He took me to his mother's

house, because she has a spare room,' Lily said quietly. 'That's all.'

She looked up at him, anxious that he should believe her—as much for Luigi's sake as her own. But he remained ominously silent.

Suddenly she found herself wondering how Vito felt. Did he care at all that she had been alone and unprotected that night in Venice, with no one to turn to and nowhere to seek refuge? She hugged her knees tighter, pressing her forehead against them and letting her hair fall forwards in a curtain around her.

He didn't care. He'd never really cared about her. A passing acquaintance had cared more for her well-being that night than Vito.

Humiliation gnawed at her. What was she doing here? Why was she here with a man who didn't care about her and didn't even have the slightest respect for her?

'Don't hide from me.'

Vito's voice cut through her misery like cold steel. She lifted her head in time to see him reaching for her—then suddenly she was standing beside the bed facing him.

'I wasn't hiding.' She tossed her hair back over her shoulders defiantly, despite the fact it bared her breasts to him again. She was completely naked, while he was almost completely dressed. But she refused to let herself think about that.

'We will never discuss the night you left Venice again,' Vito said. 'Tomorrow we eat at Luigi's—showing everyone that we are an ecstatic couple about to be married.'

'As you wish,' Lily responded stiffly, thinking that Luigi was bound to be curious as to what had happened.

'It is unacceptable that you turned to Luigi,' Vito continued, his voice throbbing with intensity. 'Mark my words—you will *never* again take our problems outside of this bedroom. Whatever happens,' he grated, 'our affairs are private.'

'You threw me out!' Lily cried in her defence.

'But now you're back.' Vito's eyes swept over her, leaving a trail of sexual awareness prickling over her naked body. 'And you must take the consequences of your actions.'

'What is that supposed to mean?' Lily stood tall, resisting the urge to fidget under his hot eyes.

'That you are mine.' His voice was loaded with sexual possessiveness. 'And you will do anything I want.'

'I've always done whatever you want,' Lily threw back at him.

It was true, she realised to her shame. Except when they'd been together it had always seemed that they wanted the same thing.

'Not always,' Vito growled, seizing her roughly and dragging her up against him. He loomed over her, plunging his hands into her hair and pulling her head back so that their faces were only inches apart. 'But now you're mine—*only mine*. No other man is ever going to touch you again.'

He dragged her closer, bumping their hips together erotically. Lily gasped at the intimate contact just as his lips closed, hot and demanding, over hers.

His tongue pushed into her mouth, stoking the sexual fire that was suddenly raging between them once more. Desire for him rushed through her veins, making her insides tingle and her legs turn to water.

A pulsing point of sensation starting throbbing between her legs, and the feel of his hands running over her naked skin was driving her wild with her own need to touch him.

He pulled away from her abruptly, and shrugged his jacket off. Lily stood shakily, taking shallow breaths as she watched him discarding his clothes. Her gaze drifted up to his face.

What she saw made her heart miss a beat.

He was furious.

She could see the anger burning in his eyes, pulling the muscles in his face taut with tension. He was still absolutely livid about her supposed infidelity, and this was an act of vengeance.

'No.' Lily took a step backwards.

'You can't back out now.' Vito moved towards her, and lifted his hand to cup her breast. His thumb toyed with her nipple, and an answering ripple of delight spread through her body. 'You are mine to take, whenever I choose.'

'You're not going to make love to me out of anger,' Lily said, trying to ignore the feel of his hand on her breast and the sensual pleasure his touch was giving her.

'I'm taking back what is mine.'

'I was always yours.' Lily's voice was small and steady, despite the turmoil of emotions and physical sensations that was assailing her.

Almost before her words were finished, he moved forwards and pulled her into his arms again. His mouth came down to kiss her, and as his tongue thrust between her lips it was as if he was staking his claim in the most basic way.

Her treacherous body was responding to his. Despite her mind protesting that this was not right—that she had to stop him if she was to maintain any self-respect—her flesh was aching with her need for him. Deep inside she was vibrating with her desire to feel him lying on top of her, thrusting into her. Making her his again.

Suddenly he pulled away.

His breathing was ragged as he stood looking at her for a moment, his expression utterly impenetrable. Then he turned on his heel and walked out.

Lily stared after him—beset by conflicting emotions.

It was what she'd wanted, wasn't it?

Then why did she feel so bereft?

Lily stood by the window, looking down at the canal below, wondering how she could make things better between Vito and herself. It was several weeks since they'd been married, and she was still having trouble adjusting to it.

It was hard to believe it was actually real, especially as Vito had hardly come near her since the night he had stormed out of the bedroom. At first she'd assumed he was simply cooling off—she'd known how angry he was. But then the wedding had come and gone, with only the bare formalities discussed between them.

It had been a small, private ceremony, and the simple occasion had scarcely caused a blip in the passage of time. It was extraordinary that such a momentous life event had slipped past without greater impact. But then it had not been a normal wedding. And as the weeks had continued to pass it was painfully clear that it was not a normal marriage.

She almost felt like she was stuck in a time warp—with nothing really changing and every day the same. Vito had continued to share the bedroom, but he worked late most nights, often coming to bed after midnight. And, although weeks had passed, he'd never touched her.

She knew he was worried about his grandfather. His instinct that his grandfather's health was not right on Lily's first day back in Venice had proved to be correct, because Giovanni had soon gone down with a nasty chest-infection. But, from the little information Lily was able to glean, that appeared to have cleared up now.

She turned away from the window, planning to sit and read for a while before going out for a walk, when a movement from the doorway caught her eye.

'Vito.' She said his name in surprise. It was barely ten o'clock in the morning—he never came home from work during the day. 'Is everything all right? Your grandfather...?'

'Yes,' Vito replied. 'In fact that is why I am here. My grandfather's health is much improved. This morning would be a suitable time for you to meet him.'

'I'll go and get my bag.' Lily walked towards the door, then hesitated as Vito didn't step aside to let her through. She held her breath and slipped past him, feeling the hairs on her arms stand up and her heart-rate increase, as she couldn't help brushing lightly against him.

She tried to ignore the feeling as she ran up the stairs to the bedroom. She paused in front of the mirror to check her appearance, and was disconcerted to see her flushed cheeks and animated eyes.

Was it the simple contact of brushing against him that had caused the light in her face? Or was it the prospect of spending a little time in Vito's company?

Whatever the case, she didn't ponder it, and as she didn't need to change her clothes she hurried back down the stairs. Ever since the first morning in Venice she had taken trouble with her appearance. She didn't want to give Vito another opportunity to humiliate her.

The walk to *Ca' Salvatore* didn't take long, and as they arrived at the baroque *palazzo* Vito took her hand in his. A charge of energy passed between them and, as Lily felt herself tremble, she realised it was the first proper physical contact they'd shared since the night they'd nearly made love.

Vito had not touched her since then, and the fact that he had chosen this moment to hold her hand made it clear to Lily that his intention was to show all at *Ca' Salvatore* that she was his. It was a reminder of how important it was to Vito that his grandfather saw them as a proper couple.

He led her into the beautiful building and up to the second-floor room where Giovanni was resting in bed.

'*Nonno*, there is someone I'd like you to meet,' Vito said. He crossed the room to kiss his grandfather's cheek. Then, putting his arm round the old man's shoulders, he helped him up into a sitting position.

'We're speaking in English?' Giovanni asked, squinting across the room short-sightedly. 'Very intriguing. I'd better put my spectacles on.'

Lily smiled. Despite her nervousness, she was already warming to the old man. His body might be frail, but his mind was certainly active.

'They're here, with your newspaper.' She slipped around to the other side of the large bed and handed his spectacles to him.

'Thank you, my dear. No, stay close,' Giovanni added, his bony hand shooting out to catch her arm and pull her closer. 'So I can get a proper look at you.'

'*Nonno!*' Vito chided gently. 'Let go of Lily, and I'll introduce you properly.'

'Formalities!' Giovanni scoffed, although he did release his grip. 'What use are formalities at my age? Tell me quickly—who is this beautiful young English woman? And why have you brought her to meet me?'

'This is Lily,' Vito said. 'And I'm very pleased to tell you that—'

'Yes, yes—get on with it,' Giovanni urged.

'That she is my wife,' Vito finished smoothly, not at all phased by his grandfather's interruption.

'Your wife?' Giovanni said. 'Why didn't I know about this?'

'You were sick, *Nonno*,' Vito said. 'I thought it best to go ahead with the wedding and tell you when you were feeling better.'

'You were married without me?' Giovanni said, sounding slightly affronted as he looked sharply at Vito, then across at Lily. 'So you've finally come to your senses and decided to settle down?'

'Yes, *Nonno*,' Vito said, hugging Lily in an open display of affection. She leant into his embrace, taking comfort from the feel of his strong arms around her, despite the knowledge that it was only for show. A whirl of conflicting thoughts and emotions was flowing through her, but she fought to keep a clear head and pay attention to the exchange between Vito and his grandfather. 'It was a very small wedding,' Vito added.

Just how significant had Giovanni's desire to see his grandson settled been in Vito's sudden proposal? Everything had happened so quickly at first, and in the intervening time she still hadn't come any closer to figuring out Vito's motivation. She had married him for her child's sake—but she didn't really understand what was in it for Vito. Especially as he seemed to be avoiding her.

'So you found the right woman after all?' Giovanni probed, leaning forward and peering closely at Lily. 'An English rose—or should I say an English lily? The name is certainly appropriate.'

'The right woman,' Vito repeated, placing a brief kiss on Lily's cheek. '*Si, Nonno*. You always told me that in time I would find the right woman.'

The old man snorted, wicked humour making his eyes brighten. 'I said that, did I? I seem to remember talking to you just a few days before I got that wretched infection,' he said. 'I told you to hurry up and provide me with an heir. Is that what this is?'

Lily barely managed to shield her shocked reaction. Her heart jerked painfully in her chest, and for a second she struggled to draw air into her lungs. Then she became aware of Vito beside her.

He had gone utterly rigid. A horrible sensation cut through her. It was as if she could actually feel his pain as his muscles tensed with agonising intensity.

'You went on a business trip to London,' Giovanni said. 'What did you do—propose to the first attractive girl you met?'

'No, *Nonno*. That's not how it happened...' Vito looked at his grandfather's face and suddenly ran out of words.

This wasn't how it had been supposed to go. The wily old man had completely wrong-footed him—and if he didn't pull himself together quickly it would all be for nothing. If he couldn't convince his grandfather that his relationship with Lily was genuine, he might not accept her child as his heir. It wouldn't make him content.

And that was what this was all about—fulfilling Giovanni's dying wish to see his name continued. What kind of grandson was he if he couldn't do the one thing that would make his beloved grandfather happy in his dying days? After everything his grandfather had done for him, this was the one thing that any man ought to be able to do in return.

His shame at his failure bore into him, burning a hole in his chest, making it hard to think, impossible to speak.

'It's true we arrived from London the day before you

got sick,' Lily suddenly spoke up, her voice quiet but clear in the high-ceilinged chamber. 'But we didn't just meet.'

'Tell me more.' Giovanni leant forward, as if it would help him catch everything she said.

'We first met nearly a year ago,' Lily said, stepping closer to the bed. 'After several months of travelling between London and Venice for weekends and holidays, Vito asked me to move in with him here. I've been living in Venice with him since Novem…'

Vito looked at her sharply as her words petered out. He'd been amazed, and very relieved, that she'd spoken up. But now she was blushing and looking down at the floor, letting her blonde hair swing forward to conceal her face.

'What is it?' Giovanni barked. 'Why did you stop talking?'

'I…it just occurred to me that you might be Catholic.' Lily looked up and continued hesitantly. 'That you might not approve of us living together. I'm sorry—that's probably why Vito never brought me here before.'

Giovanni's bark of laughter broke the sudden tension in the room.

'Now I see.' The old man spoke between chuckles. 'You were taking your time, making sure it was right. After Capricia, I can understand your caution.'

'It seemed wise to be sure,' Vito said, turning to look at Lily. He didn't know why she had said what she'd said—whether she was defending him, or simply acting out the role she had agreed to. Or maybe she was just naively speaking her mind.

Whatever the explanation, relief flooded through him, and he hugged her to him in an embrace that was entirely natural. Her guileless chatter had utterly won over his grandfather, and for that he was thankful.

Suddenly he found himself thinking how different Lily was from his ex-wife Capricia. In fact, she was different from all the other women he had ever been involved with.

Capricia's heart was as hard and impenetrable as a diamond. Her scornful face flashed unpleasantly through his mind, and he knew he could never have employed the same tactics of persuasion on her that he had used on Lily.

For some reason the thought made him uncomfortable, but he pushed it ruthlessly to the back of his mind. Just because Lily had her weaknesses did not mean she didn't deserve everything she got. He couldn't forget she had betrayed him by sleeping with another man.

'But now something has changed.' Vito turned back to his grandfather and continued speaking. 'Something that has made us look to the future.'

'What's that?' Giovanni sat up straighter, and from the sharp expression on his face Vito thought he had guessed what was coming next.

'Lily is pregnant,' he said. 'You are the first one to share our wonderful news.'

For a moment Giovanni looked stunned. It was as if the news, which he'd waited so many years to hear, was suddenly too much to take in. Then a massive smile spread across his old face.

Lily watched as his eyes started to sparkle with unshed tears and, even though she had only just met Vito's grandfather, she understood how important this was to him. Impulsively, she leant over the bed and kissed his cheek.

'You've made me very happy,' he said. 'My name will continue. There will be Salvatores living at *Ca' Salvatore*.'

Lily smiled at him, thinking how different life was

for Vito's family. After her upbringing, it was hard to imagine living in a palace that had been in the family for hundreds of years.

'What do you think of Venice?' Giovanni suddenly asked. 'People say it's old and crumbling—like me.' There was a merry twinkle in his eyes that made him look years younger, but Lily knew that the question was important to him. 'But I say there's life in the old dog yet. What do you think, Lily?'

'Oh, definitely.' Lily smiled warmly and leant forward to take his hand. She could feel a slight tremor, and despite the fact she had only just met him she knew that he was tiring. 'It couldn't be more different from the green and open countryside where I grew up—but I absolutely love it. It's beautiful, fascinating, and there is always more to see.'

'Not too crowded for you?' he pressed. 'After the quiet of the countryside?'

'I love the hustle and bustle,' Lily said truthfully. 'And if I want some space around me I can walk beside the water, or take a boat out onto the lagoon.'

Giovanni leant back against his pillows. His body looked frail, but there was a light in his faded blue eyes.

'You're tired, *Nonno*,' Vito said. 'We should leave you to rest.'

'No, wait a moment,' Giovanni suddenly said. 'Look in the top drawer—a wooden box.'

'Is this what you mean?' Vito asked, holding up a highly polished, flat wooden box that he'd found in the old chest-of-drawers across the room.

'Give it to Lily,' Giovanni said.

Vito frowned, but did as his grandfather bid. Lily took the box hesitantly, caught between the displeasure on Vito's face and Giovanni's wishes.

'Oh!' she gasped as she opened the box to reveal a stunningly beautiful necklace. 'It's exquisite!'

'Antique Venetian glass,' Giovanni said. 'It was *my* great-grandmother's. Until now I didn't have anyone to pass it on to. It's for you, my dear. Welcome to my family.'

Lily stared at the antique jewellery in awe. She'd never seen anything so gorgeous—and knowing that the glass beads were hundreds of years old, that the necklace had been treasured for generations, made it even more special.

'We can't accept that, *Nonno*,' Vito said.

'I'm not giving it to *you*.' Giovanni looked sternly at his grandson, then his watery gaze moved on to Lily. 'Your wife appreciates it. From her expression, I can see that she knows the true value of the necklace.'

'Vito's right,' Lily said, reluctantly closing the lid of the box. 'This is too much. You've only just met me.'

'That doesn't matter. You are my granddaughter now,' Giovanni said. He leant back against his plump pillows and closed his eyes. 'You may leave now. I am tired.'

Lily clutched the box tightly as Vito steered her out of the *palazzo*. It had been a morning full of surprises.

They walked home quietly. Lily had a lot on her mind. There were still so many questions—but at least some things were starting to come clear. Vito's grandfather was a wonderful old man, and she understood completely why Vito wanted to make his last days happy. But he wasn't being honest with anyone.

It wasn't long before they were back in their bedroom.

'I wish you had told me.' Lily spoke without preamble. 'That the only reason you wanted to marry me is to make your grandfather's final days happier.'

'There was no need to complicate our arrangement.' Vito spoke shortly, not bothering to deny her accusation. 'It was not your concern.'

'Of course it was,' Lily said. 'I'm involved! I'm the one carrying your child—Giovanni's great-grandchild. And I'm the one who is going to spend time with him during his last months.'

'Save that for the rest of the world,' Vito snapped. 'Endless repetition won't make it true, so stop trying to convince me that the child is mine.'

'But it *is*,' Lily protested. 'Whatever you say, *I'm* not going to stop believing it—or saying it—because it is true.'

'My grandfather is old and frail. He doesn't have long to live.' Vito brutally brought the subject back around. 'It is the *thought* that his family line will continue that he needs. Not to socialise with you.'

Lily stared at him bitterly. Despite the circumstances, she had enjoyed meeting Giovanni. He was a wonderful old man, and she was sure spending time with him would enrich her life.

'Oh my God!' she gasped suddenly, sitting down on the edge of the bed as her legs felt weak with shock. 'As far as you're concerned, this is a temporary arrangement. As soon as Giovanni passes away, you're planning to throw me and the baby out again!'

She looked up at Vito in a silent appeal, desperate for him to tell her that she was wrong. But he just stared down at her, a hard, unfeeling expression on his face.

'Your grandfather will have died happy.' At last Lily spoke her awful train of thought aloud. 'And you will have no further use for me. Or for the baby. No wonder you were able to suggest this, even though you are adamant that the baby isn't yours!'

'It was a practical solution,' Vito said coldly. 'And now you'll finally understand that it is pointless for you to continually try to persuade me of your innocence. Or to build a relationship with my grandfather. Or to put down roots in Venice. As soon as his time comes, you'll be history.'

Lily stared at him in horror as the cold brutality of his words sunk in.

'You are a despicable human being!' she cried, suddenly flying to her feet and squaring up to him. 'You don't deserve a grandfather who loves you so much!'

'I didn't deserve a lover who cheated on me.' The angry blue fire sparking in his eyes was the only sign of emotion on his face.

Lily glared at him, struggling for words. She couldn't believe Vito would really do something like this.

All the time she'd lived with him she'd thought him to be a fair and generous man. That had changed the day he'd thrown her out for getting pregnant. Then, when he'd asked her to marry him, she'd been forced to rethink her opinion for a second time.

She knew he was angry and upset because he believed she had betrayed him but after this latest, awful revelation her opinion of him had sunk to the lowest depths—into a confusing emotional mass of disbelief and disillusionment.

'Give that to me,' Vito said, lifting the antique-necklace box from her hands. 'You can't wear that.'

Lily stared at the box as he carried it away, her temper suddenly sparking again.

'No wonder you didn't want Giovanni to give it to me,' she said bitterly. 'Don't worry. I'm not going to steal a priceless family heirloom from you.'

'It's very old and fragile,' Vito said curtly. 'The high humidity in Venice makes things deteriorate quickly. It needs expert attention to ensure it won't fall apart when you wear it.'

'I won't be wearing it,' Lily said. 'It was a wonderful gift—but you've tainted it.'

She looked up at Vito, and she could see his shoulders were rigid with tension, and a muscle was throbbing insistently on his angular jawbone. Although his eyes were cast into shadow by black brows that were drawn heavily downwards, she could see that powerful emotion glittered within them.

Perhaps he wasn't as cold and unmoved by this discussion as he would like her to think, but that didn't change his intentions.

'Once and for all, it's time to make things crystal clear between us.' His voice cut through her shattered nerves like steel wire. 'Nothing you have discovered today makes any difference to our arrangement. You did very well with my grandfather this morning—and now you will continue to play your part as my adoring wife. Until I am finished with you.'

Lily glared at him angrily, unable to find words to express the horror she was feeling.

Was he really saying that she must put up with whatever unjust accusations and hostility he chose to throw her way? That she wasn't allowed to speak up in her own defence, or express her opinion about anything?

And then, when he was done with her, that he would toss her out as callously as he'd done before—except this time she'd have a baby with her?

'You lied to me,' Lily said. 'You lied to me about making a future for our baby.'

'You lied to me first,' Vito fired back at her. 'When you tried to pass that baby off as mine.'

'You really don't care at all,' Lily said hollowly. 'You said it would be better for my baby. But how can this be better? You deceived me and manipulated me into marrying you—when all the time you were planning to dump us like last week's trash.'

'I'm not lying now,' Vito said. 'And I will not go over this again. I have made the situation plain, and I will not tolerate your defiance, or your continued assertions that I am the father of your baby.'

With that he turned and walked out of the bedroom, taking the necklace with him.

CHAPTER EIGHT

LILY stared after him in stunned silence.

All she could think was how foolish she'd been to trust Vito. She'd seen his true nature the night he'd heartlessly thrown her out onto the streets of Venice. Why, even after he'd treated her so appallingly, had she let him drag her back into his life?

Because she had once thought she was falling in love with him. And then he had lied to her. And manipulated her. He'd made her believe it was the best thing for her and her baby, when all along he couldn't have cared less about them. All he cared about was taking revenge against her for something she'd never even done. And at the same time finding a way to please his grandfather.

Lily exhaled heavily, put her hands on her hips and shook her head decisively. She wouldn't stand for it. He couldn't keep her here against her wishes. She'd leave him. Take her life back. Ruin his plans.

She grabbed her suitcase out of the wardrobe and started throwing clothes into it. Everything—all the designer clothes, the jewellery. Everything he'd ever bought her. He'd told her they were hers, and this time she'd take the lot.

Suddenly she stopped. She didn't want things he'd

paid for. She'd never cared about his money. She'd only ever cared about him. And now about her baby.

If she left, her baby would get nothing. But it wasn't about money. It was about recognition.

Her own childhood had been blighted by her father's complete refusal to have anything to do with her. It had hurt her so deeply that she'd even married a man who didn't love her to spare her baby that same heartache. Staying with Vito was the best way for her to try to get through to him. He was her baby's father—and there must be some way she could prove it to him.

'Good bye, Mum.' Lily leant forward to kiss her mother's cheek as they reached the front of the queue to go through security at Marco Polo Airport.

'Passport…boarding pass…' Ellen double-checked she was holding the crucial documents, then turned to give Lily a final hug. 'Congratulations again, darling. And thank you for having me.'

'You're welcome.' Lily smiled as warmly as she could and returned her hug.

'Oh, I'd better go!' Ellen gasped, realising she was holding up the queue. She clutched the roll of Venetian marbled paper that she hadn't wanted to crush in her suitcase and grabbed the handle of her wheelie carry-on bag.

'Thanks for coming!' Lily called.

As she stood watching her mother disappear into the departure lounge, an unpleasant feeling of emptiness crept over her. She loved her mum, but under the circumstances Ellen's visit to Venice had been tough on Lily.

Living with Vito after she had discovered the truth about his plans had been difficult. And her mother's presence hadn't made it any easier.

After their horrible row, when he'd admitted he considered their marriage temporary, things had slipped back into their previous routine disconcertingly fast. Vito had kept his distance, and Lily had not wanted to rock the boat. She instinctively knew that it would be better for her to bide her time. Starting fresh arguments with Vito was not the way to prove her innocence to him, so that he would eventually accept that he was the father of her baby.

In the end Lily had invited her mother for a few days, knowing that it was a hurdle she still had to get over. It had turned out easier than expected to convince Ellen that everything was as it should be. But, although she should have been relieved, the fact that her mother had accepted her situation so readily bothered her.

They'd never been particularly close. Ellen was nervous and highly strung—difficult to really get to know properly. When she was a child Lily had been upset by the time and effort her mother had always put into her craft projects with the patients at the hospice—while she'd forgotten to attend school events or even to buy groceries for dinner.

As she grew up Lily had told herself it was just the way her mother coped. She was disappointed with her life, and felt vulnerable being in a position of dependence on a man who was ashamed of her and wanted to keep her existence a secret.

But now Lily was feeling vulnerable. Although she knew she could not confide in Ellen, the fact that her own mother had had no inkling that anything was wrong hurt her feelings.

At first she'd mentally made excuses for her. Having stayed firmly in the countryside for years, it was natural that Ellen had been overcome by Venice. She'd wanted to spend the whole time doing touristy things. In particular she'd been fascinated by the traditional Venetian masks that were on sale all over the place.

She'd talked non-stop about new ideas for her crafting projects, and it hadn't been hard for Lily to remain virtually unnoticed. There'd been no need for her to fend off questions about why she'd married so suddenly, or about why Vito was never around. Despite the fact that it was *her* life that had suddenly changed so dramatically—and *she* was the one her mother had come to visit—she'd started to feel like the invisible woman.

She sighed as her mother disappeared into the airport departure-lounge. She couldn't help being pleased she was gone. Quite honestly, having her mother around had made her feel more alone than ever.

She turned and headed across the concourse to follow the path back down to the water, where Vito's boat was waiting for her. It was June, and a plane full of Swiss tourists had just arrived at the airport. They were all pulling their cases down the same walkway to get a water bus or taxi, but with no luggage to hold her up Lily weaved her way quickly through them. She wasn't anxious to be back at the *palazzo*, but she'd promised she'd visit Giovanni before lunch.

Vito cut the connection to his assistant and slipped his mobile phone back into his pocket.

He was pleased to have confirmation that Ellen had left Venice, but he was bothered by the news that Lily had gone straight from the airport to *Ca' Salvatore*.

Before her mother's visit Lily had started going to see his grandfather every day, and now that her mother was gone it seemed that she was getting straight back into the same pattern. Giovanni enjoyed her visits, so Vito had not put a stop to them. But it concerned him, not knowing what game Lily was playing.

After their argument he had half expected her to try to leave him. But if anything she seemed to settle into her life in Venice with more determination. He didn't know what she thought she'd gain by making a friend of the old man, but it wouldn't do her any good. Vito was still calling all the shots.

'Ah, my beautiful English Lily,' Giovanni said, pushing himself up against the ornate carved headboard.

'I hope you haven't been waiting,' Lily said, hurrying across the room to help him with his pillows.

'I always wait for you.' Giovanni smiled, and Lily knew it wasn't a reprimand. Over the last few weeks, her visits to *Ca' Salvatore* had become a daily event that they both enjoyed.

However, during her mother's stay she'd only popped in once, briefly. It had been clear that the instant rapport she'd shared with Giovanni was not present between her mother and the old gentleman.

'My mum is flying home today.' Lily glanced at her watch. 'In fact, she's probably on a plane right now.'

'That's good,' Giovanni said. 'Now you can spend more time with your husband.'

Lily blinked and stared at him, momentarily lost for words.

'I'm old,' Giovanni said. 'I don't have the time to pussyfoot around, watching what I say.'

'Did you ever, even when you were young?' Lily laughed, despite the fact his instruction to spend more time with Vito had unsettled her. She liked Giovanni, and couldn't ever imagine being offended by him, no matter how directly he spoke. But of course he didn't know—he could *never* know—the truth behind her marriage to Vito.

'Hmm.' He pretended to pause and think. 'Not so much.' He flashed a winning smile at her, momentarily taking years off his age. 'But I'm serious.'

'Vito's been very busy,' Lily prevaricated, letting her gaze drift across the fabulous fresco that decorated the wall. 'Work…'

'I can see you love him, and that he loves you.' Giovanni spoke with assurance. 'But there is tension between you.'

'Well…' Lily's words dried up because she had no idea how to respond. Giovanni had seen love where there simply wasn't any. Vito's feelings for her were obviously the complete opposite of love—he'd made that plain enough. And, although she had once foolishly believed she was falling in love with him, now, after the awful things he'd said and the dreadful way he'd treated her, she'd be crazy to open her heart to him again.

'*You* must fix it now,' Giovanni said. 'My grandson is a good man. But he is proud. He won't make the first move.'

'I'll talk to him,' Lily promised, because there was nothing else she could say.

Lily walked through the twisting maze of alleys, past the fabulous jewellery shops and Venetian trinket-stores, deep in thought.

Even her favourite *gelateria*, which she often stopped at on her way home, did not catch her attention. Even though she was hungry, and ice cream was one of her favourite foods, she didn't feel like eating. She was thinking about the promise she'd made to Giovanni.

She was also thinking about her mother.

Living her life according to Reggie Morton's rules had taken a terrible toll on Ellen. She'd lost her confidence and her independence. Finally she'd become so scared of life that she'd buried herself in project after project, which in turn had left her preoccupied and unable to have a proper relationship with her daughter.

That was what scared Lily the most. She loved her mother, and knew that she was loved in return, but Ellen hadn't even realised that Lily was facing the biggest crisis of her life. There was no way that she was going to let her child grow up like she had—with no father, and with a mother who'd had her spirit eroded away to the point where she couldn't communicate meaningfully with her daughter.

Lily had married Vito for the sake of her baby. Nothing had changed about that. But Vito still refused to acknowledge the baby and, if she didn't do something to make him see the truth soon, before she knew it she'd be out on her own again with no further chance to talk to him.

She took a deep breath and steeled herself to have a proper conversation with Vito—whether he wanted to or not.

Vito was late home from the office that night. He opened the door of the bedroom quietly, expecting to see Lily lying still as a mouse in bed and pretending to be asleep. Instead he was surprised to see her sitting in a comfortable chair, reading one of her paperback books. She put the book aside and stood up immediately, automatically smoothing her hands down the lightweight fabric of her cappuccino-coloured dress.

'We need to talk,' she said, pushing her sleek blonde hair behind her and straightening her shoulders.

'What about?' Vito crossed the room without breaking his stride and tossed his jacket onto a chair.

'About us,' Lily said. 'About our marriage.'

'There's *no* "us",' he said curtly.

'But there is *our* baby,' Lily said.

'I thought you understood never to make that claim again.' Vito reached up and tugged his silk tie off jerkily. He could feel his anger at her betrayal rising once more. 'I won't tell you again.'

'Why won't you give me a chance?' She sounded calm, but Vito could see the colour warming her cheeks.

'Because you betrayed me.'

'When you proposed you said it was for the baby's sake,' she appealed to him. 'But that was a lie. You know how horrible it was for me, always knowing my father didn't want me. How can you do that to your own baby? It's unforgivable.'

'It's *not* my baby,' Vito grated.

The heartfelt emotion in her voice scratched down his nerves like nails on a chalkboard. *She* was the one who had done the unforgivable. Everything he had done was for his family—for his grandfather's sake.

'I don't know what else to say to convince you.' Lily stared at him, a feeling of helplessness suddenly looming up through her misery.

If she could never prove her innocence to him, what was the point of her staying in Venice? Had she made a mistake staying so long?

Should she give up the fight to make Vito realize he *was* the father of her baby, go back to London, and see if her old boss, Mike, would let her try out for that job? If only she hadn't given up the opportunity when it had been available to her.

'Don't say anything,' Vito said. He was studying her

in return, and she could see the tension evident in every plane of his face. 'I keep telling you that.'

'I just wish there was something I could do to make you believe that I wasn't unfaithful,' she said. 'If only I knew *why* you think you're not the father…'

His blue eyes were cast into shadow by brows that were drawn low, but she saw a flash of emotion suddenly flare within them. Emotion so raw it was as painful to witness as it must have been to feel. Then, as she stared up at him, a muscle started pulsing stubbornly beneath the dark stubble on his jawbone.

Without thinking she lifted her hand to touch his face.

A shock wave of sexual awareness surged through her, and she snatched her hand back. But not before she'd seen an answering glint in Vito's eyes.

'Can't we move past this anger and mistrust?' she asked, trying to speak calmly, despite the way her heart was beating out a furious tattoo in response to the sizzling energy that was suddenly flowing between them. 'We can't go back in time and alter what's already happened between us—but we could try to get along. Maybe then you'll be able to trust me again.'

Perhaps she was being too honest, too open about her desire to see Vito acknowledge his child. But it was dishonesty and lies that had led them to this impasse, where it seemed impossible to get through to him, and pointless for her to stay with him.

'What are you doing now?' Vito asked, his sensual lips spreading into a predatorial smile. 'You failed to convince me with your emotional appeal, so now you're trying to tempt me with another more basic form of persuasion?'

'No, I'd never do that!' Lily gasped, feeling her cheeks flame as she realised what Vito was implying.

'You're not offering sex as a way to manipulate me?' He stepped closer and lifted his hand to mimic Lily's earlier action. Except when a frisson leapt between them he didn't withdraw his hand—he pushed it further, slipping his fingers deep into her silky hair.

A shiver skittered through Lily as her body responded instantly to Vito's touch. But she couldn't let him continue to think the worst about her in every way.

'All I meant was maybe we could try to patch things up between us, find a way to build bridges. End the hostility between us.'

'I'd like to build bridges,' Vito said, sliding his free hand around her waist, and pulling her hard up against him so that she could feel his erection pushing against her. She knew what kind of bridge between them he wanted to build—and she wanted it too.

'No, that's not what this is about,' Lily said, despite the way her body was trembling with sudden, urgent desire for Vito. 'I'm just trying to find a way we can reach a truce—find a way to communicate.'

'You're right—we always communicated best through sex,' Vito murmured, leaning close so that his words tickled her ear. He paused to push her blonde hair aside and pressed his lips against the sensitive skin of her neck.

'That's not what I meant.' She drew in a shuddering breath and tried to keep her voice steady as she spoke, but it was difficult with Vito's tongue flicking a delicious trail down towards her collarbone.

'It doesn't matter what you meant,' Vito said, putting both arms around her. 'It's what you want. What we both want.'

'Yes.' Lily couldn't fight the tide of rising passion any longer. She didn't want to fight any more. She closed her eyes and leant into his embrace.

Anticipation coiled deep within her and, almost without conscious thought, she lifted her arms to loop them about his neck and tilted her face towards him. He responded in a heartbeat, bringing his mouth down over hers.

His tongue swept past her open lips and she felt herself start to melt in his arms. She kissed him back, revelling in the sinuous feel of his tongue against hers, marvelling in the glorious flood of sensations that washed through her body.

She lifted her hands to cup his face, and gently caressed his stubbled jawline with her fingertips. The feel of his masculine features beneath her fingers was intoxicating. She wanted to touch him all over, run her hands over his body in a way that she knew would drive him mad with desire—but not before she had driven herself wild with growing need.

She pulled back from his kiss breathlessly, and gazed up into his gorgeous face through a haze of longing. He was still holding her close, his hands buried deep in her long, loose hair, and for a moment she was lost in the darkening depths of his blue eyes. Then in one smooth movement he took hold of her zip and pulled it all the way down her sensitive spine.

She shivered in response, waiting to feel his hands slip inside her dress and caress her back, but instead he brought his hands up to ease the dress off her shoulders and pull the front down so that her lacy bra was revealed.

'Your breasts are even fuller,' Vito murmured, tracing their shape through the lace then reaching behind her to undo the fastening.

'A little, I think,' Lily agreed, hearing the breath catch in her throat as Vito cast the flimsy undergarment away. He guided her backwards and pushed her down so that she was sitting on the edge of the bed. Then he knelt between her knees and took one tingling nipple into his hot mouth.

'Oh!' Lily cried out. Either pregnancy had made her breasts even more sensitive than usual, or her body had gone too long without Vito's exquisite attention. But, whatever the case, wonderful sensations swirled out from her breasts, filling her body with a mounting, shuddering need for more.

As if he sensed her need—which of course he did, Vito always seemed to know exactly what her body craved—he pressed in further between her legs, and lifted the skirt of her dress up over her hips.

His tongue was still moving deliciously against one hard nipple, filling her with wonder at the incredible feelings he was creating. She hardly noticed when, without breaking away, he tugged her briefs down and tossed them to one side.

A second later he released her nipple and dropped down between her legs.

'Vito!' Lily gasped as she realised what he was doing, but at that moment his mouth came into contact with her most intimate feminine flesh.

It wasn't the first time he had kissed her there, had worked his tongue so expertly against the tingling epicentre of her desire. But her body had never responded with such an instant maelstrom of overwhelming sensation.

Her breath was suddenly coming in short, panting gasps and every conscious thought was driven from her mind. All she was aware of was a building crescendo of hot, demanding passion. It was almost too much to bear—but at the same time she couldn't get enough of it.

She writhed beneath his mouth, trying to lift her hands to hold onto his head, but her arms were caught up in a tangle of fabric, still trapped in the sleeves of her dress. There was nothing she could do but lose herself on the spiralling rush of sensation that was surging through her.

Vito lifted his hands to cup her breasts and she cried out again, letting herself fall backwards onto the bed, as wave after wave of pure bliss crashed over her and through her, carrying her on and on in an orgasm that was more powerful than any she had experienced before.

But it wasn't over yet. She had barely floated down from the pinnacle when Vito was moving over her. Somehow he had divested himself of his clothes and he lifted her further up the bed, freeing her arms in the process.

He positioned himself above her, then without hesitation he plunged deep into her already quivering body.

A sound she didn't recognise moaned from her lips, and she gave herself over once again to a miracle of extraordinary pleasure. She lifted her knees and tilted her hips, desperate to feel his hard flesh filling her to capacity. She clung onto him, his muscled shoulders bunching beneath her fingers as he rocked backwards and forwards.

Vito's head dipped against her neck, and she could feel his breath coming in hot, harsh bursts in time with every powerful thrust. Her own breathing was also keeping time with his strong rhythm—high, panting moans that revealed just how lost she was on the rush of uninhibited passion that was storming her body.

Her inner muscles were clenching hard around him, sensation was bursting through her, and once again she felt herself tipping over the edge of utter, all-consuming pleasure.

'Vito!' She cried out his name, then she felt her breath catch in her throat and she was sobbing, saying his name over and over again.

Her head was thrown back against the pillow and her eyes were squeezed shut, but tears were flowing freely down her face as her body trembled in the throes of another orgasm that seemed to go on for ever.

Then suddenly she heard a shout as Vito came to his climax. He reared up above her, his body stopping still for a long moment. Then he shuddered mightily as he reached his own release.

It took a long time for Lily to come back down to earth. She had never experienced anything so intense before, or responded so quickly and wildly to Vito's love-making.

There'd been hardly any foreplay. She hadn't needed it—or even wanted it. With just one touch she had been ready for him, bursting with desire, desperate for him to make her his again.

He was lying next to her quietly, and as she turned her head she saw he was looking at her. His blue eyes caught hers, and an instant shiver ran through her.

'Was that too rough?' he asked, rolling onto his side and placing his hand gently on her stomach.

Lily frowned, startled when she realised what he meant, and instinctively lifted herself up onto her elbows to look down at her own body. It was a surprise to see the ruin of her dress bunched up and crushed around her waist. It wasn't doing anything to cover her and, in a strange sort of way, it made her naked breasts and the exposed apex at the top of her legs appear even more wanton.

'No, I don't think so,' Lily said. Her eyes were fixed on his large bronzed hand resting lightly on her small, neat bump. She couldn't see his fingers properly as the crumpled dress was obscuring them, but she could feel the heat of his palm against her skin, and it was reawakening her sensual response to him.

'Are *you* all right?' Vito brought his gaze back up to her face, and he lifted his hand to brush her tear-stained cheek.

'Yes,' Lily said stiffly. She suddenly felt exposed and vulnerable in front of Vito. Of course he knew how powerfully she had responded to his love-making, and she was all too aware of how her body was already starting to sing again with renewed desire for him.

'You never cried before,' he said, smoothing her hair back from her damp face.

She stared at him with wide eyes, suddenly realising a momentous truth. She had tried to shut her heart to him—but her body had always remained true to her deeper feelings. It had opened to him, yearned to be one with him.

Because she loved him.

Despite everything, she had never stopped loving him. And if she didn't do something to hide it from him Vito would soon realise the humiliating truth as well.

'Maybe I missed sex,' she quipped, trying to keep her voice as light as her words. 'Or maybe it's pregnancy. They say pregnancy makes you hot.'

Her flippant response was out of character, and she tensed up inside, waiting to see if Vito would challenge her. But how well could he really know her, if he still believed she had been unfaithful to him?

'You were always hot.' In a flash he was kneeling over her, taking hold of her crushed dress and pulling it down over her hips. 'That's better—this is how I like you best. Totally naked, apart from your glorious curly hair.'

'I thought you liked it straightened.' Lily forced herself to reply even though she was crying inside. All he saw was a naked woman to share his bed. All she saw was the man who would never return her love. 'I always straightened it for you.'

'Why?' Vito asked. He rolled onto his back and lifted her astride him so that her long, loose hair tumbled down over her shoulders and pooled on his broad chest. 'What made you think that?'

'Something you said—a compliment you paid me,' Lily replied, remembering one of their early dates when, despite his reluctance to behave like a tourist in his own city, he had taken her on a gondola. He had pulled her into his arms and run his hands through her hair, saying it was as smooth as spun gold and looked like a liquid sunrise reflected in the lagoon on a glorious winter dawn.

'I don't remember.' Vito's dismissive words cut into her like a knife. She had made a habit of straightening her hair based on cherished words of flattery he had spoken to her. But it had all been meaningless to him. 'This is how I like it now,' he continued. 'Wild and wanton, like you.'

Lily looked down, letting her hair fall forward to shield her expression.

She'd just realised the most monumental fact—she loved Vito. And yet at every turn she saw again and again just how little she meant to him.

'We have a lot of time to make up for.' The words caught in Lily's throat, but she hoped he'd mistake her shaky tone for rising passion. If she was going to survive in this marriage she had to find a way to shield her heart and her true feelings from him.

'What do you want to do now?' Vito asked, running his hands over the curve of her hips and snuggling her closer to his erection.

'No more talking,' Lily said, dipping her body forward to run her tongue over the sensitive skin of his throat. Her nipples tightened as they brushed against his chest, and desire was already building within her, mercifully blotting out the pain in her heart.

She couldn't bear to hear any more words that made her realise how little she'd meant to him, even back when she'd thought they were happy. Before he believed she'd betrayed him.

He had been everything to her. He still was.

CHAPTER NINE

LILY was still asleep the following morning as Vito dressed for work. He moved quietly around the room so that he didn't disturb her. It was the first time since he'd brought her back to Venice that he'd seen her in a really deep sleep. Most mornings when he'd got ready for work she'd already been up. And most evenings, even if she'd been in bed pretending to be asleep, she'd been restless.

She made a small sound and rolled over, reaching above her head to flip the pillow over, then snuggled back down, surrounded by a wild mass of long blonde curls.

Vito smiled, recognising the action. Even in her sleep she liked the cold side of the pillow. She was such a warm-blooded creature that she always liked cool things. Iced water, ice cream. And now that she was pregnant it was like a tiny furnace was glowing inside her. He wondered how she would cope as the summer heated up. He'd take her away to his estate on the Veneto plain. Or even up to his retreat in the Dolomite mountains. But he'd need to keep her medical care in mind— he couldn't allow anything to happen to her or the baby.

He gazed down at her. Possibly for the first time in months he really let himself look, safe in the knowledge that she was oblivious to his attention. She was lying on her side with one knee drawn up and the other leg stretched out. She looked like a graceful gazelle, frozen at the height of an elegant leap.

An unexpected feeling prickled through him, and he acknowledged it for what it was: he'd missed Lily, missed what he thought they'd had together before he'd discovered her betrayal.

This marriage was all about doing what was right for his grandfather—Giovanni deserved to reach the end of his life knowing that his legacy would go on.

But if things continued like last night—their love-making had been nothing short of incendiary—it was going to be much more pleasant than he'd thought when they were still at daggers drawn.

Lily slept late that morning, and when she awoke her body was filled with the languid glow of complete sensual satisfaction. She rolled over and stretched, noticing the time with surprise. But, after the utter lack of inhibition she'd shown with Vito the night before, she was pleased he'd already left for work. She wasn't entirely sure that she was ready to face him yet.

She made her way to the *en suite* and ran herself a deep, luxurious bath. With her hair piled haphazardly on top of her head, she lay back in the soft bubbles and thought about what had happened with Vito. She could feel a blush rising to her cheeks as she remembered how wildly she'd behaved with him. His touch had sent her up in flames. They'd made love before—many, many times. But it had never been so intense.

Maybe that had been her body's way of letting her know that she loved him.

Up until last night her mind had certainly rejected that possibility, after the way he had treated her. But perhaps it was impossible to change the reality of her deeper feelings simply by telling herself what she ought to believe. Her heart still knew the truth.

However, she knew that loving him made her vulnerable. A small sigh escaped her as she stepped out of the bath onto the marble mosaic floor. She must *never* let him guess the depth of her feelings.

She dried herself briskly and set about getting dressed for her visit to Giovanni. She liked to wear something nice for him. He didn't see many people, and he often complimented her on her appearance.

Suddenly she caught sight of herself in the mirror, and stopped and stared. Her eyes were shining brightly, her cheeks were flushed, and her hair was bouncing wildly about her shoulders in a riot of curls.

She couldn't visit Giovanni looking that that! The sharp-witted old man would guess immediately what had caused such a change in the way she looked. She'd simply feel too self-conscious—like a deflowered virgin the morning after her wedding night, wondering if everyone knew what she had just experienced for the first time.

She sat down at the dressing table and pulled her ceramic straighteners from the drawer. Then she hesitated. Vito had said he liked her hair curly. If she straightened it again, it would seem like she was making the point that she didn't care about his opinion. But, on the other hand, she definitely didn't want to make it appear that she would do anything to please him—she'd already been down that route when she'd started straightening her hair because of an apparently meaningless comment he didn't even remember making.

In the end she did her hair in the same smooth style she'd worn since returning to Venice. She was already late for Giovanni, and she couldn't let herself waste time worrying about silly details. She had more important things to concern her, like whether the old man would ask her straight out if she'd managed to ease the tension that he had detected between her and Vito.

As it turned out she need not have worried. Giovanni was tired that day and spent most of her visit dozing. When he was awake he told her about the great flood of 1966. It had been more than forty years ago, but his memories were sharp and his descriptions vivid as he told her how the sea level had risen by two metres, washing right through the ground floor of *Ca' Salvatore*, and causing untold damage to the city.

Walking back home to the *palazzo*, Lily reflected on her new friendship with Giovanni. He was old, and according to his doctors did not have long to live, but Lily was so grateful for the time she was able to spend with him. He had accepted her so warmly into his family, and his personal stories about his life and the city that had always been his home meant a lot to her.

Whatever happened with Vito, in years to come she would tell her child how happy Giovanni had been, knowing his grandchild was on the way. She would remember the stories he had told her, so that her child would know about his or her Italian family—even if Vito still refused to acknowledge them.

Vito paced back and forth across his study impatiently. He'd come home to see Lily, but she hadn't returned from her daily visit to his grandfather.

She was late. And he wanted to see her now.

He'd spent the morning totally distracted, until finally he'd given into his desire to come home and ravish her.

Sex with Lily had always been good, but last night they had taken it to a new level. It had been utterly mind-blowing, and he hadn't been able to stop thinking about it all morning. Thinking about doing it again and again.

He strode over to the window, cursing himself for his lack of control.

Why was he letting Lily get to him so badly? Was it simply that he'd been too long without a woman, and now last night had reminded his body what it had been missing?

He looked at his watch, wondering again what time she would return. Perhaps he should go out in search of her, but although *Ca' Salvatore* wasn't far away there were several routes she could take home.

Suddenly he found himself questioning why she kept visiting Giovanni even though she knew there was no future in it. What did she hope to gain, either for herself or for her child?

He hadn't stopped her visits because his grandfather seemed to really enjoy them. But it puzzled him that Lily genuinely seemed to enjoy them too.

She wasn't like the other women he'd known. That was part of what had attracted him to her in the first place.

She really didn't seem interested in his wealth and status. Spending time together was all she'd ever really wanted from him.

The thought troubled him, but he pushed it to the back of his mind. He sat down at his desk and opened his laptop, determined to get himself back under control.

It was later than usual when Lily got home. As she climbed the stairs to the first floor of the *palazzo*, a strange feeling prickled down her spine, as if she was being watched.

'I've been waiting for you.'

Startled, despite the fact her senses had warned her Vito was close, she stopped mid-step and looked up to see him standing outside his study.

The sight of him lounging nonchalantly against the door-jamb, oozing self-assurance and sex appeal from every inch of his incredible body, sent her pulse racing. Her breath caught in her throat and she felt butterflies start to flutter wildly in her stomach.

'I've been to see your grandfather.' The words sounded husky and she swallowed, determined to keep her cool, even though her body and mind were suddenly beset by vivid memories of their wild love-making the night before.

'How was he?' His silky Italian accent shimmied straight through her defences, and her composure started to dissolve immediately.

'Fine, but very tired. He told me all about the flood.' She started walking up the stairs towards him, and although she tried she simply couldn't drag her eyes away from him standing in the doorway.

She watched him remove the jacket of his dark suit and loosen his tie. The effect was alarmingly dynamic—as if he didn't intend to keep his immaculate appearance for long. As if he meant business—a different kind of business from usual.

He combed his fingers through his black hair, sweeping it back from his perfectly proportioned face. His skin was lightly bronzed, and he looked the embodiment of health and vigour.

His blue eyes were intense, locked in his unbroken appraisal of her. She felt her skin warming in response to his gaze, yet despite that warmth a shiver began at the nape of her neck and tingled all the way down her backbone.

She reached the top step and still he towered over her,

shamelessly occupying her personal space. In a moment
of nervousness she thought she should carry on walking,
move past him, but it was strangely difficult to move—
or be aware of anything other than Vito. The heat of his
body burned through her dress, the sound of his breathing caressed her ears.

Maybe this was *his* personal space, she pondered
vaguely. It was his scent that enclosed her, his scent that
she pulled deep inside her with every breath she drew.

The potent mix of raw masculinity laced with his
exotic cologne, the very essence of the man himself, was
making her feel dizzy. She found herself swaying.

His hands closed on her waist. The impact was
instant. His sharp intake of breath told her he felt it
too—like a surge of electricity zinging between them.
He lifted her up the final step and stood her directly
before him.

Her head fell back and her eyes widened as she
looked up at his face, only inches from her own. His
eyes narrowed as his gaze swept over her, settling possessively on her mouth, conveying his thoughts with
devastating certainty.

She was breathing quickly in small, shaky bursts
through slightly parted lips. Her tongue peeked out
treacherously, moistening lips that were already red,
and tingling in willful anticipation of his kiss, betraying her needs to him.

'I came home to make love to you.'

His words seared through her like a liquid fire,
melting the last of her defences, whipping up the flames
of her desire. She stared up at him with wide eyes,
knowing that just how much she wanted him must be
written all over her face.

Suddenly he stepped backwards, pulling her into his

study with him. The door banged shut and he turned the key. Then he brought all his attention back to her.

'I couldn't get last night out of my mind,' he said, tugging her close to him.

'I thought about it too.' Lily's voice wavered. His hands had already found the tiny pearl buttons that fastened the front of her dress and he was making quick work of them.

'It was incredible,' Vito said, gripping the hem of her dress and pulling it straight over the top of her head. He tossed the garment aside, then his hands were on her naked skin, sweeping across her body in a way that set her trembling deep inside.

Lily gazed at him through a growing haze of sexual excitement. He was utterly gorgeous and he was going to make love to her. Her heart was racing and her legs felt weak. Just like last night, all it had taken was the merest touch and her body was on fire for him again.

She lifted her hands, tugging distractedly at his clothing. He knew what she wanted, and within moments he was standing naked before her.

Her eyes roamed greedily over his magnificent body, revelling in his pure masculine perfection, before being drawn inexorably to the proud thrust of his erection.

She wanted to touch. Needed to touch. Without a conscious decision she reached for him and her fingers coiled around his hard, jutting flesh.

'Lily!' He closed his eyes and a deep, feral sound rumbled from within his chest. Then, never taking her eyes off his face, she began to move her hand in the way she knew he liked.

His breathing changed immediately, and he dragged air into his lungs in an uneven rhythm through parted lips. His head had dipped to one side, letting his fringe fall forward, and she saw his tongue flick against his teeth.

Suddenly she ached to kiss him. Without letting go of him, she stepped closer. Then, standing on tiptoes, she pulled his head down to hers.

He kissed her hungrily, his tongue plunging into her mouth with an erotic intimacy, and all the while she was aware of her hand caressing him, felt his reaction to the movement of her fingers through his kiss.

Suddenly he pulled away, gasping for breath, and gripped her wrist to still her hand.

'No more. Not now.' His voice was as laboured as his breathing, and she knew what he meant. He wanted this to last for both of them.

Almost reluctantly she uncoiled her fingers, but then he pulled her close and spun her round in front of him, so that he could lift her hair out of the way and kiss the back of her neck.

'You are so beautiful,' he murmured, before tracing the edge of her ear with his tongue.

She trembled and leant back against him, the skin of her back pressed against the skin of his chest. And the whole time she was acutely conscious of the length of his erection behind her.

'Look in the mirror,' he murmured. 'See what I see.'

She lifted her eyes and stared at their reflection in his large mirror. He was behind her, curled over her possessively, and she was standing in her lacy bra and briefs surrounded by a shimmering curtain of blonde hair.

Suddenly his hands began to slide around to the front of her body.

It was a strange sensation to feel and watch at the same time as his large bronzed hand slipped beneath the lace of her bra. Her nipple tightened to a hard point against his palm, then suddenly he eased the stretch-lace down so that her breast came free of the bra cup.

She gasped as erotic feelings flooded through her. Supported and lifted underneath, her breast thrust proudly towards the mirror, the nipple a pert, rosy bud that drew the eye.

'Is that uncomfortable?' he asked, his breath tickling her ear so that she shivered and tilted her head towards him.

'No.' She shook her head, aware of her breast, of the way her nipple felt supercharged with the aching need to be touched.

His hand slipped beneath her other breast, lifting it out of the bra cup as well. Now both breasts were pointing shamelessly towards the mirror, tight and tingling with the need to feel Vito's hands on them.

She didn't have to wait any longer. Vito brought his palms up to knead them both gently in a way that made her moan and arch back in encouragement. When his fingers teased her nipples she gasped and closed her eyes, pressing her head back against his shoulders.

'Look in the mirror,' he whispered huskily. 'You are so beautiful.'

She opened her eyes in time to see his right hand release her breast and slide downwards, across her stomach, then lower still.

She held her breath, pure sexual excitement coursing through her as she anticipated his masterful touch. Her skin was flushed, and she could see a wild light in her eyes. Then his fingers slipped beneath the lace of her briefs, quickly locating the centre of her desire, and she was lost on a sudden rush of sensation.

It an instant her body was engulfed by marvellous feelings that pulsed right through her. She moaned, leaning back against his strong chest, and he continued to caress her, sending her higher and higher.

She rocked her hips, moving jerkily against his hand

as the feelings became increasingly intense. She twisted in his arms, almost as if she wanted to get away. But that was the last thing she wanted. He'd carried her up to the brink. And now she needed the ultimate release from the pressure building within her.

As if to prove how perfectly in tune their bodies were, he let her go for a moment to pull her briefs down. Then he bent her over his huge leather topped desk.

She barely had time to register his intention when she felt him pressing close behind her. Her legs were slightly apart, and she let herself flop forward so that her forearms were resting on the desk. He took hold of her hips to steady her, and with one expert thrust was inside her.

Her breath whooshed out of her as a sudden rush of pleasure washed through her. She felt alive and tingling in every part of her body. But as he started to move, pulling out and stroking back in, she was soon lost on a rising tide of overwhelming sensation.

Her heart was racing beneath her breast and her blood was singing in her ears. There was no room for conscious thought as her body was overtaken by the incredible experience of feeling Vito moving inside her.

She leant on the desk, resting her head on her arms, buried in a cascade of blonde hair. Vito was holding her from behind, tugging her close so they were joined as tightly as possible on each thrust. Her legs were as weak as water, but she didn't realise that Vito was holding her up.

She was only aware of the marvellous upward spiral of growing ecstasy within her, until suddenly she reached the pinnacle and her world exploded in a beautiful, climatic release.

With a perfect mastery of timing, Vito followed

straight after her, crying her name, and dragged her tighter still. Then his body shuddered and convulsed with his own powerful orgasm.

Lily lay against his chest on the leather sofa in his study, wrapped in a gorgeous warm glow of sexual satisfaction. She had never expected to come home to such an incredible experience—but she certainly wasn't complaining.

Vito was still naked—as was she, apart from her lacy bra. In a moment of self-consciousness, she had slipped her breasts back inside the cups. But, considering the fact she hadn't replaced her briefs or done anything else to cover her nakedness, she was still feeling amazingly relaxed.

'We've wasted too much time,' Vito said, running his fingertips idly up her long, creamy thigh.

'We can make up for it.' Lily smiled at him shyly. 'Especially if you come home for lunch every day.'

'This isn't my lunch break,' Vito said, letting his gaze slide over her body in a way that made her heart skip a beat. He slipped his hand under her thigh and lifted her leg over his lap, so that once again she was open for his touch. 'I'm not going back to the office today. I've taken the afternoon off.'

Lily looked up at him, amazingly feeling the heat of longing wash through her once more despite the fact that she'd felt totally satisfied a moment ago.

'How can you do that to me, with just a look?' she whispered, aware that a rosy flush of excitement was spreading over her skin again.

'Do what?' he teased, raising one hand to lift a swathe of her long blonde hair back over her shoulder so that her bra was showing. Her nipples jutted jauntily beneath the transparent stretch-lace, as if they were seeking his attention.

'Set me on fire,' she said shakily. 'Make me ache for you with every fibre of my being.'

'Maybe because that's how looking at you affects me too.' He lifted his hands to hold her face tenderly and she looked deep into his blue eyes, knowing that what he said was true.

Right at that second, Lily knew that they had just shared a powerful moment. It felt like the first time they had been totally honest with each other.

She knew it was only about one aspect of their relationship—the physical side. But that was important. She felt so much closer to Vito than she'd felt yesterday. And maybe now they would continue to grow closer still, each time they made love.

'I don't even need to look at you to want you,' Vito said, trailing his fingers deliciously down her collarbone. 'Just thinking about you makes me hard. This morning in the office I couldn't do a stroke of work.'

'Really?' Lily asked shyly. She'd always thought of Vito as totally in control, whatever situation he was in.

'Enough conversation.' Vito's voice was deep and gravelly as he suddenly pulled her round so she was sitting astride him. 'This time I'm going to take it slowly.'

CHAPTER TEN

'THANK you for coming with me,' Lily said. She blinked in the bright light as they left the hospital after her mid-pregnancy scan.

'You don't need to thank me.' Vito held her hand as she stepped down into the boat. 'It was my duty to be there.'

Lily squinted up at him, but she couldn't read his expression through the glare reflected off the water. During the scan he had seemed cold and distant, which was not how he'd been with her generally over the last couple of weeks. Since the night they'd made love things had been so different—much warmer, with almost no tension between them at all.

But that was probably because all they did together was make love, she thought with a hint of sadness. At first she'd been overwhelmed by their new-found intimacy and enjoyment of each other. He was the most amazing, generous lover, and he treated her like a princess.

Just looking at him made her heart skip a beat, and the love that she'd finally admitted she felt for him had continued to grow, like a precious secret in her heart. But as time went by she needed more. She wanted to be able to do more together than have sex.

Of course that was wonderful—but it would also be

wonderful to be able to talk to him, have a proper conversation. She was aware that whenever her comments became more than just pillow talk he found a way to silence her. Perhaps with a kiss, or a caress, or with a suggestion of something exquisite he'd like to do with her willing body.

'Did you mind it when I asked the radiographer the sex of the baby?' She delved in her handbag for her sunglasses. She wanted to be able to look at him properly, to see if she could detect any clue as to how he was feeling after the scan.

'My grandfather will be pleased that you are carrying a boy.' His tone was bland and did not reveal anything about his mood.

She found her sunglasses and put them on, then her eyes came to rest on the scan photos she had tucked carefully into her bag.

'Do you want one of these?' she asked, holding the flimsy pictures tightly, as the boat was moving and a stiff breeze was blowing.

'I'm sure my grandfather would like to see them *all*.' He pulled his mobile phone out of his pocket and switched it on to check if he'd missed any calls or emails while they'd been inside the hospital. 'Put them away to keep them safe.'

Lily gazed at him quietly. His black hair was whipping about and the jacket of his suit was billowing slightly in the wind—but his face was set in stone. He didn't look angry. In fact he looked completely devoid of emotion.

It must be hard for him, she knew, believing the child inside her was not his. She still didn't know why he thought that, but after the wonderful accord they seemed to have reached lately, at least in the bedroom, it seemed *so* wrong that he still believed something that simply wasn't true.

A few minutes later they were travelling along the Grand Canal. Even though she had been there many times before, Lily couldn't help being impressed by the magnificent array of buildings that edged the water. Recently Giovanni had started to tell her some of the history surrounding many of the important families that had owned the *palazzi* that could be seen from his bedroom window. She'd found it absolutely fascinating.

'It's already late morning, so I thought you might like to stop at *Ca' Salvatore*,' Vito said. 'Unless you're tired and you'd like me to take you home before I go to the office?'

'No, I'd like to visit Giovanni,' Lily said. 'I want to see his face when he learns he is to have a great-grandson.' She glanced at Vito, suddenly feeling slightly awkward. The comparison between his grandfather's pleasure and Vito's utter lack of interest was uncomfortably obvious.

'He'll probably start choosing names. Traditional family names, suitable for the newest Salvatore,' Vito said. 'But don't be concerned. We won't name the child anything you are not happy with.'

Lily pushed her hair back off her face and looked at him with interest. Just when she thought he was showing as much emotion and understanding as one of the marble statues at *Ca' Salvatore*, he took her by surprise. It was the first time he'd said anything that showed he took her feelings into account.

'I'd like to choose a name that makes Giovanni happy,' she said. She wasn't worried about Giovanni's choice of names for her son. To tell the truth, it touched her deeply to know that her son was truly wanted by his great-grandfather, and was important enough to be included in the family tradition of names. But in the circumstances it was a bittersweet thought. If only Vito felt the same way as his grandfather.

'I'll be late tonight,' Vito said, jumping out of the boat to offer Lily a steadying hand as she disembarked at the water entrance of *Ca' Salvatore*. 'I have a lot to catch up on.'

Lily watched as the boat eased back out into the traffic on the Grand Canal. She'd felt so happy during the scan, seeing images of her baby. But now a heavy weight of sadness was descending on her.

The past couple of weeks had been wonderful, spending time with Vito again. She had pushed her concerns about the future to the back of her mind, telling herself that the intimacy she had rediscovered with him would help rebuild the trust between them.

But this morning his reaction to the scan had told her nothing had changed. Even the awe-inspiring sight of a tiny baby growing inside her hadn't softened him. By his actions he'd made it very clear that he was just as hard-hearted towards her as ever.

The next few weeks continued in the same way. It seemed impossible for Lily to spend any time with Vito without ending up in his arms.

But she was falling ever more deeply in love with him, and a tiny seed of hope was steadily growing within her heart. If only she could convince him of her innocence maybe things could be genuinely good between them—both in and out of the bedroom.

At last, as her pregnancy advanced, life gradually began to settle into a routine similar to when Lily had first come to Venice to live with Vito. He started taking her out around the city and eating with her in restaurants again, finally giving her the opportunity to talk to him.

But, although it was what she had been hoping so for weeks, she knew she had to be careful to take things slowly, to keep their conversations on neutral ground. She was trying to build the foundations of her unborn baby's life while she had the chance. She couldn't risk ruining everything she was working towards with a rash comment.

Then one evening she was surprised to find herself being guided into Luigi's. It was the first time they had visited the restaurant since their terrible argument when Vito had been horribly suspicious of the kindly restaurateur.

She stiffened unconsciously as they crossed the threshold. It was unbearable that he had brought her here, especially after they had been getting on so well. Luigi was bound to say something, and she didn't know how Vito would react.

'Lily, Vito!' Luigi bundled over to them with an extravagant flourish. 'It is wonderful to see you again after so long.'

'Luigi.' Vito greeted the proprietor of the restaurant with a neutral tone.

'*Mamma mia!* I see congratulations are in order!' he exclaimed as his gaze settled on Lily's very obvious bump.

'Thank you.' Vito guided Lily to her chair and held it for her himself.

'And I am so glad to see you back in Venice after the last time we met,' Luigi said, addressing his first words to Lily. Then he turned to Vito, a protective glint flashing unexpectedly in his eye. 'You must have been so worried, to think that your love was roaming the streets alone that cold, foggy night.'

It was the comment Lily had been dreading. She couldn't stand it. She'd worked so hard to make things right with Vito—for the sake of her unborn son and also for her own future happiness. Suddenly, at that awful moment, it seemed easier to bear the shame herself rather than have Luigi think the worst of Vito.

'It was a silly misunderstanding,' Lily blurted.

'No, it was my responsibility.' Vito spoke calmly and placed his hand over Lily's, which lay trembling on the white-linen tablecloth. 'And I wish to thank you for taking care of Lily when I was remiss.'

'You must be so pleased to have her back,' Luigi said. He still had an assessing look in his eye, making Lily want to move the conversation on as quickly as possible.

'It's—good to be here.' She stumbled over her reply.

'She's my wife now,' Vito added, his voice deep and intense.

'Molte congratulazioni!' Luigi beamed, instantly loosing all of his sternness. He called across to a waiter to bring out a bottle of prosecco.

Lily felt Vito's hand pressing hers, and she lifted her gaze to his face. He looked as drop-dead gorgeous as ever, but she couldn't read his expression. Was he telling her that he believed that she had not been involved with Luigi?

Or was he simply letting her understand that, despite the fact that he believed she had been unfaithful—if not with Luigi, then with some one else—this was all part of the act he was prepared to play to ensure his grandfather's happiness?

But, as glasses of sparkling prosecco were poured, and extravagant Italian toasts to the newlyweds were made, she couldn't dwell on the problem any longer.

* * *

'You look terrible,' Vito said, rushing to help her up the last few stairs and onto the sofa in his study.

'Thanks.' Lily tried to smile, but she really didn't feel very well.

'I'll call the doctor,' Vito said, dropping down onto one knee in front of her to look at her properly.

'There's no need,' Lily said. 'I only went for a check-up two days ago. Everything's fine—it's just I got so hot walking back from *Ca' Salvatore*.'

With a muffled curse Vito shot across the room to the bar area, clunked ice into a tumbler and poured mineral water on top.

'I'm sorry,' he said as he handed the glass to her. 'I should have thought of bringing you something to drink right away.'

'That's all right,' Lily said, touched by his concern. 'The first thing I needed was just to sit down.'

'You shouldn't be walking in this heat,' Vito said. 'You need to rest for a few days. Then, after you are recovered, if you want to visit my grandfather you must go by boat.'

'I don't need a few *days'* rest,' Lily protested. 'I'll be all right by tomorrow. And I need to walk or I won't get any exercise at all, and that can't be good for me.'

'I'm calling the doctor.' From the decisive tone of his voice it was clear that he had already made his mind up. 'I want to know for myself what it is all right for you to do. I won't let you overdo it.'

Lily stared at him in bewildered consternation. At seven months pregnant she could still be working full-time, if she wasn't in the privileged position of being married to a rich man.

'Your ankles are puffy.' Vito knelt down to pull off her

sandals. He sat next to her on the sofa, turned her sideways and lifted her feet up onto his lap. 'Is that normal?'

'I think so,' Lily said as Vito began to stroke gently along her feet, smoothing the slight indentations the straps of her sandals had made, and then massaging up her calves towards her knees. 'Unless it gets too bad. The midwife always checks for it—but I don't know what it means.'

'I'll ask the doctor.'

'Really, I'm fine now,' Lily protested. The glass of water had refreshed her, and she really did feel fine. Better than fine, in fact. The touch of Vito's fingers, which she was certain he meant to be purely comforting, was already doing things to her libido. Her progression well into her third trimester had not done anything to curb her physical desire for Vito. 'But I think I might feel better if I freshen up in the shower.'

Before she realised what he was about, Vito swept her up into his strong arms and, holding her cradled against the broad planes of his chest, carried her upstairs to their bedroom.

He took her through into the *en suite* and set her down on the marble floor. The small mosaic tiles felt deliciously cool under her feet and, as always when she was close to Vito, Lily felt completely aware of her own body. And every inch of her skin or strand of her hair was conscious of Vito—longing to touch or be touched by him.

'Do you need any help?' he asked, and Lily could see from the darkening of his blue eyes that he knew exactly what she needed.

'I'd love some help.' She sucked in a shaky breath as he brushed past her to turn on the shower. Then, bending to take hold of the hem of her loose-fitting summer dress, he pulled it up and straight over her head.

He shed his own clothes quickly, and kicked them out of the door into the bedroom before turning back to her.

'You are so beautiful,' he said, letting his hands caress her seven-month bump as he reached for her lacy underwear.

Lily held onto his powerful shoulders as she stepped out of her briefs. He still showed such adoration of her body, even though her pregnancy was well advanced. And he was very inventive when it came to finding new ways for them to enjoy their love-making despite her changing body. The way he was treating her gave her hope for the future—maybe in time he would come to share her feelings of love.

He reached behind her to unfasten her bra. And then, totally naked, they both stepped into the shower. She sighed as Vito started to smooth exotically scented shower cream over her body. Being with him was incredible.

Later that evening Vito took Lily to his house in the Dolomite mountain-range. As soon as she stepped out of the helicopter she could feel her body relaxing in the cooler atmosphere. Although sometimes it had felt like it, she knew she hadn't really been hot all the time in Venice—the *palazzo* was air-conditioned—but there was something wonderfully refreshing about being in clear mountain air.

'It's incredible,' Lily breathed, gazing at the awe-inspiring view.

'The chalet makes a useful retreat,' Vito agreed. 'And it will be a good place for you to rest.'

'I don't exactly do much in Venice,' Lily protested, turning to look at what she presumed must be Vito's chalet. It didn't look like her idea of a chalet—but then she was thinking of the small, individual holiday-homes she and Ellen had sometimes stayed in while she was growing up. Not an impressive timber building that looked more like an exclusive alpine ski-lodge. 'I'm pregnant—not an invalid.'

'The doctor thought it would be good for you to get out of the city,' Vito said, taking her hand and leading her up the wooden steps to an impressive first-floor balcony that appeared to run right round the building. 'And I agree with him.'

He led her into the first-floor living space, which was laid out to take maximum benefit from the ravishing view that seemed to roll on and on for ever.

'Sit down and rest, while I speak to the housekeeper about dinner.'

Obediently, Lily sunk into a huge comfy armchair. It did feel good to be off her feet, even though she'd only just stepped out of the helicopter. And before that she'd spent most of the afternoon sleeping, until Vito had woken her up to tell her that the doctor had arrived.

He had confirmed that everything was fine, and had said there would be no harm in Lily leaving the city for a while. After he had left, Lily had started to say that there was no need for Vito to disrupt his work routine for her. But then she'd discovered Vito had already packed for her while she'd been asleep.

She knew that once Vito had made up his mind there was no way to change it. And also she was secretly touched that he'd taken the trouble to pack her things himself. Never in her life had anyone packed her suitcase for her. On short breaks away with Ellen, she'd always had to be the responsible one who made sure nothing essential was forgotten.

'I've brought you a drink.' Vito paused in the doorway, holding a glass of iced water in his hand, and watched at her gazing out at the view.

She looked beautiful. There was a gentle glow to her cheeks, and in profile he could see the slightly upturned tip of her delicate nose. Her hair was tied back at the nape of her neck, but long blonde curls had escaped and were coiling prettily around the side of her face.

'Thank you.' She turned to him and smiled, the expression lighting up her already radiant face. Suddenly he was pleased he'd brought her away from the city. He could have her all to himself without any distractions. Soon the child would be born and, although it was the whole point of this marriage, he knew everything would change. Lily would have a new focus in her life, and the pleasant routine they had established would be replaced.

'It seemed a good bet that you'd like a drink—you're always thirsty these days.' He passed her the glass and sat in an armchair, facing her.

'I didn't know about this place,' Lily said, icecubes clinking as she took a long drink of water. 'Do you use it often?'

'For skiing in the winter,' Vito said, grimly remembering how he had spent nearly two weeks after Lily had left at Easter hurling himself recklessly down black runs. 'And it makes a quiet place to get away from it all in the summer. It's not too far—even by road—from Venice.'

'You never brought me here,' Lily said. There was a slight crease between her brows as she gazed out at the view.

'It didn't snow until late this year, and then you had

your stomach bug,' Vito said. 'What we *thought* was a stomach bug,' he amended.

'Oh.' Lily put her hand up to smooth her blonde hair. She hesitated self-consciously, as if she'd just realised it was still a riot of curls after their love-making in the shower. He'd left her sleeping in bed, and then there hadn't been time for her to style it in her usual careful way before they'd left the city.

'I do remember saying I liked your hair smooth,' Vito found himself saying. 'It has a beautiful sheen when you straighten it, almost like polished-gold foil embedded in Murano glass.'

Lily was staring at him, her eyes wide with surprise at his confession.

'Then why did you say you didn't like it straight-ened?' she asked.

'I didn't mean that,' Vito replied, suddenly wishing he hadn't brought the subject up. 'It's just that I prefer it curly.'

'Well, that's good.' Lily put her glass down on the coffee table and stood up to walk across to him. He tilted his head back, looking at her as she perched on the arm of his chair and lifted her hand to run her fingers lightly through his short black hair. 'Because that's how it goes naturally.'

His body responded instantly. It always did. Just looking at her was enough to make him hard with desire. Hell, just *thinking* about her when he was at work was enough. She was gorgeous. Even with her body chang-ing shape, and slowing her down slightly, he still couldn't get enough of her.

'I brought you here to rest.' Looking into her face, he reached up and traced her delicately defined cheekbones with his fingertips. Her eyes glowed with a sultry sexual invitation, and hot desire pulsed through him.

'Then you'd better show me the bedroom,' she said, pulling him to his feet.

Over the next couple of days Lily honestly thought she'd never been so happy in her entire life. She'd made a conscious decision not to let her worries about the future intrude, and she focussed completely on the present, knowing it might be her last opportunity to be truly alone with Vito.

She'd never spent such wonderful, uninterrupted time with him before, and she was revelling in it. As far as she was aware he'd totally ignored his mobile phone and laptop to concentrate entirely on their time together. It was like heaven.

Vito was simply amazing. Attentive to her every need, he looked after her so well, and they visited the most incredible places each day. Then at night he took her in his arms and made wonderful, exquisite love to her.

'You are lucky to have grown up near here.' Lily sighed, rotating on the spot to enjoy the breathtaking panoramic view. Vito had brought her to a beautiful alpine meadow filled with wild flowers for a picnic lunch.

'Sit down and rest,' he instructed, spreading out a blanket on the lush green grass. 'You still have to walk back to the chair-lift.'

'I am feeling it a bit,' Lily admitted, passing her hand over her stomach protectively, then curling her spine forwards and rubbing the small of her back.

'Let me.' Vito dropped down beside her and began to tirelessly rub the exact spot that was aching, right above the base of her spine.

'Oh, that feels good,' Lily murmured, taking a long breath and enjoying the firm, hot pressure of Vito's palm on her back. 'I wish I had the energy to walk down there,' she added, gazing across the incredible landscape to the crystal-clear mountain lake.

'I'll take you tomorrow,' Vito said. 'I know a different route that will involve less walking.'

'You're spoiling me.' Lily turned and looked at him. 'But don't you have to get back to the city?'

'Business can wait.' Vito shrugged. 'Summer will be over soon and, beautiful as this place is in winter, it's not so warm and welcoming for a picnic then.'

'I can't imagine it bleak and windswept, or covered with snow,' Lily said. 'We've had such lovely weather.'

'Let's make the most of it.' Vito opened the hamper he had carried with them, pulling out a bottle of mineral water, some chilled fruit-juice and a mouth-watering array of food that the housekeeper had prepared.

'You know, I don't think we should stay away too long,' Lily said. 'I hate to think of Giovanni with no one visiting him.'

'He has visitors,' Vito replied shortly. 'He wasn't a total recluse before you came.'

'I didn't say he was,' Lily said, upset by the sudden abruptness in Vito's tone. 'Anyway, I thought you were pleased I've been keeping your grandfather company.'

'And I thought you were happy staying here,' Vito said. 'But if you'd rather go home we'll fly back this afternoon.'

'Why does it always have to be all or nothing with you?' Lily voiced her frustration without thinking. She loved the fact that Vito was a strong, decisive man—but sometimes she wished he didn't have to see everything in black and white.

'I don't know what you mean,' he said, briskly passing her a plate of food. Lily took it glumly. Suddenly it didn't look so delicious any more.

'I mean I *have* been happy here—incredibly happy,' Lily said, watching Vito's thunderous face. 'That doesn't stop me thinking about Giovanni. But I didn't mean we have to go back immediately.'

'He has people caring for him twenty-four hours a day.' Vito took a savage bite of bread and stared at the rugged mountains across the valley.

He thought about his grandfather. He owed it to him to make his last days as happy as possible. And, although for some reason it suddenly irked him, he did know how much Giovanni counted on Lily's visits to cheer him up.

He cursed his selfishness at wanting to keep Lily away from the city for his own pleasure. There was nothing for it now. They'd have to return to Venice.

'I love your grandfather,' Lily said unexpectedly, catching his full attention. 'He accepts me and he doesn't judge me.'

'He doesn't know what you've done,' Vito said in a tightly controlled voice, wishing Lily hadn't said something to remind him of her betrayal. 'I *do* know what you've done,' he added. 'But I'm not the one who keeps bringing the subject up. I know the truth.'

'Our son won't grow up knowing his great-grandfather,' Lily said, as if she was wrapped up in her own thoughts and hadn't heard a word he'd said. 'But Giovanni wants him to grow up knowing about his family history—with a real sense of where he came from and where he belongs.'

Vito stared at her, unable to believe that she was still carrying on in the same vein. He felt a muscle start to pulse at his temple, and he clenched his fists, trying to control his rising anger. *Why* would she say things that were bound to make him remember that she had been unfaithful to him?

'I never felt I belonged. My father didn't want me, and my mother could barely cope,' she said. 'More than anything I want our son to know he's truly wanted and loved. Know he belongs with his family.'

Vito gritted his teeth, not trusting himself to speak. Why didn't she seem to care, or even realise, that she was skating on thin ice?

'My grandfather is old now,' Vito said. 'You wouldn't have found him so easy-going in his younger days. He was a formidable man.'

'Of course he was. He still is,' she responded instantly, looking at him sharply. 'It obviously runs in the family.'

'Now that he's old, he knows his time is limited,' Vito continued. 'I believe that has brought his remaining wishes into very sharp focus.'

'I agree,' Lily said. 'I thought that's what we were talking about.'

'We are talking about his desire for a grandson.'

'That's what we are giving him,' Lily said.

'That's what he *thinks* we are giving him.' Vito spoke through gritted teeth. 'The fact that for the sake of my grandfather's happiness I am prepared to publicly accept the child as my own does not mean I have forgotten the truth.'

'Nor have I,' Lily said quietly. She pushed her curly hair off her face with an exasperated gesture.

'I thought we'd got past this,' Vito said. 'The pretence that the baby is mine is for the rest of the world. Don't insult me by acting like *I* don't know the truth.'

'You don't seem to,' Lily said simply. 'And I don't know why you won't give me a chance. I agreed to your wishes not to mention it any more, because I knew there was no chance we'd ever sort things out if we kept arguing. But I thought a bond was growing between us now, and I don't understand why you keep shutting out what I'm saying.'

Vito clenched his fists and dragged in a controlled breath. No matter what he said, she just kept on claiming innocence. It was starting to grate on his nerves. He would not put up with it any more.

'I know he's not mine,' he said. 'Because I know that I can't have children.'

CHAPTER ELEVEN

LILY stared at him in shock. His expression was tightly controlled, but she could see the strain he was feeling by the lines of tension around his blue eyes. Suddenly, despite the fact she *knew* he could father a child, she realised that he really did believe that he couldn't.

'Of course you can,' she said at last. 'You are. I mean, I'm pregnant and you are the father.'

'For God's sake!' Vito exclaimed, surging to his feet and raking his fingers through his short hair. 'It's time to let that ridiculous charade go.'

She looked up at him carefully, trying to see what he was keeping hidden beneath his rigid expression. She was still sitting on the rug in the meadow and he towered over her, his white shirt and black hair outlined by the blue mountain-sky.

A light breeze tugged his fringe forwards, and he scraped it back from his face again with an impatient jerk of his hand. The gesture revealed just how tightly wound he was.

Lily got to her feet, her aching back and increased size making her feel awkward, and stood in front of him. Instinctively, she reached out a hand and placed it on his forearm. The skin was warm and supple beneath her fingers, but his muscles were as hard and immovable as steel.

'I can't let it go, because it's the truth,' Lily said simply.

She saw the change in him instantly and, despite the tight rein his was keeping on his temper, she knew he was about to explode if she didn't say something to defuse the anger that was building in him.

'Why do you think that?' she asked gently. 'Were tests done?'

Vito took a shuddering breath and turned to stare in the direction of the crystal-clear lake. Lily knew he wasn't really seeing the spectacular view. He was deep in his thoughts and memories.

'Capricia and I were unsuccessful when we tried to start a family,' he said, startling Lily with his sudden candour. 'After a time we submitted ourselves to fertility testing.' He paused for a moment, but when he continued Lily could hear the strain crackling in his voice. 'I was the one who could not have children.'

'A mistake must have been made,' Lily said automatically.

'There was no mistake,' Vito said curtly. 'Sit down and eat something. Then we'll pack up and leave.'

He pulled his mobile phone out of the back pocket of his dark jeans and pressed a speed-dial number, presumably for his assistant. Without another glance for Lily, he turned his back and walked away a few steps as he talked, effectively shutting himself off from her.

She sat down on the rug, watching him with a troubled expression. Suddenly everything that had happened was starting to make sense.

He believed that he was infertile—so when she'd become pregnant he'd assumed that she'd been unfaithful. In his mind, that was logical. He thought there was no other way she could have conceived. That explained his anger towards her—but it did *not* excuse it.

If he had told her the truth that Easter weekend, she would have tried to reason with him, persuade him that there'd been a mistake. He could have had the results of his fertility tests double-checked. Obviously there must have been a mix up. Or maybe something had changed. She wasn't an expert on fertility, but she *knew* that she was pregnant, and that he was the *only* one who could be the father.

She looked at him talking on his phone. Standing there with the awe-inspiring backdrop of the Dolomite mountains behind him, he looked as magnificent as the noble terrain. But he was also as cold and uncompromising as those harsh, jagged peaks that soared above the verdant valleys.

She understood that his belief that he could not have children must have hurt him—especially when he was the last surviving man in his proud Italian family. But he had hurt her—throwing her out onto the street when she had done nothing wrong, and then coercing her into a marriage that he'd never meant to be permanent.

He should have told her the truth. Instead he'd misled her—first making her believe she was responsible for birth control that in reality he thought was unnecessary. Then making vicious accusations when she had never, ever given him any reason to doubt her. Then finally, worst of all, he had shamelessly used his knowledge of her troubled childhood to manipulate her.

Suddenly a wave of anger rose up out of nowhere, startling her with its intensity. He'd trusted a medical report over the woman he had shared his life with. He'd never given her a chance.

She stared up at him balefully. He had treated her appallingly, and she had let him get away with it. Well, not any more.

At last he finished his conversation with his assistant, slid his phone back into his pocket and sat down on the rug.

'You haven't eaten,' he said, finally looking at her again.

As she met his gaze a crackle of energy passed between them.

His eyes widened in surprise, and she knew he had recognised the anger that was building inside her.

'When we get back you must have the fertility tests repeated.' The sound of her own voice thrumming with intensity startled her. But she continued to stare him down, determined to make him see that she meant business.

'Why would I subject myself to that humiliation again?' Vito bit out, the planes of his face tightening as he spoke. 'In the circumstances, don't you think it would be better to let sleeping dogs lie? Or are you simply masochistic enough to want incontrovertible proof of your infidelity?'

'I want proof of my innocence!' Lily snapped. 'And, if you won't have those tests repeated, I'll get a DNA test after the baby is born.'

'Are you mad?' Vito demanded. 'If I won't submit to a fertility test, what makes you think I'll be party to a DNA test?'

'I'll go to Giovanni,' Lily declared. 'His DNA will prove a family connection.'

Vito cursed violently in Italian and surged to his feet, hauling her up by her arms.

'You go too far!' His words throbbed with barely contained fury, and suddenly Lily felt herself quaking under the sheer force of his rage. Of course she'd never do anything to hurt Giovanni, but Vito's refusal to listen to reason was driving her to distraction.

Then, with one powerful arm around her waist and one hand gripping her upper arm, he started marching her away, back in the direction of the chair-lift.

Everywhere they made contact she could feel Vito's thunderous energy burning into her body. It felt like she was caught up in an escalating storm, still waiting in trepidation for it to reach its maximum force.

In barely any time they reached the main footpath, and Vito eased his grip slightly as two young male hikers approached them. He hailed them in English, then quickly switched to fluent German as he identified their nationality.

Lily couldn't catch everything he was saying, but, as he thrust a wad of euros their way and pointed back to the abandoned picnic-hamper in the meadow, she understood what had just transpired. Vito was so used to issuing orders and being obeyed that apparently he'd thought nothing of paying the young men to clear away their mess.

She didn't have time to ponder what it must be like to be Vito—so powerful and self-assured that he expected complete strangers to jump to do his bidding—because at that moment he continued walking her briskly towards the chair-lift.

They flew back to Venice in virtual silence, and the days that followed were miserable for Lily. Refusing point-blank to engage in conversation with her, Vito kept well away. He left for work early, returned late at night, and only spoke to her when absolutely necessary.

She felt like she was trapped in a nightmare, and

there was no escape that she could see. At first she thought she must leave Venice—but it wasn't that simple. It wasn't just the gnawing ache that filled her soul at the thought of leaving Vito, there were other things to consider.

Her pregnancy was too advanced for it to be easy to travel, and the idea of arriving in London with a baby due to arrive so soon was frankly terrifying. At least here in Venice she was already under medical care.

And the other thought that kept plaguing her was how devastated Giovanni would be. She knew the baby *was* his true great-grandson—but if she left she didn't know what Vito would tell him. Although she still felt horribly betrayed by how Vito had used her, she shared his desire to make his grandfather happy. So she'd have to wait for the baby to come before she could do anything.

As the days went by, the anger she'd felt towards Vito in the alpine meadow slowly ebbed away, and she was left feeling dejected and lonely.

Time seemed to drag on interminably, sometimes making it feel like she was going to be pregnant for ever. She still had more than a month to go, and she honestly didn't know how she was going to get through it.

She visited Giovanni every morning, travelling on the canals both ways, and in the afternoons she took refuge in her supply of paperback books. She slept a lot. And, in between sleeping, reading and visiting Giovanni, she sat in the baby's nursery, trying not to think about the implications of Vito's stunning revelation that he believed himself to be infertile.

At first it had been like a light switching on in her mind, because it finally explained why he'd assumed she'd been unfaithful. Then she had felt anger at his lack of trust in her. Now she felt something different.

Unwanted.

If Vito hadn't believed himself infertile, *he would never have married her.*

Right from the start she had understood that Vito wasn't interested in a serious commitment to her. At the time it hadn't mattered to her. She'd been overwhelmed just by being with him, and had assumed his 'no commitment' rule was not a reflection of what he thought about her but simply a rule he lived by.

Now she knew differently. It *had been* about her.

She'd been good enough to be his lover, but not good enough to be his wife. Not until he'd seen an opportunity for her to give him, for his aging grandfather, something he thought he couldn't get anywhere else.

And even then it had taken the time pressure of his grandfather's failing health to bring him to his decision. She couldn't forget that when she'd got pregnant he had ruthlessly thrown her out of his life without a second thought.

But, after they were married, she had realised that she loved him. She had clung to the hope that maybe, if she managed to convince him that she had never been unfaithful, he would start to open his heart to her. She had to believe that there was something between them, a tiny little ember that could be brought to life in the right circumstances.

However, now she knew he believed himself to be infertile, all hope seemed to be gone. It really was only circumstance that had prompted him to marry her. Once he discovered he was not infertile there would be nothing tying him to her any more. He could have any woman he wanted.

* * *

'You look tired,' Giovanni said, taking his spectacles off and laying them down with his Venetian newspaper beside him on his large bed.

'A little,' Lily admitted, easing herself down into the comfy chair Giovanni kept near his bed especially for her visits. 'I don't know why. I'm not doing much these days.'

'What do you mean?' he exclaimed. 'You are growing my grandson inside your body—that is something!'

Lily smiled. Her visits to Giovanni always lifted her spirits.

'Not long now, and you'll get to meet him,' she said, hoping that it was true. The doctors had been pleased with how stable Giovanni's health had been lately, but he was still a very frail old man.

'I won't watch him grow up,' he said. 'But I'm not going anywhere until I've seen him with my own eyes.'

Suddenly Lily felt tears welling up. She blinked them away, feeling self-conscious, but Giovanni hadn't noticed. He was gazing forward with a smile on his face.

'I promise I'll teach him everything you told me about your life and Venice,' she said, keeping her voice steady with a determined effort.

'You've made me a very happy old man,' Giovanni said, turning to look at her. 'Only the very lucky can live long enough to see their great-grandchildren. I don't know if I've ever told you how pleased I am that *you* are to be the mother.'

'Thank you. You've always been so good to me,' Lily replied, hearing her voice tremble with heartfelt emotion.

'You were worth the wait,' he said with a lively smile. 'You know, after Capricia, I was worried my grandson might not have good taste in women.'

'Really?' Lily asked, her curiosity piqued even though she knew it was potentially a controversial subject. 'But if they'd stayed together, and if they'd started a family, you would have had longer to get to know your grandchildren.'

'Capricia's children?' Giovanni said in disgust. 'I never understood why he married her. She might have been Venetian, but she was not a good wife for him. And I doubt that she would have agreed to motherhood for a long time.'

'What do you mean?' Despite her better judgement telling her to keep off the subject of Vito's first wife, Lily wanted to know more.

'She was far too busy living it up—enjoying her selfish existence, spending his money on frivolous things,' Giovanni said. 'She's still the same, except now she's in Rio de Janeiro spending her Brazilian lover's money—if what my contacts tell me is true.'

'Contacts?' Lily smiled, trying to appear lighthearted even though her heart felt anything but light.

'What do you think?' Giovanni sounded affronted. 'Just because I'm old and in bed I know nothing?'

'Of course not,' Lily laughed, but she couldn't help wondering what he knew about her and Vito.

'But don't think about Capricia,' Giovanni added. 'Vito never loved her the way he loves you. Anyone can see you two are soulmates—like me and my dear Anna Maria.'

Lily forced a smile and looked down at her hands clasped in her lap, feeling heartsick. She knew now that Vito had never loved her at all.

'I nearly forgot—I have a surprise for you,' Giovanni said.

'A surprise?' Lily repeated, pleased at the distraction. She didn't want to bring Giovanni down by looking dejected. But she hoped he wasn't going to make things awkward for her with Vito by giving her any more family heirlooms. She loved the antique necklace he'd given her the first day, but she hadn't seen it since Vito had taken it away from her.

'Yes. Talking of my Anna Maria reminded me...' He smiled, and Lily knew from his dreamy expression he was still thinking of his wife. 'I remembered her favourite thing when she was pregnant, and I thought you might like it too.'

Lily smiled expectantly, intrigued to get another glimpse of the woman who had so clearly captured Giovanni's heart.

'I can't come with you to see how you like it,' he said, pressing a button to call a member of his staff. 'But you must tell me when you visit tomorrow.'

At that moment his housekeeper came into the room and he told her to show Lily to her surprise. From the way she responded to the instruction, she had obviously been involved in the arrangements, and as Giovanni settled down for a nap she led Lily away to a part of the *palazzo* she had never seen before.

Down two flights of stairs, across an absolutely delightful courtyard complete with citrus trees in giant terracotta pots, and in through another double door, Lily found herself gazing at the most inviting thing she had seen for days.

A cool, blue swimming-pool.

'Oh my!' she sighed, suddenly aching to ease her tired body into the water.

The housekeeper explained how Giovanni had had the pool repaired and refilled, showed her where the changing and showering facilities were, and finally presented her with a collection of maternity swimwear.

Just minutes later Lily was floating on her back in

the blissfully cool and supportive water. She rolled over and slowly swam a length of the pool, admiring the detailed mosaics beneath the rippling water.

She loved Giovanni for this gift to her. It was absolutely perfect in every way.

Suddenly tears sprung unchecked to her eyes.

Vito's grandfather had shown her unstinting kindness like no one in her life ever had before. He treated her with respect and as an individual he genuinely wanted to get to know. Her own father had never done that. He didn't even want to know her at all.

And now Vito, her husband, didn't seem to want to know her either.

Vito strode through the narrow Venetian streets impatiently. It was late afternoon, and he'd come home from the office early for the third day in a row only to find Lily was not at the *palazzo*. Since they'd returned from the mountains, she'd started spending more and more time at *Ca' Salvatore*. In fact she was rarely at home these days, and it was beginning to bother him.

He knew that his grandfather had refilled his swimming pool for her, which he acknowledged was a very thoughtful gesture. And apparently Lily loved swimming—which was something he hadn't known about her. But surely she couldn't be spending *all* day in the pool?

Suddenly the memory of their conversation in the meadow loomed large and uncomfortable in his mind. He swore under his breath, cursing himself for telling her about his infertility. Things had been progressing smoothly between them up until that point, and he wished he hadn't chosen that moment to upset the balance of their relationship.

He didn't understand what had driven him to come clean, but blamed it on Lily. He'd spent so much time alone with her that she had whittled her way through his defences. He had quite simply let his guard down. He wouldn't make that mistake again. He shouldn't have made it this time.

He remembered all too well the scornful look on Capricia's face when she'd waved the doctor's report stating his infertility under his nose. It was unbelievable that he'd been foolish enough to put himself through the same humiliation twice.

He'd been young and naive when he'd married Capricia, hoping that she would be the perfect Venetian wife to bring up the next generation of Salvatores. It hadn't worked out that way. But he'd thought he had learnt something from the experience—to protect his pride if nothing else.

His infertility had driven a wedge into his first marriage. To alleviate her disappointment in his failure, Capricia had thrown herself into a wild life of socialising and travel. They'd grown apart, but he hadn't made any effort to hold onto their marriage. When Capricia had finally left, he'd been pleased. With her gone there should have been no reminder of his shame.

But, no matter how hard he'd tried, he hadn't been able to forget what had happened. He was accustomed to success, and his failure as a man continued to burn into him mercilessly.

Dealing with the unrelenting sense of humiliation was the hardest challenge he had ever faced. So he'd vowed never to let a serious relationship compromise his defences again. He could not father a child—therefore there was no point in long-term commitment.

It was only his grandfather's dying wish that had made him reassess his decision, and that had led him to marry Lily.

Lily was not like Capricia—she hadn't responded with scorn when she'd discovered he was infertile. But the shock of the news had made her show her true colours. And the way she was acting now told him what she really thought of him.

He knew he'd knocked the ground out from under her. She was no longer able to cling to her story that she hadn't been unfaithful. She'd seemed stunned at first, but that had been quickly followed by anger—presumably because he'd made her look a fool.

But, whatever her feelings, it was part of their agreement that she kept them to herself. He didn't appreciate the message she was sending his household by spending all her time at *Ca' Salvatore*. In the daytime it was fine—but not in the evening when he was expected home from work.

He was still deep in thought as he strode into the old courtyard at *Ca' Salvatore*. Lily was sleeping on a recliner under the protection of the cloistered passage that led to the entrance to the pool.

He stopped and gazed at her. She looked beautiful— utterly enchanting, but also achingly vulnerable. She was turned slightly on her side, with her silken hair spread out behind her like an angel's wings, and her arms were folded protectively over her stomach.

As he gazed at her, all the bad feelings that had built up during his walk from the *palazzo* melted away. How could he feel angry when presented with a vision of such celestial beauty?

He had missed her—had missed the time they'd spent together.

He sat down beside her on another chair, suddenly content to wait until she awoke naturally. She must have only been dozing, because she started to stir almost immediately.

'*Ciao,*' he said, reaching out to tuck a blonde curl which had fallen forward behind her ear. 'I thought I'd find you here.'

'How long have you been sitting there?' Lily asked, groggily pushing herself upright.

'Not long. In fact I just arrived,' Vito said, twisting on his chair to glance around. 'You know, it's years since I was in this courtyard. I used to play football here.'

'Really?' she said, looking at the citrus trees in terracotta pots and the curved marble benches arranged around the trickling fountain-pool in the centre. 'There's a lot of obstacles.'

'Good for my dribbling skills.' Vito smiled as he remembered. 'There's nothing like getting tackled by marble bench—it gets you right in the shins.'

Lily blinked and rubbed her eyes, still feeling half asleep.

Why was he being so nice all of a sudden? His smile completely changed his face, erasing the vertical crease that had been gouged between his eyes in the weeks since they'd returned from the mountains.

'There's a lot of windows too,' she added, trying to ignore the way his smile tugged at her heart. She couldn't let herself start to fall for him all over again every time he decided to turn on the charm.

'Yes—I smashed quite a few of them,' Vito said. 'The housekeeper covered it up at first, but when my grandfather found out he certainly took me to task.'

Lily gazed at him, trying to imagine what he might

have looked like as a boy. For the housekeeper to have covered up broken windows he must have been quite a charmer, even back then. She wondered if he had photos. It would be intriguing to get some idea what their son might look like.

An unpleasantly cold feeling washed over her. Vito wouldn't show her photos because he was still denying the possibility that he could be the father. She slumped back on the recliner, suddenly feeling weary and washed out.

'Are you all right?' Vito's voice sounded genuinely concerned.

'I'm fine. Just tired.' She picked up her glass of water, deliberately not letting herself look at his face. She knew his expression would reflect what she had just heard in his voice. If she saw that concern, combined with his heart-stoppingly good looks, she knew her defences would start to melt.

'You look sad.' Vito reached out to touch her arm, and the gesture of comfort sent a wave of warmth through her which was at odds with what her brain was telling her. 'Why are you unhappy?'

'Because you only married me for the baby inside me,' she said, the honest words coming out as a reaction to the conflict she was feeling inside.

'You knew that—I told you that from the start.' Vito let his hand drop from her arm abruptly. 'Why is that an issue now? Are you saying that you thought there was another reason?'

'I thought—I hoped—there was *something* between us, more than just the child inside me that you still refuse to even consider is yours.' She put her feet down onto the marble flagstones, looking beside the recliner to locate her flat sandals. 'Now I know I was wrong. All I am to you is a convenient baby-machine.'

She rammed her feet into her sandals and pushed herself quickly to her feet.

Suddenly she felt a strange sensation inside her, followed by a gush of warm fluid down her legs. She stared down at the puddle on the ground in a moment's bewilderment. The baby wasn't due for another month. Then she heard Vito's voice, strong and reassuring.

'Your water just broke,' he said, sweeping her up into his arms and striding swiftly to the *palazzo's* water entrance. 'We're going straight to hospital.'

CHAPTER TWELVE

LILY stared in awe at the baby sleeping in her arms. He was utterly beautiful. Her heart ached with how small and perfect he was, and she didn't think she'd ever be able to take her eyes off him again.

He had arrived so suddenly. By the time they'd reached the hospital her labour had already been well advanced. But everything had gone smoothly and he'd been born at nine-thirty in the evening, weighing a healthy six pounds.

Vito had been amazing during the labour and delivery, an absolute tower of strength and encouragement. He had known exactly when to hold her or rub her back, or whisper fortifying words of comfort in her ear. He had never left her side for a moment—until now, when she'd had to urge him to go and call his grandfather.

The door of her private room opened and she looked up, expecting to see Vito returning. But instead it was the doctor.

'I gather the baby has already fed a little,' the doctor said. 'That's good. He's a strong little fellow for his size. But I'm afraid I must disturb him to take a small sample of his blood.'

'What for?' Lily asked, assuming it was some kind

of routine test done for all babies. 'Why do you have to do it now while he's asleep?'

'I think it best to find out whether he has inherited his father's rare blood-type as soon as possible,' the doctor replied, talking as if he thought Lily knew what he was referring to. 'Being delivered at thirty-six weeks we wouldn't expect any problems,' he continued. 'But in the circumstances it's prudent to know the facts regarding his blood type.'

'I don't understand what you are talking about,' Lily said, hugging the tiny baby protectively to her. At that moment Vito returned and she stared up at him, a wave of panic rising up within her.

'I was just explaining about the situation with your blood type,' the doctor said to Vito as he crossed to Lily's side.

'You didn't *explain*.' Lily flashed her gaze anxiously between the two men. 'You just told me we needed to find it out, in case something went wrong!'

'Just a precaution,' the doctor said, pulling up a chair next to her and placing the equipment he needed to draw a blood sample on a small tray on the table beside them.

'Why didn't you tell me about this?' Lily looked up at Vito accusingly, still keeping her baby out of the doctor's reach.

He stood as straight as a ramrod with an unreadable expression on his face, but Lily knew the answer to her question. He hadn't told her because he'd thought it was irrelevant—he didn't believe the baby was his.

'I'm sure he just didn't want to worry you,' the doctor said. 'It's extremely unlikely that the baby will have inherited it.'

'What if he has?' Lily asked, fear ripping through her.

'Well, as you are obviously aware, your husband is as strong as an ox. It only becomes an issue if he needs a blood transfusion.'

'What happens then?' Lily pressed.

'It's harder to find suitable donor-blood. That's why we want to be prepared, so we don't have any surprises at a time we could do without them.' He reached up gently to ease the blanket away from the infant. 'If you can hold him steady, we'll get this over with as painlessly as possible.'

'But what if you can't find the right blood to give him?' Lily asked, feeling increasingly anxious. It all sounded very complicated and worrying.

'There's no reason at all to think we'll *need* blood for a transfusion,' the doctor said firmly. 'But, if for some reason we do, then of course we'll find it. It's just that we may have to search further afield.'

Lily took a deep breath and lowered the baby unto her lap. She unwrapped the blanket so that the doctor could take the blood sample.

As the needle pricked his fragile skin he opened his eyes in horrified protest. A moment later he opened his mouth and started crying.

Lily felt her lower lip start to tremble in response, and she hugged her son close to her. It was unbearable to see her baby upset.

'I'll get this sample off to the lab,' the doctor said, taking his leave.

'Lily…I…' Vito was standing close to her, but she didn't look up. For the first time ever, she thought he sounded uncertain—but right then all her attention was on her newborn baby.

'Leave me alone,' she said, feeling like she had been punched in the stomach.

She unbuttoned her nightdress and tried to offer the baby up to her breast. But the position wasn't right, and after a frantic moment of silence as he rooted unsuccessfully for her nipple he started crying again.

Without a saying a word, Vito dropped down on his knees in front of them. He cupped the baby's head gently and guided it forward to Lily's breast. Just as the baby opened his mouth as wide as possible to let out a mewling cry, Vito nudged his head forward and he latched onto the nipple successfully.

Lily looked down at her baby suckling contentedly, and took care to keep his position steady. Vito had rocked back on his heels, but his eyes were still locked on the infant.

'I asked you to leave me alone,' she said quietly, lifting her eyes to meet his. Vito's gaze was troubled, but she was too angry with him to give it any thought.

'But—'

'I don't want you here,' she said, hearing her own voice crackle with ice. 'Your pride has made you selfish. I can't believe that you were so arrogant and stubborn that you let your lack of trust in me make you ignore something that could affect our baby's wellbeing.'

Vito paced up and down his study, looking repeatedly at his fax machine, waiting for it to whir into action.

He'd had a miserable night. The worst night of his life—even harder than when he'd forced Lily to leave Venice back in March. That night he'd been upset, but he'd focussed his anger on what he'd thought of as her betrayal. He hadn't been forced to look in the mirror at his own decisions and actions.

Now, everything was different. His personal demons

were howling round the room with him, unrelenting in their attack on his well-built defences.

What if he'd been wrong?

Wrong about everything?

The thought plagued him, constantly looming up in his mind. He tried to reject it, the way he'd always successfully rejected Lily's claims. But now it seemed as if she was finally getting through to him.

What if he really was the father of the baby?

The look of fear on her face when she hadn't understood what the doctor was saying about his rare blood-group haunted him. And the cold look of disgust on her face when she'd thrown him out of her hospital room stabbed into him like a jagged blade.

Suddenly the fax machine came to life. He was rooted to the spot, watching as the sheet of white paper curled out.

A copy of his fertility-test results.

All those years ago he'd never read them for himself. The disdainful look on Capricia's face had seen to that. His pride hadn't been able to stand it. Even providing the sample in the first place, letting his virility be put to the test, had been hard to bear. He'd never considered getting a physical examination or second opinion. The brutal assault on his masculine pride had been unendurable.

He reached for the fax and hesitated, blood pounding in his temples.

He was terrified at what he would read.

Would the results show that he had been right all along, make him relive his humiliation yet again? Or would he find out that Lily had been telling the truth—that he was guilty of treating her appallingly when she didn't deserve it? And that her beautiful baby boy was his son?

He picked up the document and looked at it.

His heart thudded in his chest and his palms were suddenly damp with sweat.

Results: every likelihood of excellent fertility at this time.

Lily lay on her side in the hospital bed watching her newborn baby sleeping in his crib. The nurses had made her put him down, told her that if she didn't sleep when he did she'd become exhausted and her milk wouldn't flow. But, even though she'd been awake all night, sleep would not come.

Vito had left when she'd asked and he'd never returned.

She didn't know what she had expected—she hadn't exactly been thinking straight at the time. But despite the fact he had proven once again just how little faith he had in her, she wished he were there with her.

She couldn't stop thinking about how wonderful he'd been during the birth. She couldn't have asked for more. It must mean something. Maybe, although love was not part of the equation for him, he did care about her a little.

But now she had sent him away.

She squeezed her eyes shut, wishing sleep would come and ease her misery. But then she heard a quiet sound and, although it could have been a nurse returning to check up on her and the baby, she knew it was Vito.

She rolled over and tried to sit up, but after the rigours of the birth she was stiff and sore. Vito was by her side in a second, gently helping her into a comfortable position.

'Thank you.' She looked up at him standing beside the bed, and her eyes widened with surprise as she took in his appearance. He'd showered and shaved since last night, but his face was ashen and painfully troubled.

'I'm sorry.' His voice was deep and rough, as if it had been difficult for him to say that word. Or maybe it was because he was so tired. But, whatever the case, his expression was contrite as he gazed down at her on the bed.

'What for?' she asked simply.

'For everything,' he said. 'For the way I've treated you. For not trusting you. For making you marry me even though I didn't mean it to last.'

'Do you believe me now?' Lily asked, looking at the lines of stress etched around his eyes.

'Yes,' Vito said. 'I got Capricia's doctor out of bed at an ungodly hour this morning, and had him go straight to his office to fax me a copy of the results of my fertility test.'

'I don't understand,' Lily said, ignoring the wave of sadness that washed over her as she realised it wasn't anything *she* had said or done that had convinced Vito. It had taken Capricia's doctor. 'How did that make any difference? You saw those results years ago.'

'I never read them myself,' Vito admitted.

Lily stared at him in frank disbelief, too startled to mask her reaction. For a moment he actually appeared to wince with embarrassment.

'You never read them?' she gasped. 'Surely you followed up the result—repeated the test or got a second opinion?'

'No.' Vito hung his head for a moment, then took a deep breath and looked her in the eye to continue. 'I was devastated. All my dreams of becoming a father, of continuing the Salvatore line, were shattered. It seemed like an assault on my very existence.'

'Why did she do it?' Lily asked. 'What would make Capricia lie to you like that?'

'I don't know,' Vito said. 'I've been wracking my brain all night, trying to work it out. The only solution I have is that she didn't want children. I knew she didn't want to come off the Pill—but I thought I'd persuaded her to try to start a family. Presumably she just carried on taking the Pill all along.'

'I think you're right.' Lily thought about how Giovanni had described Vito's first wife. It was ironic that the old man had got her measure better than Vito. 'It must be painful to realise that the woman you loved tricked you like that.'

'I don't know if "painful" is the correct word,' Vito said. 'I'm furious with her. Furious that what she did led me to hurt you so badly.'

'You should have read the results yourself,' Lily muttered. She knew it was harsh to point that out. But she couldn't help noticing Vito had not denied loving Capricia—a woman who had deceived and cheated him. For some reason that really hurt.

'I'm sorry,' Vito said again. 'I've treated you unforgivably.'

Lily gazed at him sadly, swallowing against a hard lump in her throat. She ought to accept his apology. He was the victim of a wicked deception. If Capricia hadn't lied to him, he would never have treated *her* so badly.

But none of it was her fault. The only thing she'd ever done wrong was fall in love with Vito.

'Nothing's changed in the way I feel,' Lily said miserably. 'You never trusted me—you had to get Capricia's doctor to send you proof.'

'Something did change yesterday. I saw your fear when the doctor took the blood sample.' Vito sucked in a deep, shuddering breath and raked his hands roughly through his black hair. 'I spent the night in an agony of confusion. Once I'd admitted the possibility that you might be telling the truth, I was desperate for that to be the case. But, after Capricia left, I spent so long denying my feelings that it was almost impossible to get out of that rut. The security of encasing your deeper feelings in a layer of cold rock is hard to give up.'

His heartfelt outburst tugged at Lily's sympathies, but it was a cruel kind of torture to listen to him describing how he'd battened down his emotions after Capricia had left.

'You must have loved her very much,' she said.

'Capricia?' Vito looked at Lily in surprise.

Her hazel eyes were wide in her pale face, and the dark shadows of fatigue around them accentuated their size. She looked so small and vulnerable, sitting there in the white hospital bed, that his chest contracted painfully.

'I don't think I ever loved Capricia,' he said. 'Not really.'

'Then why did you marry her?' Lily asked.

'I was young,' Vito said. 'She was beautiful. Venetian. And at the time I foolishly thought she'd make a good wife and mother.'

Lily didn't reply, but he could see in her face what she thought of his judgement. It was terrible. It had always been terrible. In business it seemed he could do no wrong. But, in his personal life, *everything* he'd done was wrong.

Until one day, in a moment of good fortune, he'd met Lily. And then he had set about ruining that too.

'I'm sorry. I've ruined everything,' he said. 'It wasn't necessary to force you into this. I've married you when I didn't need to.'

Suddenly he saw her eyes fill with tears. As the liquid

pooled and spilled down her cheeks it felt as if someone had ripped his heart from his chest.

'Don't cry,' he said, sitting on the edge of the bed and taking her hands in his. They felt pitifully cold in his grip. 'I know we are married—but I don't see how I can hold you to that now.'

'But what about your grandfather?' she said, her voice uneven with the sound of crying.

Vito held her hands, gently warming them between his palms. Then suddenly he realised something.

Lily was more important than his grandfather.

His desire to see Giovanni end his days in contentment was still powerful. But not at the expense of Lily's happiness.

'My grandfather doesn't need to know,' Vito said carefully. 'You've given him the heir he desired. And, with your friendship, so much more than that. I can't ask you to give up your life.'

He looked at her sad face, his heart contracting painfully at her distress, and suddenly all he wanted was to take away her sadness.

'Don't cry,' he said again, leaning forward to kiss away the salty tears that were streaming down her cheeks. 'You're tired. It will seem better later. We'll work things out.'

'How *can* we work things out?' she sobbed. 'You don't need me any more. You never needed me.'

'Of course I need you!' Vito exclaimed. 'I've always needed you. From the very first time we talked I knew I had to make you part of my life.'

He cupped her face and looked at her puzzled expression. She'd stopped crying and was looking at him in confusion.

At that moment it hit him.

Like a punch in the solar plexus, he suddenly knew the truth.

He loved her.

He'd *always* loved her. That was why her pregnancy had hurt him so deeply, why he'd forced her to marry him, and why the thought of letting her go now was grinding into him like a steel bar.

He let his breath out with a whoosh, and smiled at her.

Love. That must be causing this ground-rush of emotions that was rising up to meet him as the clouds of doubt fell away, finally revealing the woman he loved.

'What?' she whispered, looking anxiously into his face. 'What is it?'

'I love you,' he said.

'But…' Lily stared at him in disbelief. Where had that suddenly come from? A moment ago he'd said he planned to divorce her—which she'd expected, now he had finally accepted he was not infertile.

So why had he said he loved her? Had she even heard correctly?

'I love you!' he said, hauling her into his arms and nearly crushing her with his exuberance. 'Oh, my God! Why have I only just realised it?'

'It can't be true,' Lily said. She couldn't let her hopes be raised. It must be guilt for what he'd put her through making him momentarily lose his common sense.

'It *is* true,' Vito said, cupping her face with gentle hands again and looking deeply into her eyes. 'I've never said anything more true in my life.'

'But…' Lily didn't know what to say. She looked deep into his sky-blue eyes, trying to suppress the tingle of excitement that was bubbling inside her. It was what she'd yearned to hear for such a long time that she hardly dared to believe it. 'Why are you saying this now?'

'I only just realised,' Vito said. 'I think I was so closed off to my feelings that it took me a long time to realise the truth. Even though it was staring me in the face all the time.'

'What do you mean?' Lily asked.

'Back before Easter, when you went to the doctor with your stomach bug,' Vito said. 'I was so worried about you.'

'I remember you waiting for me,' Lily said, thinking about the black cashmere sweater she had tossed into the canal.

'You came home looking white as a sheet, and I thought something might be seriously wrong with you.' Vito took a breath. 'I couldn't bear that thought. It cut me like knife.'

'I didn't know that,' Lily said. 'But I remember how kind you were to me. Until…'

'Until I lost my mind with jealousy,' Vito said. 'I couldn't bear the thought of you with another man. I think I lost my reason for a while.'

Lily gazed at him, the lines of his distress clearly etched onto his face.

'It's all right,' she said. 'It turned out all right.'

'Thank God for Luigi,' Vito said. 'And for your friend Anna.'

'I would have been okay,' she said. 'I don't need someone to look after me.'

'I know,' he said seriously. 'You are the strongest person I know. When I think how you dealt with all the appalling difficulties I threw your way… I'm sorry.'

'Please, stop saying that,' Lily said, placing the flat of her palm against his chest. She could feel his heart beating beneath her hand, and the power of its rhythm gave her hope. 'We can't turn back the clock. Let's go forwards.'

'Will you stay with me?' Vito asked. 'Give me another chance?'

'Of course I will,' Lily said, feeling tears of happiness start to well up in her eyes.

'Why are you crying?' Vito leant forward to brush his thumb across her damp cheek.

'Because I love you too,' Lily answered. 'I've always loved you.'

A smile of incredulous happiness broke across Vito's face. Then the next moment he was crushing her in his arms again.

'I can't believe it.' Vito's voice was muffled against her hair. 'Last night I was despairing that things could ever be right—and now all my dreams have come true.'

His words reflected exactly how Lily was feeling, and she clung to him tightly, feeling like she'd never let go again. But a moment later a tiny, mewling cry from the cot interrupted them.

'He's awake!' Vito's voice was full of love and pride, as if waking up was the cleverest thing any baby had ever done.

'Would you like to pick him up?' Lily watched as Vito lifted the baby out of the cot. His gentle hands seemed almost as big as his son as he gazed down at the crumpled, newborn face with adoring eyes.

'What does he need?' Vito turned to her for advice.

'I don't know,' she replied honestly. 'I'm new at this. Perhaps I should try to feed him.' She unfastened the top few buttons of her nightdress and held out her hands for the baby. Vito placed him gently in her arms, then doing the same as the previous evening, guided the little head towards her nipple.

'Ah, that's the idea. I like to see a little bit of teamwork.' Lily recognised the doctor's voice and lifted her gaze to see him walking into the room. 'We have the results of the blood test,' he continued. 'Unfortunately it seems this little fellow is following in your footsteps with a rare blood-type.'

Lily looked at Vito's face to see how he would respond to this physical proof that he was the baby's father. To her surprise a worried frown marred his features.

'That's a blow,' he said. 'I was hoping he would have taken after his mother.'

'There's nothing to worry about,' the doctor said. 'Your wife and I talked some more last night, and she understands now that it won't be a problem. It's just something it pays to be aware of.'

He walked over to the bed and gave a satisfied nod as he saw how well the baby was feeding. 'I'll be back to check on you later,' he said as he left them alone again.

'I thought you'd be pleased,' Lily said. 'Pleased to have concrete proof of your paternity.'

'I didn't need it.' He turned and held her gaze with serious eyes. 'I have all the proof I need, in here,' he said, placing his hand over his heart.

Lily felt her lips quiver again as once more her eyes filled with tears of happiness.

'I love you,' she said.

'And I you,' Vito replied. 'With all of my heart and soul.'

EPILOGUE

'MY GREAT-GRANDSON,' Giovanni breathed, looking down at the little baby cradled carefully in his arms.

Lily sat next to him on his huge bed, feeling tears well up in her own eyes as she heard the tremulous notes of awe and gratitude in his voice.

'He's called Giovanni,' she said.

The old man lifted his head to stare at her with sparkling blue eyes, momentarily speechless as the information sunk in.

'Thank you,' he said. 'Thank you for making me very happy.'

'It's an honour to do so,' Lily said, leaning forward to kiss his paper-thin cheek. 'I can never explain what your kindness has meant to me. How delighted I am to be part of your family, and how much pleasure I have knowing that my son will carry on your family name.'

'You are wearing the necklace,' he said, suddenly noticing the exquisite piece of antique jewellery that was fastened round Lily's neck. 'When you never wore it I thought it was not to your taste after all.'

'Oh no, I love it,' Lily said, reaching up to trail her fingertips over the smooth beads. 'Vito was having it checked by antique jewellery experts to make sure it was strong enough to wear. I didn't want to damage it.'

'But today is an important occasion, *Nonno*—introducing you to my son,' Vito said, gazing at his wife. She was the most beautiful thing he'd ever seen, and just looking at her made his heart swell with the great love he felt for her.

He was embarrassed that he'd kept hold of the necklace for months after it had been restored, but somehow he had never been able to find the right time to return it to her. But then she had asked for it this morning, smoothing away his awkwardness with tender kisses, and making him fall in love with her all over again for her kindness and understanding.

'Yes, it is,' Giovanni said, his eyes focussed back on the baby again, but Vito could tell he was beginning to grow weary.

'We'll leave you to rest now, *Nonno*.' He lifted the baby gently out of his grandfather's arms. 'Don't worry—we'll come back tomorrow.'

'See that you do,' Giovanni said, but the abruptness of his words was softened by the fact that his eyes were already starting to close as he leant his head back against his pillows.

Vito led the way down to the canal entrance of *Ca' Salvatore* and, once Lily was safely on the boat, he passed baby Giovanni down to her.

'You've made my grandfather very happy,' Vito said as he stepped down into the boat and sat next to her. A thick autumn fog was rolling in from the Adriatic, and the city was taking on an eerie quality. It made him want to hurry home and snuggle his little family up, safe and warm inside.

'I meant what I said to him.' Lily looked up through

the fog at the magnificent façade of the baroque *palazzo* as the boat started to move out into the flow of traffic on the Grand Canal. 'About being proud that my son will be part of this family.'

She dropped her gaze to look into the gorgeous face of the man she adored, and as their eyes met a little frisson of pleasure ran through her. She was tired from looking after their newborn baby, but she had never felt so happy in her entire life.

'I love you. And I am so proud to have you as my wife,' Vito said, slipping his arm around her and hugging her gently. 'You belong here in Venice. You belong with me.'

'I love it here,' Lily said as the boat turned off the Grand Canal to head towards home. Tendrils of fog were creeping into the smaller waterways, and the boat driver was taking it carefully. 'But, more than that, I love *you*. And I'll always belong with you.'

THE MILLIONAIRE
BOSS'S BABY

MAGGIE
COX

The day **Maggie Cox** saw the film version of *Wuthering Heights*, with a beautiful Merle Oberon and a very handsome Laurence Olivier, was the day she became hooked on romance. From that day onwards she spent a lot of time dreaming up her own romances, secretly hoping that one day she might become published and get paid for doing what she loved most! Now that her dream is being realised, she wakes up every morning and counts her blessings. She is married to a gorgeous man and is the mother of two wonderful sons. Her two other great passions in life—besides her family and reading/writing—are music and films.

To Evelyn, John and Stephen with all my love

CHAPTER ONE

IT HAD been a long, seemingly endless journey—the most ambitious drive Georgia had undertaken in ages. Her saving grace was that she adored driving and prided herself at being quite good at it. With her Labrador Hamish in the back behind her she had the best companion she could wish for, next to her brother Noah. Now, well into the summer evening, she drove silently, with the radio off, her gaze lapping up the extraordinarily beautiful landscape of the Scottish Glens, tiredness banished by what had to be one of the most heavenly sights on earth.

Everywhere she looked she was treated to the most incredible beauty—sunlit lochs, mountain peaks and shimmering green fields. Even Hamish seemed to perk up as he looked out of the window, as if silently contemplating the large open spaces in which to romp and run free with eager relish. It was a far cry from the overcrowded London suburb where Georgia lived.

Already she sensed the accumulated knots and kinks of tension in her back start to unravel a little.

They had made quite a few stops during the long journey, for food and drink, but they had still made very good time. Now, Georgia knew, by the map opened on the seat beside her, as well as her new boss's very precise e-mail directions, that there was not too much further to go before they reached Glenteign—the large country estate of which he was Laird.

'No wonder Noah loved working here!' she declared out loud, and Hamish wagged his tail enthusiastically as if to agree.

Her brother had assured her that she would grow to love Glenteign too. He'd recently spent six months there, in his capacity as a freelance garden designer hired to help work on the formal gardens. It was a place where a person could really *breathe,* he'd told her, his passion for nature and beauty spilling over into his voice. And in his opinion Georgia wouldn't regret leaving London behind for a while, with its continual gridlocked traffic and polluted air. Working as the Laird's temporary secretary, while his permanent secretary recovered from a bad fall, she would have some breathing space from the grinding commute into the City every day. She would find out what a different way of life it was up here—a much more relaxed, 'sane' way of life.

She had accepted the job because she wanted so much to believe him, but Georgia still had some reservations about her decision. What would it be like working for a man who had probably never had to worry about where the next meal was coming from in his life? A man who, because of his status, epitomised the old feudal system of 'Lord of the Manor' while those around him were mere serfs?

She didn't exactly have a problem with the concept of inherited wealth—she begrudged nobody their comfortable circumstances—it was just that she was so weary sometimes of her own struggle to keep the wolf from the door, and the idea that somebody could just be born into such good fortune and not have to do anything to earn it was apt to rub salt into the wound. Still, no doubt the wealthy Laird of Glenteign had his own problems…they just didn't come in the same shape as Georgia's. But— problems or no—surely he couldn't fail to take solace in so much wonderful scenery?

When her reliable but old Renault finally drew into the grounds of Glenteign, Georgia switched off the engine, leaned her elbow on the window's ledge and considered her surroundings with a flare of wonderment in the pit of her stomach.

The house immediately proclaimed its historic past—its impressive edifice of Pictish stone, with its turrets reaching towards the presently cloudless azure sky, reminding Georgia of an ancient impenetrable fortress that had survived every onslaught both nature and man could throw at it and still there it stood, proud and inviolable, with an almost defiant grace. Turning her head, Georgia viewed the lushness of emerald lawns rolling out into the distance like an expansive glittering carpet, and over to the right a high stone wall that perhaps led to the formal gardens that her brother had been working on for the past half-year.

She couldn't deny she was eager to see them— not just because of the work Noah had done there, but because he'd told her they were incredibly beautiful. Moving her gaze further afield, a grove of tall firs captured her attention, stretching endlessly beyond the exquisite perfection of the immaculate lawns. There was just so much land! It didn't seem feasible that one person could own all of this. She began to realise what a prestigious opportunity this was for Noah, coming to work here. And now, because of the success he had achieved, he was working at another large estate in the Highlands—a commission he had secured on the Laird's recommendation because he had been so impressed with what he'd done at Glenteign.

She felt a flicker of love and pride. Every sacrifice she'd made to help Noah get his business off the ground had been worth it…

'You found us, then?'

Abruptly lured away from her reverie, Georgia found her glance commanded by a pair of eyes that were so faultlessly, intensely blue that for a moment no speech was possible on her part. The rest of the features in the masculine face before here were not exactly difficult to look at either. It was as if they might have been sculpted—the planes and angles so strongly delineated that they were surely the loving work of an artist's reverent hand? But Georgia wasn't the only one who was transfixed... The man's unflinching perusal of her own face came as a shock.

She wasn't used to being regarded with such uncommon directness and everything inside her clenched hard in sudden self-consciousness. But before she could find her voice, he was opening the driver's door and standing aside for her to step out onto the gravel.

'Yes...hello.' She held out her hand, then awkwardly withdrew it almost as soon as her skin came into contact with his. *Such an acceptably polite gesture shouldn't feel as if it was bordering on intimacy but somehow it did.* As he considered her further, his gaze no less direct, Georgia silently bemoaned her travel-worn appearance. After several hours' travelling her clothes must resemble unironed laundry, she was sure. The cream linen shift dress she wore, with its scooped neckline, had been cool and fresh when she'd donned it early this morning, but it definitely didn't look like that now.

'Did you have a good journey?'

Beneath the polite questioning Georgia thought she detected a slight strain—as though he neither welcomed nor enjoyed this kind of inconsequential chit-chat. Her heart sank a little.

'Yes, I did. The directions you gave me were spot-on.'

'Good.'

'I presume you must be the Laird?'

'Yes, I am… And you are Georgia…Noah's sister.'

It was a statement of fact, not requiring a reply.

'How do I address you?' she asked, her voice determinedly bright.

'The correct title is "Chief," but I would be quite happy for you to call me Keir—the same as I told your brother. Talking of which…I have to say I can hardly see a resemblance between the two of you.'

'People usually say that.'

'Then I'm sorry to be so predictable.'

He was still a little perturbed by the handshake they'd shared—although the contact had been less than brief, Keir had been genuinely taken aback by the warm electrical 'buzz' that had flowed straight through him. It had been a very arresting wake-up call, and now he sensed his attention magnetised by

Georgia Cameron's lovely face. He was surprised that she was so different in colouring from her tall, blond, blue-eyed brother, and perhaps more pleased than he should be by the contrast. Anybody with a penchant for beauty would admire such dazzling green-gold eyes, but in a face as animated and compelling as hers, with its high, elegant cheekbones and wide, generous mouth, it was hard not to elevate them as perhaps the most beautiful he'd ever seen...

But Keir could hardly attest to welcoming such distracting assets. It was her professional skills he was interested in, not her looks. He had employed her because her brother had assured him that if he was looking for a first-class secretary, he should look no further than his very capable sister. He'd said she was temping with an agency in the City, and her current job would be coming to an end soon, so she could start at Glenteign practically straight away.

Way behind with the administration of running such a large estate, after reluctantly inheriting the mantle of Laird from his brother Robert, who'd been killed in an accident abroad, Keir was in urgent need of some first class secretarial and organisational skills. Doubly so since his own secretary Valerie had unfortunately tumbled down the stairs and broken her leg. *Only the next few days would tell if Noah Cameron had exaggerated his sister's capabilities or not...*

'I expect you'd like to go straight to your room and freshen up?'

'There's something that I really need to do first if you don't mind?'

'What's that?'

'I need to take Hamish for a bit of a walk. The poor creature's been cooped up for too long in my small car, and to tell you the truth I feel the same. We won't be ages…is that all right?'

'That's fine. I should have thought of it myself.'

Keir moved to the passenger door behind the driver's seat of Georgia's dusty little car, pulled it open and invited Hamish to jump out. The Labrador was ridiculously grateful, leaping up at him excitedly and wagging his tail at a rate of knots.

'Oh, my gosh—he's taken to you straight away! He doesn't do that with everybody…he must sense that you're friendly.'

Georgia's smile was genuinely delighted.

Being the unexpected recipient of such a fulsome expression of joy, Keir stared—caught between wanting to arouse more of the same rather beguiling delight and needing to assert some formality between them pretty quickly. The truth was he suddenly found himself having serious reservations about the wisdom of employing this rather disarming woman to work for him…even though the post was only temporary.

He decided to try and keep her gestures of friendliness at bay as much as possible. Theirs was a strictly business relationship, and if she didn't come up to scratch then Keir would have no compunction in telling her she was no longer needed. And he wouldn't cut her any slack just because her brother had impressed him either. James Strachan certainly wouldn't have. A less compassionate and sentimental man would have been hard to find anywhere! And, even though his father had shown evidence of relenting his rather austere manner towards the end of his life, the die had been cast. His efforts to try and forge with his younger son an emotional bond that had never existed before had come too late, Keir acknowledged with some bitterness. It had certainly come too late for his brother Robbie...

'I wouldn't read too much into it,' Keir said, deliberately pushing his hands into the pockets of his light coloured chinos, as if signalling that he wouldn't be paying the animal any undue attention while he was there. He had agreed to her request to bring the dog with her, and that should be enough. 'He's just grateful to be let out. You can walk anywhere, but I'd be glad if you kept the dog away from the flowerbeds. Is your stuff in the boot? All the staff in the house are busy, so I'll take it upstairs to your room. It's on the second floor. I'll leave the door open so that you know which one it is. Dinner is at eight, and I like people to be prompt. Enjoy your walk.'

Her smile gone, Georgia frowned and murmured, 'Thanks.' And if the withdrawal of that smile made Keir feel as if he'd deliberately deprived himself of something extraordinary, then he told himself he deserved it. Watching her collect Hamish's lead from her handbag beside the driver's seat and walk away, he opened the car boot and lifted out her luggage to carry it into the house.

Freshly showered after her walk round the grounds with Hamish, Georgia sat on the bed in her room and examined the employment contract Keir had left for her to sign. *He didn't waste much time, did he?* What did he think she was going to do? Run away after driving since the early hours of the morning to get here?

Even though she might have briefly entertained the thought, after the distinctly frosty way he'd shut down on her following her remark about Hamish liking him, Georgia was not about to give him the satisfaction. She would show Keir Strachan, Laird of Glenteign, that she was a reliable, efficient and skilled worker—and most of all that she kept her word when a promise was made.

Signing her name with a deliberate flourish, she laid the paperwork aside, then shook her damp hair free from the towel she'd wrapped it in. Pushing her fingers through the dark slippery strands, she let her gaze wander over her new surroundings. The room was the height of elegance, with plenty of loving feminine touches everywhere—from the rose-pink velvet curtains, with their matching gathered tie-backs and deep swags, to the rather grand mahogany dressing table with its gleaming surfaces, ornate lace doilies and sparkling oval-shaped mirror. The drowsy scent of late summer pervaded the air, and there was a breathtaking bouquet of white roses in a pink vase arranged on top of a polished satinwood chiffonier that made Georgia's heart skip with pleasure.

She wondered who had been responsible for such a delightful touch. Noah had told her that Keir wasn't married, so it must be some other female… Georgia felt vaguely annoyed that she was even speculating about it at all. She should be concentrating on getting ready to present herself to her new boss; that was what she should be doing!

Jumping up, she went to fetch her hairdryer from her almost empty suitcase. Realising that it was almost ten to eight, an unwelcome twist of anxiety knotted her stomach at the recollection that her new employer expected people to be 'prompt' for dinner. Trying to quell the feeling of rebellion that the thought surprisingly inspired, she turned her mind instead to the prospect of meeting the other staff who worked in the house.

Noah had told her how fond he'd grown of Keir's housekeeper, Moira Guthrie, while he'd worked there, and if the woman was as friendly as he had described then perhaps she needn't be as daunted as she was feeling at present at the idea of living in such a grand, impressive residence. Not to mention acting as secretary to a man who appeared to welcome gestures of friendliness with about as much enthusiasm as finding a viper in his bed!

Unlike her bedroom, the dining room had plenty of masculine touches in evidence—from the array of shining swords placed strategically round the walls to the several portraits of presumably past lairds who overlooked the proceedings with a definitely superior air. Breathtakingly impressive, the room was decorated in true baronial splendour. In fact, as she'd followed the very amiable Moira Guthrie inside, Georgia had half expected a fanfare to sound.

She bit down on her lip to suppress a smile. Under its high-raftered ceilings and candle sconces on the walls, and seated at the long refectory table with its burnished silverware and elegant cream dinner service, it was easy to imagine herself transported to a much more elegant and mannered era. All this finery was a far cry from Georgia and Noah's ridiculously small dining room at home, with its well-used pine table bought at a local second-hand store, and the four matching chairs that were in urgent need of refurbishment…

Glancing briefly down at her simple pink cotton dress, worn with the heart-shaped rose quartz pendant that her mother had left her, Georgia couldn't help musing that her employer might expect much more elegant attire in her dressing for dinner in his imposing house. Oh, well… Noah hadn't seemed to worry about such things, and nor should she. Neither of them had ever been able to afford elegant clothes even if they'd desired them. Most of the time they had been too busy just trying to survive.

Bereft of both parents since Noah was fourteen, Georgia, just five years his senior, had taken over her brother's care from that too young age, and worrying about finances had dominated her life for more years than she cared to remember. Even to the point of sacrificing any opportunity for a loving relationship, according to her concerned friends. But there was no real sacrifice in Georgia's mind. She would do it all again tomorrow if she had to. Still, she couldn't deny that the valuable commission to help work on the gardens at Glenteign had literally arrived in the nick of time.

Georgia had sunk every spare penny she'd had after paying the bills and running their home into

Noah's fledgling gardening business. With her blessing, he was intending to reinvest as much of the cash he'd received from that commission into making the business even more viable… In a couple of years' time maybe they would both be able to relax a little where money was concerned, instead of working practically every hour God sent.

'Don't worry, my dear…we won't be so formal every night,' Moira assured Georgia, having seen the doubt flicker across her face. 'We do like to do things properly at the weekends, but during the week we're very informal. There's a smaller dining room, just down the hall from the kitchen, and we usually eat in there. Now, if you'll excuse me for a second, I'm just off to see where Chief Strachan is. I expect he's busy finishing off some work and has forgotten the time. God knows the poor man's been up to his eyes in it since he came back here! And what with poor Valerie breaking her leg, you haven't arrived a moment too soon, lassie, and that's a fact!'

Georgia breathed a sigh of relief when the other woman exited the room. She couldn't deny she welcomed a few moments by herself, to reflect on where she'd landed. Considering the job in hand, there was no doubt in her mind about her secretarial abilities passing muster—but, having finally met her new boss, she did have some concerns as to whether they would get along. Lord knew, it could be frankly exhausting working for someone without a sense of humour, and quite honestly Georgia had been hoping for a breakthrough in that department. People in London these days seemed so uptight, with most of them consumed by long working hours and making career goals their God, that it made working as a temporary secretary for such driven individuals sometimes frankly hellish.

Sighing, she got up from her chair to examine the paintings that bedecked the walls. Turning up her nose at the stern male portraits to rest her gaze instead on the more genial scenes of pastoral serenity that were so invitingly displayed alongside them, she felt a little of the anxiety she was holding in her body ease from her shoulders.

'My apologies for keeping you waiting.'

She turned at the sound of that richly attractive and commanding voice, her gaze diverted by the sight of Keir walking straight to the head of the table in a brisk manner, straightening the cuffs on his open-necked white shirt, as though about to head up a board meeting instead of sitting down to dinner. Surprisingly, he was wearing denim jeans, and the faint aura of some classic male cologne lingered in the air as he moved.

Catching the briefly intense flare of the searching azure glance that immediately came her way, Georgia felt her stomach react as if she'd just plummeted several thousand feet without a parachute. Noah should have warned her that the Laird was so…so compelling! But perhaps it was understandable that younger brothers left out such important details when describing another man to their sisters!

Feeling ridiculously annoyed that she should be so thrown off-centre by her employer's good-looks, when she wasn't remotely an easily impressed girl at all, Georgia lightly shrugged her shoulders.

'Not at all. I was just enjoying looking at your beautiful paintings. The portraits are a little too severe for my taste, if you don't mind my saying…but the country scenes are lovely.'

'You like art?'

'Of course.'

The surprise on her face held the unspoken question. *Doesn't everybody?* and Keir found himself inordinately pleased by her vehemence.

'There are many paintings in the house—some by some very famous Scottish artists indeed. Perhaps when we're not so busy there might be an opportunity for me to show them to you? Now, please…sit down. There's only the three of us this evening as some of the staff are off duty, so there's no need to stand on ceremony. Moira, why don't you tell Lucy that she can serve the soup?'

As the older woman turned hurriedly away again, Georgia felt her cheeks burn with indignation beneath Keir's disconcerting scrutiny. She arranged herself in her chair. Didn't he know it was rude to stare? She swallowed hard, irritated with herself that she should let herself be so affected by the way he looked at her. She'd worked for attractive bosses in the past...of course she had. But none had bothered her sufficiently that she couldn't think a single straight thought without feeling flustered!

Reaching for her perfectly folded napkin, Georgia shook it out and laid it in her lap. 'This is such an incredible house, and the grounds—from what I've seen so far—are quite breathtaking! You must love living in such a beautiful place,' she commented conversationally.

Her blood ran cold as ice water at the look in his eyes. 'That is your assumption, is it?'

'I only meant that—'

'Don't be so quick to make careless judgements, Miss Cameron,' he advised broodingly. 'Have you not heard the adage "never judge a book by its cover"?'

CHAPTER TWO

'WHAT DO YOU MEAN?'

She found herself trapped by his glance for an almost excruciatingly long moment, and Georgia wondered what she'd said that was so wrong. There wasn't just irritation in his chastising glare. She was sensitive enough to detect some deep unhappiness there too, and for some reason her stomach turned hollow. There was such strength of will and vitality in Keir's strong, handsome face, and the idea that such an indomitable visage might be hiding some profound hurt behind it disturbed her more than she considered natural for somebody she'd only just met, and she didn't know why…

'It doesn't matter. Have you heard from Noah recently? No doubt you know he's coming for a visit next weekend?'

The swift change of subject caused her smooth brows to draw momentarily together. 'Yes, I know.

He rang me yesterday. We speak on the phone every couple of days.'

'And has he told you how he's getting along?'

Even as he asked the question Keir knew it wasn't Noah's welfare that was uppermost in his mind. He admired the younger man, of course—his professionalism, ability to work hard and deliver on a promise were commendable. But right then Keir was actually dwelling on the obviously close relationship he enjoyed with his disarming sister. To speak on the phone so often when they were away from each other was hardly something he could have imagined doing with his own brother.

He and Robbie had drifted apart many years ago—with Robbie preparing to take on the mantle of Laird after their father, with all that that entailed, and Keir leaving Glenteign just as soon as he could, to pursue his determination to go into business for himself and put his less than joyful childhood memories firmly behind him. Talking to his brother on a regular basis would only have reminded him of that dark period in his life, and Keir definitely didn't want reminders. The fact that he was back at Glenteign now, after all these years, and had inherited the role of Laird of the estate himself when he'd never wanted anything remotely to do with it again, was a twist of fate he hadn't foreseen. He was still learning to live with it…

'He seems happy enough…settling in and immersing himself in the job that has to be done.' The edges of her mouth lifting in a tentative smile, Georgia laid her hands one on top of the other in her lap, as if considering her words very carefully.

Sensing that his cutting remark had made her nervous, Keir told himself he should have been more guarded. Usually he was. After all, shielding his true feelings from others had become second nature to him since childhood.

'It was very good of you to recommend him to your friends in the Highlands,' Georgia continued. 'He's grown to love Scotland, and I know he would have found it a wrench to leave. Also, I don't think I thanked you for offering me this job of filling in for your own secretary. It's good to get out of London for a while. How is she, by the way? Your secretary, I mean?'

'Recovering slowly. It was a bad break, unfortunately, with some complications. She may have to have another operation to put it right.'

'I'm sorry to hear that.'

'That's why I needed someone who could step in and competently take over where Valerie left off. I've only been back at Glenteign for nine months myself, and what with organising the work on the gardens and getting them up to scratch again after the death of my brother… Well, there's a lot of work involved in running an estate like this and it doesn't get done by itself. Come and sit down, Moira… Is Lucy bringing the soup?'

'She'll be along directly.'

Georgia felt relief that the other woman had re-appeared. Even though she'd been shocked and sympathetic to hear that Keir had so recently lost his brother, and she longed to learn more, she was also wary of saying the wrong thing again. Hunger was also gnawing at her. Fast food at a motorway service station was no substitute for good home-cooked food, and that was a fact! She was honestly looking forward to her meal.

Sitting opposite Georgia at the beautifully laid table, Moira let her friendly brown eyes focus kindly on her.

'I just wanted to tell you, lassie, that Hamish has had the food you left for him, and is now curled up by the range in the kitchen. He was looking quite content when I left him, so there's no need for you to worry. I'm sure he's going to settle in just fine!'

'Thank you. It was very good of you to see to him like that. I'm sure he's loving every bit of all the extra attention he's been receiving!'

'He's a wee lamb, that's what he is! It's lovely for us to have a dog about the place again…isn't it, Chief Strachan?'

'If you say so…' Refusing to be drawn, Keir

glanced impatiently at the doorway just as the soup arrived, carried on a large solid silver tray by a very pretty auburn-haired girl who couldn't have been much older than seventeen.

When she would have served Keir first at the head of the table—as no doubt she usually did—surprisingly he directed her down to Georgia instead.

A brief smile touched the corners of a mouth that seemed somehow reluctant to utilise that gesture too often, and his gaze was wry. 'No doubt you're only too ready for your meal after your long drive, Georgia, and we won't keep you waiting any longer to fulfil your great need!'

Although pleased by his apparent thoughtfulness, Georgia was slightly embarrassed too. Perhaps he'd seen her relieved glance at the bowls of steaming soup on the tray Lucy carried and secretly thought it unseemly somehow that a woman should so unwittingly display her hunger? She was inhabiting a whole new world of manners and formality that she wasn't used to, and she would probably have to learn to be a little less impulsive and less apt to reveal her feelings.

'Well, it smells absolutely delicious! Carrot and coriander, if I'm not mistaken?'

'That's right lassie. So…do you like to cook yourself?' Moira asked politely.

Daring a swift glance at Keir from beneath her

curling chestnut lashes, Georgia picked up her spoon, waiting for both he and Moira to do the same before she started eating. 'I've always tried to prepare fresh food for me and Noah when he's at home, and, yes, I do enjoy a bit of cooking… But it's not always possible when we're both busy working and invariably get in quite late. I usually try and do something nice at the weekends, though…like a roast on a Sunday, with a home cooked pudding to follow. Apple crumble is Noah's favourite.'

'There's not many young women of your age who know a lot about cooking in my experience,' Keir commented thoughtfully. 'Apart from your brother, do you often cook for other people?'

In the flickering candlelight, his blue eyes glowed like the glint of fireflies, and for a moment Georgia felt as if they were the only two people in the room. 'No, not really. Like I said…' Her cheeks throbbed and burned beneath his unflinching cynosure. 'I'm usually busy working…both outside and in the home.'

'Are you telling me that you don't have a social life?'

Where was this leading? Georgia wondered, a sense of panic flowing through her bloodstream. All she wanted to do was enjoy her soup and assuage her hunger—not answer too awkward questions that made her feel vaguely as if she was being interrogated.

'I see my friends, and we do the usual things—like going to the cinema or eating out… So, yes—I do have a social life.'

The fact that she hadn't done any of the above for quite some time now, because she'd been too busy working hard, worrying about finances and fretting about Noah's welfare, was Georgia's private business and not the kind of thing she would remotely want to discuss with people she'd just met…however curious.

Keir saw the slightly agitated rise and fall of her chest in the unremarkable pink dress and didn't know why he was suddenly fishing for details about her private life. He was only aware of a disturbing tension deep inside him whenever his glance happened to settle on her beautiful face, which it seemed to be doing at a rather compelling rate. He should have quizzed Noah more about his sister. He should have somehow learned that she had the ability to mesmerise with her eyes, her smile, her voice…he should have learned that she blushed easily when discomfited or embarrassed, and that her smooth, silky skin glowed like satin in the flickering candlelight… If Keir had known these things before he'd gone ahead and hired her—then he might never have agreed to her coming to Glenteign at all. Georgia Cameron was too much of a disturbing distraction. Especially when there was so much that had to be done.

As much as he didn't want to be back in the family home, now that Robbie was gone he had a responsibility to carry on in his stead. Besides that, there was also the livelihood of the staff to think of, as well as the local people in the surrounding villages who had lived and worked on this land since time immemorial and had certain expectations of their Laird.

Glenteign had been in Keir's family for generations, and now there was no one left but him—and a distant ailing uncle in Cape Town, who was hardly interested or even desirous of coming back to Scotland after spending the majority of his life tending vineyards in South Africa. Keir had to be focused and committed to the task in hand if he was going to win the respect of people who looked up to him, and he needed to inspire the help and support that was necessary to help him do that. No…it wouldn't help his case one bit to become too friendly with the bewitching Ms Cameron…

'Let's eat, shall we? Or the soup will get cold.'

Directing a final rueful glance Georgia's way, Keir deliberately diverted his attention to his meal…

Rising early the next morning, Georgia pushed the memory of last night's slightly strained atmosphere at dinner determinedly out of her head. Today was a new day, she told herself, and she and her new boss needed time to get to know each other's ways before they both relaxed their guards a little around each other and felt more comfortable.

Although she didn't think it was likely that someone with the responsibility of such a large country estate and the weight all that must place on his shoulders would ever really relax their guard around anyone.

Nevertheless, Georgia was even more determined this morning to make things work. She'd been given a great opportunity to get out of London for a while and live in the countryside, which had always been a longed-for dream, as well as earning the best salary she'd made in ages, and she wasn't going to waste even a second filling her head with self-doubt about whether she'd done the right thing or not.

Allowing her lips to curve with pleasure at the thought of being able to explore her new surroundings at her leisure on her day off, she hurriedly washed and dressed. Throwing on jeans, trainers and an old sweatshirt of Noah's that she had commandeered a long time ago, she headed off to the kitchen to collect Hamish for his walk.

The rest of the house was as silent as a church as she carefully undid the sturdy locks on the front door and stepped outside. It was a rare morning, as her dad would have said, and a fine mist clung like a draped silken cobweb over the mountain peaks that edged above the tall firs in the distance. For a disturbing moment Georgia knew a pang of longing so great that she stood stock still, with Hamish gazing expectantly up at her, her hazel eyes awash with tears.

'You'd love it here, Dad,' she whispered softly beneath her breath. 'The air is so sweet you can almost taste it.' Resolutely scrubbing away the moisture on her cheeks, she raised her chin and walked from the great house with a spring in her step. As she feasted her hungry gaze on a landscape that would stir emotion in even the stoniest of hearts, she thought how she could easily live here and never set foot in another city or town again.

Overjoyed at being outdoors, and released off his lead, Hamish bounded across the springy emerald grass and headed off towards the magnificent sentinel of trees that stood guard in front of the mountains up ahead. And as Georgia followed behind him, at a more leisurely rate, the tensions she'd experienced on her first evening at Glenteign faded away...

Back in the house an hour later, she declined the cooked breakfast that apparently Keir was enjoying in the smaller dining room, to share a pot of tea and a plate of hot buttered toast and marmalade with Moira Guthrie, in the expansive country kitchen.

As the two women sat companionably together at the family-sized pine table, the owner of Glenteign walked in.

'Georgia…I'd like a word, if I may?'

She started to rise to her feet, caught off guard by his sudden appearance and almost too aware of the innate sense of authority he brought into the room with his presence. With his lean, yet muscular build, everything he wore looked tailor-made for him…not to mention expensive. Even away from this amazing house and its vast grounds there would be an air of exclusivity about Keir Strachan that would always make him stand out from the crowd.

Suddenly Georgia's appetite disappeared, and she tucked a wayward chestnut curl behind her ear with less grace than she would have liked. 'Yes, of course.'

'When you've finished your breakfast will do. I'll be in my study. Moira will show you where it is.'

He'd gone again before she'd even voiced a reply. Sitting back down in her chair, Georgia inadvertently released a sigh.

'A word about the young Laird, my dear,' Moira said, resting her elbows on the table. 'He may come across as rather brusque at times, but he has a lot of responsibility on his shoulders. Not only is he Laird here, but he also has a business to think of. No matter what you might think he does have kindness in him, so don't judge him too quickly—will you, lassie?'

Georgia was still dwelling on what the housekeeper had told her when she stood outside Keir's study door a short while later. To her surprise he answered her knock almost straight away, and ushered her inside. Experiencing a deep jolt at the definitely masculine ambience of the imposing room she found herself in, Georgia couldn't help feeling she was somehow intruding.

Keir turned his deep blue gaze towards her.

'I trust you slept well? I know it's not always the case the first few nights in a strange house, but I'm sure you'll quickly get used to things.'

Surprisingly, Georgia *had* slept well. No doubt the long day's drive to get to Glenteign and her trepidation about what things would be like when she got there had contributed to her near exhaustion when her head had finally hit the pillow.

'Yes, I slept very well, thank you.'

'And your room is to your liking?'

'It's lovely.'

'Moira takes care of all that sort of thing…always has. She's been housekeeper here since my father's time, so if you need anything at all or want to know where anything is she's the person to ask.'

Seeing the question in her clear hazel eyes and sure he hadn't misread it, Keir held Georgia's glance with a wry twist of his lips.

'Unfortunately there's no Lady Glenteign to help exert that essential feminine influence that makes a house a home. So apart from my bedroom and this study—a room that I view strictly as my own domain—you'll no doubt see evidence of those important female touches everywhere else in the house courtesy of my housekeeper.'

Vaguely discomfited by the fact that he'd practically read her mind, Georgia moved her glance to the opened casement window opposite Keir's desk and back again. 'You mentioned last night at dinner that your brother had died? I just wanted to say how sorry I was to hear that. It must be devastating to lose someone so close in your family.'

'We weren't as close as we might have been, but, yes…it was quite awful to lose him.'

Seeing the sympathy on her concerned face, Keir felt strangely at odds admitting something so personal to a woman he'd only just met—like trying on a suit that didn't fit—and was frankly surprised that he'd allowed himself to be so uncharacteristically candid. But sometimes the pain of losing Robbie and remembering the bleak reality of their childhood was so crushing that he thought he might go mad if he didn't ever speak his feelings out loud. Yet he knew in reality that he couldn't afford to show even a hint of such weakness to anybody. In his illustrious family it just wasn't done.

'Was he married? Did he have a family of his own?' Georgia ventured.

'The answer is no, to both of those questions.

Thank you for your condolences, but I really do need to get on.'

'Right.'

He saw her own guard come up, and immediately regretted it.

'So? Presumably you wanted to talk to me about work?'

She crossed her arms over her chest in the too-large navy blue sweatshirt she wore, with its recognisable sports motif, and Keir realised that it had probably belonged to her brother at some point. The realisation immediately reminded him of how close the two of them must be, and he knew again a faint yet disturbing pang of envy.

Because Robbie was dead, and he would now never have the chance to be close to him even if he wished it, and because he'd been forced to return to Glenteign when he'd rather be a million miles away, Keir's pain spilled over into sudden irritation.

'I know it's Sunday, but we're going to have to make a start on things today. Everything's got far too behind to be left until tomorrow, so the sooner we start to tackle the backlog, the better. If you had any plans to look round the gardens or drive into the village, then I'm afraid you're going to be disappointed.'

'I didn't make any plans to go anywhere, and I'm perfectly aware that I came here to work. It's no problem for me to work on a Sunday… I've done it many times.'

'Good. Then might I suggest that you change into something a little more appropriate for work, and come back here in…' he gave a perfunctory glance at his watch '…say twenty minutes?'

'I'm only dressed like this because I took Hamish for a walk!'

'The shirt is your brother's, I take it?'

'Is that a problem?'

For a moment Keir saw mutiny in her surprised glance, and as his gaze descended from those flashing hazel eyes of hers to her softly bare mouth an unexpected jolt of sexual heat zig-zagged hotly through his insides. The sensation staggered him, arising unbidden as it did—and in what could hardly be deemed a 'provocative' situation.

'I don't have time to stand here bandying words with you, Ms Cameron… Just go and do as I say, will you?'

CHAPTER THREE

THE SLIGHTLY COOLER evening air that breezed in through the open casement windows arrested Georgia's attention with the ravishing floral scent it brought with it. Seated at the absent Valerie's desk, immersed in typing yet another long and involved letter regarding estate business, she briefly closed her eyes and inhaled deeply. The hypnotic perfume of roses in full bloom was almost soporific, and undeniably sensual as well. Lifting her arms, she stretched like a contented cat, her breasts pushing against the Indian cotton of her blouse, and the ache in her back from sitting too long eased.

'When you've finished that letter we may as well call it a day.'

Her eyes flew open again at the sound of Keir's rich, cultured tones. They'd worked alongside each other mainly in silence save for a couple of telephone calls he'd had to make, with Keir and herself only speaking when it was absolutely essential. Having been quite content with this arrangement, Georgia had to reacquaint herself with the sound of his arresting voice.

A brief surge of disturbing heat flowed through her in response, and she quickly dropped her arms and turned her head to look at him.

Having observed her unknowingly seductive stretch, and seen the points of her breasts strain the material of the soft white blouse she wore, Keir reeled from the thunderbolt of desire that shot through his insides at the sight. In fact, he'd plainly detected a husky inflection in his voice that had been the direct result of that moment of unexpected sexual excitement.

'Are you sure? I don't mind working on for another hour or so, if you need me to,' she replied.

He was sorely tempted to agree. If only to hope that he might glimpse such an unwittingly sensual little manoeuvre again… *Good God, he had been working too hard!* Suddenly impatient with himself, Keir got to his feet and swept the pile of correspondence he'd been diligently sifting through deliberately aside.

'Enough is enough,' he said gruffly, raking his fingers through his straight dark hair. 'Besides…dinner is at seven on a Sunday, and no doubt you'll want to take Hamish for a walk before you go and get ready.'

'He's not the only one who could do with a stretch of the legs.' Georgia smiled. 'I feel as if I've been welded to this chair, I've sat in it so long!'

'Finding the going too tough already? This is only the tip of the iceberg. The week ahead will be even harder.'

His mocking words completely demolished her smile.

'It's not too tough at all! I'm used to a fairly punishing pace, and I can handle it so please don't worry on that score.'

'I'm glad to hear it. Tomorrow morning we've got a hundred and one things to get through, not *least* catching up with the rest of this wretched correspondence! It seems to have grown into a veritable mountain since Valerie's accident. I also need you to liaise with Moira and the kitchen staff about a couple of dinners that I'm giving at the house which are coming up. After that I need you to familiarise yourself with the local post office in Lochheel, because I'll need you to take the post there at the end of each day, and after that…' He paused, to make sure she was keeping up with this itinerary. 'In the evening I'll need you to come with me to Dundee, where I'm attending a classical concert. It's a charity benefit, organised by a friend of mine, and as I have an invitation for two I thought you might as well come and enjoy the evening with me. Did you bring anything suitable to wear to a black-tie event?'

He was asking her to sit through an entire concert with him? Listening to some blissful classical music would not be in the least bit arduous, but spending the evening with a man who seemed not to even know the meaning of the word 'relax' definitely would! Even though they had worked together in relative peace, she had still easily sensed the tension in him. Every time he'd moved, even a little bit, he'd practically made her jump! And, reflecting quickly on the contents of the suitcase she had brought, Georgia knew straight away that she didn't possess the kind of sophisticated outfit that he was no doubt hoping she possessed to wear to this event.

'No...I'm afraid I don't,' she told him. 'I didn't expect that I'd need—'

'In that case I'll have to talk to Moira. There are a couple of vintage dresses that have been in the family for years. I'm sure there must be one in your size. I'll ask Moira to show you, and you can try them on.' His relentlessly blue eyes narrowing impatiently, Keir frowned. 'If they're not suitable then we'll just have to add shopping to our itinerary and get you something.'

Georgia's spine stiffened in protest. *She didn't want to spend money on an expensive evening dress she might never wear again just so that Keir Strachan wouldn't be embarrassed by her lack of suitable attire on just one occasion!*

'Perhaps I could just sit and wait for you outside the concert hall?' she suggested, thinking how that would be infinitely preferable to enduring a shopping trip she couldn't afford with a man who put her so on edge she would be apt to buy the first unsuitable dress she set eyes on because he distracted her so!

'Out of the question! Don't you enjoy dressing up on occasion? Most women I know don't find it such a great hardship.'

Surprised to find amusement lurking in his compelling eyes, Georgia did not smile back. 'I'm afraid I manage on quite a tight budget that doesn't run to buying lots of expensive clothes. I have a brother, a house and a dog to look after, as well as myself, and that takes quite a bit of financial juggling I can tell you!'

He was frowning again as she finished speaking, and Georgia's heart was thumping too hard inside her chest at having confessed her situation so candidly. But one thing she didn't want to do—even to save face—was pretend. In her book it was always best to tell the truth…no matter what. Her parents had drummed that fact into both her and Noah from almost as soon as they could talk.

'I agree that London can be an expensive place to live,' Keir commented. 'But isn't Noah's gardening business paying its way yet?'

'Glenteign was his first really decent commission. Every spare penny we've both earned has gone back into the business. It's early days yet, but Noah is such a brilliant designer I'm sure it won't be long before people are flocking to his door to get him to come and design their gardens!'

'Judging from what I've personally experienced of his abilities, I'm sure you're right.'

'Well…I'll just finish this letter, then I'll go and walk Hamish.'

'Georgia?'

'Yes?'

'I'm sure Moira will come up with something to save the day.'

Feeling heat rush into her cheeks at the unexpected kindness in his voice, Georgia turned her attention back to her typing.

Watching her slender fingers fly across the keyboard at a rate that was definitely impressive, Keir silently acknowledged that so far everything that Noah had said about his sister's secretarial skills was true. She'd coped with everything he had thrown at her today, and she hadn't flapped…not *once*. *He regretted it if he'd embarrassed her about a dress for the benefit concert, but he'd appreciated her candour.* Not many people would have had the guts to tell him the truth about their finances—and without any sense of feeling hard done by either, just simply stating facts.

'Good. That's settled, then.'

Going to the door, he stood there for at least half a minute, staring at the way her long chestnut hair curled so provocatively at the ends and remembering the way her flimsy cotton blouse had outlined her very arresting figure as she'd stretched. By the time Keir turned away to leave the room he found himself to be in a state of highly aroused tension, and the only sensible thing to do to alleviate it was to put some distance between his new secretary and himself as quickly as possible…

'And where are you off to this fine morning, my dear?'

Keir's friendly housekeeper waylaid Glenteign's newest employee as she was about to get into her car the next morning. The day was seasonably warm and bright, and Georgia was wearing a dark lime cotton sweater with white tapered linen trousers, very conscious since his remark about Noah's shirt not to appear too casual for her employer's liking.

Pushing her sunglasses onto the top of her head, she smiled, already feeling very much at home with the older woman.

'I'm off to Lochheel. I need to go to the post office for the Chief. He was going to take me himself, but he's got several phone calls to make this morning and can't spare the time.'

The truth of it was—because he'd definitely got out of the wrong side of the bed this morning, judging by his extremely tetchy mood—Georgia was glad to be going on her own. It would also give her a chance to enjoy some of the spectacular countryside without having to make stilted conversation with her new boss.

'That's usually the way of it…' Moira sighed. 'The man just always has so much to do! Considering he's scarcely been Laird here for two minutes, it's an absolute credit to his skill and dedication that he's already achieved so much!'

Georgia frowned, thinking. 'So his brother was Laird here before him? Is that right?'

'Until he was killed in that terrible car accident in America…yes, he was. Nobody thought that Keir would ever come back here again…even for a visit! But Robbie's death changed everything for him.' The kind brown eyes of the other woman crinkled with concern around the edges for a moment, as if she'd inadvertently revealed more than she should have. 'Look at me, standing here chatting away when I need to get on! Enjoy your drive to Lochheel, lassie. No doubt I'll see you again later.'

For a few moments, as the housekeeper bustled away to get on with her own busy tasks, Georgia stood stock still on the gravel drive beside her car, her mind captured by what Moira had said about nobody thinking that Keir would ever come back to Glenteign and how his brother's death had changed everything for him. Was that why he had warned her during their first dinner together that she should not be so quick to make 'careless judgements'?

Having clearly assumed that he must love living at Glenteign, Georgia was now getting the distinct impression that he didn't, and that there were good reasons why he didn't... But how tragic—to live in such an amazing place, with all the advantages that most people could only fantasise about, and yet secretly wish you were somewhere else.

Sometimes the ironies of life just got to her—they really did. There was Georgia, living in a small cramped house in Hounslow, directly beneath the flight path of the planes out of Heathrow, struggling to keep her head above water, dreaming of the peace and quiet of a place like this and wishing that money wasn't such an issue. And there was Keir, living with the complete antithesis of her own situation and yet apparently deeply unhappy. How was anybody supposed to make sense of it all?

Shaking herself out of her reverie, she got into the car, briefly studied the map she'd left on the seat, then gunned the engine and drove off. Although she would take great pleasure in enjoying the scenery as she drove, she would find Lochheel and locate the post office as quickly as she could—then get back to

Glenteign to at least try and alleviate some of the burden of work that was clearly getting her new boss down…

They'd scarcely taken a moment to even glance at the cups of tea Moira had brought them at varying intervals that afternoon, they'd both worked so hard. Now, as Georgia sat in front of the elegant Victorian mirror on her dressing table and applied a deep plum lipstick, she told herself she was feeling far less tense at the idea of accompanying Keir to the classical concert than she had been earlier.

Working alongside him, seeing how effortlessly he seemed to get the measure of situations and handle them, how diplomatic and concerned he could be when addressing more sensitive issues presented to him both by letter and on the telephone, there was much to admire about the man. And that was apart from his brilliantly azure eyes and his firm, handsome jaw…

Catching the flare of her own dark pupils reflected back at her, Georgia momentarily stilled, her fingers gripping the slim metal case of her lipstick and her cheeks suffusing with heat.

Years of celibacy must have made my mind deranged if I can think for even one minute that he and I could—

She shut off the thought abruptly, already too disturbed by the erotic image that presented itself so temptingly in her mind, dropped her lipstick into her make-up bag, and pushed to her feet.

Crossing over to the bed, to fetch the black-fringed Spanish-style evening shawl that Moira insisted went with the dramatic black evening dress she'd borrowed for the evening, she almost jumped through the roof at the loud knock that sounded at the door.

'Georgia, lassie?'

It was Moira herself. Sighing with pure relief, Georgia put her hand to her chest to still the sudden disconcerting surge of her heartbeat. For one dreadful moment there she'd thought it might be Keir. She felt quite a different person in the beautiful borrowed dress, and she needed some time to compose herself before she faced her boss. She picked up her purse.

'The Chief is waiting for you outside in the car,' the housekeeper continued cheerfully. 'He asked me to come and tell you to please hurry up!'

In the middle of Barber's *Adagio for Strings*—a piece of music that always reminded him that the things of this world were ultimately fragile and did not last, Keir glanced at his companion's rapt profile and experienced a searing stab of need so great that it actually caused his heart to race.

Georgia Cameron looked so stunning that she

provoked powerful stirrings of desire and longing in Keir that he could not ignore. Neither had he been blind to the admiring glances that had come her way when they'd walked into the early nineteenth-century building that was housing the concert tonight. And it was perfectly true that his male ego knew a certain sense of pride at being her escort.

Her compelling dark beauty highlighted the impact of the dramatic black satin dress she wore even more and Keir could not imagine that anyone had looked half as arresting in it before. Whoever had first bought it had had good taste, though. The black dress had an ultra-feminine style that was definitely from the 1930s or 1950s, and it was subtly sexy in a way that most twenty-first-century women's clothing was not. Its nipped-in waist made the most of Georgia's womanly curves, and the elegant neckline exposed flawless skin that no beauty product could hope to emulate in a million years.

Keir wondered if Georgia even guessed at the riveting impression both she and the dress were making on the people around them. Several of his acquaintances who were in the audience this evening had glanced their way with frank curiosity many times after Keir and Georgia had left their company to circulate the room—when they'd thought he wasn't aware of them looking. They were all too polite to suggest openly that his stunning compan-

ion might be a bit more than just his temporary secretary, and the normally intensely private Keir found
to his surprise that for once he didn't actually mind
the silent speculation that was going on.

Since his return, gossip in the local community
had been rife about whom he was or was not dating.
Although he was a well-travelled businessman, there
was an unspoken preference around Glenteign that
any girlfriend of the Laird should definitely hail from
closer to home. The older folk especially were
always hoping for a wedding, and for the young
Laird to settle down with his eventual new wife and
start a family. They had been disappointed when
Robbie had not been able to achieve that, and now
naturally they expected Keir to do what his brother
had not. That was the way of it when you lived
amongst a community steeped in history and tradition. *It was a ball and chain that he could live
without...*

That was why, when it had come to looking at some
new fresh designs for the formal gardens, Keir had deliberately chosen a young, innovative designer like
Noah Cameron, instead of someone more obviously
traditional. It was important to move with the times.
And, no matter what his respect for what had gone
before, he was his own man and would *not* be dictated
to as to how he should run the estate by *anyone*.

As the sweetly sensual fragrance Georgia wore

caused another flare of acute electricity to silently implode inside him Keir had to secretly attest to a fascination for her that seemed to be gathering strength as the evening went on...

During the interval, as he accepted a glass of champagne from a black-tied waiter and Georgia selected sparkling mineral water instead, Keir endeavoured to find them a more private corner in the crowded room.

Above them, suspended from the high, ornate ceiling, was a rather spectacular chandelier, its crystal teardrops shimmering like the most fabulous diamonds. To add to the indisputable grandeur that surrounded them, the walls were covered in portraits of illustrious Victorians with—it had to be said—expressions that had little joy in them.

'How are you enjoying the concert?'

For a few moments her interested glance seemed to alight on everything else in the sumptuously beautiful room but *him*—as though all the treasures it held had to be given the proper time and consideration they deserved.

'Do you know what a gift you've given me tonight?' Her green-gold eyes were shining. 'The music just swept me away! In my opinion doctors should prescribe classical concerts at least once a month rather than Prozac...then I'm sure most of the population wouldn't be half so depressed!'

Her words were so passionate and her eyes glowed with such intensity of emotion that Keir could find nothing to say for the moment. He simply stared. Rarely did he meet anyone who expressed their love of the arts so vociferously. *What would it be like to have a relationship with such a woman?*

He had dated many women over the years, but had never enjoyed a true connection—a deep bond of mind, body and soul—with any of them. Keir knew that the fault more than likely lay with him. He had got too used to covering up his true feelings and was just not capable of sharing the real man behind the mask, with anyone.

'I'm sure you're right—although the National Health Service would soon be bankrupt if they did!'

His smile was genuinely amused, but the gesture did not fully reach his compelling blue eyes, Georgia saw. The tenuous nature of it underlined her opinion that being wealthy did not help keep the psychological discomfort of life away. She couldn't help wondering what demons dogged him. The loss of his brother had to be one, but what were the others?

Georgia intimately knew what her own were: the fear of something dreadful happening to her or Noah, losing their house, becoming sick and not being able to work. And ending up alone…that was a biggie. She sighed, not liking the sudden wave of melancholy that engulfed her when only moments ago she'd been so elated.

'I read a quote somewhere that most people's troubles arise from the fact that they can't sit alone in a room in silence. Maybe they're afraid to face what might come up? It's probably like stirring a great soup…you don't know what might rise to the surface…and that's why people have to stay busy to distract themselves. What do you think?'

'We live in a world of commerce and achieving. We don't all have the time to sit and contemplate our navels.'

His caustic comment privately pained her, but even so Georgia could tell that her reflections had disturbed Keir.

'Well, then…it's just as well that sometimes we're fortunate to have opportunities like tonight—to sit and listen to sublime music that feeds the spirit and helps us contemplate other things besides the world of commerce!' There was deliberate challenge in her tone. 'I for one would go mad if I wasn't able to find some peace somewhere!'

Georgia had seen how moved Keir had been by the music, even though he might hurry to deny it. She would have registered his response even if she *hadn't* turned briefly to glance at his riveted profile. The emotional tension in him had been *palpable*. It had made Georgia aware that there were hidden depths to this serious-minded businessman and Laird, and driven her to speculate that perhaps he *did* possess a

less harsh and guarded side. A side he was determined not to expose to the world. *Was he afraid of
being hurt somehow?* It was a *provocative* idea, even
though Georgia told herself she'd be a fool to explore
it any further.

'Yes—peace. I suppose that's ultimately what we
all want.' Surprisingly, he acquiesced, 'So tell
me...what other things besides music do you enjoy?'

'Oh, there isn't any lack of occupations. It's just
having the time to do them that's the problem.'

'For instance?'

'Well...' Georgia's smile was as disarming as that
of a little girl who'd just been told she was to be a
bridesmaid for the first time. 'Reading is a great
passion—I love to lose myself in a good book... I also
enjoy a bit of gardening myself from time to time...tiny
though our little plot is! I also love hiking and swimming and going to the movies. Can I have a couple
more?' She sucked in a deep breath and laughed.
'Taking long rambling walks with Hamish, and—
finally!—spending time with my brother of course.'

'You must be greatly looking forward to seeing
him at the weekend.'

'Oh, yes!' Her eyes sparkled with undisguised
longing. 'I've missed him very much!'

Keir was mesmerised by the animation in her
face.

'How long has it been since you last saw him?'

'At least three months. He came back home one weekend at the end of May for a brief visit. You were in New York on business—I remember him telling me.'

Keir remembered too. He'd been meeting with officials regarding Robbie's car accident. His rental car had been hit side-on by a drunken driver. He hadn't had a chance of saving himself. Keir's gut clenched hard as iron.

'Have you and Noah always been so close?' he asked, the pain ebbing a little as he forced himself to concentrate on Georgia's answer.

'We lost our parents one after the other in the same year. Noah was fourteen and I was just five years older. We have no other living family, so I was determined to take care of us both.'

Her cheeks had turned an impassioned pink, and Keir absorbed what she had told him with a sense of shock—for a moment his own pain at the memory of Robbie's death was banished.

'That was an amazingly brave thing to do at nineteen,' he said with admiration.

Georgia's eyebrows flew up to her hairline. 'It wasn't brave at all! What else would I have done? Let them take him away from me? My own little brother? Let him go to strangers who wouldn't love him like I do?' Her hazel eyes sparkled with unshed tears. 'I could never have lived with myself if I'd done that!

And my parents would have turned in their graves! Families should stick together…especially when times are tough. Don't you agree?'

CHAPTER FOUR

THERE WAS NO DOUBT in Keir's mind that she meant emotionally and not just physically. But since his own parents had never been there for him or his brother in that way he could not immediately give Georgia an answer.

His mother had drunk herself to death when Keir was just eleven—no doubt to escape the foul black tempers of his father which had become increasingly worse and more threatening as the years had gone on.

Robbie had been terrified of the old man, and Keir had defied him as much as he'd been able to—he'd worn the bruises to prove it—but nothing had made any difference to how James Strachan treated his sons. Not until he'd become ill himself and seen the gates of death beckoning. By which time, of course, it had all been too late. How Moira Guthrie had stayed working for such a man—never mind nursing him after he'd got ill—Keir had never understood. He'd asked her once, and her reply had frankly stunned him.

'I saw that he had good in him,' she had asserted, in her quiet yet forthright way, and Keir had had to acquiesce that the woman had far more forbearance and forgiveness in her than he could ever hope to have.

For himself, he couldn't ever foresee a time when he would be able to forgive James Strachan his transgressions. The man had simply not been fit to be a father.

A muscle throbbing at the side of his temple, Keir grimaced before answering Georgia's question. 'In an ideal world I suppose families should stick together,' he remarked. 'But as we both know this world is far from ideal, and people who have no business even contemplating having children sadly do, and screw up their kids' lives as well as their own.'

And God only knew what pretty Georgia Cameron with her passionate adherence to family loyalty and love would have made of his completely unnatural family! He shuddered to think.

'Ladies and gentlemen, would you please find your seats as the concert will resume in three minutes' time…'

Relieved by the instruction that meant their conversation had to come to an end—because it was touching upon things that made him uneasy—Keir inclined his head briefly towards his companion. 'Time to get back.'

'Yes.'

Seeing a look that might have been concern in her pretty eyes and steeling himself against it, Keir took Georgia's glass, deposited it beside his own and, unable to resist the opportunity to touch her, put his hand beneath her elbow to steer her back towards their seats.

'All the worry and stress has gone from your eyes.'

'Has it?'

Her relaxed stroll coming to a stop on one of the myriad footpaths throughout the gardens, Georgia turned to regard her tall, blond, blue-eyed brother, and couldn't suppress the effervescent bubble of happiness that rose up inside her at the sight of him.

He'd arrived at Glenteign only last night for the weekend and she had been thrilled to see a familiar, smiling face.

'This place has done wonders for you...I can see that.' Looking thoughtful, Noah reached out and fingered a curling tendril of her chestnut hair. 'You're a different girl...and you've lost that grey London pallor!'

'Who wouldn't love it here?'

Turning slightly away from him, Georgia leant

forward to smell the scent of a drowsy yellow rose, drooping heavily on its stem beside the footpath. The path was resplendent on all sides with foliage, plants and flowers—some past their best, since September was swiftly approaching, but still lovely all the same.

Roses had always been her favourite. She supposed it was because her mother had loved them so, and had always brought one or two into the house from the garden to light up a room when she was feeling a little melancholy. Even though she and Noah had been on their own for years now, Georgia still found it hard sometimes to realise that their mother was no longer there...her father too. They had been such wonderful, loving parents.

For some reason just at that moment the memory crept into her mind of what Keir had said at the concert. Something about not living in an ideal world, and how some people should never have children because they not only screwed up their own lives but their kids' as well. Was that what had happened to Keir and his brother Robbie?

Her brow creased with renewed concern. She'd already concluded that the Laird of Glenteign was not exactly the happiest of men. Sometimes she glimpsed such singular sadness in his riveting blue eyes that she longed to be able to banish it for good... But she knew it was a very dangerous impulse, and one that should definitely be curbed if she didn't want to find herself not just hurt but out of a job too…

'And what about the Highlands? What about where you're working now?' she asked Noah, determined to focus on her brother's visit above all else while he was there. 'Do you like it as much as Glenteign?'

'Oh, it's beautiful enough, all right—and the couple I'm working for are very down-to-earth…despite being landed gentry! But I enjoyed perhaps some of the best months of my life working here.' Noah lapsed into a reflective stroll again and Georgia joined him. 'Keir was great to work for. Easy to discuss my ideas with, and very fair. I enjoyed his company. How are you finding him, Georgie?'

'Oh …' She shrugged to deflect attention from the hectic colour that she knew had rushed into her cheeks at the mention of her boss. 'There were a few awkward moments at first, but now we're getting along just fine. He's off to New York on business again on Monday, so we've been very busy the past few days trying to do as much as possible before he goes.'

It was odd, but when Keir had announced the day after the benefit concert that he was going away, Georgia's stomach had turned strangely hollow. No one she'd ever worked for had had such a peculiar effect on her before.

'Oh, well… You'll enjoy being your own boss for a while, won't you?'

'Yes, I'm sure I will.'

Georgia wondered what Noah would think if he knew that the big masculine study where they worked together already seemed strangely desolate even with the idea of Keir not being there with her. The man was such a presence that the big house would not seem the same without him.

'Anyway…' Linking her arm in his, Georgia grinned. 'Guess what's for dessert at dinner tonight, in your honour?'

'Not apple crumble?'

'I asked Moira if she could arrange it as a special treat.'

'Be still my beating heart!'

Keir heard the laughter from the open study window and, drawn there away from the sheaf of legal documents he'd been busy perusing at his desk—he glanced out over the ledge towards the ground below. His heart gave a jolt at the sight of Georgia in a white summer dress, her shining chestnut hair arranged in a loose, girlish ponytail. She looked very young and carefree. Beside her was her brother, and together they made an eye-catching pair, the striking blond Noah and his darker, bewitching sister.

A slash of envy curled almost painfully in the pit of Keir's stomach. They might have lost their parents, but he could see that the bond between them was an extremely close and affectionate one. Again he thought of Robbie, and how the distance between him and his brother had grown ever wider over the years. Back at Glenteign—the root of all his early misery and pain—Keir had never felt more emotionally isolated than he did right at that moment. The sight of Georgia and Noah's delight in seeing each other merely reconfirmed that he'd made the right decision in electing to go to New York on business.

The matter that called him there was hardly urgent—he had good people working for him, who were quite capable of dealing with it—but Keir found he was glad of the excuse to go away again for a while. Being around Georgia Cameron was just unsettling him far too much, and perhaps with some real distance between them he might get things back into perspective. She was only at Glenteign temporarily, until the dependable Valerie recovered from her injury and came back. It wasn't wise to get too used to having her here, and in New York there was a girl Keir had met on his last trip. He'd vaguely promised to get in touch with her on his return…

* * *

After Noah and Kier had left, Georgia was greatly unsettled. To alleviate the restlessness that had come upon her, after work each day, and at the weekend, she walked for miles with Hamish, exploring and enjoying her breathtaking surroundings.

One day, after scrabbling over some challenging rocky crags, her back damp with perspiration and her clothes sticking to her beneath her waterproof— while Hamish had made comparatively light work of the same arduous climb beside her—she came upon a shining silvery loch, exquisitely positioned amidst tall pines. It was like discovering paradise... The sight so undid her that Georgia immediately burst into tears when she saw it.

Sitting back on a rock, she put her arms around Hamish and held him there, her gaze enthralled. She was moved almost unbearably by the spectacular scene in front of her. Did Keir ever come up here? she speculated. If he didn't, then he should. Surely the sight of all this wild, unfettered beauty would have the power to chase away all his heartache? Her own heart turned over at the memory of his strong, serious face, and she sincerely hoped that whatever he was doing in New York he might find some comfort there from the worries that beset him.

Perhaps there was a woman there who might

provide that comfort? The thought was like the viper in the Garden of Eden.

'No!'

Hamish pulled away from her in surprise. She hadn't meant to voice her disapproval out loud, and Georgia was shocked by her own unrestrained outburst.

'What am I saying?' she muttered crossly, getting to her feet and wiping loose grass from her corduroy jeans. 'He means nothing to me other than that I just work for the man! I have no right to be jealous if he's seeing some fabulously beautiful woman in New York! Why should I care? Come on Hamish…time to get back! We don't want to be late for dinner!'

Determinedly banishing thoughts of Keir from her mind, she started to negotiate the climb back down the rocks again. But a melancholy had descended that she couldn't shake, and it stayed with her for the rest of the day until she went to bed later that evening…

A few days later, the sultry weather they'd been having finally broke at around ten to midnight. An almighty crack of thunder vented its fury above the turreted rooftops of Glenteign, and Georgia sat up in bed in shock as a streak of lightning lit up the room, briefly and eerily illuminating all the previously dark corners and making her clutch at the thin cotton sheet which was all the covering her overheated body could bear.

She had a love/hate relationship with thunderstorms. While she had a secret admiration for the passion and fury they displayed, which reminded her that no matter what humankind achieved it could *not* control the elements, they frightened her deeply. Of course she'd never displayed that fear to Noah— not when he was young and had naturally relied on her to help him feel secure. But when she was on her own, as she was now, it was hard to keep her anxiety completely at bay.

She'd suffered an agony of tension all day because she'd known that a storm was threatening, and she'd guessed it would come tonight. And while Georgia despised the fear that it evoked in her, which she couldn't entirely control, she found herself wishing that Keir was at least at home, in his room down the hall from hers. It would have given her a measure of security just to know that he was there. But Keir was still in New York, and she had received no word as to when he would be returning.

Something that sounded vaguely like a door opening and closing broke into her consciousness. But as the rain started to lash with some ferocity at the casement windows with their lavish undrawn curtains Georgia wondered if she'd imagined it. Her ears strained for a repetition of the sound, or some follow-up to it, but all she heard was the rain pounding relentlessly at everything it touched. She let out her breath slowly and forced herself to try and relax.

All of a sudden she was certain she heard someone walking about in the corridor outside, and her heart leapt into her mouth. *Was it Moira?* But the housekeeper's room was on the floor below hers. What reason would she have for coming up here in the middle of the night? A new, more terrifying thought occurred.

What if they were being burgled? What if the sound she'd heard hadn't been a door innocently being opened and then closed by one of the staff, but the sound of someone breaking into the house instead?

What better distraction than a fierce thunderstorm to drown out any sound of broken glass caused by climbing through a downstairs window or breaking and entering through a side door somewhere?

Trembling hard, Georgia shoved the cotton sheet aside and slid smoothly and quietly out of bed. Switching on her lamp, dim light flooded the room. That at least reassured her. Reaching for the thin pink robe hanging over the end of the brass bedstead, she pulled it on over her bare body and swiftly tied the belt. Then, tiptoeing across the carpet, she reached for the iron poker that lay in the old-fashioned fireplace. Surprised at how heavy it was, clutching it between her hands as though it were some kind of broadsword, she crossed the room slowly to the door.

She didn't know exactly what she intended to do, or how on earth she was supposed to deal with some burly thug bent on thieving something valuable—she only knew that this was Keir's *home* that was being violated whilst he was away, and that Moira and the other staff slept on oblivious downstairs. Clearly someone had to do something!

The sound of footsteps was no more, but she thought she heard a muttered expletive—a man's voice, low and harsh. Georgia's heart began to pound so hard that to her sensitive hearing the sound drowned out the noise of the heavy rain that was pelting the windows. *Oh, dear God...* Muttering a swift prayer for help, she turned the doorknob and wrenched open the door. The light from her bedside lamp escaped into the darkened corridor and cast an eerie yellow glow.

'Just what the hell do you think you're doing?' she demanded, her gaze latching with fright onto the six-feet-plus frame of the menacing individual hovering outside Keir's bedroom door.

'I might ask you the same bloody question!' came back the irritated and furious reply.

'Keir!'

'If I were you, Georgia, I'd put down that extremely lethal looking poker before you drop it on your foot and break a couple of bones!'

'I thought you were a burglar!'

'You thought *what?*' His hard handsome face was glistening with moisture from the rain, and his jacket and trousers were darkened in several places from the spreading damp. Keir's disbelieving blue eyes regarded Georgia as though she was deranged.

Her heart slowing to a more normal beat, she pushed still shaking fingers through her tousled dark hair, her relief too immense to be measured. 'You should have rung to let us know that you were coming home!' she said accusingly.

'Why?'

Studying her with a mockingly sensual grin, Keir let his gaze drop deliberately to the thin, inadequate robe that was clearly outlining the very feminine contours of Georgia's body. Of course he must know that underneath it she was naked.

'Are you telling me that you missed me?'

What a question! Her gaze cleaving to the darkly brooding expression on his hard-hewn features, Georgia felt as if her breath had been suddenly snatched from her lungs. She'd missed his presence, yes... But surely not in the way he was implying? She quickly laid the heavy poker down on the casement windowsill beside her, as though it were now something distasteful, and curled her fingers into the flimsy edges of her robe around the neckline. Her skin was hot and prickling beneath his mocking regard.

'You're the owner of this house... I'm sure—I'm sure everybody notices it when you're not here.'

'That's not what I asked, and you know it!'

Impatiently Keir threw off his sodden jacket, uncaring where it landed, and scraped his hand through his equally damp dark hair as if too furious to contain his rage.

'And if I *had* been a burglar, what exactly did you think you could do against some threatening thug twice your size? Even *with* a poker? You could have got yourself killed or badly injured! Didn't it occur to you to phone the police if you suspected someone was breaking in? Dear Lord! Don't you have any common sense?'

An explosive crash of thunder overhead leached the colour from Georgia's already pale face. Coupled with the tension that was already holding her stomach in a vice, it made hot, frustrated tears spring readily to her eyes.

'Stop shouting at me! I was scared—scared of who you might be, *and* of this hateful storm!'

Needing to get away, Georgia fled back into her room and slammed the door behind her. *Awful, horrible, ingrate!* It would have served him bloody well right if burglars had ransacked the whole house and stolen everything he held dear!

But even as the tears started to roll down her cheeks, the door opened behind her and Keir came into the room. Georgia turned and clutched at her robe in shock. She watched dry-mouthed as he carefully closed the door again, his straight, broad-shouldered physique seeming to suck up all the oxygen in the room with its indomitable presence, leaving her very little left to breathe. The expression in his eyes was not one she recognised either.

'You should have said you were frightened of the storm.' His voice was gruff but not in an unkind way.

Georgia's heartbeat skittered.

'Are you crying?' he demanded.

Before she could reply, he strode up in front of her and touched the palm of his hand to her damp cheek. With the pad of his thumb he brushed away the slippery track of a tear and his warm breath drifted over her. *Had she ceased breathing?* It certainly seemed as if she had. Her senses held in thrall by his touch, the storm that raged outside all but forgotten, Georgia gulped down air and exhaled raggedly.

Keir's chin, with its hard, masculine cleft, was just inches from her forehead, and she had to look up to meet his searching gaze...

Staring into her mesmerising tear-filled eyes was like seeing the sun glinting gold above the green of the Glens… Her exquisitely feminine scent seemed to saturate his senses, and Keir hardly dared move lest he somehow shatter something irretrievable.

He'd stayed away longer than he'd needed to in New York because of this woman. In the couple of days following their attendance at the concert he had found it almost impossible to be in the same room as Georgia without needing to touch her. His desire had almost grown into a compulsion. She'd drawn his gaze wherever she went, and he'd barely been able to concentrate on the work that had to be done. It was a distraction he'd found hard to deal with. That was why he had grabbed at the chance to go to New York. But even when he'd been an ocean away she had dominated his thoughts. Now, home again, he realised that this budding attraction was developing into something nearer to obsession.

'There's no need to be afraid. The storm won't hurt you *or* this house. Can you imagine how many storms Glenteign has endured over the years? In an hour or so it will have blown itself out, and everything will be calm again.'

'You probably think I'm behaving like a complete coward!' Her mouth quivered, and Keir's hungry glance latched onto it as though it were heavenly perfection itself.

'Don't be ridiculous!' Even though his tone was gently mocking, he smiled and moved his fingers through the soft fall of her hair. 'You? A *coward?* You could have done someone some serious damage with that poker because you thought they were breaking in!'

'I wouldn't have used it!' Georgia looked aghast for a moment. 'Maybe I was being more stupid than brave, now that I come to think of it.'

'Why did you do it?'

'Because I didn't want anyone stealing anything of importance to you,' Georgia replied quietly, swallowing hard.

'Nothing I own would be worth risking your life for, Georgia.' His voice lowered tenderly, and Keir tipped up her chin, intent on nothing else but to fulfil the compelling, growing need inside him to feel her soft, inviting lips opening beneath his own.

As her warm sweet breath feathered invitingly across his mouth, there was a loud knock at the door.

'Georgia? Are you all right, lassie? I heard a noise from up here and thought you might be up and about because you were worried by the storm.'

'Damn!' Cursing harshly, Keir stepped away from Georgia, a sudden irresistible need to break something flashing through him with almost violent demand.

'It's Moira,' Georgia said, her expression torn. She unconsciously moistened her lips with her tongue and made Keir suffer the agony of heightened frustration—because he could not enjoy the same delectable privilege.

'Yes...I heard.'

She saw both exasperation and resignation written across his riveting features. She hurried past him to open the door, unable to deny her own frustration that Moira should choose that exact moment to check if she was all right.

The incredible realisation that she'd *wanted* Keir to kiss her flooded through her. How much had she craved the touch of his mouth on hers when the opportunity had presented itself? Even now her body still had tremors flooding through it because he had touched his palm to her cheek.

'Moira...hello,' she said, smiling awkwardly at the housekeeper, who was standing there in her long plaid dressing gown with her silver hair in curlers.

Georgia caught hold of the edge of the door and pulled it closed behind her as she joined Moira in the corridor. Apart from the occasional flash of lightning reflected in the casement windows, the area was plunged into near darkness. *What on earth would Moira think if Keir should come out of her room right now?* She prayed he wouldn't expose her like that and make the housekeeper suspect the worst. Over the past few days Georgia had come to set a lot of store by the other woman's friendship and respect. Alienating her because she thought something might be going on between her and Keir would not be good at all...

'I'm perfectly all right, thanks. I thought I heard a noise too, and I went out into the corridor to investigate, that's all.' Shrugging her slim shoulders guiltily, Georgia started to explain what had happened. She despised the need for subterfuge of any kind. It wasn't in her nature to be dishonest, and this didn't sit well with her.

'And when I came back in, the wind must have made the door slam. Maybe that was the sound you heard?'

'Aye...that must be it, then. Well, as long as you're all right. This storm is enough to put the fear of God into anybody!' Moira replied.

'They've always made me a little jumpy,' Georgia agreed.

Her back was sticky with perspiration and prickly heat at the knowledge that Keir was waiting in her room, and she worked hard at containing her anxiety and not arousing any suspicion from the other woman that something else might be bothering her aside from the weather.

'Please, Moira...go back to bed. Thank you for your concern, but I'm honestly fine. I'll see you in the morning.'

'Goodnight then, my dear.'

As the housekeeper turned away to return down

the darkened corridor to the grand curving staircase at the bottom, Georgia touched her hand to her forehead and was not surprised when it came away moist. Biting her lip, she turned the catch on the door and went back inside the room.

Keir was standing with his back to her at the window, seemingly engrossed in watching the torrential downpour that was sheeting the glass and everything else in sight. Hearing her come in, he immediately sought her out, his blue eyes as piercing as any bright searchlight.

'She's gone,' he remarked soberly.

'Yes.' Georgia stared at him, her brow furrowing. 'You don't think she heard us talking, do you?'

CHAPTER FIVE

'AND DISCOVERED THAT the Laird was home again and up to no good in his secretary's bedroom?' His smile was taunting. 'No, Georgia... I don't think she heard us. And even if she did... Moira Guthrie is the soul of discretion and wouldn't bat an eyelid.'

He'd been kind before, when he'd thought she was afraid of the storm, and he'd been going to kiss her, Georgia thought a little forlornly. But now his mood seemed to be altering...almost as if he blamed *her* for Moira knocking at the door!

'How was it that you arrived home so late?' she asked, needing to say something to ease the palpable tension between them.

'I got a flight out of Newark at the last minute. I'd concluded my business earlier in the day and simply decided to come home.'

He walked towards her, his expression as impenetrable as the rugged stone that made up the impressive walls of his ancestral home. 'For the first time in my life I actually looked forward to coming back here...did you know that?'

'Really?'

She dropped her chin and stared at the floor. A wave of heat swept upwards through her body in a dizzying rush. What was he saying?

'Why have you never looked forward to coming home before?' she asked quietly, hardly daring to move in case he denied her the answer. An answer she found she very much longed to know.

'There was nobody here that I wanted to see before.' He shrugged, his mouth twisting wryly at one corner.

'Not even your brother?' Georgia asked the question even while all her senses were in uproar at what he'd just confessed.

'I told you we weren't close.'

A dark look had crept into his eyes.

'Why weren't you close?' Her voice was barely above a whisper. 'Did you have a fight or something?'

A muscle visibly showed itself contracting in the dark shadow of his sculpted cheekbone. 'No...we didn't have a fight. The tension between me and Robbie was an unspoken thing.'

'And you weren't able to heal that tension before he died? Is that it? Is that why you seem so troubled?'

'It might be late, Georgia, but trust me—this isn't the time for night-time confessions! Especially the kind that are apt to make me want to leave this cursed place again.'

'I don't want you to leave.'

'What did you say?' Appearing startled, Keir stared and Georgia could have bitten out her tongue. Why on earth had she come out with that? But she really didn't want him to leave again… She just didn't want him to get the wrong impression about what she'd said and why she'd said it.

'What a night you chose to return!' she declared, deliberately trying to lighten the atmosphere.

'I know…and I'm sorry if I gave you a fright.'

Surprising her, Keir reached out to touch her, and as his hard, warm fingers curled round her chin to raise it she was seized by such trembling that she could barely conceal it from him.

'Next time I'll be sure and ring you to let you know that I'm coming home,' he promised, his voice threaded with a hushed and sensual undertone that riveted her.

'Maybe next time you go away I'll be back in London because I won't be working here any more.'

'Are you in such a hurry to leave me, Georgia?' His tone was slightly mocking and his grip tightened a little around her chin.

'It's not that… It's just that Valerie will be back sooner or later, and I—'

'You have a life in London, waiting for you... I know.' His voice threaded with apparent dissatisfaction, he dropped his hands down to his sides. Immediately Georgia felt bereft of his touch, as if some integral part of her had suddenly been ripped away.

'Does that include a man, perhaps?' he demanded.

Shadows seemed to shift in his penetrating glare, and Georgia wished she could look away—but she couldn't.

His question threw her into a state of near panic. If he knew...if he even *guessed* how little experience she'd had of intimate relationships he probably wouldn't be able to believe it. He might mock her, or simply conclude she must be lying.

Fiddling with the neckline of her skimpy cotton robe, she was certain her lack of experience must show. Because it was so hard to contain her reaction to him and keep it hidden neatly away, like a secret letter stowed amongst her personal things in a bedroom drawer. His nearness was making her feel as if she stood too close to a scorching fire, yet at the same time she desired it above all else...

'You're right. This isn't the moment for night-time confessions, and I really think you should go now. We both need to go to bed... I mean to go to sleep... In our—in our own beds is what I mean!' Her face went beetroot red at the hash she was making of what should have been a simple statement.

In response, Keir looked grim. There was certainly no amusement evident at her clumsy phrasing.

'I had better go, then,' he announced clearly. 'Before I finish what I started to do before my loyal housekeeper knocked on the door and ruined everything. An event that with hindsight you will probably no doubt welcome!'

He left her then, shutting the door with deliberately firm emphasis behind him, and Georgia stood frozen for a full minute, locked in the myriad emotions that welled up inside her. She no longer felt afraid of the storm that vented its fury outside because her head was too full of wild, heated thoughts to be fully aware of much else but her own disquiet.

Keir was wrong about her welcoming the interruption from his housekeeper…so wrong.

'Good morning, Moira.'

'Georgia, my dear!'

The friendly housekeeper glanced up from the cooking range as the younger woman entered the large bright kitchen. Immediately she observed the telling signs of a sleepless night on Georgia's slightly paler than usual face.

'You look like you had as restless a night as I had,

love. Goodness gracious, but that was some hullaba-
loo last night, wasn't it? Come and sit down, lassie,
and I'll make you a nice rejuvenating cup of tea.'

'Thanks, I'd really appreciate that… And I'm
sorry if I added to your sleepless night with that
slamming door.'

'Think nothing of it. The truth is it gets harder to
get a decent night's rest as a body gets older so I'm
not blaming you. Now, sit yourself down and I'll get
you that cup of tea.'

Pulling out a shaker-style chair from the large
pine table, Georgia picked up a pot of marmalade
standing with the rest of the jams on the square
placemat which had a picture of the Scottish
Highlands imprinted on it, and absently read the
contents label—her mind preoccupied with the fact
that her boss could walk through the door at any
minute.

During the night, after he'd left, she'd been kept
awake far more by thoughts of him than the thunderous storm. Her lips had ached without cease for the
touch of his mouth against hers, for his inviting, addictive taste, and she wondered what would have
happened if Moira hadn't knocked at the door when
she had. What perturbed Georgia even more was that
she would have *welcomed* Keir's kiss instead of re-
pelling it. *What did that mean?*

She'd always avoided becoming involved with

men she worked for and for very good reason. She was responsible for her brother, and that responsibility took precedence over everything else. She had to give Noah the sense of security that had been so devastatingly snatched away from him by the deaths of their parents. And trying to make a living and keep a roof over their heads and not get into debt was hard enough, without making things even harder by getting romantically involved with her boss!

But now it seemed as though all her previous common sense was suddenly coming under serious fire. *It must have been the storm,* Georgia told herself… That was why she'd acted so uncharacteristically. Storms were her Achilles' Heel. Plus the fact that she had truly believed someone had broken into the house. If she hadn't been so jumpy and on edge about those two factors she would never have allowed Keir to even *enter* her room…let alone comfort her and then try to kiss her!

But even as her mind tried desperately to defend her actions, she knew she was only kidding herself. The fact was that she had seriously missed him when he'd been away in New York, and she hadn't been able to wait for him to return. Even though she knew her feelings weren't at all sensible, or even welcome, Georgia couldn't help them. She just hoped that in the cold light of day what had happened wouldn't make things too awkward between them for them to continue to work together. The bottom seemed to drop out of her whole world even at the thought that she might have to leave Glenteign sooner than she'd planned...

'Oh, by the way...the Chief is back from New York, dear. He returned late last night in the middle of that terrible storm! What a homecoming! Come to think of it...it was probably him coming home that woke me up! I don't suppose there's much chance of you having a quiet day today with him back, though, dear. He had his breakfast and then went straight out to see if there was any damage to the gardens. That wind was fierce! No doubt there'll be a few branches thrown about the place—and he was concerned about some rare plants and shrubs that your brother planted too. Anyway, he came back a little while ago, and he's in his study now.'

Swallowing hard, Georgia contemplated the news that Keir was already in his study with mounting trepidation. 'Well, then, I'll have my tea, give Hamish a quick walk, and then join him. By the way, where *is* Hamish?'

Glancing around her, Georgia guiltily realised that she'd forgotten all about the Labrador. *That was how distracted Keir's appearance last night had made her!*

Moira was quick to reassure her. 'Young Lucy came in early, to help me prepare a few meals I've got planned for the next few days. She asked if she might walk Hamish, and I'm afraid I told her yes. Was that all right, dear?'

Georgia rose to her feet again wanting to delay facing Keir until she'd got herself properly together, and saw her last excuse emphatically disappear now that Lucy was walking Hamish.

'Of course it was all right. Be sure and thank her for me when she gets back. Don't worry about the tea, Moira. I'll get one later. I'd better just go and see if the Chief needs anything.'

Keir was surprised to see Georgia enter the room when she did. He hadn't expected her to make such an early-morning appearance—especially when he knew intimately what sort of a disrupted night she'd had. God knew she'd 'disrupted' *his* night too…in more ways than one.

But now, as she carefully closed the heavy oak study door behind her, Keir's examination of her eye-catching figure, and her slim, tanned legs in the knee-length red linen dress, was swift and hungry. Because of that, and because his desire had been frustratingly thwarted last night, his tone was brusque.

'Nobody instructed you to make such an early start. Have you had breakfast?' he demanded.

'I'll get something later.' She frowned as if it was hardly significant. 'Chief Strachan, I—'

'*Chief Strachan?*' Unable to keep his mockery at bay, Keir twisted his lips grimly. 'Is this how things are going to proceed between us, then? Are you forgetting that I was in your bedroom after midnight, drying your tears because of your terror at the storm, with you dressed in a robe that barely concealed the fact that you were naked underneath it? Under the circumstances, don't you think it a little ridiculous to resort to calling me "Chief Strachan"?'

Georgia's face paled. 'I wasn't deliberately wearing what I was wearing to entice you! And I didn't ask you to come into my room...you just came in anyway!'

'For goodness' sake, don't look so damn offended! What you wear or don't wear to bed is your own business, and I wasn't trying to cast aspersions! Now, what was it you started to tell me?'

Deliberately dismissing her indignation, Keir exhaled on a heavy sigh and got up from his chair. The instant he did, the scent she was wearing caught him with a slide tackle he hadn't seen coming, and it all but brought him to his knees. An innocent and light fragrance had no right to be so powerfully alluring...but on Georgia it clearly was. Not that she needed any artifice to heighten her already immense appeal...

'About last night...'

'Are we going to labour the point all day,

Georgia?' he asked with exasperation. 'Because, strange as it may seem, we do have work to do!'

There was no point in any further discussion about the matter as far as Keir was concerned—even if he *had* left not knowing whether she had a man waiting for her back in London or not. If she had he really didn't want to hear about it, because it would only make this inconvenient attraction he'd developed for her even worse.

Last night he'd realised he was on very dangerous ground. Apart from nearly kissing her, he should never have confessed that he'd missed her as he had. Recalling his mood, he would have perhaps said other things too—things that in the cold light of day he might have regretted.

Whatever mixed-up emotions he was currently feeling, he couldn't afford to lose a perfectly good secretary because of it. Glancing at his appointments diary earlier, it had seemed a certainty that it was going to be another busy week, after having been away, and the last thing he needed or wanted was to have to hunt for another replacement. Yet even though realistically he knew he would have to curb his 'extra curricular' interest in Georgia if he wanted to keep her at Glenteign, he already intuited it would be a near impossible task. There was something about her that kept making him want to let down some of the usual defences he employed around people, and his blood still simmered hotly with the need to make love to her.

In New York he'd had plenty of opportunity to spend time with the beautiful girl he'd promised to get back in touch with when he returned there. Yet each time Keir had deliberately avoided the chances to be more intimate that had been presented. Even his demanding sex drive had not been able to persuade him to take advantage of the situation.

'Look...if you think this can't work any more, and that my being here is causing some kind of problem for you, then I'll simply pack my case, put my things in the car and get out of your hair for good.'

Her chin had lifted with determination and her hazel eyes were flashing. Keir saw that Georgia was quite capable of carrying out her threat. This wasn't how he'd envisaged the start of their morning together at all, but now—because of his frustration and general irritation—a scenario was threatening that he definately did not welcome.

'Oh, no, you don't! You've signed a contract that's binding, and barring illness and acts of God you're obligated to stay here and fulfil it!'

'There's no need to threaten me! I'm fully aware that I made a written promise when I signed my name, and I have always been a person who has kept her word, but—'

'No buts! I need a secretary, and I want you to stay, so let's have no more nonsensical talk about leaving!'

Shaking his head at her as if she was the most irritating woman on the planet and was driving him to complete distraction, Keir strode back to his desk. Staring at the back of his head, Georgia decided that no matter what she said or did there was just no pleasing this man this morning, so she might as well give up trying. She just couldn't work him out. One minute he was acting as if her mere presence was like a thorn in his side, and then last night he'd nearly been going to kiss her!

Just as her heart leapt at the stirring memory, Georgia recalled him asking her if she was in a hurry to leave him. The answer to that was definitely no. She'd only said what she'd said just now because his coldness towards her had upset her. No matter what the Laird of Glenteign thought of her, Georgia couldn't turn her back on him…not yet. Not until it was really time for her to go.

There was obviously a reason he sometimes seemed to shut her out, and the clue lay with his past—she was certain of it. She wanted to help him, so she would stay.

Certain about her decision, she felt her anger dissipate. 'All right,' she agreed. 'I won't talk about leaving any more. We just got off on the wrong foot this morning, that's all. I can see that now.'

She was interlocking her fingers, staring down at them, when she heard the creak of the leather chair that Keir was occupying. When she glanced up again, he had swivelled it round to regard her. Not having entirely finished what she'd been going to say, Georgia sucked in her breath and continued, 'To make things a little easier for both of us, apart from working with you during the day I'll keep out of your way as much as possible at all other times. Then we won't have to make polite conversation with each other when we don't feel like it.'

'That won't be necessary.'

'I don't mind—'

'Didn't you hear what I said? I said that won't be necessary!'

'Oh, for goodness' sake!'

Throwing her hands up in the air in exasperation, Georgia stared at him in disbelief. There was clearly *something* about her that was pressing all the wrong buttons with him this morning—something she just didn't get. Either that, or he was unhappy about something that had happened on his trip.

As soon as the idea had planted itself in her mind, she found she needed to have it confirmed. Georgia didn't want to add to his troubles—all she wanted to do was help alleviate them. Her nature was that she always tried to help.

'Did something go wrong in New York?'

'What?'

'Is that why you seem so on edge?'

Georgia was beginning to wonder if it was a woman that was at the root of his bad mood, and she didn't include herself—in spite of Keir's suggestion last night that he'd looked forward to coming back to see her. Had there been a woman Keir liked in New York? A woman he might even be in love with? Had that woman rejected him?

Jealousy vying with fear inside her, Georgia had to work hard to keep her expression impassive.

'Nothing went wrong in New York, Georgia…other than the fact that I didn't really want to be there!'

'But you seemed in such a hurry to go there!' she exclaimed.

'Did I?' His handsome brow creased as though he were perplexed.

'You really are completely impossible!' Georgia accused him, frustrated that she clearly wasn't going to get any answers that made any sense to anything today. Dropping her hands to either side of her shapely hips in the red linen dress, she sighed heavily.

'That aside…perhaps we should both just get down to the business of the day and restore a little peace to the morning? We've had enough storms of one kind or another for a while—wouldn't you agree?'

'Fine! What would you like me to do for you first?' Her temper helplessly simmering, Georgia tossed back her hair and waited for instructions.

Silently surveying him for a moment, she saw a distracting dimple appear at the corner of Keir's disturbing mouth.

'That could take us into a whole new interesting arena if I were deliberately to misconstrue that question.' He grinned. 'Want to ask me again? But perhaps this time with a little less provocative passion?'

CHAPTER SIX

A SHAFT OF SUNLIGHT beamed in from a small side casement window and created a pool of light in the middle of the floor. It lit up the muted reds and golds of an old faded Persian carpet that had been unfolded there a long time ago—possibly even before Keir had been born. Round the edges of that eye-catching pool of light were some of the now superfluous remnants of his family's past.

In one corner were a pair of discarded Tiffany lamps that had once resided in his father's study—the study that now belonged to Keir—and next to them an old oak dresser-cum china cabinet, long empty of any fine display of porcelain and pottery, and now home to a generous coating of dust.

Piled around the room in general haphazard fashion were myriad cardboard boxes, splitting at the seams with books and ornaments and trinkets, and possibly somewhere in amongst all that the beloved chess set that his mother had surprisingly presented to him one Christmas when his father had been away on business. It was a gift that had often been utilised as a means of escape and distraction from James Strachan's sour temper, and its home had nearly always been this attic.

Robbie and Keir would steal away up here as often as they could, to shut the door on their parents' terrible rows, and locked in the strategy of the game would briefly escape the trauma that seemed to underline their childhood. After their mother had died there'd been no more refuge in the attic to play chess.

Both boys had gone to a local public school, as their father had done before them, but they hadn't been allowed to board like most of the other pupils. If they had, Keir sometimes wondered if the bleakness of his home life wouldn't have scarred him quite as badly—but James had seemed to take particular delight in demanding that his sons came home at the end of each school day, just so that he could remain in rigid control of every aspect of their lives and plague them further with his meanness and ill temper.

Made to do various jobs round the house as well as work on the estate, they'd also regularly had to listen to his various rants and small-minded prejudices over the political situation, or his belligerent belief that 'people just don't know their place these days,' and that they should show the gentry more respect. When Keir had invariably started to disagree with his point of view and dared to express his own his father had demonstrated his fury with his fists...

Feeling slightly nauseous at the relentless tide of unwanted memories that washed over him—each one like a stinging cut that had never healed—Keir moved with trepidation into the room and accidentally trod on something hard underfoot. Looking down to see what it was, he picked up a once lovingly painted miniature replica of a nineteenth-century Scottish soldier. For a few moments he scarcely breathed. Then, his palm curling tightly round the small toy, so that the metal edges dug painfully into his flesh, tears stabbed the backs of his eyes like dagger points.

'Robbie...' he murmured fiercely, a thick, merciless ache inside his throat. 'I'm sorry, Robbie...I'm so sorry...'

'Georgia! Are you bringing that coffee?' Keir bellowed.

Turning towards the thickly carpeted staircase, with its almost Gothic carved figures on the newels, Georgia was careful to balance the silver tray she carried as she ascended the stairs. As she went, she took a deep breath in and scowled.

'I wonder whatever happened to good old-fashioned manners?' she grumbled.

Even after the little talk they'd had earlier, her boss had been like a wounded bear all morning, and his mood was showing no sign of improving any time soon. Just as she reached the landing and approached the study door, she saw Keir's tall, broad-shouldered figure impatiently pacing the floor. His dark straight hair, sticking out a little at odd angles, attested to the fact that it had taken the brunt of his impatience. Immediately honing in on her presence, he didn't trouble to conceal his irritation.

'For God's sake, don't hover! Just come inside, will you?' he commanded.

Just about holding onto her own temper at his belligerent mood, Georgia reluctantly crossed the threshold into the study.

'If you remember to say please, I will,' she retorted smartly.

Her glance colliding with his steely blue glare, Georgia's heart bumped indignantly as she carried out his request, her jaw set mutinously to show her displeasure.

So much for restoring some peace to their working morning! The half an hour's breather Keir had taken earlier to—in his own words—'get his head straight' clearly hadn't done much good. Maybe she should suggest he spend some more time on his own?

'I can take the letters into the library and do them there, if you need some privacy for a while?' she offered, thinking that that would probably be the best arrangement. There was a spare computer all set up in there, and it wouldn't be a chore.

She loved the lofty elegant room, with its studious yet inviting ambience, and it was filled to the rafters with books of all kinds. The shelves that contained them were made from oak inlaid with maple, Moira had told her, and some of the books had been in Keir's family for centuries. With its worn but lovely carpets and its big overstuffed sofas and chairs it was a room to sit and dream in, or while away a rainy day in unashamed comfort.

But Georgia saw the flicker of a dissenting muscle in Keir's chiselled cheek and knew that her helpful suggestion had gone down like a lead balloon.

'There's no need for you to go anywhere else. This is where I work, and this is where I expect my secretary to work!'

Standing next to her, he slammed his hand down onto the desk to emphasise his point. The sudden violent movement dislodged the tray Georgia had just placed there, and as he reached out to try and stop it from crashing to the floor the full-to-the-brim silver coffee-pot toppled over, splashing its scalding contents all over his wrist.

'Arrgh! Damn!'

Georgia acted immediately.

'Let's get you to a bathroom. We'll go to the one

across the hall.' Already with her hand at his back, she started to push him towards the door.

'I don't bloody believe this!' he muttered furiously.

Examining his shocked face, Georgia led him into the marble-tiled bathroom and hurriedly turned the cold tap full on. As the water gushed out from the faucet she held his arm beneath it, watching it soak into the coffee stained sleeve covering his forearm. She wouldn't be attempting to peel back the material until she was certain that no skin would come away with it.

'We need to do this for at least ten minutes,' she told him, her heart racing fast at what had happened. 'Thank God the coffee wasn't quite boiling hot… By the time I'd brought it from the kitchen and came up the stairs it would have cooled down considerably. I don't think you'll need to go to hospital, but it will probably sting like crazy for a few hours or more. Are you okay?'

Acting purely on impulse, she pushed back a lock of his midnight-dark hair. But seeing him flinch, she wondered if she had taken a liberty she shouldn't have.

'I'm fine.' His breath exhaled on a ragged sigh, Keir turned to glance sideways at Georgia, a surprising lift at one corner of his mouth. 'I didn't know you were a trained nurse in one of your previous incarnations,' he commented wryly.

'I did some first-aid training with the St John's Ambulance organisation. When you're left to raise a fourteen-year old boy all on your own, you need to know some basic first-aid skills, let me tell you!'

'Ouch!' He blanched as Georgia gently moved his arm, to make sure the water was reaching the entire area where the coffee had been spilt. 'I'm lucky that you were around and knew what to do,' he remarked.

It struck Keir then that he felt total confidence in Georgia's healing skills. She was capable and firm when she needed to be, and yet exceedingly gentle too. As her calm voice washed over him and her soft skin inevitably came into contact with his, where she held his hand and guided his forearm beneath the splashing water, he was aware that even though he was in considerable pain he very much *liked* this sudden enforced closeness with Georgia.

Moira Guthrie put her head round the door just then, her flushed round face bearing rosy evidence that she'd rushed up the stairs.

'What on earth has happened?' she asked breath-lessly, coming into the room. 'I was in the hall and I heard you cry out. Oh, good gracious! Was it the hot coffee, lassie?'

As she saw that Georgia had clearly taken charge, and knew what she was doing, some of the anxiety drained out of the housekeeper's face.

'It spilled across his wrist. Just a little longer,' Georgia told Keir, when she saw him flinch again in pain. 'Believe me this will help. Moira, do you think you could find me a clean, dry dressing? And if you wouldn't mind going into my bedroom and getting my handbag? I've got some arnica in there, which is good for shock. We'll wait here.'

'Stupid bloody thing to happen!' His expression fierce for a moment, Keir shook his head from side to side as if in disbelief.

'I've often found that when I'm angry I end up hurting myself somehow,' Georgia shared with him gently, not wanting to inflame his temper any further, but needing to make what she hoped was a helpful observation. 'Perhaps you need to find a safer way to release the anger you're holding on to and let it go?'

'No doubt you're right.'

He reflected on his reluctant yet compelling visit to the attic earlier—the first in the nine months since he'd been back at Glenteign. He'd been searching for something… exactly what he didn't know…but something that might give him some clue as to how he was going to overcome this great weight of sorrow and pain in his heart. But Keir had not left that room of memories feeling much forgiveness or any closure in his heart about his past. Instead, rage had welled up inside him afresh at what he and Robbie had endured, and the indelible scars it had left him with.

He was only beginning to realise now, after suffering this stupid accident, how dangerous it was to let that rage dominate his emotions. Georgia—in her surprising wisdom—was absolutely correct with her sage advice. Except that Keir didn't know how he could begin to 'safely' release the rage and hurt he felt inside. Since he'd been back at Glenteign he'd almost felt like a prisoner there, locked inside his painful memories, with reminders at every turn, instead of a man in charge of his own destiny. He knew that such a debilitating state of affairs could not go on...

'But there are some things that are almost too damn hard to do and, I can't help the way I feel,' he continued, his mouth a thin, bitter line. 'What? You're not going to tell me I should try harder?'

There was something so bleak in his riveting blue gaze as he trained it directly on Georgia's face that her heart constricted in pain. She tore her glance from his with difficulty, and focused once more on the running water splashing onto his arm.

'I wouldn't presume to tell you what to do. I think you just need to try and stay calm. It won't help the pain if you get yourself more agitated...no matter whether you're hurting inside or out.'

Minutes later, Moira appeared with a small first aid kit, from which Georgia selected a dressing of the appropriate size. She instructed Keir to sit down in the cane chair next to the bath so that she could apply it to his arm. Thankfully, she was able to peel back the soaked material without any detrimental effect to his scalded skin. The wound looked red and angry, but she could already tell that in a week to ten days' time it would heal nicely, without even leaving a scar.

Relief ebbed through her in a thankful wave and, tipping out an arnica tablet from the packet she had taken from her handbag, she gave it to Keir. 'Put this on the end of your tongue and let it dissolve. It will help with the shock. I'm just going to put this dressing on for you, and then you should go and put your feet up for a while. Perhaps you could lie on one of the big sofas in the library? They're nice and comfy. Then I'll bring you up a cup of hot, sweet tea.'

'Oh I can do that for the Chief, lassie! I'll find some of his favourite biscuits too.'

Glad to have something else to do other than stand by and watch Georgia put Keir's dressing on, Moira bustled out of the room again.

Finishing her task, Georgia sat back on the edge of the bath and smiled. 'I think you'll live to fight another day!'

'Thanks to you.' Grimly examining the stark white dressing covering a large area of his forearm, Keir quickly moved his gaze to look at Georgia instead. 'My own private nurse as well as my very efficient secretary… Does your after-care extend to tucking me into bed tonight, I wonder?'

'Definitely not!' Although her retort was smart, Georgia sensed a wave of heat suffuse her cheeks.

'Pity.'

There was the semblance of a rueful smile about his lips, but his piercing blue eyes could not disguise his longing.

Trying to convince herself that it must simply be the aftermath of shock, or the surge of adrenaline that came with it, Georgia regarded his hard handsome face with renewed concern. With its sculpted lean angles and the firm cleft in the centre of his rather arrogant chin, there was something about it that was so compelling that she was filled with the strongest, almost irresistible desire to touch him. Not just with the gentle ministrations of a healer either. But with the almost overwhelmingly demanding need of a woman who knew herself to be dangerously beguiled by him…

'You really should go and lie down for a while!' she exclaimed, jumping up from the edge of the bath. 'We have to be careful that shock doesn't set in. You can be quite ill otherwise. Shall I help you into the library?'

It was quite remarkable to Keir that he could be in so much pain from his scald and yet so imbued with desire for the woman who had tended him that he could scarcely think straight! So much so that he didn't want to go and lie down alone. If Georgia came with him, then that would be quite a different matter entirely...

Yet even as the thought grew into the most compelling demand, Keir already guessed that she would refuse him. She would no doubt have a raft of principles behind her refusal too. Number one being that he had hired her as his temporary secretary, and that was the only obligation she'd come to Glenteign to fulfil... Not to alleviate any carnal desire her boss might have!

She was clearly a woman of integrity, and he couldn't fault her for that—even though it didn't help his case right now one little bit.

'I don't need your help to walk down the corridor into the library, dammit!' he replied irritably. 'I've scalded my arm, not broken my leg!'

As he got up and went through the door, Georgia stared at him in astonished disbelief. 'Well, I'm so happy to see that your accident hasn't curtailed in any way your ability to be as cantankerous and belligerent as ever!' she declared out loud to his back.

Turning at this daring attempt not to be browbeaten by his temper, Keir felt his blood throb with renewed heat as he confronted her beautiful indignant face. Driven to act by purely primal instinct— he crossed the floor in one fluid stride and with his uninjured arm yanked her hard against his chest.

'This has been coming for a long time,' he ground out, just before he covered her mouth passionately with his own.

The hard yet compelling mouth that took command of her lips was bordering on the brutal with its untamed, ravenous demand. But as the velvet magic of Keir's hot silken tongue ruthlessly seduced her, causing an explosion of untrammelled sensation throughout her body, Georgia felt an answering cry of profound need ring out in her heart. To feel such raw physical need was a revelation to her. She'd suppressed so much that to have those potentially dangerous feelings blown apart now by this man's expert, ruthless kiss, was deeply shocking and yet wildly liberating at the same time.

She had been guarded all her life. Always, always she had thought of her brother's welfare first, and of how his upbringing might be jeopardised should she allow herself to fall in love and commit her future to someone else. What if the man she fell in love with could not find it in his heart to be kind to Noah? What if he didn't understand the closeness between brother and sister and sought to end or destroy it?

These questions had always loomed large whenever she'd nursed fantasies about meeting someone special...someone she wanted to spend the rest of her life with.

Now, the heated addictive pressure on her mouth

started to ease, degree by tormenting degree, and Keir's arm slackened a little on her waist. To Georgia's surprise his kiss became gentler, kinder—more seductive even—and her chest was tight with emotion and yearning. When he finally withdrew his lips from hers, she saw such raw, unfettered need reflected there in his amazing blue eyes that it made her feel almost faint with longing.

'I think I *will* go and lie down on one of the sofas in the library,' he teased gently, his nostrils flaring a little. 'I seem to have acquired a sudden added complication in that my blood pressure has just gone sky-high. What remedies do you have for bringing it down again, Nurse?'

Now it was Keir's turn to sweep back a lock of hair from Georgia's brow, and the tender way he did it elicited such joy inside her that it made her light-headed. Perhaps she ought to be furious with him for taking such a liberty as to kiss her so uninhibitedly and brazenly. But of all the emotions that were sweeping through her right then, fury did not feature at all.

Clearing her throat with difficulty, her lips still throbbing from his hungry, fiery kisses as though they would never cease to ache, Georgia wondered if her compliance showed in her eyes. 'Rest,' she advised softly, her hazel glance reflecting myriad greens and golds. 'Plenty of rest. I'll tell Moira to take your tea into the library.'

'Thank you.' Smiling ruefully at having to leave her, Keir finally set Georgia free with a light brush of his hand against her cheek.

His touch felt as if it burned her. She watched him move towards the door as if she were in a trance.

'I will see you later,' he promised. And leaving her, he made his way down the hall to the library…

CHAPTER SEVEN

HE'D BEEN DEEP in the throes of the most erotic dream he'd ever had… Now, stirring to wakefulness on one of the old overstuffed sofas in the library, his brow damp with perspiration and the very devil of a searing pain in his arm, Keir sat up feeling dazed, and rubbed his hand round his studded jaw.

It was hard to tell which pain was worse… The scald he'd acquired from the hot coffee, or the strong throbbing ache in the region of his groin… The dream had been so damn real that Keir could swear he'd been making uninhibited passionate love to one dark-haired, hazel-eyed sorceress who, in turn, had done things to him that would make a grown man sink down onto his knees and give thanks that he had been incarnated as a male in this lifetime…

'Bloody hell!' He exclaimed out loud. Not because he shouldn't be nursing such lascivious thoughts about his temporary secretary, but because she wasn't there with him to carry out his fantasy for *real*...

Keir reflected that now he had enforced an intimacy between himself and Georgia that there was probably no turning back. Perhaps it had been reckless of him, but even *his* infamous iron will could not resist the pure temptation that was Noah Cameron's shapely, beguiling, sister. Things had really started to get out of hand when she'd pushed back that lock of hair from his brow. Her touch had been so exquisite, so infinitely kind, that Keir had been undone by it. No one had ever touched him in such a tender, almost *loving* way...

He froze at how dangerously his emotions seemed to be unravelling. *What the hell was he thinking of?* Georgia Cameron fascinated him, and he definitely admired her as a person—how could he not when she had so many amazing qualities?—but right now he had only onc goal in mind as far as shc was concerned, and that was to simply seduce her. Anything beyond that—especially anything remotely appertaining to emotional need—was simply a fantasy on Keir's part, no doubt brought about by what had just happened to him.

Yet, even if that most basic physical need were fulfilled, would he find it that easy to let her go? He wanted more from this woman than mere sex— although he hesitated to confirm in his own mind what that something 'more' was.

He'd always found it difficult to relate to the concept or even the possibility of needing a deeper response from anyone. He even kept his platonic friendships as uncomplicated and commitment-free as possible. There was a deeply held belief inside him that somehow the taint of his unhappy past would ultimately end up destroying those friendships, and so inevitably he did not allow anyone to get too close to him. There were very few, if any among his acquaintances, who could really say that they knew him.

Now, glancing down at his watch, Keir experienced mild shock when he saw the time. Had he really slept most of the afternoon away? As he made himself stand, he tried to shake off the slightly unreal and stuffy feeling in his head that made him feel as if he'd been drugged. He was thirsty, he was hungry, and his burn throbbed like merry hell! Had anybody in the household come to check on him whilst he'd been sleeping?

As he reached the door and wrenched it open with a disgruntled frown, Keir knew full well the person he'd hoped would have undertaken that task was Georgia.

Georgia had set off walking about half an hour before dinner, to try and get her head straight. She'd hardly had any peace since Keir had kissed her, and now her feelings were in absolute turmoil.

Walking in nature usually provided a release from such inner turmoil, she'd found, and so she'd resorted to the one thing that might help her. But now she realised that the inevitable spell of the mountains and lochs had weaved their magic too potently around her senses, and the distance she'd inadvertently covered because of her enchantment was too great to allow her to get back to Glenteign in time to sit down to the evening meal with everyone else.

Damn!

Even Hamish looked up at her with reproach in his big dark eyes, his great tongue lolling as he panted hard at his exertion. Dropping down onto her haunches, Georgia affectionately stroked back the champagne coloured fur on his head and sighed heavily.

'I'm sorry, Hamish! I just lost track of time. Never mind—you'll have your dinner as soon as we get back to Glenteign, I promise. We'd better get our skates on, though, because it looks like it might rain again!'

Glancing up at the darkening grey clouds that were gathering so threateningly in the previously flawless blue sky, Georgia sensed sudden fear knife through her. The last thing in the world she wanted to do was to be caught out in a storm to equal the one they'd had last night! It was one thing being inside, watching it safely from a bedroom window, but quite another witnessing the full brunt of its elemental passion outside in the open!

Falling into a jog, she nervously increased her pace as a sudden spot of rain splashed onto her face…

'Where the *hell* has she got to?'

The harshly expressed question did not fail to conceal the underlying anxiety in Keir's voice as he paced to one of the huge dining room windows and glanced out.

Watching his stiff back in the dark cashmere sweater, and feeling the tension in him transmit itself to the other members of staff in the room, Moira silently admitted to her own concerns about the young secretary since she'd failed to turn up for dinner. She'd seen her go out with Hamish shortly after she'd finished work—and she hoped the girl had not gone and got herself lost. It was easy to do if a person didn't know their way well round these parts. The mountainous region around Glenteign was so vast that even an experienced guide could easily make a wrong turn. Now the Chief's obvious anxiety over Georgia's absence was putting her on edge as well. Especially as outside the rain had started to pour as though it would never cease, and they'd all heard that angry rumble of thunder vent its spleen above them only moments ago.

'Someone had better go and find her.'

Standing up from the dining table in the smaller, more intimate dining room where they'd just had their meal, Moira glanced across the polished maple-wood table at one of the young gardeners employed on the estate—a lad who worked alongside his father, who was head gardener there. Both men knew the area well.

'Euan, will you go? The lassie told me she was a bit nervous of storms, and she might get disoriented trying to find her way back in the rain.'

'*I'll* go.' Already at the door, and pulling it wide, Keir turned briefly to glance at the others round the table. 'She's probably not far away.'

'Get a mackintosh from the mudroom before you go, Chief. You don't want to be getting soaked to the skin or get that dressing all wet after your accident today!'

On her feet as she started collecting up the plates to take them into the kitchen, Moira didn't hesitate to advise him.

Without a word, Keir turned and went out.

Just as he reached the bottom of the concrete steps that led down onto the gravel drive, he saw a blur of vivid colour in the distance and realised that it was Georgia, jogging towards the house, Hamish slightly ahead of her. The relief that washed through him could not be measured.

But even as he sensed the tension ease out of his shoulders a scissor-flash of lightning slashed through the sky with an ear-splitting crack, and Keir saw Georgia pause to look up. She started to run again, but a moment later she seemed to trip and pitch forward in the middle of the glistening emerald lawn. Immediately the faithful Labrador ran back to be with her.

Without another thought, Keir started to run towards her. The driving rain pummelled at his clothing where he hadn't bothered to do up the waterproof he'd quickly donned on the way out. When he reached her, Georgia was starting to struggle to her feet, her red linen dress covered in loose wet grass and splashes of mud. Her long dark hair was tangled, and almost plastered to her shocked face, and her hazel eyes couldn't contain their fear.

'What have you done to yourself?' he demanded, concern making his tone gruffly impatient. 'You haven't hurt your ankle?'

'I just slipped on the wet grass,' she replied, shivering. 'I'm all right…really.'

She might not be hurt physically, but Keir easily detected that the lightning strike and the thunder had shaken her up badly. Giving no thought to his own injured arm, he swept her up against his chest and started to hurry with her towards the house.

'You don't have to carry me!' Georgia protested,

shocked. 'Keir, I'm quite capable of walking... really!'

But he carried her just the same, his dark face stoic and determined as he held her, his racing heart attesting to the maelstrom of emotion that was going on inside him at being able to hold her so close, uncaring that her own soaked clothing was making his even wetter.

By the time they reached the house and Keir had ordered the faithful Labrador to go round to the back door Moira was at the front, her face amply illustrating her anxiety and relief.

'What happened, lassie? Are you hurt?' The kindly housekeeper reached out to help her from Keir's arms, but the Laird's almost warning glare made her drop them down by her sides again immediately.

'I'm not hurt. I'm fine—honestly... I told Keir I was fine! I simply slipped on the wet grass because I was hurrying to get out of the storm, that's all.' Her teeth chattering, but on her feet once more, Georgia glanced at the other woman with what she hoped was a reassuring smile. 'Can I ask you if you'd mind seeing to Hamish? He's gone round to the back door. I just need to get out of these wet clothes and go and get a hot shower.'

'Of course I will, my dear! You go and get yourself dry before you catch your death!'

'Thanks…I appreciate it.'

Withdrawing from them, hating being the centre of attention, Georgia stepped quickly away from the protection of Keir's warm, hard body to cross the chequered entrance hall and start ascending the grand winding staircase.

'I've put your dinner in the oven to keep warm,' Moira called up behind her. 'You come down and have it when you're ready.'

Even though the spray from the shower had been wonderfully reassuring and hot, Georgia sat in her towelling robe on the edge of the quaintly old-fashioned brass bed and sensed her body shiver as though it might never stop.

What had possessed Keir to pick her up and carry her like that? As though he wanted to put himself between her and harm? The threatened storm might have secretly terrified her, but she was far more scared of the torrent of wild feelings that gripped her whenever he came near.

Staring at the wall, she recalled the look of surprise on Moira's face when she'd reached out to help her and Keir had somehow dissuaded her with just a single determined glance. Things were beginning to get complicated, she realised. As if some unstoppable force was having its way and there was nothing she could do about it… Unless, of course, she decided to leave…

Her heart racing, Georgia glanced across at the casement windows of her room, at the rain that was still rattling the little square panes. A disconcerting emptiness and a yearning that she didn't want to name gnawed at her, and the depth and power of the sensation almost drove her to tears.

'Georgia? Is everything all right?'

At first she was disorientated, not knowing who spoke, then in almost the same instant she realised that the extraordinarily compelling voice could only belong to Keir. Standing up to go to the door, she tidied the front of her robe, making sure she was adequately covered, at the same time cursing silently that she hadn't dressed straight away—because once again she was at an embarrassing disadvantage.

But there was no need to open the door, was there? Georgia could merely assure him that she was fine and he would quickly go away again.

'Yes…everything's okay. I'll be down shortly. I'm just—I'm just getting dressed.'

'Open the door, will you? I want to see you.'

So much for *that* plan! Feeling her breath grow tight inside her chest, she briefly wiped her palms down the sides of her robe before reaching for the door catch.

'What is it?'

Her aim had been to simply open the door just a little—enough for him to see for himself that she was fine—and Georgia was unprepared for that decision being immediately taken out of her hands.

He swept decisively through the opening, then shut the door firmly behind him, and the sheer physicality of the man simply overwhelmed her as she found herself staring up into his starkly handsome face, his searing blue eyes burning her with the force of intensity she saw glimmering there. Helplessly suspended in the tension of the moment, her limbs feeling peculiarly as though they no longer belonged to her, Georgia went very still. Her heart continued to beat but she didn't know how…

Before so much as another word or even a breath had left her lips, she felt herself seized by Keir's strong muscular arms and impelled almost roughly up against his chest.

'I only needed a temporary secretary,' he commented, almost with disdain, as he glared down into her shocked face. 'And now I can't even *think* about work with you around distracting me! Just what the hell am I supposed to do about you, Georgia?'

CHAPTER EIGHT

HIS MOUTH WAS on hers before she could utter a word, and suddenly their breath was one breath. His kisses tasted of the Glens, with their intoxicating pure fresh air, and almost made her high. His body against hers was like tempered steel, hard and honed, with an almost desperate undercurrent of need that wouldn't be constrained.

He'd demanded to know what he was supposed to do about her, and Georgia knew the question was equally true for her. *What was she supposed to do about her growing feelings for him?* The spellbinding magnetism that was created whenever they were near each other now indubitably held sway. It was as she'd observed…an unstoppable force that knew no bounds.

Helping Keir earlier, when he'd scalded himself with the coffee, Georgia had automatically acted to do what she could—but, as well as hopefully alleviating his agony, she couldn't deny the intense pleasure she'd received at being able to touch him without question.

Now her gaze cleaved to his resolute jaw as he slid one arm beneath her knees and the other behind her back, then carried her across the carpeted floor to the sturdy, old-fashioned brass bed.

'Be careful of your wound!' she pleaded urgently, her voice almost breaking.

A rueful smile touched the corners of his mouth as he carefully laid her down on the bed. '*What* wound?' he joked. 'I hardly feel any pain any more. The only ache that's disturbing me now is my wanting you, Georgia... You know that, don't you?'

Her heart skipped at his very serious concentrated expression. 'I know that... But do you—do you have something to...' She couldn't help it. Her face flamed because she'd had to ask him the question. A question she'd never asked another man before in her life...

Wordlessly he removed a small packet from his jeans pocket. He laid it down on top of the small oak cabinet beside the bed, next to the suspense novel she'd brought from home to read. Then, stripping off his shirt, he held her gaze with his piercing blue eyes as a fierce shining star commanded and held the blackness of the night.

Georgia wanted Keir so badly that if a spaceship

had materialised in the room during those electrify-
ing moments, she wouldn't have noticed. Her eyes
ate him up as she watched him undress. The more he
revealed of himself, the more her heart pounded with
ferocious joy. Confronted with his breathtaking masculinity, registering the impact of his strong, fit
physique, she felt her senses utterly enraptured by
him. Her gaze lit too on the stark white dressing on
his arm, and she silently commiserated anew with the
pain he must have endured.

Her breath was released on a soft onrush of air as
he came to her, unfastening the tie of her robe with
hands that were sure and strong, then peeling the
garment easily from her body. Before he could say
anything Georgia lifted her arms and wrapped them
around his neck.

Hearing the ragged sigh that broke free from his
lips at the contact with her bare soft skin, she whispered, 'I know we shouldn't be doing this...but I
don't want to stop.'

'If it's what we both want, then there's no reason
to stop... Have you never given into pure naked
desire before, Georgia?'

She didn't want to answer that question lest it in-
criminate her. She was walking a tightrope of
tension, despite the heady rush of adrenalin and need
pulsing through her body, but she did not intend to
let fear or doubt rule the day. *It would be all right...*

It *had* to be all right. For once in her life she was thinking of no one else's needs but her own.

The sudden sensation of his firm warm silky skin next to hers made Georgia's insides tighten with longing, but instead of fearing this new territory she was venturing into she found herself welcoming it. Her mouth slipped over his with unselfconscious eagerness, tasting moisture, heat and demand in one divinely erotic press, and her body knew no dissent only a deeply carnal hunger when he tipped her back onto the bed and covered her nakedness with his.

Readily allowing Keir's hands to explore her, Georgia heard her own breathless sighs drown out the steady repetitive hush of the rain that accompanied them. His mouth languorously tasted her velvet-tipped breasts—taking his time, giving her pleasure and receiving it, sucking and caressing them until her whole being was consumed with fierce tingles of the most erotic joy. Was this how a flower felt...opening for the first time to the miracle of rain...the caress of sunlight? As if its very being was created anew by that seductive, addictive touch? Even Georgia's quite considerable imagination had not prepared her for the river of hot sweet delight that poured through her veins at Keir's touch.

Her hand brushed against his strong, hot erection with curiosity and lust, and she heard his almost painful groan in response. Inside, answering heat drenched her. Without another word he moved her hand away, and started to unwrap the little foil package he'd left on the bedside cabinet. When he'd sheathed himself in the contents, he started to slowly press himself inside her. Holding on to the broad, muscular slopes of his shoulders, Georgia stared into Keir's eyes and felt as if she was being consumed by electric blue fire so intense was the gaze that commanded hers.

Silently she told herself to relax. She knew all she had to do was surrender to the powerful melting tide that was softening her hips and making her breasts throb in an agony of desire. *She'd been made for this...* Any momentary hurt would quickly pass, and then all she would know was the pleasure...

When he finally penetrated her all the way, Georgia was unable to hold back her cry of pain. Keir's surprised glance searched her face with stunned enquiry, and his hard jaw momentarily tightened.

Moving her hand behind his head, Georgia leaned up towards him and pulled his face down to hers. In less than a moment he was kissing her with renewed passion, her pain forgotten, his demanding thrusts inside her body growing deeper and harder, enforcing a rhythm between them that built with urgency at each passing second.

Just before she sensed his whole body tense and

then finally let go, the muscles in the tops of his arms bunching like iron as she held on to them, Georgia rode the sweetly fierce tide that swept her up in its powerful current and felt as if she was flying. Ripples of intoxicating delight ebbed through her body, again and again and again. A strange kind of calm stole over her in its dizzying aftermath. Dazed, she accepted Keir's final powerful claim on her body, and then he stilled and laid his head against her chest. She sensed him shudder violently with his own release. She shut her eyes in silent awe…

What had he done? His heart feeling like a bass drum, pounding out its rhythm inside his chest, Keir rolled away from Georgia and lay on his back, breathing hard. *Good God!* He'd never in a million years anticipated such an unbelievable surprise. As soon as she'd cried out he'd known that this was her first time…her *first!* Astonishingly Georgia Cameron, until a few minutes ago, had been a virgin. And Keir had accepted the gift of her innocence with scant hesitation—choosing to ignore the gravity of the deed to achieve his own lustful satisfaction.

He knew why. Lately, instead of the common sense he could usually summon so easily to his aid, he'd let down his guard and allowed himself to be driven by emotions and feelings as far as this woman was concerned. It was a definite first.

Now, as he turned to regard her, the dark silk skeins of her hair tousled on the pillow behind her, Keir saw that Georgia's eyes were curiously closed. Had she retreated into her own private world perhaps to make her peace with what had happened between them? He only hoped that she wasn't regretting it. What if she'd secretly had some idea of saving her virginity for the love of her life? A flicker of the most profound unease assaulted his insides at the thought. Then he reminded himself that she hadn't repelled him at any point. She'd been as eager as he had for them to make love...

Reaching out, he captured one of the shining soft brown curls that lay coiled against her shoulder and saw her start. Her hazel eyes opened in surprise and studied him, glazed with the hazy softness of lovemaking. Her words, nonetheless, belied what had just taken place between them. 'Moira will be wondering where on earth I've got to. She was expecting me down for my dinner,' she said calmly.

It was a ruse. Instinctively Keir knew that she was delaying the inevitable moment when they would have to discuss the momentous event that had just taken place between them, and he sensed her anxiety.

'You should have told me,' he said quietly, withdrawing his hand.

'Should I?' Her voice faltered a little and she bit her lip. 'Would it have stopped you making love to me if you'd known?'

'I'm not saying that. But you should have mentioned it at least!'

'Why? Do you have something against virgins?' she asked mockingly, her expression unable to mask her hurt. 'Don't most men think we're such a *prize?* Admittedly, twenty-eight-year-old virgins are probably fairly thin on the ground, but sometimes it's good to break the mould...don't you think?'

Before he could stop her, she'd grabbed the linen sheet, wrapped it round her naked form, and moved away across the room to the window. Presenting her back to him, Georgia gazed out at the teeming rain as though it hypnotised her.

Confused and angry at her blasé attitude, Keir collected his boxers and jeans and hurriedly pulled them on over his own nakedness. Barefoot, he strode across the luxuriously thick carpet to join her. Before she could say anything, he spun her round and forced her to look at him.

'Why?' he asked her, his gaze hard.

'Why what? Look...you're really making a mountain out of a molehill, you know!'

At Keir's answering glower, Georgia shrugged.

'All right then. You want to know why I stayed a virgin up until now?' There was a small but discernible quiver of her prettily shaped top lip. 'After taking care of Noah, earning my living has always had to be the top priority in my life. I simply didn't have the time or the energy to devote to an intimate relationship.'

'Other people manage.' Keir was striving to understand her.

'Well…other people have different situations and priorities. Since my parents died, mine has been taking responsibility for Noah, making sure that the mortgage and the bills are paid and that we have enough to eat.'

'After your parents died, didn't you and Noah inherit the family home?'

'We did…but it wasn't paid for. We only inherited the mortgage.'

It seemed to Keir as if her beautiful green-gold eyes clouded over with sadness for a moment.

'My father got into trouble with his business and accumulated quite a bit of debt before he died…that's why. I had to work hard to help pay that off too.' She shrugged, clearly uncomfortable at having been made to reveal such a precarious situation.

Now that he knew her reason for staying a virgin for so long, Keir was stunned. She'd sacrificed a life and a relationship of her own for her brother, as well as taking on her parents' debts. Rarely, if ever, had Keir encountered such selfless love and devotion. Absently he laid his hand on his flat, lean stomach and rubbed it, a myriad of conflicting emotions flooding through him at that moment.

'And just how long did you intend to carry on putting Noah's needs before your own, Georgia?' he gently enquired.

'It's not a question of—'

'How long?' Keir insisted.

'I didn't have any finite date in mind! When someone is depending on you, you just get on with things! I know he's a man now, and the business is starting to take off, but I suppose I just got so used to doing what I was doing that it became a habit not to think about a—a relationship with someone.'

She held the sheet tightly in front of her breasts, as though to protect herself.

And even though he clearly saw that she was vulnerable right then, Keir almost wanted to shake her. He could scarcely believe that she'd been willing to put her brother's welfare above her own for so long. When he thought of his tense relationship with his own brother—a factor that maybe he should have been more diligent in trying to improve—Keir silently confessed to feeling slightly ashamed.

'But you must have dated men, surely? Didn't you ever let anybody get close?'

'I went out on a couple of dates, but I never encouraged the men concerned to take things further,' she replied flatly, pushing her fingers through her tumbled locks. 'I was always worried that the energy it would take to commit to a relationship might encroach on what I had to do to survive.'

'But this is your *life* we're talking about, Georgia!'

Yes, it *was* her life—and hearing Keir say the words out loud made her realise that it was about time she started to consider what she really wanted for herself. The momentous event that had just occurred had awakened her as thoroughly as though she'd been asleep for the past twenty-eight years— and finally woken up to reality. Transported to another realm by the hot tide of lust and urgent carnal demand that had gripped her body so emphatically in Keir's arms, Georgia had at last discovered her own sensual nature. And, more profoundly, she'd discovered that she wanted to be loved by a man. She didn't want to spend the rest of her life alone.

Her parents' death had cost her dear in more ways than one. She'd expended so much time, energy and devotion on taking care of Noah and keeping their family home together that she'd honestly doubted she was capable of committing herself totally to a relationship—but now a real flicker of hope was burning inside her, and she didn't want to let that flame of hope go out.

'I'm quite aware that it's my life… And if you imagine that I don't have hopes and dreams of my own then you're wrong—because I do!'

Tears were horrendously close, boiling up behind her lids, while her throat felt as if she'd swallowed razorblades and hot water.

'Noah is a lucky man to have such a devoted sister. You're an amazing woman, Georgia…and the man that you eventually end up with will be a very lucky man too.' His expression was unrelenting in its intensity, and Keir knew he meant every word of that compliment. Even if the idea of her ending up with someone else seemed to trigger an avalanche of hurt inside him.

'And what about—?' She seemed to hesitate to pursue her question. 'What about what just happened between us?'

God, she was so innocent! Keir's heart seemed to stall inside his chest at the realisation.

'It was probably inevitable! You can't suppress your own needs for ever…eventually something has to give!'

'So…'

He saw her absorb what he'd said with what seemed like distress. 'What you're saying is I could have gone to bed with anybody? It just happened to be you?'

'No! I'm not saying that at all! It's obvious that we're more than a little attracted to each other, and you are a very desirable woman. Good God! I almost knocked your door down to get you into bed—have you forgotten that?'

It was a cast-iron certainty that Keir hadn't! Even now his body ached with an almost unholy ache to be inside her again. Touching Georgia, making love to her, drowning his senses in the hypnotic intoxication of her body's sweet perfume, had brought him the most indescribable delight. Nothing he'd experienced in a long time could compare with it. And then there was the fact that he was her *first*. He would always be the keeper of that precious gift she had given him, and he couldn't deny the surge of jealousy that all but cut a painful swathe through his insides at the thought that she might ever make love with someone else.

Now, seeing her shoulders drop a little, Keir had to own the surprising feelings of protectiveness and warmth towards her that were assailing him.

'Georgia? Did you hear what I said?'

'Yes…I heard. I'd better get dressed. Moira will be—'

'How can you think of food at a time like this?' Unable to conceal the need that had been growing inside him even as they were talking, Keir knew his desire must be written all over his face as he stared down into Georgia's beautiful startled eyes.

'I didn't get to eat my dinner, remember?'

'Come back to bed.' He hooked his finger in the front of the linen sheet she'd wrapped round herself, at the place between her breasts, and tugged until the two ends came apart and the material slithered down her naked body.

'Keir! We can't. What will—what will everyone think if we don't go downstairs again?'

Keir didn't need to see the sudden delightful contraction of her soft pink nipples to know that she was as turned on by the idea as he was...

'To hell with what anybody else thinks! They don't even know that we're together. I told Moira that I had some work to do. If anybody knocks at your door, then you can just call out that you're tired and having an early night. Later, when the rest of the house is asleep, I'll take you downstairs to the kitchen and we'll raid the fridge together!'

Secretly delighted by this previously unseen playful side to his nature, nonetheless Georgia was doubtful. 'I can't let you do that.' She tried to tug back the hand he had captured.

'What?' His expression was deeply amused. 'Raid my own fridge?'

'I didn't mean that. I came here to work for you, remember? I know it's too late to undo what's just happened, but we shouldn't be making things even more complicated by repeating it!'

'Do you regret the fact that we made love?' he demanded, his vivid blue eyes attesting to his sudden doubt. 'Would you have preferred it if the man you gave your virginity to was the man you were in love with?'

Keir's words were akin to setting off a small earth-quake inside her, and Georgia almost swayed. What would he say if he discovered that she *had* given her virginity to the man she was in love with? Finally admitting the truth to herself, she felt the realisation rock her very soul to its foundations.

'I don't regret it at all!' she exclaimed. 'And I had no grand plan about saving myself for anyone! I've already told you why things were the way they were. I'm simply trying to be sensible about this. I know it's a bit like putting the cart before the horse, but we have to work together until your own secretary returns and I don't want to ruin things.'

'Nothing will be ruined,' he insisted, impelling her forcibly into his arms. 'We're both adults, aren't we? We'll just carry on as normal and nobody else has to know anything unless you want them to.'

Even as he said the words Georgia felt uneasy. What if Keir's housekeeper found out? Or one of the other members of staff? What if they thought that she was taking advantage of her situation working for the Laird? She would hate any of them to imagine for even one second that she was some self-seeking un-principled opportunist! *And she wasn't convinced by Keir's statement that nothing would be ruined.* He had no idea that she had realized she was already in love with him, and that just made the situation even more precarious!

'I really think that we should put the brakes on here.'

Easing herself out of his arms and stooping to pick up the sheet again, Georgia held it to her front. Inside her chest, her heart thrummed with regret and pain that she couldn't easily curtail her instinct to be sensible and allow Keir to take her back to bed again. Her only consolation was that given time he might thank her for behaving more rationally.

'Okay. I can see that you've made up your mind about this. Even though I would do a hell of a lot to persuade you differently.' Touching his knuckles tenderly to her cheek, Keir turned away from her with an audible sigh.

Wishing she could just relent and tell him she'd changed her mind, Georgia watched him go over to the bed, pick up his shirt, then leave the room without saying even one more word…

CHAPTER NINE

IN SEARCH OF some strong black coffee the next morning to chase the 'fog' from his brain because he'd hardly slept the night before for thinking, Keir strode into the large country-house kitchen only to find Georgia already there.

She was wearing a long tunic-style lilac shirt over matching loose trousers. Nonetheless, the silken cloth lovingly outlined her shapely hips and *derrière* as she reached up to the old-fashioned dresser for a mug. Mesmerised, Keir fancied the material was like a living rippling sea over the sensual island of her body, and a surge of pure lust gripped him with a vengeance. The impact was dizzying, yet straight afterwards his head cleared almost miraculously, and he secretly marvelled at how just the mere sight of this woman could effect such a dramatic change in him.

Before Georgia had come to Glenteign he had

been angry and resentful at being forced to return to his family home, even though he'd always known that he would do his duty there. Mired in the past because of his surroundings, and the hurtful recollections triggered by his brother's unexpected death, most of Keir's attention had been consumed by his situation. But now—now he found his mind transfixed instead by the allure of this lovely woman...

Drawn by the pure rush of need that pulsed in his veins like one of the fast-flowing inlets that wound its way down through the Glens, Keir crossed the flagged kitchen floor to join her, walking up behind her without a word and sliding his arms around her waist.

'Good morning,' he greeted her softly, his voice deliberately lowered and his lips a mere half-inch from the tender place just behind her ear that smelled so divinely of her sweet erotic essence.

'I was just going to make some tea,' she said breezily, slipping from his arms as easily as though she were some silken will o' the wisp. 'Would you like some?'

Keir did not welcome the tumult of powerful rejection that kept his feet rooted to the floor. Her moving away from him like that was not the scenario he'd anticipated, and immediately his temper surfaced.

'You should know by now that I only drink coffee in the morning!' he snapped.

'My mistake,' she replied, unoffended and gave him a little half-smile. 'If you want to sit down at the table I'll make you some. Moira has already left to go grocery shopping in Dundee, so if you want breakfast I'll make that for you too.'

Regarding his stony expression, Georgia wished she hadn't been so hasty to free herself from his unexpected embrace. His hard, masculine body had felt so good pressed up close to hers, and his warm, enticing breath and the hypnotic blend of his aftershave had whispered seductively over her skin. But the truth was that she hadn't known how Keir would greet her this morning, after yesterday's events, and she'd steeled herself for the possibility that he might be a little bit cool with her.

After all, she had rejected his invitation to go back to bed, and with hindsight he might easily have concluded himself that it was better if they didn't sleep together again. Plus, he had made it quite apparent that what they had was merely something fleeting, and not something that heralded any right future for them both. Why else would he have told Georgia that the man she eventually ended up with would be lucky to have her?

'I don't want any breakfast. I'll just have some coffee.' Assessing her with an almost accusing glare, he seemed to suddenly and chillingly assume his role of somewhat distant employer, and Georgia's insides cramped in protest. 'You can bring it into the study when it's ready. I'll be in there working.'

'Keir?'

But he was already walking out through the door as Georgia called his name, and he did not bother to wait and hear what it was she had been going to say...

'The dinner party on Saturday night... Did you do a final count of all the acceptances and inform Moira how many were coming?'

Hating the deliberately formal tone he'd adhered to all morning—as if she were truly just someone who worked for him and had never been remotely anything else—Georgia briefly licked her lips before turning in her chair to reply.

His handsome face was unsmiling, yet no less compelling for the frown that creased his brow. Keir's annoyance was tangible.

'It's imperative that everything is right,' he interjected. 'Some of the "great and the good" from the local community are coming, and this is the first big dinner we've held at Glenteign since work on the gardens was completed. Apart from the curiosity and criticism that that in itself will provoke, you can be sure they'll be scrutinising everything in the house with a fine tooth comb... From the silver plate decorating the dining table to what kind of tissue paper we put in the bathrooms!'

'There's no need to worry. Everything's been arranged. I got up early to go over it all with Moira before she went into Dundee shopping this morning, and we'll do a final check again tomorrow.'

'And did you remember to tell her that the Dean likes his beef very rare?'

Georgia had already told him yesterday that she had. Now it was her turn to frown. She got the distinct feeling that he was spoiling for a fight. Was it solely because she hadn't been as warm as she could have been earlier, when he'd embraced her in the kitchen, or was it something else?

'I did. I told you—there's nothing to worry about.'

'I think I should be the judge of that!'

'What's the matter? Is your burn causing you pain? Why don't you let me take a look at it and change the dressing?'

On her feet before he could answer, Georgia walked straight over to his desk, despite his expression being less than welcoming and even seemed to be warning her off. A wave of deep unhappiness descended. She didn't want them to continue on for the rest of the day like this...like sworn enemies either side of a high wall. They had shared something wonderful yesterday...something Georgia would always remember. She hoped that Keir would too, after she'd left Glenteign.

'It's fine.' He held up his hand to indicate that she

stay where she was, his firm jaw clenched ominously tight. 'Why don't you just get back to work? I really don't need you to fuss over me!'

'Why are you being like this? I thought that—'

'You thought that because you let me seduce you, you should now be receiving some kind of special treatment?'

Georgia could hardly believe what she was hearing. Her cheeks burned with embarrassment and hurt. 'I thought nothing of the kind! And I didn't "let" you seduce me! It was entirely mutual…you know it was.'

Holding her gaze for long seconds, Keir finally turned his face away with a muttered expletive under his breath. 'Then why did you push me away earlier? As if my very touch burned you?' he demanded.

In the deep recesses of his mind Keir despised himself for allowing his acute sense of rejection to get the better of him. But when Georgia had not responded with the affection he'd desired, and had instead deliberately moved away, it had catapulted him right back to the centre of his childhood pain. Both his parents had been past masters at rejection.

Elise Strachan had been affectionate one minute and cold as ice the next, and when drunk had often pushed him and Robbie away. And if either of the boys had hurt themselves in any way, instead of comforting them, his father would admonish them with,

'You need to learn how to take a few hard knocks…stop snivelling and toughen up!' This from the age of three…

'Your touch did burn me, Keir… But not in the way you think.' Georgia's hand came down on his arm, and he sensed her heat radiate right through the linen sleeve of his shirt so that his whole body became instantly inflamed with desire.

'Then come here and kiss me!'

Suddenly Georgia found herself in Keir's lap, and he was holding her face captive as his mouth plundered hers. The wildly addictive taste of him made her writhe and yearn for him to touch her the way he had touched her in bed yesterday.

Just as his hand found her breast beneath her silky top and hungrily cupped it, the loud ringing tones of the telephone made them both spring apart.

'Stay right where you are.' Breathing hard, Keir scrubbed a rueful hand round his jaw before reaching for the receiver.

All the while he spoke to whoever was at the other end of the line his gaze cleaved to Georgia's with such riveting intent that her heartbeat refused to slow down, even though he was no longer kissing her or touching her. When he'd finished the call, his smile seemed to melt the very marrow in her bones as he lifted her hand to his lips to plant a kiss there.

'Now, where were we?' he teased. Glancing away, her mouth still tingling where he had ravished it only moments ago, Georgia suddenly turned ridiculously shy. Here she was, sitting in her boss's lap, letting him do the most delicious, delectable things to her with his eyes, his mouth and his touch, and she felt like the most gauche, inexperienced teenager. She might be a highly professional and competent secretary, a woman who had taken successful charge of her own and her brother's life from a very young age, but right now none of those attributes readily came to her aid...

Nobody had ever told her that falling in love could scramble your brain so much that when faced with the object of your desire it was impossible to even string two lucid thoughts together! Her glance fell almost with relief on the small metal figure of a soldier lying at the side of the blotter on the desk. She picked it up and examined it.

'Does he belong to you?' she asked lightly.

Georgia sensed Keir's body grow briefly rigid. When he didn't answer straight away, she wondered if she'd done something wrong.

'It belonged to my brother Robbie.' He took the miniature figure from between her fingers and sighed. 'It was one of a dozen. Robbie painted them all with painstaking care when he was about seven or eight...he spent hours and hours on them.'

'What happened to the others?'

'My father flung them into the fire in a temper, because Robbie hadn't been quick enough in bringing him his morning newspaper.'

'Oh, how cruel!'

Georgia's eyes had actually filled with tears, and Keir's lips twisted sardonically. 'You think that was cruel, do you? Well, James Strachan surpassed that particular act of spite many times, let me tell you! You wouldn't believe just what despicable depths the man could sink to when it came to the treatment of his family.'

Reaching across Georgia to get to his desk, Keir opened a drawer and dropped the figure of the soldier inside. Closing it again, he quickly fielded the pain and rage the memory inevitably engendered, and studied the ravishing girl in his lap with a blend of sorrow and regret. Even talking to her about the smallest part of his past he somehow felt that he was sullying her. This beautiful, innocent woman who had single-handedly raised her fourteen-year-old brother and sacrificed her own plans and dreams for love of her family...

That kind of pure, untainted love was a million miles from Keir's own experience. That was why he knew deep down in his soul that he couldn't expect their affair to go any further once the time came for her to leave. He wasn't the man for her...no. She

deserved someone much more whole and psycho-
logically intact than he was…

'I'm sorry that you and your brother had such an
unhappy time when you were young, and I'm sorry
your father was so cruel. I can't imagine what that
must have been like. I only ever knew love and
kindness from my own parents when they were alive.
Was that why you told me not to judge a book by its
cover when I first came here? Because this house
doesn't hold happy memories for you even though
it's so beautiful?'

She was regarding him with what Keir could only
describe as infinite tenderness in her lovely green-
gold gaze, and he couldn't deny the almost overwhelming wave of warmth that flooded his heart in
response. Yet at the same time he knew it was dangerous to keep succumbing so easily to the compas-
sion and caring that Georgia so naturally displayed.
One day soon he would have to live in this house
without her, and he'd better not encourage her to
become more involved in his personal life than she
was already. Ultimately it would be easier for them
both if she didn't.

'I'm sorry…' He put a hand on her back and indicated she should get up. 'I really have a lot of work
to do, and enticing as you are…I can't afford any
more distractions today.'

To Georgia, Keir's words were akin to somebody

throwing a bucket of ice water down her back. Just when he had been opening up to her, sharing some of the pain of his past, he had all too suddenly closed down again and shut her out. Even though they had slept together. Was he subtly reminding her that she was after all only his secretary—and a temporary one at that? He was Laird—an important man in his community—and when he finally decided to settle down with a woman it would no doubt be with someone from his own class and background. The sooner Georgia accepted that and divested herself of any secret hopes she might entertain of becoming closer to Keir the better.

On her feet again, she crossed her arms in front of her chest and nodded towards the glimpse of white bandage beneath his sleeve. 'What about your dressing? I really think I should change it for you.'

'It can wait until later.'

'I only want you to be more comfortable.'

'I'm fine. Like I said…we have a lot to do, and the work won't get done by itself.'

Pursing her lips, Georgia turned regretfully away. 'Okay… But nobody can say I didn't try…'

The last thing she had expected was an invitation— though it was more akin to a command—to join Keir at the dinner party on Saturday evening.

For the past couple of days he had been kind

enough towards her, but there had been no more incidents like the one when he'd spontaneously pulled her onto his lap and kissed her, and—more pertinently—no late-night visits to her bedroom.

Georgia knew she wasn't imagining the distance he seemed to be deliberately putting between them. Telling herself that he must badly regret making love to her, she barely knew how she kept herself sane— but reverting to her usual saviour of hard work helped. And when she wasn't working alongside Keir in his study she helped Moira and the other staff in the kitchen, or ran errands for the household into Lochheel or Dundee.

She'd begun to understand that this dinner party was to be a bit of a 'statement' for the new Laird. Not only had he returned to Glenteign when he'd always vowed he wouldn't, but he'd also acted like a new broom—first getting the administrative side of the household up to scratch and inspiring new confidence in his staff, and secondly organising the bold new designs for the formal gardens.

Moira had told Georgia that the house had never looked as beautiful, and the younger woman believed her. Everywhere she looked polished surfaces gleamed, carpets and floors had been swept and vacuumed to within an inch of their lives, picture frames had been dusted, artefacts and ornaments fairly sparkled with the loving devotion they'd received, and the dining room and drawing room of a duke or a king could not have looked as decoratively elegant, she was convinced.

Georgia felt a bit like Cinderella learning that she was going to the ball. Now she'd realised how important this event was to Keir in terms of his reputation and standing in the community, she decided she couldn't let him down by borrowing the same dress she'd worn to the classical concert shortly after she'd arrived. So she went into Dundee early on Saturday afternoon and, after a frustrating two hours of not finding anything she particularly liked or could afford, found the most exquisite black cocktail dress in a small retro boutique down a cobblestoned side-street. She was delighted when it fitted as though it had been made for her.

When the time finally came for her to wear it, Georgia had spent a good half an hour beforehand in a scented bath, and had washed her dark chestnut hair until the little lights deep in the colour gleamed like tints of burnished copper. She took great care with her make-up too, and when there was nothing else to do other than drape her burgundy pashmina round her shoulders and take a final morale-boosting glance in the wardrobe mirror she left her bedroom to head down the long silent corridor to the staircase.

* * *

Keir was in the huge chequered hallway, greeting his guests as they arrived back at the house after being shown round the gardens by the head gardener Brian. There was a smartly attired member of his staff waiting beside him with glasses of champagne ready to place into their hands after Moira Guthrie had taken any unwanted coats and jackets to the down-stairs cloakroom.

As if he'd been intimately attuned to the very moment she would appear at the top of the grand winding staircase Keir glanced round to see Georgia standing there. Everything inside him rejoiced at the sight of her. He had always considered her beauti-ful, but tonight in his opinion her loveliness excelled that of Venus herself. As he observed her one side of the Pashmina shawl slipped a little down one shoulder, and the smooth radiance of her perfect skin was inadvertently revealed in a black strapless dress—including the soft, sensual swell of her breasts. He hardly knew how he took his next breath he was so transfixed.

'Come and join us,' he invited, over an almost tinder-dry throat.

His gaze tracked every tread as she descended the staircase. When she reached his side, his blue eyes devoured her as though he would swallow her whole.

'You look stunning,' he told her, uncaring that the mingled guests drinking their champagne overheard him. Turning, he lifted a fluted glass full of the fizzing, sparkling wine from the waiting tray and placed it into her hands. 'Let me introduce you to my guests.' He smiled.

Georgia told herself she must be dreaming. But even amidst the spellbinding grandeur of the gleaming hallway, the champagne, and the interested glances of the other smartly dressed assembled guests, it was the man who stood beside her that held her attention above all else. His riveting features and commanding physique were captivating enough without the benefit of being dressed in the most exquisitely tailored tuxedo, so that he resembled the elegant hero of a bygone old-fashioned movie… Georgia's heart throbbed so hard she thought she might faint.

But Keir was leading her up to one person after another, and her dazzled brain was barely able to recall their names as they were introduced to her even in the very next second after they'd been voiced—because she was so enthralled by the man at her side…

'You'll be seated next to me,' he whispered in her ear, just after he'd suggested they all go in to dinner. And, with his hand thrillingly at her back, so that she felt the heat from his palm burning her through her clothes, Georgia just about managed to smile and nod her agreement.

CHAPTER TEN

CURIOUSLY, KEIR HAD not elaborated upon who she was to his guests, other than to say, 'Georgia.' And as the lavish dinner progressed, and the wine and the champagne flowed, she sensed the interest in her presence at his side gain momentum.

Finally, the elderly Colonel sitting to Keir's left, where he sat at the head of the table, leaned across and announced rather pompously over his wine saturated breath, 'You've done well for yourself, catching the eye of our young Laird, what? All seems a bit of a mystery, though, if you don't mind my saying. Where are you from? Who are your people? Do we know them?'

Everything inside Georgia froze. She knew that everyone at the table must have heard what the man had said, because suddenly other conversations around her seemed to die as abruptly as though a conductor had tapped his baton and ordered a silent pause. As she slowly let out her breath and the blood started to throb hotly again in her veins, she glanced across at the slightly piggy eyes examining her so relentlessly, as though she were some daring unwanted usurper at this dinner party. With all her dignity she said quietly, 'There's no mystery. I'm actually working for Keir—Laird Strachan. I'm from London, and my "people" are mostly gone, I'm afraid—but even if they were still living I doubt if you and they would have moved in the same circles.'

A hand slid over hers and gripped it tight. She almost jumped out of her skin until she realised it was Keir. He was looking directly at her inquisitor, and in the flickering candlelight there was something about the set of his jaw that told Georgia he was furious, even though his expression was outwardly benign.

'Colonel…I think your opinions are a little on the presumptuous side…if you don't mind *my* saying. Georgia is my guest this evening and I would have you respect both her feelings and mine by not interrogating her as though she were some kind of miscreant. As for your enquiry about her family—I can tell you personally that Georgia can claim parentage of the very highest caliber. I hope that satisfies.'

'Of course… Meant no offence. Do forgive.' Blustering, his cheeks momentarily as pink as the

rare beef that the Dean of the Cathedral had just
been served, the Colonel took hurried refuge in his
generous glass of claret and the conversations around
the table began to hum again, as though somebody
had switched a radio back on.

Under cover of the other talk, Georgia turned her
anxious gaze immediately to Keir.

'Perhaps I'd better go? My presence might be
making it awkward for you and I know how important this dinner is for your reputation.'

'Don't run away.'

'I'm not! I'm just—'

'To hell with my reputation! If I can bear this, you
can too.' He drew her hand onto his firm thigh,
encased in its fine tailoring, and his heat instantly
transferred itself to her body. It made her yearn to be
alone with him, instead of having to endure this
endless tension filled dinner with people she didn't
like, and who were clearly judging her behind their
falsely bright smiles. He was right…she *did* want to
run away.

Her admiration for Keir increased tenfold,
because he could endure such an ordeal and not show
even by the merest glimmer of an impatient look or
turn of phrase that he'd far rather be doing something
else than wining and dining the local 'great and the
good,' as he'd put it.

'Stay with me.' His voice lowered to a husky

command as he briefly and urgently roamed her candlelit features. 'I need you here...don't desert me.'

There had been no dilemma about whether he should spend the night with Georgia or not. In the end, Keir had simply had to admit that he had zero resistance as far as she was concerned, and part of him had thought to hell with the consequences. Increasingly throughout the dinner she'd been all he could think about.

Oh, he'd done his bit. He'd discussed the house, the gardens, the local politics in the community, and he'd smiled and been diplomatic. But after what the Colonel had said to Georgia Keir had made it very apparent that he would not tolerate any further speculation about either her person or her presence beside him at the table.

Thank God the event was over. His well-fed guests were now on their way back to their various homes, their effusive and complimentary remarks as they'd left, about the house and the gardens, still ringing in his ears.

And leave it to the Colonel to have the last word. 'Your father would have been proud of you, my boy!' he'd declared, as he'd unknowingly gripped Keir's wounded arm and all but made him cry out with the agony of it. The comment had elicited an ironic grimace on its own merit, though. Keir doubted very much if anything he'd achieved at Glenteign would have made James Strachan proud—but quite frankly he no longer cared whether he would have had his father's good opinion or not. The man was dead, and he was beginning to see that as far as the estate was concerned he could write his own history now that he was in charge.

Having told Georgia to go up to bed ahead of him, Keir now let himself into her room unannounced, and saw straight away that she stood in the golden light of just one small bedside lamp, wearing the same distracting short, silky robe she'd been wearing the night he'd returned from New York...the night of the storm. His heartbeat quickened at the curiously shy glance she gave him.

'It's got quite chilly tonight, don't you think?' she remarked.

'I've got something that will warm us up.' Keir held up the bottle of cognac he'd brought from the drawing room, along with two crystal-cut brandy glasses.

Approaching the bed, he placed the bottle and the glasses carefully down on the little oak cabinet beside it and pulled off his tie. The sound of the silk sliding against the stiff linen of his shirt collar was unwittingly sensuous to Georgia's ears. Knowing intimately what the impressively taut musculature beneath that expensive tailored shirt looked like, and remembering how his hard body had felt pressing down on her in bed, she knew she didn't have a cat's chance in hell of hiding the need that poured through her bloodstream right then.

Her cheeks burned so bright she must appear to him as though she had a fever.

'The food tonight was wonderful, wasn't it?' she chattered. 'And Moira did an incredible job of making everything look absolutely—'

'Here…drink some of this.'

A glass of darkly golden cognac was put in her hand, and Keir's long fingers briefly glanced against hers. Because she was so spellbound, Georgia lifted the glass to her lips and tasted some of its fiery contents without question. When the brandy's burn reached her stomach and ignited there, her whole body was infused with the most delectable melting heat.

'It's delicious.' Cupping the thick crystal tumbler between her hands, she glanced almost nervously at Keir.

After he'd whispered in her ear just as his guests were getting ready to leave that he intended to spend the night with her she'd hardly known how to get up from the table, because the sheer anticipation of his visit had rendered her limbs as weak as a lamb's. Now face to face with him in the softly lit bedroom, the gentle diffused lighting making his handsome features appear even more formidably compelling than ever, she knew she was utterly lost. Already, his gaze and his body—never mind his highly seductive voice—had made her incapable of refusing him anything. And she yearned to chase away some of the pain that she sometimes witnessed in his incredible blue eyes. Now that she knew some of the story of how that pain came to be there she craved that chance even more.

'What have you got on under that robe?' he asked her now, a dark eyebrow lifting ironically as he removed his jacket and then started to unbutton his shirt. 'If you want to make an already enslaved man even happier please tell me it's not very much...'

'I don't have anything on underneath.'

'Really?' With a slow, knowing smile, Keir moved towards her and took the glass of brandy out of her hand. Silently he placed it beside his own on the oak cabinet. When he turned back to Georgia he said huskily, 'Open your robe...I want to see.'

Seeing the shy hesitancy on her face, Keir took pity on her. 'Maybe this will help.' He bent and switched out the lamp, so that the only light left illuminating the room came from the silvery rays of the nearly full moon that filtered in through the open casement windows.

With the softest of sighs Georgia undid the belt on the flimsy little garment and stood there unmoving as Keir glimpsed the tender globes of her breasts and the smooth flat plane of her stomach. Gilded by moonlight, her long dark hair curled prettily against her shoulders. Any poet worth his salt would write sonnets to her.

'Any more instructions?' she joked, and he saw her shiver a little.

Again he smiled knowingly. 'Yes... Take off your robe completely and get into bed.'

As she did so, Keir turned to the swift removal of his own clothing. He had a delectable glimpse of Georgia's perfectly peach-shaped bottom bathed in moonlight before she quickly lifted the counterpane to slide underneath it, and he wanted her so badly that he practically hurt with the need. When he got into bed beside her, all her hesitation and self-consciousness seemed to vanish and she immediately welcomed him into her arms...just as if she was welcoming him home again. Having not experienced such an addictively seductive feeling in his entire life up until now—from any quarter—Keir was infused with an almost unbearable sense of rightness and a bone-deep pleasure.

Now, as his lips sought hers and he hungrily reacquainted himself with her extraordinarily sensuous taste, he sensed the oppressive weight of all his cares and darkness slip away as though by magic.

'Thank you for staying with me tonight…you made the whole thing bearable,' he breathed, gazing down at her rapt face. 'And I'm sorry you had to endure the Colonel's little outburst. The man was an old friend of my father's, and as you could probably tell he's still living somewhere in the Middle Ages as far as some of his views are concerned.'

'It's only natural that friends and associates expect you to be seeing someone from your own background, I suppose.' Her smile a little unsure, Georgia considered the man looking down at her with a sudden flicker of doubt in her hazel eyes.

'It's nobody else's business but my own!' Keir replied a little gruffly, hating the idea that she might think he was influenced in any way by other people's expectations of him.

'It's mine too, Keir. Don't forget that.'

'I would never take you for granted, Georgia…I promise. Now, where were we?'

When he would have captured her lips again, Georgia put her hand against his chest and stopped him. 'You were amazing tonight,' she whispered, her fingers playing lightly against the dark silky hairs coiling on his chest. 'The perfect host and the perfect Laird. Glenteign wouldn't be the same extraordinary place without you.'

'I never wanted to come back here again. I never thought I would…' His expression darkened a little.

'But you did, and everything's going to be all right, Keir. You do know that, don't you?'

'Is it? Somehow I can almost believe it when *you* tell me.'

Moving his hand downwards, he lightly stroked her breast, fiercely enjoying the soft gasp of pleasure that feathered over his already exquisitely aroused senses. As far as he was concerned the time for talking was ended…words were not what he craved at all. Forgetting everything but the lovely woman in front of him was what he wanted right now…that, and losing himself for a while…a long while…in the sheer enchantment of her.

Not for the first time in the few weeks since the dinner party did Georgia tell herself that this magical hiatus from real life that she was enjoying with Keir—working alongside him during the day and sharing his bed at night—would sooner or later have to come to an end.

He hadn't discussed the topic with her at all, and neither had either of them mentioned his permanent secretary Valerie's eventual return. It was clear that they were both keeping their own counsel about things—perhaps not wanting to risk spoiling what they had right now with worries about the future. But, even though he'd assured her that he wouldn't take her for granted, Georgia was afraid to ask Keir outright what his intentions were lest she sign her own warrant to heartbreak.

Autumn was upon them. There were signs everywhere, both on the estate and in the picturesque surrounding areas. She saw it each day in the rolling pastures and heather-clad mountains when she walked out early in the morning with Hamish. She saw it in the burnished leaves lying underfoot, and sensed it in the distinct nip in the air. Georgia also registered the changes coming in the magical dawn mists that covered everything in a blanket of icy ethereal silver.

It was a water-colourist's paradise, and some of the scenes she saw would stay in her mind and heart for ever, but not knowing what would happen, and almost dreading the prospect of going home again—even though she knew she had to—Georgia felt like a small sailing craft in the middle of a vast, unpredictable ocean, with nothing to protect her but God's grace from a possible storm at sea that would capsize her.

For the first time in her life she was in love. So in love that there was only one topic that never tired of recurring in her mind…Keir. She had never wanted anything in her life more than him. In the past all she'd wanted to do was provide a sense of security and happiness for Noah. She had hardly dared allow any personal wants or needs to come into the picture at all. Her deepest hopes and dreams had been put on hold for so long that she'd almost forgotten that she'd ever dreamed them. But now, with Keir, they had surfaced in glorious Technicolor to taunt her.

Leaning over the stunning old-fashioned claw-toothed bath in her bathroom one evening, Georgia trailed her fingertips in the steaming scented water. Satisfied that the temperature was just right, she went to the equally old-fashioned and beautiful gilt mirror there, and pinned up her tumbling chestnut hair in front of it before removing her light pink cotton sweater, then her lacy white bra. Folding the items over the white rattan chair next to her, she straightened again. Just as she did so, she experienced a wave of acutely hot tingling in the tips of her breasts. The sensation was almost painful.

Wincing in surprise, Georgia studied her body carefully in the reflection before her—as carefully as a scientist staring down a microscope at some fascinating sample on a slide. The dusky pink area around her nipples appeared significantly darker, and even with her own surprised gaze she could see that her breasts definitely looked a little larger. Cupping them, she felt a sharp stab of shock slice dizzyingly through her as she realised that they felt heavier too. Staring into the mirror as though transfixed, Georgia's clear hazel eyes easily registered the repercussions of shock that were ebbing through her.

'It can't be...can it?'

Moving to the rattan chair, she sank down into it, her arms crossed protectively across her chest as if to ward off even the possibility that she might be pregnant—because even with her lack of experience in these matters Georgia realised that that was her state. *But how could she be pregnant?*

Staring at the pink wall, with its tasteful cream border patterned with tiny pink roses just above the steaming bath, she made herself remember in detail all the times that she and Keir had made love. It wasn't difficult. There were days when she seemed to be able to think of little else. She wasn't on the pill—not yet—but he had always used protection...even when passion consumed them and threatened to make them reckless. Something must have happened that they'd somehow overlooked. Georgia had read that sometimes it could, even with the safest protection.

She shook her head with a groan. Why hadn't she paid better attention to her periods? They were always so regular, and the fact that she was at least eight days overdue should have told her that something was amiss. But her mind had been all over the place, and she hadn't even noticed. Now what was she going to do? She wasn't in a position to have a baby! Financially and practically, every which way, it wasn't a possibility. She had a home to run, bills to pay, Noah's business to support whenever she could. It just wasn't feasible that she could do all that and raise a child as well! If she attempted it she could potentially lose everything she had worked so hard to attain.

But, inevitably, the biggest question in Georgia's mind was Keir. What on earth was he going to say when she told him that she was pregnant with his baby? At this moment in time she didn't even know if he'd planned on seeing her again after she left Glenteign…let alone if he desired a proper committed relationship with her. Even the prospect of a relaxing scented bath to ease away the stresses and strains of the working day did nothing to release the tension inside her as she wondered just how she was going to break the news…

CHAPTER ELEVEN

GEORGIA DIDN'T FIND the opportunity to speak to Keir that evening, because after dinner he told her that he'd had an impromptu invitation from a friend to join him for drinks at his club in Dundee. Inevitably he would be back late, so she had tentatively suggested that it might be better if he slept in his own room that night and she in hers. Albeit reluctantly, Keir had agreed.

She'd made the suggestion less because of the fact that he might disturb her coming in late, and more because she'd convinced herself that it was probably wise to get some proper rest and sleep on things before broaching the subject. Her decision promoted the most disturbed night she'd had since coming to Glenteign—barring the night of the storm.

Nightmares of a baby crying and harsh voices telling it to be quiet, then a small boy curled up in the corner of an empty, dusty room, as if hiding from some lurking dark threat had sheened her body in icy perspiration when she'd woken, her face wet with tears, and she'd been struggling all morning to try and shake off the shroud of melancholy that inevitably lingered. And, as well as suffering the ravages of her nightmares, it was hard to think straight when the secret she carried had the potential to impact on her own and Keir's life so dramatically.

Georgia just had no clue how he would take the news at all. Now, watching him across the room from her desk as he put down the telephone receiver on his umpteenth call of the morning, she felt her heart slam almost sickeningly against her ribs as she decided that now was as good as any moment to break it to him. But still she hesitated. Eyeing him with a profound stab of longing, she concluded that he looked almost too beguiling for words, in a navy blue cable-knit sweater and black corduroy jeans, his slightly mussed dark hair reminding Georgia of a schoolboy who had rushed out of the door in the morning without remembering to comb it.

In her mind's eye she could see him as a young boy. With those amazing azure eyes of his and that perfect face, he must have been the most beautiful, adorable child. It was inconceivable that his father had ill treated him as he had. It was inconceivable to

Georgia that *any* adult could mistreat a child. Children were so precious…

The earnestly felt thought brought her anxiously back to her own astonishing news.

'Keir?'

'Hmm?'

'I was—'

'What?'

'I was wondering if you had an enjoyable evening last night, at your friend's club?'

Georgia grimaced at her own unhelpful diversion. Just where was her courage this morning?

Nonplussed, Keir glanced distractedly towards her. 'It was fine. Nothing remarkable.' But his expression had suddenly became more animated, as if recalling something of far more interest than whether or not he'd enjoyed the evening at his friend's club. 'I was going to show you some paintings—remember?' He was on his feet and opening the study door before Georgia could gather her wits and waylay him.

'Paintings?' She frowned.

'The illustrious Glenteign family legacy,' he mocked with an enigmatic smile. 'Let's get out of here before that bloody phone rings again!'

That day he showed her around rooms she'd never looked into before. There were so many of them—

anterooms and apartments full to the brim with paintings and priceless artefacts, all lovingly kept dusted and cleaned by Glenteign's devoted housekeeper and her staff. To Georgia, following Keir around like some enthusiastic and interested tourist, it was really like having access to your own personal museum.

'Look at this.'

He touched her elbow and diverted her attention from a regal-looking portrait of one of his many ancestors to the stunning gold harp leaning, against the door to yet another undiscovered room.

'Oh, how lovely!' Georgia declared, moving swiftly towards it. 'Did someone in your family play it?'

'No.'

He was smiling inscrutably, and she glanced up at him in confusion.

'Touch it,' he suggested.

As Georgia bent low to obey him, she realised it wasn't a real golden harp at all and she reached out to confirm it in amazement.

'It's what they call a "trompe-l'oeil." It's a painting…an illusion…of a three-dimensional object that looks completely real. As children, me and Robbie were fascinated by it.'

'It's amazing!'

As she straightened up to her full height again, Georgia saw the delight in Keir's face at her obvious pleasure in the illusion, and her heart swelled anew with love for him. Her feelings must have revealed themselves for a moment, because the next thing she knew he was pulling her into his arms and kissing her with a slow-burning hunger that made her toes curl.

When he finally withdrew his lips, she knew that her cheeks were surely glowing as pink as any chrysanthemum.

'What was that for?' she asked, her voice soft.

'Because I missed not being in bed with you last night. Would you have minded me coming in and waking you up?'

'I wish you had.' Her face troubled for a moment, Georgia let herself revel in the feelings of safety and protection that Keir's strong arms so tantalisingly engendered. 'I had a couple of really disturbing nightmares, and I couldn't go back to sleep after the second one.'

'Oh?' Now it was Keir's turn to look troubled. He brushed back some soft chestnut hair from her smooth forehead, his gentle touch eliciting a small explosion of delicious tingles up and down her spine. 'What were they about? Want to tell me?'

'No. I think it would upset me too much.'

And there was still the small matter of her pregnancy to discuss... Georgia sighed and started to free herself from his embrace. She walked across the elegantly varnished wooden floor to the other side of the room, pulling the opened sides of her soft grey cardigan together across her pink T-shirt and black skirt as if suddenly feeling the cold.

'I need to tell you something…'

'Sounds very serious!'

There was the ghost of a smile on his compelling mouth, and he shrugged his shoulders as if she might possibly be exaggerating just how serious the matter was. For an instant, Georgia wanted to delay telling him the news, and instead encourage this unusually happy mood he seemed to be in. But, as great as the temptation was, she knew she couldn't put her confession off any longer.

'It is serious, Keir. I think I'm pregnant.'

'What?'

The previously teasing light in his eyes seemed ominously to go out.

Georgia's hand subconsciously went to her stomach, as though to protect herself. 'I haven't done a test yet, but the signs are all there.'

'I'm sorry, but you'll have to give me a few moments here…' His hand absently touching the side of his temple, Keir appeared genuinely stunned. 'I always used protection,' he said, shaking his head slightly. 'How can that be?'

He doesn't believe me, Georgia thought, and for a long, interminable second she was sucked into a vortex of pure blind panic. Her own inexperience suddenly made her very afraid.

'I don't know.' Her hands curled into the material of her skirt and her mouth went dry as chalk. 'Perhaps we weren't always as careful as we might have been? Sometimes that can happen…' Her voice trailed off, and she hardly knew how she confronted the shock that clearly marked his handsome face.

'How long have you known?'

'I only found out yesterday… My—my breasts were tingling, and I suddenly realised that my period was over a week late. They're always so regular, and I should have noticed… But I—I haven't exactly been thinking straight these past few days.' Her glance was clearly distressed, and she pulled it away from the disbelief she was convinced she saw on his face, looking anywhere but at him.

'Well, clearly we have to address this—don't we?'

'Address it?' Georgia's knees began to feel weak. He sounded so cold…so unemotional…so detached. It was like a nightmare.

'We have to come to some decision about what we're going to do.'

Was he going to suggest a termination? Now she really did feel as though her legs wouldn't hold her upright. As shocking as the realisation that she was pregnant was, not to mention the glaring hard fact that her life was about to change beyond all recognition because of it, she knew she would never voluntarily travel down that particular road of anguish. She was certain, too, that when Noah found out he would not want that for her either.

'You're upset,' she said, her voice cracking a little as she looked up at him again. Her heart longed to bring back the seductive humour he had so captivated her with only a few short moments ago, but she thought that perhaps she would never be treated to such an event again. The assessingly clinical glance Keir gave her in return did nothing to reassure her.

'Upset? That's an understatement! How did you expect me to react, Georgia?'

'Well, how do you think *I* feel?' Georgia burst out, her eyes sparking with sudden fury. 'What do you imagine being pregnant means for me, Keir? I'm a single woman, supporting myself as well as helping my brother build up a business! How do you think a baby is going to affect my ability to earn a living? My God, you men can be so bloody selfish sometimes!'

Before he could answer her, Georgia ran to the other side of the room, pulled opened the door and rushed out.

The Strachan family portraits that gazed back at her from their gilt frames on the corridor walls seemed to mock her distress as she quickly passed them, as if to say, *Did you really think that someone like you could be part of this great family?*

In that moment Georgia was certain that she'd lost her ability to trust another human being for ever. She'd hardly known how Keir was going to react to her news, but she honestly hadn't expected him to act so coldly. It occurred to her that perhaps he thought she was trying to trap him somehow, because of his wealth and position, because of Glenteign. Maybe he thought she'd seen a chance to stop working so hard and live a far easier life? The thought was apt to make her want to lie down and die.

As she hurried, dazed, back down the grand staircase, Moira was coming up the other way. She carried a pile of folded laundry in her arms, and she didn't hold back on the warm, genuinely fond smile she bestowed on the younger woman.

'Hello, lassie! Where are you off to in such a hurry? Is everything all right?' She peered closer at Georgia's stricken preoccupied face.

'Yes…I'm fine.'

'Are you sure?' Moira's frown told Georgia she didn't believe her. Glancing round to check that Keir wasn't following her, and feeling secretly heartsick that he wasn't, Georgia sighed. 'I've got a bit of a headache, actually. I think I'll take a walk down to the beach and get some fresh air, try and clear it. I won't be long.'

'You do that, my dear, and take your time. When you get back I'll make you a lovely cup of tea. That'll soon help put everything to rights again.'

'Thanks, Moira…you're very kind.'

Although the temperature was a little warmer today, there was a distinct crispness in the air. Before she knew it Georgia would be home again. Keir's permanent secretary, Valerie, would be reinstalled at Glenteign, and everything would be just as it had been before Georgia had ever set eyes on the estate— or the charismatic man who owned it.

Inhaling a long, shaky breath, she started to walk down the almost deserted beach. Save for an elderly man, who watched his pet terrier dart in and out of the foaming sea, she had the wide sandy shoreline with its craggy rock formation to herself. Folding her arms across her grey cardigan, her long black skirt billowing about her ankles, she finally allowed the feelings she'd been desperately trying to keep at bay until she got there free rein.

All this time… All this time and she'd never known she could love a man as she loved Keir. She'd given herself to him because she loved him. Her virginity hadn't been such a burden that she would have given it to just any man she was attracted to. And now she was going to have his baby. By rights she should be feeling on top of the world. Except for Keir's hurtful reaction to the news of her pregnancy Georgia told herself she would be. But now she knew that despite their passionate connection, and her love for him, there was no future for them as far as he was concerned.

Probably one day, soon after she had gone, another woman—a woman from a similarly privileged background to his—would see his face next to hers when she woke in the morning in their bed. Another woman would come to know that sometimes he was haunted by his past, would learn to forgive him for his occasional black moods... And another woman would lie in his arms, her head against his chest, and feel loved and protected as she'd never felt loved and protected before...

Georgia pulled herself up short. But Keir didn't love her. That was the whole point. If he had cared for her in the slightest then he wouldn't have behaved like some aloof, distant stranger towards her when she'd told him she was carrying his baby. He would at least have reassured her that he would stand by her, come what may...wouldn't he?

She had no indication of who was behind her until the golden Labrador flew past her in a flurry of sand and wet fur. He stopped just ahead of where she stood, panting hard, his long tail wagging, his black eyes as bright and liquid as a seal's as he gazed happily up at her.

'Hamish!'

Immediately bending low to pet him, Georgia felt her heart lift at the sight of the animal, despite her sorrow. Turning her head, she looked up the beach, expecting to see Lucy or perhaps Euan jogging towards her. Both young people had taken quite a shine to the Labrador, and occasionally walked him for Georgia. But the tall, dark figure walking towards them wasn't either of Glenteign's younger staff members.

Georgia froze, convinced for a moment that her eyes must be deceiving her. Why was Keir walking Hamish? He'd never done it before. She didn't even know if he liked dogs!

She remembered when she'd first arrived his definite withdrawal when she'd suggested that the dog had sensed he was friendly.

Drawing near, he dropped his hands to his hips and blew out a breath. A gust of wind tousled the thick silky strands of his strong black hair and blew them across his indomitable brow. Georgia straightened and pushed her own windblown hair away from her face.

'When I was nine years old I had a Labrador very much like Hamish,' he started to tell her.

Transfixed, Georgia hardly dared breathe.

'I did something to displease my father… I can't even remember what it was now. Probably I just looked at him the wrong way. It didn't take much.'

He shrugged and glanced away from her for a moment, his blue eyes glittering.

'To punish me, he had the dog taken away. I never knew where he had gone and he wouldn't tell me. I loved that animal more than I cared for either of my parents…but, frankly, that wasn't hard to do. I think I've indicated already that they weren't the most affectionate people you could meet. Anyway, I vowed from that day on not to get too close to either another human being or an animal again. I'm afraid I even included poor Robbie in that vow…something that I've come to deeply regret. But then you came along, Georgia, and there was something about you that got to me straight away.'

For a moment his lips looked as though they duelled with a smile.

'You fascinated me right from the start. In fact I'd never reacted so strongly to a woman in all my life! It didn't take long for my feelings towards you to deepen into something even more compelling. How could they not when I learned of the sacrifices you had made for your brother? I was in total admiration. I'd never known anyone who'd acted so selflessly before…certainly I'd never known anyone who was capable of loving someone as much as you appeared to love Noah. When we first made love I was overwhelmed by the discovery that you were a virgin. And if I'm honest I wanted you to be mine right from that moment. I'm asking you now Georgia…will you be mine for ever?'

Her mind hungrily trying to absorb everything he'd told her, hardly daring to believe what he was asking her, Georgia trembled so hard she felt giddy. 'But what about the baby, Keir? You seemed so upset when I told you I was pregnant.'

'I admit I felt that I'd been hit by a hurricane at the news.' With a wry grin, he pushed his hands into his jeans pockets. 'But first of all I was cursing myself for not taking better care to protect you…and secondly I was totally overwhelmed at the idea of being a father. Having not had the best example of fatherhood myself, I naturally wondered if I was capable of being the kind of father I would want for our baby…can you understand that?'

Seeing her expression soften, Keir knew immediately that she did. Perhaps it was selfish and even arrogant of him to believe that she would forgive him for not immediately welcoming the news when she told him, but even so he didn't take Georgia's forgiveness for granted. She meant far too much to him ever to commit such a folly. Everything he had just confessed was true. She had turned his life around with the love she radiated so unselfishly, and Keir knew he would never be the same brooding, solitary, emotionally repressed individual again. She had even helped him to see Glenteign with new, far less jaundiced eyes. And now, with the advent of their baby, hopefully a whole new more joyful chapter would begin for the grand old house and its occupants…

'I do understand, Keir, and I already know that you'll be an incredible father. You've nothing to fear in that regard.' Tucking her windblown hair behind her ear, Georgia ventured a smile. 'But first I need to know that you really do want this baby, and that you won't feel that I've trapped you somehow.'

'Trapped me?' Taking a step towards her, Keir impelled her urgently into his arms and his gaze hungrily roved her upturned face. 'Sweetheart, you trapped me practically the moment I set eyes on you! I love you—and I only want the best for you. I want you to live life on your own terms, Georgia. I don't want you to put your own needs last on the list ever again—do you hear me?'

'I hear you.'

'Well that's settled, then.'

'What's settled?'

'We're going to be married.'

'We are?'

'If you think for one moment that I'm going to live in sin with you, then you'll have to think again! This family has certain standards to maintain, you know,' Keir teased.

'So you want me to marry you?'

There was a definite tremor in her voice, and

Georgia's heartfelt gaze clung to the riveting planes and angles of Keir's darkly handsome face as if she really couldn't bear to look anywhere else.

'Didn't I already say?'

'But you didn't even ask me properly! And you didn't ask me if I loved you either!'

For one horrendous moment, Keir was filled with doubt and dread. 'Well? *Do* you love me, Georgia?'

'Very much, Keir.'

Relief and desire shone from his glittering blue eyes with equal intensity. 'Then will you marry me, and make me even happier than I ever hoped or dreamed was possible?'

'Yes, my love…I think I will.'

Before he could say another word, Georgia threw her arms around his neck and eagerly raised her face towards his to receive his passionate, tender kiss…

Keir was indulging in another one of his very beguiling erotic fantasies. Only this time the shapely, hazel-eyed brunette who was inevitably the star of the show, wearing some flimsy, barely there scarlet lace concoction that he ached to peel from her body—preferably with his teeth—was only too real. And she had driven his desire to a whole new category of its own.

That seemed to go with the territory as far as his feelings for Georgia went, and since their marriage a week ago those feelings had intensified to practically fever pitch. In Paris for their honeymoon, they had scarcely left their luxurious hotel room, and Keir was beginning to wonder how they would ever describe the famous sights most people came to see to their friends on their return. But he really didn't care what anybody else thought. This woman, this kind, beautiful, radiant brunette, had turned his world upside down and he never wanted it put right again.

'Keir?'

'Yes, sweetheart?'

'I think I'm going to make you very happy.'

'You've already made me happier than I could say, my love. How you can possibly exceed that I can't guess.'

'Then you haven't got much of an imagination—that's all I can say! What about if I do this?'

Georgia peeled the flimsy scarlet panties she was wearing down her firm, slender thighs and took them off. Then she threw them over her shoulder and grinned wickedly. Keir groaned as she deliberately wriggled her bottom against his hips, and arranged herself to sit astride him on the deeply luxurious bed. Before he could utter a word, she bent and kissed him lazily and luxuriously on the mouth. Her lips tasted of wine, and the aromatic Italian coffee they'd enjoyed earlier and by the time she lifted her head and came up for air, with a sexy, seductive smile that would have stirred lustful feelings in a stone statue, Keir was so turned on that he physically hurt.

His pretty, virginal wife had discovered a real talent for seduction since they'd been sleeping together, and Keir had teased her about making up for lost time. Only he didn't want any other man to realise her entrancing new talent but him. And he planned on staying married to Georgia for ever…

'And how about if I do this?' She wriggled a little more, taunting his already burgeoning manhood with her warm, scented, moist flesh. His sanity already at stake, Keir locked his hands onto her slender arms and pulled her down towards him for a hard and voracious kiss of his own. As she sighed and moaned against his mouth he found her core, stroked his fingers inside and out, then positioned his sex at her entrance. Catching her lower lip between his teeth, he plunged deep inside her.

'And how do you like it when I do this, My Lady Glenteign?' he teased huskily, watching the gold and green flecks in her eyes turn into liquid heat as he thrust deeper, feeling her satin walls tightly enclose him.

'I like it…very…much…' Georgia replied breathlessly, her dark hair spilling over her shoulders and framing her enraptured face.

'Then you won't mind if we continue in this fashion for the rest of the evening?'

'I need to eat too!'

'Then I'll order strawberries and champagne from Room Service and feed them to you in bed. What do you say to that?'

'I say that you have some wonderfully inventive ideas for someone so—so steeped in tradition,' she panted, her breath coming quicker as her body convulsed above his.

Beneath her, about to surrender to his own passionate release, Keir was suffused with wave upon wave of unbelievable love for his beautiful new wife.

'That's because you inspire me, my darling… more…much more than I can ever tell you!'

It was strange returning to Glenteign as Keir's wife. But as they drew up outside the magnificent entrance and saw Moira with a few of the other staff, and Noah as well, all lined up to greet them, Georgia sensed that she would soon feel at home again. Every one of those people waiting to welcome them had an affectionate place in her heart. She'd grown close to them all in the weeks leading up to her marriage to Keir, so it wasn't as if she were returning to start a new life amongst strangers.

She had legally made the house in Hounslow over to Noah, and now it was his to do with as he willed. She'd even suggested to him that he sell it and put some of the proceeds towards his business. They had both moved on, and so had Keir. They had all left the past behind, and there was only an increasingly bright future to look forward to.

Now, after their intense two weeks in Paris, when she and Keir had shut out the world—for a little while at least—their thoughts had turned more and more to the coming baby. Whether boy or girl, they both knew that their child would have all the love, affection and support that Keir and his brother Robbie had so sadly lacked in their own childhood.

'You look absolutely ravishing, sis!' Noah caught her in one of his fierce brotherly hugs, and Georgia held onto him tightly for a moment before pulling back to look up into his endearingly handsome face. 'Do you think that the ugly duckling has turned into a swan, then?' she teased.

'Ugly duckling, my foot!' Noah shook his head. 'You were always beautiful, Georgia—but that's because you have such a beautiful heart. I'm just glad that you've found someone who appreciates you for all your assets!'

Turning round to catch her husband's eye, Georgia saw him smile at her unreservedly. She knew without a single shred of a doubt that Keir loved her more than she'd ever dreamed she could be loved by a man, and indeed appreciated every one of her 'assets'!

There was one more member of the household yet

to greet them, and as the big Labrador bounded round the corner from the direction of the recently redesigned gardens and made a beeline for the master of the house Georgia saw how delighted her husband was with Hamish's effusive greeting. He dropped down to his haunches to make a fuss of the family pet, and for a moment Georgia had a glimpse of the lonely little boy he had once been. Her heart all but leapt out of her chest with love for him.

'I told you he loves you!' she called out, laughing. Lifting his head, Keir grinned at her, and laughed right back...

THE PRINCE DEMANDS AN HEIR...
AND WHAT HE WANTS, HE GETS!

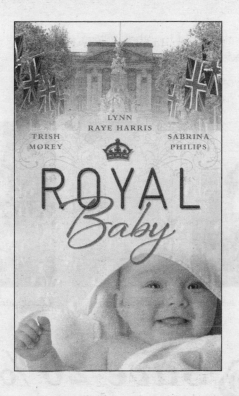

Let us treat you like a queen—relax and enjoy three glamorous, passionate stories about privileged royal life, love affairs...and scandalous pregnancies!

www.millsandboon.co.uk

Mills & Boon® Online

Discover more romance at
www.millsandboon.co.uk

- **FREE** online reads
- **Books** up to one month before shops
- **Browse our books** before you buy

...and much more!

For exclusive competitions and instant updates:

 Like us on **facebook.com/millsandboon**

 Follow us on **twitter.com/millsandboon**

 Join us on **community.millsandboon.co.uk**

Visit us Online Sign up for our FREE eNewsletter at
www.millsandboon.co.uk

WEB/M&B/RTL5